CONDITION
BLACK

CONDITION BLACK

STU JONES & GARETH WORTHINGTON

Edited by Christopher Brooks

DROPSHIP PUBLISHING

Copyright © 2020 Stu Jones and Gareth Worthington

Cover design by Gareth Worthington.
Interior design by Dorothy Dreyer

ISBN 978-1-954386-00-6

DROPSHIP PUBLISHING

Published by Dropship Publishing
www.dropshippublishing.com
Printed in the United States of America
10 9 8 7 6 5 4 3 2 1

For my son, Nikolaj—if only all people could see the world as you do, with constant wonder and intrigue.
– Gareth Worthington

For the steadfast military and law enforcement peacekeepers across the globe, boldly defending our way of life— and for the best of them, who never came home.
We salute you.
– Stu Jones

Acknowledgements

Creating another story, especially one so influenced by real experiences is no small feat. Even in the times when we go at it alone the process still requires the support of many hands that help to lift the work up along the way. To our friends and family who love us and put up with our madness, to our beta and proofreaders as well as our brilliant editor, Christopher Brooks, who brought so much more to this book, and to our steadfast literary agents, Italia Gandolfo and Renee Fountain—thank you.

Also a special thanks to Sean Dickson whose input helped to form the foundations of Billy Vick. We're grateful for all the support. Cheers.

CHAPTER ONE

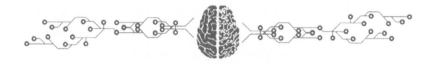

Somewhere in Syria

Through the lens of her SLR, Marie Weyland couldn't pry her gaze from the morbid scene as it unfolded some two hundred feet away. Another twist of the objective and the image in her ultralight mirrorless camera became crystal clear, even in the fading evening light of the Syrian sun: a man, his hands bound with coarse rope, sucking with erratic breaths at the cloth bag over his head. The fabric molded to the shape of his quivering lips and stuck there for an instant before being blown out again. He cried out as two masked assailants forced him to his knees. A whimper emerged from beneath his hood, followed by a muffled plea for mercy. Unwavering, the men stood in a line behind the captive, their AK-47 rifles pointed to the sky. Above them all, a black flag, inset with white Arabic script, fluttered like a pirate banner in the desert wind.

A young man carrying a beat-up camcorder scurried onto the scene and set up his tripod. He fiddled with his equipment, then gave a thumbs up. One of the soldiers stepped forward and pulled a curved blade from his belt. He called out and pointed to the camera, stabbing the air with the long knife. For a moment, he seemed to look right at Marie. Her heart faltered and the hot

1

prickle of perspiration dampened her forehead.

Marie lowered her camera and eased farther into a small depression in the side of the hill, perfect for both observation and concealment. "Don't be tree cancer," she whispered to herself. A strange phrase, but one that had proved invaluable during her long and storied career as a war correspondent. A Marine Corps scout sniper had offered her this golden nugget of advice during a stint in Afghanistan. Master of short-range reconnaissance, he'd spotted her crouched in a ball, peering out from behind a twisted stone pine tree. After approaching undetected, he'd whispered in her ear: *Don't be tree cancer.* Marie had nearly jumped out of her skin. She later discovered the phrase referred to an observer drawing attention to themselves by standing out from the world around them.

The voice of the knife-wielding man rose in pitch. Marie shuffled for a better view and raised her camera once again.

The knife man jerked the hood from the captive's head.

A chill crawled down Marie's spine.

Glen Bertrum, the American relief worker kidnapped three months ago from the outskirts of Aleppo, shifted on his knees. With a brutal shove from his captors, the terrified relief worker flopped to his side, squirming. The knife man descended on Glen, then sawed at the relief worker's neck with the blade. Blood sprayed against the sand. Glen screamed for what seemed an eternity, the sound morphing into a horrible sucking wheeze.

His gore-drenched knife dripping, the murderer yanked Glen's head free and held it aloft.

The men shouted in victory, thrusting their weapons into the air.

"Shit," Marie said, lowering the camera.

The cruelty and barbarism of humankind knew no end, and these zealots had a way of making it even uglier, spreading their jihad across the globe like a pestilence. Without raising the SLR again, she watched the terrorists conclude the recording and march away, leaving Glen's decapitated body to rot.

Marie's stomach knotted, and she tried to swallow away the tingle of nausea in her throat. *This isn't why you're here*, she thought. A beheaded aid worker wasn't news, even if she had met the man before. Such things hadn't been news for a long time. The war had escalated, far beyond Syria and the Middle East, beyond single hostages and beheadings. Terrorist cells were now a pandemic, spread across the globe and embedded in every country. There was no central faction anymore. No IS or al-Qaeda, or Allah's Blade. The war against the west was now an idea, a disease infesting the world. Anyone anywhere could be an enemy—the core vision metastasizing, traveling to every corner of the Earth and there propagating.

Major cities now operated under war-time policy; curfews and rationing to prevent too many people congregating in any one place, such as a supermarket or a major sporting event. Aerial surveillance and street-level military patrols did their best to keep people safe, but a cage was a cage. In some ways, Marie felt free out in the world, even if it was in the enemy's backyard. Yet while hate for terrorists was justified, as in all wars the enemy wasn't the only one capable of terrible things. So too were the allied forces—the people who stood against terror and extremism—and *that* was why she was in Syria.

The little jaunt Marie had undertaken was unofficial. Her boss would kill her if he knew she'd conducted this op. After flying into Istanbul and crossing the border south of Daruca, she'd spent the better part of the past three days moving from checkpoint to checkpoint, working her way along Highway 7 through northeastern Syria. With dark features and perfect Arabic, she hid with ease among the local population.

Marie pulled a tablet from her backpack and keyed up the map she'd gotten from her contact. The coordinates were correct. A tiny civilian village in Northeastern Syria. This ramshackle settlement was little more than a speck on the map, and from what she was told by her contact, this place was of zero military significance. No base, no known weapons caches, no landing strips. The small cell of terrorists she'd just found were likely that: a small cell. Little more than a coincidence, and by no means justification for this village to be firebombed back to the stone age.

Unless they'd found something of significance.

Marie scanned the scene below. A boy herded goats across a nearby hillside. Two women with children ambled between an assortment of ramshackle metal, cinderblock, and mud dwellings. Around the outer edge of the village a few wind-blown canvas tents appeared to house families displaced by the fighting.

In just a few hours, all of these innocent people were going to die in a rolling ball of flame. Mark 77C kerosene fuel-gel based flames, to be exact. Not as archaic as napalm, MK-77C bombs contained white phosphorus, a gel, and multiple oxidizing agents for a longer, more sustained burn that was impossible to extinguish. It was supposed to be illegal.

Marie bit her lip, then unscrewed the cap from her canteen and took a long slow drink. There was only one large building in the whole village. She'd watched men dressed in black entering and exiting the structure almost non-stop for the past two hours. She'd bet a year's worth of paychecks the building housed a secret for which the U.S. government would break international convention and murder civilians. Marie had planned to wait for the cover of darkness for an opportunity to sneak in. If she was lucky, she could be in and out in minutes—with some solid evidence.

Settling into her sandy ditch, Marie watched a handful of roe deer in the distance, ambling across the open desert terrain. The wind picked up, dusting the arid landscape in yet more sand. Marie pulled her arms beneath her and curled into a ball. She resolved to close her eyes for just a moment, hoping not to replay the horrors of Glen Bertrum's brutal death, and wait for nightfall.

Marie jerked awake.

Though the sun was already rising, a sharp chill cut the air. The sky above was a smeared watercolor painting, the blue wash of night bleeding into the orange glow of dawn. A pale crescent moon clung to the edge of night. Marie fumbled with her sleeve, her fingers numb and clumsy as she checked her watch: 4:17 a.m.

"Fuck," she blurted out, then scrambled to her feet.

The town was quiet and still, save for the prattling of a few old generators brought in by the militants. The warm glow from lamps and firelight slipped out between shadowed structures. A militant sentry wandered along the outer edge of the village.

Marie slipped her tablet into her pack along with the camera and stashed them beneath a wiry bush. She checked her garb, complete with hijab, concealing the functional military-style pants with plenty of pockets for anything she may find. As Marie adjusted her outfit, her knuckles glanced the heel of the small but razor-sharp three-inch ESEE knife. A gift from her husband, Evan. Marie had no intention of ever using it in violence against another human being. She brought it along in her luggage when she traveled to appease Evan and to keep from having to hear another one of his safety sermons. All she'd ever used it for was to open packages or spread condiments. Though here and now, far from home and separated from Evan, who loved her, as she prepared to enter an active terrorist camp, Marie paused. She released the knife from its kydex sheath and looked it over. *Be prepared*, she could hear Evan say, wearing his trademark crooked smile and holding up three fingers like an over-sized Boy Scout. After a moment of deliberation, she snapped it back into place along the front of her belt beside the smartphone tucked into its pouch. Marie pulled the hijab down over her head.

Heart thumping in her chest, Marie descended the hillside with smooth strides, dropping into and traversing the natural depression of the landscape. As she moved, she reminded herself over and over that this story was of vital importance. The truth had to be known. She owed that much at least to Glen Bertrum and his family.

Arriving at the outer edge of the camp, Marie hesitated, listening. She could now make out the faint sound of music and the grating sounds of a dispute. Marie checked her clothing one last time, stood, and walked with a casual stride into the village.

She progressed with purpose, staying close to the first row of conical mud-based structures, and just inside the edge of the shadow cast by a pale crescent moon. She paused at each dwelling she passed. A quick peek through a crack in a wooden door or window left ajar served to confirm the village was full of civilians. She eyed her target, the long, low roofed block building straight ahead near the center of town.

A door on her left jerked open. Marie straightened and continued forward as another woman stepped into the lit doorway of the beehive dwelling, her arms full of bedding. The woman said nothing, her gaze severe and scrutinizing. She watched Marie continue on in cautious silence for a moment before shaking the blanket over the doorstep and shutting the door with a *creak* and a *clunk*.

Marie blew out a controlled breath. It was time to see what she needed to see and get out. She continued on, stepping from one pooling moon-cast shadow to the next. The sound of men talking grew louder.

At the central building, dusty alleys snaking down either side of it, Marie leaned against the windblown cinderblock and stood on tiptoes to peer through the crack in a window frame. It was too narrow and the shutter was latched tight. *Damn.* She listened, shoulders hunched against the chill of the early morning breeze. On the other side of the building, the generator rattled and clanked, the sounds echoing off the nearby dwellings. The soft, garbled voices of some radio program filtered from the room. There was the sound of a chair scraping across the floor, the voices of men, some laughing, others arguing.

Stepping from the window Marie took another nervous look around and, seeing no one, scurried toward the opposite side of the building. A quick glance around the corner revealed the alley was clear. She shimmied to the door and waited a moment. Steeling her nerves, she twisted the door handle, but found it locked.

"Dammit," she whispered.

Still, locked doors meant things worth protecting. Head on a swivel, she moved to the adjacent window. With numb fingers, she managed to pry open the aging shutter but couldn't reach the latch.

7

In a moment of inspiration, she unsheathed the blade on her belt and used it to disable the latch. The knife snapped back into the kydex sheath, and Marie popped open the window. She scrambled up the wall and snaked through the opening, then dropped into the darkened room, lit with a single flickering tea-colored bulb. She scanned the room, listening for something beyond the scurrying of nearby desert rodents, and searched in the dim light for anything out of place in a room littered with junk.

"Jackpot," Marie whispered.

On a tabletop, amongst what appeared to be stolen military radio equipment, was a series of charts and maps of the region, each marking positions held by extremists, as well as those held by allied bases. Marie pulled her phone from her pouch, initialized the camera, and snapped a barrage of photos, ensuring the detail was legible in each shot.

Men shouted in the next room. The arguing grew over some perceived slight, an accusation of cheating amidst their game of Risk.

Marie's heart skipped. Innocent games had a way of turning to bloodshed in this part of the world, and she didn't want to be around when whoever it was lost their opportunity at global domination. For a moment it struck her how ironic and tragic for these people to be enthralled with a game that so closely mirrored the violent struggle of their homeland, but then again, maybe it was the familiarity of conflict that drew them to it.

She focused and scanned the documents scattered across the table a little closer. They weren't maps of Syria, but of Russia, lined with flight paths and covered in Cyrillic that Marie couldn't read.

Why would the U.S. be willing to wipe out a village for some maps? There has to be something else, Marie thought. Careful not to make any noise, she moved about the room now illuminated with blades of early morning light through cracks in the doors and windows. She stopped at a nearby table, her gaze landing on a scarred metal case. Studying the object, she touched a deep depression in the lid. A bullet strike. Crouching, she eyed the disengaged biometric locking mechanism inset with yet more Cyrillic lettering. Somehow these terrorists had found a way to disable the security.

Judging by the Cyrillic words and the state of the case, this had to be stolen from the Russians. Was the U.S. helping the Russians? Or did they want to rid the world of what the Russian's possessed? Her mind reeled at the implications. She stared at the case, suddenly recalling a military transport plane shot down in northeastern Syria a few weeks back. She didn't know much about the incident other than there were no survivors. The plane, suggested to be Russian, illegally crossed over into Syrian airspace. Russia denied any involvement and stated the craft wasn't theirs, but everyone suspected otherwise.

Was this on the plane?

Marie reached for the lid, then pulled her hand back and cracked her knuckles. She reached out again and carefully pushed open the lid. A digital screen flashed red inside the case, showing what looked like some sort of warning. Marie initiated her camera phone again. She snapped pictures of the case, the labeling, and the error message. Leaning close, she examined a metallic cylinder sitting in a cradle. Smudged fingerprints suggested it had already been handled. The device didn't look like anything she'd seen before; cold and alien with sensors attached to the end caps as if to monitor something inside. Whatever the hell this thing was, the whole mess stunk of a cover up. It would make one hell of a story.

Marie snapped a few more photographs, then reached out

again to rotate the cylinder. Perhaps there were more markings she could capture. Her eyes narrowed. There was a fissure snaking across the cap of the cylinder. She rotated the device toward her, raising her phone.

A loud *zip* shrieked from the cylinder. Aspirated liquid peppered her face.

Marie screamed.

She fell back, wiping at her eyes and mouth.

The strange fizzing device clunked to the floor alongside her phone. Marie gagged, the oily substance coating her face in a greasy film. Through blurred vision she groped for her phone, grabbed it, and stuffed it in her pocket.

The door to the room burst open and a man charged forward screaming at her. He grabbed Marie by the throat and pinned her to the wall. She pulled at his hands, gasping an apology for her accidental intrusion.

The man bared his teeth and tightened his grip.

The edges of Marie's vision grew dark as the man squeezed, spittle frothing on his lips.

A sudden shriek of jet engines overhead. A rushing swell of flame flashed across the windows and was gone, replaced by a rising, white-hot, glow. Outside, half of the village had disappeared –immolated in a writhing inferno. Her attacker straightened, his eyes wide. He shouted something Marie couldn't make out.

Wild with fear, the attacker's hands still about her neck, Marie came alive. Jerking the knife from the sheath on her belt, she raised it high and plunged it deep into the eye socket of the man. Blood and ocular fluid sprayed across her clothes as the man let out a shriek, his hands clasped to his face. He stumbled, knocking over a nearby table, and pitched forward onto the floor, the knife still protruding from his head.

Gasping, Marie clambered to her feet. A burning sensation gripped her eyeballs and bored into her skull. She hacked out a cough, a greasy metallic taste filling her mouth. With a moan, she crashed through the door, fell to her knees in the street, then rose again. The cold dawn air was alive with the flicker of fire and the screams of the dying. Running stumbling, falling, and rising again, Marie fled for what she hoped was the edge of the village. Each breath felt ragged, her lungs gurgling as they filled with fluid. All she could think of was how bad she wanted to see her husband's face one last time.

As Marie reached the edge of the village, another shriek from above caused her to duck her head. A second blast of MK-77C engulfed the village. The command center she fled disappeared behind her in a blast of sticky fire and churning black smoke.

Up over the rise where she'd surveilled her target, Marie grabbed her day pack, slung it over her shoulder and ran. A third blast struck the village, drowning the screams of women and children in a vast wave of liquid fire.

Her eyes bleary with a mixture of the oily substance and her own tears, Marie stumbled down the far side and fell into a gully. She scrambled to her feet and somehow made a hasty half mile trek to the drop point, where she was sure her ride would no longer be waiting.

Crawling out of the ditch and up to the road on all fours she located the small, idling, dust-covered compact car.

"Thank God," she coughed. "You're still here." Marie threw the rear door open and slung her bag inside.

The young man behind the wheel leaned back, swallowed, and looked at her with terror-filled eyes. "Y-you pay and say to wait, so

11

I try, but…" He licked his lips. "What happen?"

"Just…" She coughed again, the words sticking in her throat. "Get us the hell out of here."

Marie exhaled hard, panic and fear replaced with gratitude for being alive. Maybe she'd get to see her sweet Evan's face one more time after all. She slumped against the dusty cloth of the seat as the vehicle's back end swung around in a sharp U-turn, tires sliding on sand.

Marie's eyes burned, moisture building up and running in streaks down her face. A throbbing headache radiated between her temples, and spikes of pain like surgical needles stabbed into her brain. She let her head fall back to rest on the seat and lifted the phone to swipe through the photographic evidence she'd captured. She wiped her face and squinted, cursing her impaired vision. As she flicked through the images, Marie's diaphragm convulsed, the pain causing her body to shudder in spasmodic waves.

She fought against the urge to cough and cough, gasped in a shallow gulp of air, blinked hard, and pressed the secure cloud-storage icon on her phone's home screen. A small colored wheel began spinning.

"Open, damn you," she groaned, lamenting the area's unreliable cell service. She touched the icon again and again. A violent cough erupted from deep in her chest.

"Are you sick?" the driver asked.

Marie couldn't answer. Heart hammering, she touched her sleeve to her lips, and watched large globs of crimson fluid soak into the fabric.

CHAPTER TWO

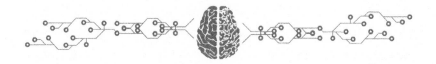

Johns Hopkins University, Baltimore

Ink seeped from the pen into Evan Weyland's mouth. The bitter flavor, like fermented vegetable juice, jolted him from his trance. He tried to scrape the taste away with his teeth, though it only served to make his saliva blue, just like his tongue. *Great*, he thought, *that will be there the whole day*. And he needed to look his best, because today was a special day: Marie was coming home.

He pulled up the sleeve to his white lab coat and checked the impact-resistant digital watch she'd bought him six birthdays ago. 12:43 p.m. An hour and forty-three minutes late. She was supposed to have landed at eleven and then call him. Just like always. Marie was good like that. Calling him when she said she would, and not a minute later. Even if Evan didn't speak to her for days while she was in the field on assignment, she gave him a specific schedule on an Excel spreadsheet so he knew each day when she would call. That made the long absences bearable.

He snatched a tissue from the box on his desk, wiped his tongue and the inside of his mouth. He checked his watch again. 12:45 p.m. Evan tapped his foot on the floor. It was far too long after their scheduled contact. Something was wrong. He switched off the computer monitor, threw the busted pen in the garbage, then ensured his desk was clean and tidy. Keyboard perpendicular with the screen, mouse parallel to the keyboard, mousepad lined up with the light hashmarks he'd made on the desk in pencil. Coffee mug already washed and dried and back in its place next to the potted plant. Evan stood, slipped off his lab coat and hung it on the same peg he did every day, second from the left. The first one belonged to his boss, so Evan couldn't take it.

"Wait. You're leaving?"

Evan turned to Lai Sim, still wearing the headgear and clasping two hand-held accelerometers.

"Yes," Evan replied.

Lai stared at him through thick-rimmed glasses for a few moments.

Evan stared back, though his gaze was fixed on the bridge of Lai's nose. A method Marie had taught him since making eye contact was hard, uncomfortable even. It worked well. People couldn't tell he wasn't looking them in the eye. At least not for a while. The real trick was to look away occasionally. Evan still forgot to do that part.

"Seriously?" Lai pressed. "Like this? I'm still rigged up and we need to finish this test run." He nodded to the small drone still hovering mid-air above a complex assault course complete with tunnels, channels, bridges, and membranes stretched between multiple towers.

"Marie's late," Evan replied.

Lai sighed. "I'm sure she's fine, Evan. Delayed flight or something."

Evan shook his head, then pulled out his smart phone. "No, it says right here. Landed 11:00 a.m."

"Look, I'm sorry, Evan. I know Marie's been gone a while this time, but we really need to finish here. We're behind by six months. The system just doesn't interface well, and it needs to. It was a condition of the contract. We assured them we could fix it."

"Works fine with me," Evan replied.

"I know it does," Lai said, a slight irritation in his voice. "And that's great. It's why we got the funding, but now we need to make it work for everyone else."

"I guess."

"You guess? Just help me finish this one test and then go, okay?"

Evan glanced at his watch: 12:52.

"Okay," Evan said. "At one p.m. I go."

Lai nodded. "Sure thing."

Evan slipped on his lab coat and sauntered to his desk. The screen came back to life, the readout still up and running right where he'd left it. The electroencephalograph and both electromyographs were online and operating within normal parameters. No spikes. Lai was calm.

"Ready?" Evan asked.

Lai huffed and wriggled into a more comfortable position. Then he pulled the VR goggles over his eyes and initiated them.

On Evan's screen Lai's visual readout popped up in the corner: a drone's eye view of the assault course. "You can start now," Evan said.

Lai held out his hands in front and gave his fingers a slight twitch. The drone buzzed forward, through a tunnel and along a bridge before making a banking U-turn and dropping below and under the same bridge. It zipped along in a straight line, into a very narrow causeway, headed for the nearest membrane. This part of the course was always tricky. If the drone was to touch either wall of the narrow causeway, the test was over. Flying through at speed was better because, like riding a bicycle, it was harder to maintain a perfectly straight line when trundling along. Too fast, though, and the drone wouldn't stop in time, causing a puncture in the membrane at the end.

That was worse, and the test would be rendered an even bigger failure.

Evan managed to complete the course multiple times. No mistakes. No punctures. But no one else had been able to do it. His brainwaves were different; altered gamma oscillations and asynchronous alpha waves, but neither really explained why he could do it and they couldn't. He was just better at processing visual stimuli. Processing it and feeding it to the computer. The EEG was enough for him to be able to command the drone. For his colleagues they'd had to combine it with EMGs, tying brain and musculature together in a complex algorithm. They weren't even truly controlling it. The drone's flight path was pre-programmed, and all Lai had to do was tweak it along the way. Error-related potentials, or ErrPs, were brain signals that occurred when humans noticed mistakes. When Lai noticed the drone going off course or too fast, the EEG system registered the ErrP and stopped the drone so Lai could correct it. So far, the time delay from drone, to ErrP, to stoppage, to correction was far too long. At least it was when Lai was the operator.

Evan longed to utilize the big rig stored in the basement—a crane-like arm in which he'd be gripped and maneuvered a little like a rag doll, in sync with the drone or whatever he controlled at the time. Full immersion VXR.

A wet ripping sound drew Evan from his thoughts.

Lai cursed, pulled off his goggles, and stared at the membrane

16

that now flapped like a torn flag on the breeze. "Son of a bitch, I can never get through that section."

"Sorry," Evan said, though he wasn't quite sure why. It's just what people said.

"How do you do it, man?"

Evan shrugged. "You're better with the reports."

It was true. Evan struggled with words. He often floundered to find the correct word or phrase that was suitable for any given situation. Even objects sometimes lost their label, and he'd have to search a soup of syllables to find the right ones. And because his brain worked so visually, they appeared in his mind's eye like alphabet soup, swirling in front of him in such a way that he had to swim through the mess to catch them. Sometimes he'd audibly scroll words until he got to the right one. Marie thought it was cute. Still, it took time, and, more often than not, the conversation had moved on.

Spatially, though, he could run rings around everyone else.

As a child he would build elaborate train-track railroads all over the living room, using anything and everything to transverse the furniture. The whole thing balanced on a network of makeshift pylons and suspension cables that would have impressed Thomas Telford. At work, Evan could feel how the drone moved; know the speed, direction, and position all at once. He'd said that once out loud, and was forever stamped with the nickname anti-Heisenberg. AH for short. He didn't like it.

Evan's smart phone chimed in his pocket. He fumbled with it and checked the screen. It wasn't Marie, but instead an unknown caller. Evan slid the answer key. "Hello?"

"Evan Weyland?" He didn't recognize the woman's voice.

"Yes?" Evan said.

17

"This is Josephine Harkness," the woman said, "with the CDC. I'm calling about your wife, Marie Weyland."

Evan stood straight, his limbs stiff, spine rigid. "Where's Marie?"

"We have her in isolation, Mr. Weyland."

"Isolation?" The word floated around Evan's mind. It wasn't one he'd heard used often. It took him a moment to figure its meaning. "Is she sick?"

"Yes, Mr. Weyland." Harkness said. "We need you to come to the quarantine station in the new facility just outside Dulles Airport in D.C., as soon as you're able."

Evan checked his watch. Numbers were easy. Dulles was sixty-one miles from his lab at Johns Hopkins. Factoring in traffic at that time of day, and the military check points, he calculated the time it would take to make the journey. "Two hours and fifteen minutes," Evan said.

"I'm sorry?" Harkness said.

"I'll be there in two hours and fifteen minutes."

"Great, thank you," she said. "Please—"

Evan cut the call, then paused for a moment. *Damn*, he thought. He forgot to let her finish or say goodbye. Marie always reminded him it was more polite to end calls by saying goodbye.

Marie. Evan jolted into action. Without acknowledging Lai, he pulled off his lab coat, hung it, then half walked, half ran from his lab to the parking lot, climbed into his new Toyota electric car—which without the sound of an engine, was a godsend for Evan—and headed straight for Dulles.

18

The journey took two hours and eighteen minutes. Under normal circumstances he'd be proud of that. Something to tell someone. But today he was hyper-focused. He needed to see her. There were few things in the world Evan focused on so intently. His research was one. Marie was another. His wife of seven years, Marie was the most supportive, wonderful woman he'd ever met. He'd never thought such a woman could love him. He wasn't sure anyone would, bar his parents. Evan was well aware he was different. He wasn't witty or charming or gifted with romanticism—the usual things that seemed prerequisite for a meaningful relationship.

Marie didn't care about those things. She had a way of looking at him that peeled back his onion-like layers of awkwardness and confusion, allowing him to reveal to her who he was deep down. No judgment or criticism followed. She accepted what she found inside and loved him just the same. It was a gift he'd never been able to repay.

Evan thought back to the first time they'd met in a crowded bar. It wasn't the sort of establishment he frequented because he liked the loud music, gaudy disco lights, and clumsy drunk people; quite the opposite. Bars were training grounds for him. A chance to practice not getting overwhelmed by too much sensory information. He would sit on a stool with a lemonade, take a deep breath, and attempt to stem the feeling of sensory overload— manage the stream of information attacking his mind. On that particular night it was an inoffensive jazz band. Marie had taken a seat on the stool next to him and made a comment about how bad the lead singer was. Evan hadn't responded, instead admiring her big brown eyes and long dark hair.

She'd offered a big toothy grin, and said, "You wanna take a

19

picture?"

Without thinking, he'd blurted out the first thing that came into his head: "You're beautiful."

It seemed Marie liked that. He'd used the word *beautiful*. Not *hot*. Not *sexy*. Nothing vulgar. Simply, beautiful. Marie chatted to him for a while and of course it was very one sided. She talked, he listened. She was a war correspondent for the *Washington Post*. The Baghdad bureau chief, to be precise, though her job took her all over the Middle East. Her career meant she spent months away at a time, and then months back at home in D.C. Relationships were hard, with most men wanting to control her or rescue her from her dangerous vocation. But most of all, in Marie's line of work, she was tired of liars, cheaters, and narcissistic flakes. Evan's straight to the point attitude and pure honesty was so foreign and refreshing, it had won her over.

After that initial meeting, they met every few days at the bar. She would talk and Evan would listen. Only when the subject of his job arose did he launch into a more interactive back and forth. She was fascinated with his work as a medical engineer, working on a joint project with Johns Hopkins and MIT, with funding from the Department of Health and the Department of Defense— even if he wasn't allowed to disclose much. She'd laugh, and he'd laugh, a shared feeling of genuine warmth between them. He liked it most when she'd throw an arm around him and squeeze him tight or plant a kiss on his cheek.

Their meetings went on for a few months, until it came time for her to leave again for Baghdad. He drove her to the airport and walked her to security, where he would have to say goodbye. She'd turned to him, backpack slung over one shoulder, and said: "When I get back, you wanna get married?"

The answer was obvious. She was amazing and kind and intelligent, and most of all she accepted him for who he was. "Yes, I do," Evan had replied.

True to her word, six months later she returned and they were married at St. Leo's in Baltimore. A small but pretty Roman Catholic church with high white walls and fresco painted ceilings. Marie had looked stunning a simple white dress. Standing at the altar, she'd taken his hands and looked deep into his soul. The moment dragged on for an eternity, Marie waiting on Evan to say something.

Eventually she'd just smiled and said, "I love you."

"I love you, too," Evan had replied.

Evan caught his reflection in the glass door to the Dulles CDC quarantine lab. His short, ash-blond hair was too messy, and his hazel eyes were bloodshot from crying in the car on the journey. He stuck out his tongue and found it to still be blue. He was a mess, and that wouldn't do. Evan stopped off at the bathroom, wet his hair to get it to lie down, then rinsed and scrubbed his tongue. Satisfied he was presentable, he made his way to the quarantine station.

He needn't have bothered.

Once identified as Marie's husband, he was led to the isolation room by a young woman whose name he didn't even bother to ask. He peered through the thick glass wall at his beloved wife, laid unconscious with tubes and wires entering and leaving her body from all manner of devices. His stomach clenched.

"She's on a respirator," the woman at his side said.

Evan registered his escort's voice but couldn't peel his gaze from Marie.

"We spoke to her manager at the *Post*," the woman said. "She

21

was on assignment in the Middle East. Is that what you understood?"

"Baghdad."

A quick side glance and Evan noted the woman wore a white coat similar to the one he wore at the lab.

"Right. Except, she wasn't in Iraq, she was in Syria," the woman pressed. "Do you know what she was doing there?"

Evan turned, forcing himself to look at the bridge of the woman's nose. "No. Why are you questioning me?"

"We need answers. This is serious."

"Who are you?" Evan said.

"Josephine Harkness, we spoke on the phone," she replied. "I'm a fellow in the EIS program—Epidemic Intelligence Service."

"How sick is she?" Evan asked, fixing his gaze back on Marie.

Josephine sighed. "Very. She's on life support. Her systems are shutting down. We have her under heavy sedation. All we know right now is she came in on a military contracted flight out of Damascus. Maybe bribed her way on with her press credentials. The soldiers said she became delirious on the plane, talking about a broken cannister."

"That's all she said?"

"Well that, and she asked for you, apparently," Josephine said, gesturing to Evan.

Evan rubbed at his short hair, a self-soothing activity that today brought no comfort. "I want to go in."

Josephine shook her head. "I'm afraid not. We've had to put everyone else on the plane in quarantine until we can figure out what's wrong with her. You don't have any idea why she was in Syria?"

"Will she be okay?"

The woman didn't answer for a moment, and Evan couldn't bring himself to meet her stare again.

"I don't know, Mr. Weyland," she said finally. "We're running tests, but we need to understand what she was exposed to. Anything you can do to find out why she was in Syria would help us a lot."

Evan turned and started toward the exit.

"Mr. Weyland?" Josephine shouted after him.

"You'll call if you move her again."

"Yes, but... where are you going?"

"Home," Evan called over his shoulder without breaking his stride. "I have to go home."

CHAPTER THREE

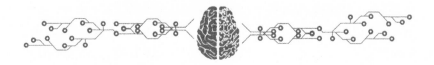

Interstate Checkpoint Three, Maryland

T he windows to Evan's electric car glistened with steam, the glass warm on the inside with his breath, but cold outside with a crisp November breeze. Lost in thought, he watched droplets of condensation run down the inside of the windshield. Without the rumble of a combustion engine, which had stopped being mass produced for vehicles a while ago, his own thoughts felt like a battery of clanging cymbals in his head.

What was wrong with Marie? Why was she in Syria? She always told him where she would be, that was part of their arrangement. Not knowing was torture. He needed her schedule, the predictability of it a thread through his life to which he strung all other aspects. His daily routine was crafted around Marie's calls, messages, and video chats.

She'd tried lying once about where she was, right at the beginning of their marriage. She hadn't wanted him to worry. She'd said she was in Istanbul, but on the video call it was obvious she was in Iraq. Evan had done his research, studied all there was to know about the Middle East. Details others might miss. In the back of Marie's video that day was a Basra Reed Warbler—a small bird of the genus *Acrocephalus*. Ninety percent of this species was to be found in the marshes of Iraq and Israel. Turkey had the Great Reed Warbler. The two were often mistaken, but the Basra was smaller, had whiter underparts and had a longer and more pointed bill. He'd pointed the distinction out. Marie didn't get angry. Instead, she accepted she'd been wrong and told him his honesty was why she loved him, and she owed him the same. She hadn't lied to him since.

If Marie lied, or didn't tell me where she was going, there must be a good reason, Evan thought. They'd developed a protocol for such a situation. In the event she ever lost contact or was in imminent danger of being taken hostage, the plan was for Marie to drop a message in an encrypted cloud folder only Evan could access.

A knock at the window.

Evan pushed a button and the window slid down. A refreshing gust of cold air rushed into the now uncomfortable warmth of the small passenger vehicle. Using his peripheral vision, Evan could make out a soldier, wearing camouflaged fatigues, helmet, and a high-collared flak jacket. The automatic rifle slung over his left shoulder shifted as he bent down and peered into the car.

"Identification, please, sir," the officer said, leaning to make eye contact.

"Here," Evan said, handing over his card without looking up. He hated the checkpoints. It was as if they were designed to attack him. A lot of pressure, questions, and most of all some unspoken directive that he should meet their probing stares—as if that would give credence to the notion he might or might not be a terrorist.

"Where are you going, sir?" the officer asked, inspecting Evan's license.

"Home," Evan said.

"And where's home?"

"Fells Point."

"Baltimore?" The man checked his watch. "You're cutting it close for curfew."

"Curfew is at seven p.m. It's now 5:47," Evan offered, again without looking up. "The remainder of the trip is thirty-seven minutes including one more checkpoint on the I-95/I-395 intersection. I can make it."

"Are you being funny?"

"No."

"You want to look me in the eyes when you answer?"

Evan exhaled. He could only look Marie in the eyes. Perhaps it was because she loved him, or perhaps they were the most beautiful eyes he'd ever seen. Either way, he found everyone else's to be cold and hard, and invading. He turned to the officer and fixed his gaze on the man's nose.

The officer squinted, studying Evan. "Where are you coming from?"

"The CDC quarantine station, at Dulles Airport," Evan replied.

"The quarantine station?" There was an edge to the man's voice. "You work there?"

"No, I work at Johns Hopkins. I was visiting my wife, Marie. She's in isolation." *Too much information*, Evan thought. *Only answer what you're asked.* That's what Marie had told him. *It's not lying, it's just keeping it brief.*

"Isolation? And you came from there? Do you have a release to show you had clearance to leave?"

Evan didn't have a release. Did he need one? "No," he said, though he wasn't sure if that was the right answer. What had he been asked again? His breathing accelerated, loud in his ears. The winter zephyr gusted through the street, ruffling the officer's clothing with a scratchy, irritating noise.

"I'm going to need you to get out of the car, please, sir."

The digging claws of mental paralysis scraped at the edges of his brain. Evan's eyes widened. *He wants me to get out?* The edges of Evan's vision darkened, his pulse strong in his neck. The officer's controlled breaths, misted in the air, long and labored. Evan was sure he could feel them on his face. "Out?" he said.

"That's right," the officer said. "Exit the vehicle and keep your hands in plain sight."

Evan placed his Toyota in park, switched off the electronics, then fumbled for the door handle. It gave a click and he shoved the door, perhaps a little too hard. It swung open, almost catching the soldier in the knees. Evan stepped out on rubbery legs to find the muzzle of the weapon leveled at his chest in the low-ready position.

"What's your problem?" the soldier barked.

"I... I don't... have a p..." Evan stammered.

"What the hell is going on here?" came another voice.

"Potential infectious situation, sir," the soldier said. "He just came from the quarantine station at Dulles. No release papers."

Evan couldn't remove his stare from the cold dark barrel of the rifle trained on him, its muzzle like a stovepipe. He sensed a broad man in camouflage fatigues approaching.

"Release?" the newcomer said. "He won't need release if he was just—oh, Evan."

Evan adjusted his focus, peeling it away from the M16 to focus on the new man—George. Evan managed to nod in acknowledgement, his heart rate slowing at the sight of the familiar commanding officer.

"What the hell are you doing?" George said to the soldier,

forcing the weapon down with an open palm. "Are you okay, Evan? I apologize about this."

Evan exhaled, the onslaught of external stimuli fading to levels he could manage. "Yes, I'm fine."

"You were at the airport CDC station?" George asked.

Evan nodded. "Marie's sick. She came back unwell. I was visiting."

"Ah, damn, Evan. I'm sorry. Is she all right?"

Evan disliked the question, because he had no idea. "I don't know," he said.

"You're going home now?" George asked.

"Yes." Evan nodded again. *Only answer what you must*, he thought.

George checked his watch. "It's getting late. You better get moving if you're going to make it home in time." He jerked his head at the car.

Visual cues were the best. No ambiguity.

Evan climbed back into the car, closed the door, and pressed the start button. The interior hummed to life with electric-blue holo-gauges. The military barrier lifted and Evan pulled away. As he did, he caught the tail end of the soldier's conversation through his open window.

"That's Evan Weyland," George said. "He comes through here all the time, dropping his wife off at the airport."

"What's wrong with him?" the soldier asked.

"He's harmless," George replied. "He's on the spectrum. A bit odd, but clever as hell. He's a researcher at Johns Hopkins. The guy doesn't deserve a gun in the chest. You get me?"

"Yes, sir, but if he's autistic shouldn't he carry a medical card or something?"

"A medical card? Why? Do they make you carry one that says *asshole* on it?"

That little incident added extra minutes to his journey, but Evan still made it home before 7:00 p.m. The declaration of martial law by the president last year in the wake of the widespread terrorist attacks occurring stateside, and mounting fear as zealots somehow divided the world, was turning out to be more than a little inconvenient—not to mention scary.

Evan stared through the windshield at his house. Double income and no kids meant they could afford a nice home in a good neighborhood. The car slid into the driveway of their detached two-story home. Evan overrode the auto-controls and popped the door open to a host of warnings before the wheels had even reached full stop.

He powered the vehicle down, climbed out of the car, and rushed to the porch door. A wave of his key, together with facial recognition, and it swung open. He made for the den—Marie's office. The mess of papers, pinned photos, and hand scrawled midnight epiphanies mirrored her chaotic thinking process, an astute ability to link seemingly unrelated things together in a spider's web of intricate trails. It's why she was a good reporter, able to see what others couldn't. Maybe that's why she understood him so well, and his need to visualize everything in his mind's eye.

Evan's office was upstairs, and by comparison the space was the epitome of immaculate. Organized, clean, and structured. It had to be. Not finding something he needed could become frustrating to the point of madness. He'd lost his wedding ring once. It took him four straight hours to find it, turning the house inside out. It had been in the fridge on top of a Tupperware box of leftover King Ranch Chicken. Marie was prone to put things away when she saw them out, regardless of details like a ring sitting on the lid.

Evan sat at Marie's desk and shook the mouse, waking the computer and monitor. He typed in the password, then searched the desktop for the folder he wanted. It wasn't there. She'd moved it again. Annoyed, Evan searched the hard drive for his own name since the folder was named *Evan*. His hunt released a plethora of files, most of them photos of him or them as a couple. Pictures of carefree trips to the park, eating at his favorite noodle place, and their occasional vacations—though her job meant that they'd only had two in the last seven years. One to Hawaii, which Evan didn't like because of the heat, and one to Iceland, which he adored. He smudged his finger across the screen on a photo of them taking a selfie in front of the Northern Lights. Marie's huge grin and soft cheeks smushed up against Evan's serene face.

Tell me you put something in the folder, Evan thought.

The folder he sought sat at the bottom of the search list.

It had been moved to the desktop for some reason. He double clicked the icon. It pulled up a Word document with a single link embedded. He clicked on that, too. This took him to the secure cloud-based storage.

Evan searched the desk, lifting wads of notes, maps, and books until he found the VXR ultralight headset. Worn much like a pair of glasses, the VXR clear screen wrapped around his face and ears, covering everything except his mouth. The display came alive with augmented reality. If he desired, he could look at any object in the room and the system could tell him what it was, what it contained,

30

or where to buy it. But today, he needed it to open the drop box.

The password system had been devised by Evan and Marie, based on the fact that he preferred spatial problems to word-based ones. This type of password made it extra secure, as most people would not have a clue how to even begin deciphering the unique set of repeated gestures and environmental and virtual targets.

Evan rifled through the password protocol, adjusting his head position, gaze, and finger taps in the air with lightning precision. The folder, which appeared much like a dodecahedron-shaped Rubik's cube on his visor, burst open. Evan used more air gestures to pull out the contents. Most of the files flashed red. They were corrupted, perhaps due to an interrupted upload, or maybe they were so large that the connection couldn't handle them. He pushed the useless broken links to one side.

Two files had glowing green ticks next to them—partial successful uploads.

A quick air tap and the first file opened: an image. A close-up shot of some kind of cannister in a case. The case itself was more than just a metal housing, confirmed by an inset readout with flowing red Cyrillic letters. *Great*, Evan thought. *Not just words, but foreign letters.* He tapped on the Cyrillic but kept his finger there, like a long-press on a smart phone. A menu popped up. He selected *Augmented Translation*. The red Cyrillic became English. The word *Biohazard* in capitals now hovered above the cannister.

A cold sweat broke out on Evan's forehead.

Biohazard. While not a word used in daily life for most people, and thus one that Evan would struggle to connect a meaning quickly, he worked at the biomedical division at Johns Hopkins and knew well what it meant. He zoomed in on the picture of the cannister to study it further. He had to know what was inside. Evan long-pressed the cannister image and again brought up the menu, from which he selected *3D Rendering*. The system's AI confirmed, and within a few seconds had brought up a 3D image of the object. While of course it couldn't know what was on the entire surface of the cannister, it could approximate and give depth to the visible scratches, bumps, stamps, and markings.

Evan rotated the hovering image, Marie's office blurred in the background. It wasn't a design he'd seen before, but its structure was consistent with a refrigerated biocontainment unit. There was a fissure in the narrowed end around a possible seal. *Maybe an attempt to force it open? Was that how she became exposed?*

He moved the object around and around, spinning it like a top. He cocked his head, so that he could examine it side on, using a single eye. Sometimes removing his depth perception helped him see an object in a new light.

It worked.

Running along the edge of the seal was a serial number: BDS-2433-G.

He ran a search through the VXR.

A serial number for a coffee maker. The registration ID for someone's dog in Connecticut. Someone's fake social media handle. Nothing of interest. Evan bit his lip. Another tap and the second file opened with a dialogue box hovering over it:

File corrupt. Attempt repair?

Evan tapped *Yes*. The file popped open. It was audio. He pressed play. The sound crackled and garbled for a second until he heard the warmth of his wife's voice in mid conversation with another man. It made his heart flutter.

"You're sure about the location?" Marie said.

"Yes. A small village in Northeastern Syria."

32

"And you can't tell me why?" Marie asked.

"It's classified. I'm not cleared to know why." The man sounded frustrated. Maybe even guilty.

"Then how do you know at all?"

"I'm flying the mission."

"It's not a drone hit?"

"No," the man said, his tone resolute. "We have orders to blanket the area with Mark-77Cs. We have to record mission specs for our flight but they can be… adjusted. Drones have embedded electronic data. You can't touch that and the ops are too visible by too many people. This order was given verbally. You get what I'm saying?"

"Mark-77Cs? You mean incendiaries?" Marie asked. "The U.S. government is hitting a civilian settlement with incendiary bombs?"

"That's what I'm telling you."

"This is good," Marie said, her voice tinged with the excitement about a story. A tone Evan knew all too well. "But I need more information."

"I don't have any more. You're a reporter, you figure it out," the man snapped.

"Wait, why are you telling me this?"

A long pause followed. Evan raised his finger in preparation to scrub back to the beginning.

Then the man spoke again. "Intel suggests there are children in that village," he began. "I do my job and I follow orders, but this one… all of it feels wrong. You don't refuse an operation like this. It's a career ender and I have a family to feed and a retirement to think about. I can't stop this, but… maybe you can expose it."

"Okay," Marie said. "Thank you."

The audio file stopped playing.

Evan's heart thumped like a percussion instrument in his chest. For a moment he wanted to play the file again just to hear Marie's voice, but that train of thought led straight to an image in his head of her lying on a gurney at the CDC quarantine station. The U.S. government had plans to incinerate a civilian population. Marie went to Syria to find out why and that's how she was exposed to a biohazard. He had to tell the CDC. Evan closed all the files, cleared his screen, and then brought up his recent call list. One number was Marie's, the other was Josephine Harkness—the woman he'd met with at quarantine. Evan's finger hovered in indecision over the call button.

This drop box was secure for a reason. Only Evan was supposed to see it. That's what Marie had said. Evan was then to take any information and go straight to her boss, Jack Carter. Normally, that would have made sense to Evan. Jack was a good man and he'd freed Marie from a number of tight spots over the last years. Tight spots often meant foreign detention facilities. He had good political connections. But a bioweapon and a U.S. government air strike on civilians in another country? No, he'd call the CDC, tell them she might have been exposed to some sort of biological agent. Then he'd talk to Lai. Their project was funded by the Department of Defense. Maybe they would know something about that serial number. Marie's well-being was all that mattered.

Evan pressed *Call.*

A dial tone hummed for two cycles, then the line connected.

"Josephine Harkness." Her voice was weary.

"It's Evan Weyland."

"Oh, Dr. Weyland," she said. "Something of interest for me, I hope. It's been a long day."

"Yes, yes, I do."

CHAPTER FOUR

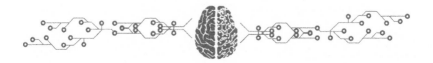

Quantico, Virginia

Billy Vick sat bare chested in his silkies at the edge of the bed, the lean, stacked musculature of his shoulders, chest, and back clenched tight. Warm orange-yellow rays of early morning sun pushed through slits in the closed blinds scattering rectangles of golden light that might otherwise cause a person to forget it was November and there was frost on the ground outside. Billy's shoulders heaved up and down with his labored breathing. With an intense gaze, he studied the off-white variations, ridges, and micro bubbles in the paint of his bedroom wall. A wall that always seemed to remind him of a battlefield stained with the blood of the fallen. Somehow, staring at it calmed his nerves.

For the fourth time this week he'd woken up to the sounds of Pete screaming. Like grim shadows from the past, the voice of his friend called out to him, his anguished cries refusing to allow Billy to live in peace. Billy looked down at the thick scarred knuckles of his hands, his fingers vibrating with the slightest tremor. He clenched the trembling digits into a fist.

"You were my brother and I love you, but that was eight years ago, Pete," Billy whispered. "You've gotta let me move on."

"Talking to yourself in here, Captain Vick?" a soft voice said from across the room.

Billy jerked his head up. His wife, Rosie, leaned against the bedroom doorframe. In her arms, she carried a bundle of still warm, washed laundry that radiated the soothing smell of whatever softener she'd used.

"I was just, um…" Billy stood from the bed and shrugged. A prickle of embarrassment tingled across his scalp.

"You don't have to explain," said Rosie. She crossed the room, placed the laundry next to him, and took his hands in her own.

Billy searched the soft caramel eyes of the woman he loved and found no judgment there.

"Hands shaking again?" she said.

"Yeah."

"I can feel it. Here," she said, as she picked up the bundle of laundry and pushed it into his hands with a smile. "Give them something to do."

Billy took the folded bundle of his shirts and pants and underwear and tucked it against his chest.

Rosie clasped his salt-and-pepper stubbled chin in the palms of her little hands and gazed into his eyes. Billy searched the face of his bride, her face framed by long dark tresses. Seemed like a lifetime ago that they'd met in a small town café while Billy was on micro-drone recon assignment along the Belarusian-Russian border. The rest was history. Together, he and Rosie had been through the hell of his multiple deployments and a career in the military. She never gave up on him, not then, and not now.

"Look at me," she said, kissing his face. "You are home, you are safe, and you are loved."

Billy tossed the folded clothes on the bed and pulled his wife's petite hourglass frame against him.

"Oy!" she yelped and smacked his shoulder, causing him to squeeze her tighter. "I just folded those!"

"I don't care. I'll refold them." Billy breathed in the sweet scent of her neck, relishing her embrace.

Twenty minutes later, dressed in an old Army pullover sweatshirt, faded and tattered jeans, and a pair of soiled gray tennis shoes, Billy descended the stairs. He took a moment to revel in the comforts of home, a far cry from the desert hell from which so many never returned—a desperate place that nearly claimed him as well. Feeling his heart rate ticking upward, Billy forced himself back to the present.

He took in the scent of seasonal spice, turning leaves, farm grown pumpkins, and other various autumnal decorations adorning the porch, entryway, and every other open surface he could lay eyes on. Thanksgiving was just weeks away. It wouldn't be long before all this was swapped out for the loads of Christmas decorations waiting piled in boxes in the attic. Rosie was a fanatic when it came to decorating for the holidays, and even under rationing order—too many people crowding at market places was now banned for fear of bombings—she managed to save up for months in order to give their home a feeling of freedom. Billy figured it was only due to his urging that Rosie kept it in check. They lived on base after all. He had to maintain a reasonable level of professionalism for those who might be watching.

The smell of warm cinnamon rolls, fresh from the oven, reached out from the kitchen. He swallowed back a sudden flood of saliva and shuffled toward the island. "You're killing me."

"Aww." Rosie made a pouty face. "I know. Sorry, baby, but those boys of yours have a way of wearing me down. Used the last of the cinnamon for this batch." She tottered past with a wink and set the iced buns down on the countertop.

Billy turned, half following the buns, half following the sway of his wife's hips. He was greeted by his three boys—Danny, Cade, and Luke—perched on stools, already stuffing their faces with Rosie's prize-winning rolls.

"Sorry, Dad," Danny said around a cheek full of chewed cinnamon roll, icing still on his lips. He smirked, glancing at his two younger brothers. "Sure you don't want one?"

"Yes... no." Billy rubbed his jaw, now sorely regretting having committed to a thirty day no-carb challenge. "I don't know." He managed a wry smile as he gave Danny a little shove, then put Cade in a headlock and, with his free hand, pulled Luke playfully by the ear.

They grumbled and fought back.

"Ah, ah, owww." Five-year-old Luke winced, a half-chewed glob of cinnamon roll almost falling from his mouth.

"Just don't antagonize your old man too much or there might be consequences," Billy said.

Rosie swatted at his backside with a wooden spoon. "Leave them alone. I put them up to it."

Billy released his boys and gave Rosie a scolding look. "Of course you did."

She plated a pile of steaming scrambled eggs with a smattering of cheese and two strips of bacon and handed it to him. "Sorry, we're low on cheese, and bacon, too. The fridge has an order scheduled as soon as more is allowed by the rationing center."

Little Luke, eyes wide, stuck his tongue out and panted like a dog as the bacon went past.

"Nope," Billy said, sticking a piece of bacon in his mouth. "This plate is for me, you little sneak."

Billy's work phone buzzed on the countertop. He reached out, flipped the device over, and glanced at the screen. It was the Army's Criminal Investigation Command unit on base. Billy silenced the call and returned to his breakfast. This was *his* day. *Screw 'em*, he thought. The world would keep spinning. It always did.

"Dad, you're coming to my game today, right?" twelve-year-old Danny said, wiping his mouth. "We got special permission to have a game, on base. Only one parent is allowed, so I asked for you."

"Of course, buddy. I gotta see the star wide receiver do his thing," Billy said, and took another bite of cheese eggs.

Danny shrugged. "I'm on second string, Dad. I'm not the star."

"That's up for interpretation," Billy said, then sipped his coffee.

"Hopefully it won't get canceled again," Rosie said. "Lockdowns, even on base? It's gotten a little crazy."

"Mmmphh." Billy nodded his agreement behind his mug.

"What do you have planned for your day off?" Rosie asked as she hovered about, taking care of her boys.

"Well, *we*," he eyed each of the boys, "are going to be doing some much needed yardwork." He pointed downward. "Hence the crappy ten-year-old tennis shoes."

An assortment of groans and grumbles.

"Room and board isn't free here, boys. Got to earn your keep." He winked at Rosie who returned a little smile.

She looked to the boys, still grumbling about how unfair life was. "It's good quality time with your father. Think of it that way."

The phone buzzed again, shifting across the counter with small vibrations. This time Billy ignored it. A moment later the buzzing stopped, followed by a short chime indicating a new voicemail.

"You, my love? What do you have going on today?" Billy said.

The golden morning light spilled in through the windows of the breakfast nook, glanced off the island, and seemed to give Rosie's face a certain radiance. "Well," she said, taking a sip of her tea. "I received a subpoena over a client of mine earlier this week. While you boys are preoccupied, I'm going to stop by the office and review his file. After that, I'll take care of a few things and be looking forward to watch Danny's game on the monitor." She stopped behind her eldest, taller than his mom even while sitting on a stool, and kissed him on the cheek.

Not too grown up yet to get cuddles from Mom, Danny leaned from the stool toward her and got the hugs he was looking for.

Billy smiled and his chest swelled at the sight of his family. There was a time he feared coming back from the desert, a place that stole so many men from their families. All too often, he heard stories of guys making it home only to realize they were unable to deal with civilian life. The guilt of their brothers in arms deploying again while they enjoyed good things at home, more than they could bear. It was hell to go and hell to be stuck at home when your boys went back without you. *No one escapes*, Billy thought.

Billy's phone buzzed a third time, jittering its way across the counter. He swore under his breath and met his wife's gaze.

"I have to answer it," Billy said.

"I know," Rosie replied, giving him a pat on the arm as she stepped past.

Billy picked up the phone. It was the same number. Three times now someone had called him from the office. In his line of work, it wasn't a good omen. He swiped the call open and held the phone to his ear. "I'm on my first day off in three weeks. This better be good."

"I'm sorry to disturb you, Cap. We've got a lot of intel coming in about a possible containment situation stateside. I wanted to make you aware."

"Stand by," Billy said, and walked away from the kitchen. He caught Danny's withered expression. Billy held up his hand in a gentle plea for understanding, then disappeared into the living room. Billy could hear Danny asking his mom if Dad was going to have to miss his game, *again.*

"Go ahead, Adam. And ditch the formality."

There was a pause on the other end from the first sergeant. "It doesn't look good."

"Did I hear you say a containment situation?" Billy asked.

"Yeah. A sick woman from the press came into Dulles on an international military flight. Somehow, she wrangled her way aboard. She's been quarantined but may have exposed the entire plane to an unknown pathogen."

Billy blinked and shook his head. "Okay, contaminations happen all the time. The containment protocols are on the CDC and EMA, and any enforcement is business as usual for the locals and Feds. Was it a deliberate act of terror?"

"Not that I can tell, but—"

"Dammit, Adam. You call me on my one day off for this bullshit? We've been on station together for years now. This is day-one stuff we tell the new guys. Bio terror investigation is one element our job. One element. And it must have a military nexus. You know this. Army CID can't just inject itself into a civilian containment—"

"There's a nexus," Kurkowski interrupted, stopping Billy's rant short. "And I think it's going to come back to us..."

Billy swayed, the muscles of his gut tightening.

"Dad?" Cade called from the kitchen.

Billy raised a hand to silence his son and turned away lowering his voice. "Come back to *us* as in, the Army?"

"Affirmative. But maybe on a personal level as well. This one feels bad all the way around."

Billy's skin prickled. In the past their work often involved pretty routine tick-box investigations. With the presidential declaration of martial law and the mess that followed, the past year had been a doozy from the start. Then came the secretive and dangerous military program his unit had to shut down. Nothing could top what he'd had to endure over that.

Billy cleared his throat. "How in the hell could it come back to us personally?"

"I don't want to talk on an open line, Cap." Kurkowski paused, nervous. "You know the drill. You know I wouldn't do this if it wasn't important."

Billy's jaw tightened. "All right. Call in everyone else, too. I want the whole team on this one."

"Roger that."

"I'll be there in fifteen," Billy said, and, not waiting for the reply from his counterpart, terminated the call.

Billy took the turn off Russel Road onto Talmadge on two wheels, the tires of his blacked-out Ford Explorer squealing like a cheaply produced chase scene off an old episode of *CHiPs*. His vehicle's auto-drive assistant would never operate the vehicle like this, which was why he'd had to take manual control.

The information Kurkowski described turned over and over in an endless loop in Billy's mind. *It couldn't be Omega, could it?* Command knew about the plot behind the program and had axed it. Important heads had rolled. There was no way it would get activated again. *So, what then? Kurkowski sounded concerned.*

He pulled up to the gate, brought the car to a stop, and lowered his driver's window.

"Captain." The camo clad MP at the gate offered a quick salute. "I thought you said you had a few days off?"

"Hey Marquez. Yeah, you and I both." Billy shrugged. "Someone should have told me Army CID works all the time. Maybe I'd have done something different with my military career."

Marquez shook his head with a smile as he scanned Billy's ID card. Another MP with an explosive detection K9 conducted an exterior sweep of the vehicle. "No sir," Marquez said. "Then you'd be stuck somewhere on gate duty scanning people's ID cards."

"Fair enough." Billy put on his best smile and accepted his ID back from the MP. "You boys be safe."

"Yes sir."

The Russel-Knox building loomed ahead, all right angles along its red and cream brick façade. Billy pulled into a spot and exited his car. He caught his reflection in the window glass and realized he was still wearing his crappy yard work clothes beneath an old faded Army pullover. *Damn, hope there aren't any brass around,* he thought, then shrugged it off and headed at a trot to the entrance. He swiped his ID card at the terminal and stood still while the monitor conducted a scan.

"Body scan complete," the security AI said. "Authorized issued weapon detected. Facial recognition complete. Welcome, First Captain Vick."

With a click the exterior door popped free. Billy gave it a yank and squeezed through the gap. In a few strides, he arrived at the door to CID and was asked to present his card yet again. As he waited for a second body scan, he eyed the U.S. Army Criminal Investigation Command Division seal on the wall by the door. The motto beneath it, a phrase he'd heard ten thousand times in the course of his career, leapt out from the image: "Do what has to be done."

Damn straight.

The door released and Billy leaned back to pull it open. "Well, come on. Don't leave me in suspense," he said to the entire office.

First Sergeant Adam Kurkowski, a ruddy faced man with rounded shoulders and a short crop of fire red hair, stood from his workstation. "You're not going to like this."

"What have you got?"

"I was able to pull some things. Passenger manifest for the plane, some intel on the infected female and others showing signs of contamination, things like that." Kurkowski wiped his forehead.

"Wait," Billy held up his palms. "I'm not jumping into this with you mid-stream. Start over. Give me the thirty-thousand-foot view."

Kurkowski nodded and took a moment to compose himself. "Patient zero, her name's Marie Weyland. A well-known war correspondent, the Baghdad bureau chief as a matter of fact, for forty-four-forty out of D.C." He held up an index finger. "Except this time, she was off the reservation. Acting on a confidential informant's tip without the official go-ahead from her boss."

Billy sighed. "What the hell does this have to do with us, Kurkowski?"

"I'm getting to that," Kurkowski said, swiping open a digital file on the tablet he held in his hands. "I've got records of her flight into Istanbul. Then she goes dark, until a few days later she pops back up on a military-contracted flight headed into Dulles from Damascus. The pilot reported they may have an infectious medical situation aboard the plane. When they arrived at Dulles the plane was quarantined and the passengers were detained by the CDC for screening. By that point, Weyland was unconscious. No one else showed symptoms."

"Wouldn't they have diverted?"

"Not necessarily," Kurkowski said. "They were well into a transatlantic flight before Weyland was unable to hide her symptoms any longer."

Billy exhaled slowly. "Go on. I'm still not seeing our nexus."

"That's just it. On the surface, there doesn't appear to be one. Not until you dig into *why* Marie Weyland was in Syria."

"Okay?"

"Did you hear about the village that was hit with incendiaries over in Northwestern Syria? Confirmed bad guys. Exigent circumstances."

Billy shook his head. "That's every week these days…"

"Exactly. So, nobody took notice. Except Marie. While digging into the terrorist threat there, she discovered they were embedded in a settlement of Syrian refugees." Kurkowski let that last part hang in the air. "I'm talking about civilians, Captain. A lot of them."

Billy scrunched his brow and examined the screen on Kurkowski's tablet. "Those ops with high likelihood of major civilian casualties always get screened out and denied."

"This one didn't."

"Hang on." Billy held up his hands. "Are you saying the Army

45

knew it was full of civies and they still hit it? Are we talking about a war crime here?"

Kurkowski nodded. "Our nexus."

Billy shook his head. He suddenly felt hot, smothered. "But why?"

"That's what Marie Weyland wanted to know," Kurkowski said. "And now that she's comatose, there's no way for us to find out."

"There's no way it's a coincidence she's sick with an unknown infectious disease after visiting an encampment that our people wiped out without regard to innocent casualties."

"My thoughts exactly," Kurkowski said, swiping to another screen and handing the tablet over. "I got this data from the CDC. They were tight lipped and refused to speculate, but look at the initial symptoms…"

Billy scanned the readout. He looked at Kurkowski. "Don't tell me with a name like Marie Weyland…?"

Kurkowski nodded. "Third generation. Maternal grandfather."

"Son of a bitch," Billy pressed his teeth together. "And the others on the plane?"

"That's the thing. They're missing. Once they were cleared by the CDC, they were let go. None of them ever made it home."

"Adam, if we're looking at a military orchestrated cover up…"

Kurkowski shook his round head. "That's the least of our worries if this is—"

"Don't. Don't even say it." Billy turned and marched into his office, powering up his workstation. Behind him Kurkowski stopped at the door.

"Cap, everyone is going to be asking questions."

"Get our guys chasing down leads on this, but keep it quiet.

When we blow the lid on this it better have been air tight up until that point. Covering up an airstrike is one thing, heads would roll, but... but if the reason is what you're suggesting..." Billy couldn't bring himself to say the words out loud.

"Roger that, sir," Kurkowski said.

"I want you to head it up, Kurkowski. Focus on the airstrike and the war crime angle since that's our nexus. Once I know what you know and have your file, ASAP, then I'll go to the Major. Not before."

"Roger."

"Listen to me, Kurkowski." Billy sighed, pumping a squirt of sanitizer into his hands and rubbing furiously. "Our asses are going to take fire for this, so we've got to be sure. Understand? If there was high-altitude drone footage of the strike—I want it for close examination."

"They're not going to want to release that."

"If they stonewall us, go for the high-res satellite imagery. Get creative."

"And what about you, sir?"

"I'll track down more info on this Marie Weyland. We have to know what she knows and determine definitively what she's infected with. If it really is related to Omega, we'd better hope to God it's contained." He flicked his gaze at the First Sergeant. "Go on. Get to it."

"Yes, sir."

Billy leaned back in his chair. Was it possible the Omega protocol had somehow activated even after everything he'd done to see that it never saw the light of day? If that was true, it would mean someone high up had taken matters into their own hands— and played God in the process. Billy let out a long stream of air that whistled through pinched lips. This whole damn mess, conspiracy or not, revolved around Marie Weyland. He needed to get to the CDC isolation unit, and he needed to get there now.

CHAPTER FIVE

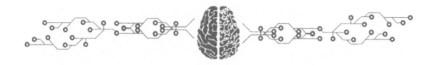

CDC Isolation Facility, Dulles Airport, Washington

Evan paced the corridor of the sterile fluorescent-lit white and gray CDC facility, a Styrofoam cup of cold machine coffee clasped in both hands. It had been two days and he was still feeling anxious about the men in suits who kept coming to his home and knocking on the door. He'd yet to speak with them; the thought of getting grilled and having to answer their questions was just too much for him to take right now. He had to focus on Marie. She was all that mattered.

The problem was, Marie was not only unconscious and unresponsive to any form of antibiotics, her organs were shutting down, too. Evan hadn't even been allowed in to be close to her. Instead, he was made to stare through a window and watch the life ebb away from the pale near-corpse of his beloved.

Josephine, the woman in charge—totally unqualified and far too young for such responsibility, to Evan's mind—had been less than useless. She only seemed capable of following CDC protocol to the letter, offering weak platitudes and thin words of hope that the next round of treatment would yield a result. Evan liked people who were direct and got to the point. This woman was neither.

The information he'd given the doctor, at least about the bio-container, seemed to have confirmed their initial diagnosis: it was a bacterial infection. But one they had never seen before, and one that seemed to make little sense, with regard to who it affected. Apparently, there had been more people on the flight, all screened and released. Given the virility of the infection, the CDC were at a loss as to why only Marie was symptomatic.

Evan stared through the window to the isolation room in a growing state of despair. Marie lay there, her chest slowly rising and falling as commanded by the respirator. The monitor at her side blipped along at a steady, slow pace. There was a hole in Evan's chest, a void usually filled with her kindness, her smile, and the warmth of her embrace. He felt her slipping away beneath a looming shadow of fear and regret for all the things he had never been able say to the woman he loved.

"Dr. Weyland."

Evan didn't respond. The tone of Dr. Harkness's voice meant she had nothing good to say.

"Evan," the woman pressed.

"Mhm," Evan managed.

"We need to talk," she said, placing a hand on his shoulder.

Evan turned to meet her dark eyes, however uncomfortable it made him.

"Perhaps in another room?" she said.

The doctor turned and ambled away, carrying the laptop case that went everywhere with her. There was purpose to her stroll—clearly, she wanted to get to a quiet room, give him the bad news, and then get the hell away from him as fast as possible. Evan followed, dread filling his core, his limbs heavy and uncooperative.

Dr. Harkness opened the door to a small stark room with a single square table and two metal-legged chairs that screeched as she pulled them across the tiled floor. Evan and the doctor sat in painful silence. Normally Evan would relish the quiet, but today the hush seemed to scream as loud as any bar he'd frequented.

"I think you may need to get your wife's affairs in order," the doctor began.

Evan frowned.

Josephine sighed. "It won't be long," she said, clamping her hands together.

"She's going to die," Evan said, the words almost not making it out—the stone in his throat growing larger by the second.

The doctor nodded.

"Why can't you treat a bacterial infection?" Evan asked.

"It's like nothing we've ever seen, Evan," she replied. "We can barely get a sample of it. It's not hanging around in the blood stream. And even when we do, we can't culture it. It forms protective layers and goes into suspended animation. Something in your wife's biology keeps it alive within her, but we don't know what. If we can't culture it, we can't test treatments on it. And we've dosed Marie with every known antibacterial in our arsenal. You have no idea how upsetting it is to have to admit defeat here—" The doctor's words trailed off as she realized the folly of her statement.

Evan wasn't listening. He'd locked onto something she'd said a moment earlier. "The infection isn't in her blood?"

"No."

"Then where is it?" Evan pressed.

The doctor pulled the laptop from her case and opened it. A quick boot up, then she initiated an app that held all of Marie's files. She clicked on a fluorescent scan. The image on the screen was of his wife's brain. The doctor toggled the mouse wheel, and

51

the image altered, showing different slices of Marie's brain moving from the frontal lobe to the cerebellum and occipital lobe.

The medulla was lit up. Luminescent blue, as if all the bacteria had called a town hall and the brain stem was the meeting place. From every angle, through every pass through the image of his wife's brilliant mind, the medulla looked like Las Vegas at night.

"They've accumulated here," the doctor said. "We've considered every scenario. Even flushing out the brain stem, but we have no idea how effective that would be or what damage we would do to the medulla. We could ruin her control of her heart and lungs—not that I have to tell you."

Evan stared at the image, struggling to comprehend losing his wife. Even though she was constantly in some Middle Eastern war zone, somehow, he always knew she would come home. But this, this was new. An enemy no one understood. His sweet Marie was out of time.

Think, Evan. In the end, all biology is a physical process. That's how Evan understood it so well. He could see everything and how it happened. The human body was just a machine, from the arms and legs to the tiny ribosome crawling along mRNA to build proteins. Evan focused on the rhythm of his diaphragm, then stared at the fluorescent image once more. He pulled the brain scan from the computer screen into the virtual space of his own neural synapses, his hyper accurate mind's eye, and examined it in three dimensions—turning and twisting it every which way.

"Dr. Weyland?" Dr. Harkness said, though her voice was muffled as if she spoke to him from behind glass.

Of course, he thought.

"Dr. Weyland?" Harkness repeated.

"What if I could cut them out?" Evan said.

"That's what antibiotics do, you know that. Target bacterial cell walls, ribosomes or DNA, and prevent normal cell function, but none are—"

"No, I mean *cut* them out," Evan said, mimicking a knife with his hand.

Dr. Harkness frowned. "Like physically? No surgeon in the world can operate at cellular level. You can't just take a scalpel and—"

"I have to leave," Evan said, already on his feet.

"I'm sorry?"

"I need to go. I'll be back. But right now, I need to go."

"Dr. Weyland, I don't think you understand."

"Life support will keep her brain alive and her organs working?" Evan said.

"Yes, but that's not life. That's not how you want your wife to live…"

"That's all I need for now."

Evan pushed through the door without a goodbye and began his march down the corridor to the elevator. He needed to get to his lab. He needed to talk to Lai—*he* would understand. He could help. Evan cursed himself for not thinking of the idea earlier. How stupid could he be? Of *course* this was the answer. Lai would help him; he'd have to. Why wouldn't he? Marie's life was at stake.

Head down, Evan crashed into someone. His train of thought obliterated, Evan looked up to meet the steely gaze of a well-built, clean shaven man in a dark suit. The man radiated intensity, and though shorter than Evan, had the presence of someone twice his size.

The stranger said nothing for a moment, his stare roving over Evan with calculating judgment.

53

"I'm sorry," Evan said, attempting to shuffle past.

"Dr. Weyland," the man said. It wasn't a question. "Marie Weyland's husband. You're a hard man to reach."

Evan turned, fidgeting, his own stare now fixed on the man's shoes gleaming with mirror-like polish.

"I'm Billy Vick, I'm with the U.S. Army's Criminal Investigation Command." He extended his hand, revealing scars across the knuckles. "My unit is investigating your wife's case."

Evan shook the agent's hand and managed to bring his focal point to the well-pressed shirt covering the man's broad chest. "I need to go," Evan stammered.

"I'm sorry, Dr. Weyland, but I really do need to ask you a few questions, about your wife."

Billy stared at Evan Weyland standing before him, the fellow's eyes averted as if searching the floor for imperfections. Billy took in the rigid posture and starched, obsessively clean appearance. "Hello? Can you hear me?"

"Yes," Evan said, not raising his eyes.

Billy frowned.

An assertive looking woman, athletic with arresting green eyes, wearing business attire and a guest badge, entered the hallway and moved with purpose to push past on her way to the quarantine sector.

"Do you mind?" she told Billy, who stood in the middle of the cramped hallway.

He waved her past. "Sorry about that." Billy turned his

attention back to Evan, still and silent as a statue. "You *are* kin to Marie Weyland?"

"Yes."

"Okay…" Billy scrunched his shoulders, lowering his head in an attempt to get the odd fellow to look at him. Two days of trying to track this guy down, only for him to act like this? *Guilty conscience*, Billy thought. Guilty of what, he didn't yet know, but he'd find out. He always did.

"I know it's a difficult time right now, but the questions I have for you are just routine, information-gathering sort of stuff. It may help us determine what happened to your wife." Billy hoped his tone was relaxed enough.

Nothing.

Billy raised his eyebrows.

Evan turned on a dime, as if anchored on the spot. He raised a hand and pointed half-heartedly in the direction of the isolation ward. "My wife is sick. I want to stay close to her," Evan said.

Billy nodded. "Of course. We'll stay close. There's a room just off the lobby used for medical consultations. It might offer us a little more privacy than this. Does that work for you?"

After a moment, Evan nodded, running a hand through his close-cropped, ash-colored hair.

"Right this way." Billy crossed the lobby and with a swipe of the labeled guest keycard, disengaged the latch.

Evan, slim and taller than Billy by about six inches, brushed past and took a seat. Billy shut the door behind him, pulled over a chair and positioned it between Evan—now white as a sheet and glistening in a sheen of sweat—and the door.

"I want to ask a question," Evan said in a clipped tone as Billy set his notepad on the coffee table to his right.

A little surprised at the outburst, Billy sat back in his chair. "Sure."

"Why is an Army criminal investigator interested in my wife?"

"A fair question," Billy said, interlacing his fingers. "One I'm not at much liberty to answer in detail, I'm afraid. It's quite complicated, I assure you. Just know that we have an interest in your wife's condition."

Evan Weyland looked at the gray carpeted floor, the ceiling tiles, the short lamp on the end table. His gaze seemed to take in everything in the small, pale blue room, everything but Billy's person.

"Marie isn't in the Army," Evan said with an air of finality. "She's a news correspondent."

Billy smiled. "Correct."

"I don't understand why you're here."

"Maybe if I could just ask you a few quick questions," Billy said, "I can resolve my business and leave you to care for your wife."

After a moment, Evan gave a reluctant nod.

"Good." Billy pulled the steno pad into his lap and clicked down on a ballpoint pen. "Do you have any idea what your wife was looking into on her trip overseas?"

"No." Evan shook his head.

"No clue? No speculation?" Billy asked, and made a few notes.

"I don't like speculation."

Billy frowned, watching as Evan fiddled with the buttons on his shirt. "All right. Can you tell me if you have any knowledge at all about where she traveled to, or where she might have been?"

"No."

"But, you're her husband," Billy said.

"Yes."

Billy took a breath. Was this guy trying to screw with him? "So, she never told you anything, where she was going? Anything like that?"

"She traveled to the Middle East," Evan said.

"I'm aware of that part," Billy said. "Anything else?"

"I had her flight itinerary. I knew something was wrong when her flight didn't come in on time. Then I got the call about her being quarantined here."

Billy jotted down a few notes, more to look like he was taking notes than anything. He tilted his head. "You sure you don't know anything else, Dr. Weyland?" He clicked his ballpoint pen in and out four times. Then again, another three.

"I'm sure."

Billy leaned forward and clicked his pen a few more times. "I have a hard time believing your wife, who you seem quite devoted to, wouldn't tell you anything about what she found."

"I'm sorry," Evan said, rubbing at his ash-blond hair again.

Billy perked up. "What are you sorry for, Dr. Weyland?"

"I'm sorry you don't believe me."

The skin at the base of Billy's neck prickled and clicked his pen a half dozen more times. "Are you playing games with me? Because this is very serious."

"I'm aware it's serious," Evan said, still rubbing his head.

"I'm not sure you are, sir. You've deliberately avoided me and my men for two days. You look everywhere in this room but at me, which is a sign of evasiveness. Then you want to dance around my questions and give me non-answers. So, I'm not convinced you understand the gravity of what you and your wife are caught up in. It could be serious—as in prison-time serious. And with habeas corpus suspended, there's no telling when you might see a trial…"

Billy let his voice trail off.

"But you're with the Army, you can't—" Evan started.

"Arrest you?" Billy said. "Actually, I can. You must have missed congress passing the Hugh Lowery National Defense Authorization Act last year. Posse Comitatus has been temporarily suspended and military personnel deployed stateside have the authority to detain, arrest, and enforce both state and federal law." Billy clicked the pen over and over.

"Can... can you stop that, please?" Evan asked, staring at the pen.

Billy looked at his pen. "This?" He clicked it a few more times.

"Yes." Evan pinched his eyes shut.

Billy clicked the pen twice more. "You're lying to me, Evan. I know your wife told you something or passed on secure information to you. I have her phone data records. She uploaded something to a secure cloud. Only she and one other person have access to that space. Want to take a guess who that is?" Billy, confident his words had struck a chord, sat still and stared. Evan blinked a few times and rubbed his head again. He looked down, then back up, his gaze rising to Billy's face, and sat still as a statue with his hands folded in his lap. A minute of total silence passed.

Billy squinted, searching Evan's face. It was almost as if this Weyland guy stared at his nose. Billy leaned forward clicking his pen over and over. "Hello? Evan? You still there?"

"Yes."

"Well?" Billy said.

"Well what?"

"Dammit, you know *well what*. How about you start giving me straight answers or I'll see you arrested for conspiracy and you can explain yourself under oath in federal court. Is that what you want?"

Evan stared straight ahead, his lips moving but no words coming out. His face was pale, as if all the blood had run out of it, his gaze far away. For a second Billy thought the man might faint. Instead, to Billy's great surprise, Evan Weyland stood from his chair and walked to the door.

"Whoa, hang on a second." Billy rose, his hand outstretched. "We're not quite done here."

"Am I under arrest?" Evan said, his tone flat.

Billy considered his answer. He could do it. He could detain this man right now with very little cause, but was that American? If he was going to do this, he wanted to do it right.

"Right now," Evan said. "Am I under arrest *right now*?"

Billy motioned for him to calm down. "No. You're not under arrest at this time, sir."

"Then I'm leaving. Marie needs me." Evan stepped around Billy and flung the door open. With a *click* the door shut behind him.

Left alone and tingling with irritation, Billy went over the interaction in his head—three, four, five times. He'd played it all wrong; mistook Evan Weyland's restless and strange behavior as weakness. Billy needed more, needed to know what was in the secure cloud storage. This Dr. Evan Weyland knew a hell of a lot more than he was letting on.

59

CHAPTER SIX

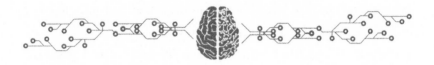

Interstate Checkpoint Two, Maryland

The checkpoint was taking far too long. *Could that military guy be on his way to take me into custody,* Evan thought. He didn't have time for that. In fact, he had no time at all.

"Attention, your vehicle is stopped in traffic," the car's onboard computer said in a genderless tone. *"Auto-drive Assistant estimates another twenty-five minute wait. You may also choose to take manual control and arrive at your destination by another route."*

Evan punched the dismiss key on the console, silencing the message. He glanced at his watch: thirty-six minutes without any progress. He powered down the car door window and poked his head out. What was the hold up?

A young man dressed in skin tight jeans and an oversized Ravens jersey, smoking a cigarette, wandered up to Evan's window. "Bomb threat," he said. "Someone called it in."

"What?" Evan replied without looking up, his nose wrinkled at the stench of tobacco.

"Bomb," the guy repeated, again. "I heard it on my scanner. I like to keep in the know, you know?"

Evan checked his rearview mirror. The car behind had the driver side door wide open, a young woman in the passenger seat.

This guy must have been the driver, also stuck in the line.

"We'll be here for a while. This is the third time this week. But don't worry, if it were real, they'd have evacuated us by now. This is just *the man* showing they control us, you know?"

"Oh," was all Evan could muster.

Whatever the problem, it paled in comparison to his wife's. Evan needed to get to the lab, and this hold up was not helping. He gripped the steering wheel tighter, trying to block out the incessant talking of the man at the window, but his voice became a drone that grew in intensity, like a beehive becoming louder and louder with each worker that arrived home, until Evan thought his brain might explode. He sucked in a breath to yell at the smoking self-proclaimed bomb expert, when the lungful of air was knocked from him. His car rocked in the wake of stunning overpressure.

Evan looked to where the man at the window had been standing, but he'd either run off or been vaporized. Ears ringing, Evan turned his focus back to the traffic jam. Half a dozen cars ahead, a fireball rose into the sky, followed by a blistering shockwave. The windshield of Evan's Toyota shattered into a mosaic of a thousand tiny shards, but remained in place. Evan's heart raced in his breast. *If I die, Marie dies, too.* He had to make it to the lab, it was all that mattered. He pulled on the door handle and stepped out. The searing atmosphere scorched his face and waves of thick, dry air pushed against him—demanding he flee for his life. "Marie," he said, his mouth filled with the growing cloud of ash.

Another explosion sent glass scatting across the asphalt. Car alarms wailed through the smoke, while people ran screaming in every direction. Evan clamped his hands over his ears to muffle the auditory barrage, his eyes screwed shut to block out the orange flames licking at the clouds.

A stunned woman missing a hand stumbled past, her clothes on fire, skin blackened and charred. She let out a horrible, prolonged moan, then fell face first into the concrete and laid there unmoving. Fire crawled up her body and caught her hair alight. Three men, civilians who'd been farther back in the queue, rushed forward slapping at the flames with their jackets and blankets. The smell of burned flesh and singed hair made Evan want to vomit.

He pushed off into a sprint toward the burning wreckage of destroyed family cars and the mangled military checkpoint.

The screams grew louder and the squeal of warping metal became unbearable as disfigured vehicles burned and melted. Evan covered his ears and squinted until he could barely see. A soldier wielding an M16 shouted something at Evan, but it was white noise against the catastrophic backdrop. Only Evan's own breathing seemed to rise above the din. He used it as a focal point, pushed on past the twisted metal heap of a burning Tacoma sitting in a small crater, and half walked, half ran along the edge of the highway. At this pace, he calculated it would take him two hours to make it to the lab.

He made it in an hour and a half.

Out of breath, covered in a layer of sticky gray dust and muscles burning with lactic acid, Evan fell through the main entrance to Johns Hopkins Hospital. As he moved through the building, he grabbed for every door handle, railing, and wall to support his aching body. He had to get to the lab.

The door swung open and clanged against the coat rack behind it. Evan stumbled in, dazed and exhausted. He fell against his desk and slumped into his chair, sucking at the filtered air.

"Evan?"

A slow and pained glance up. It was Lai.

"Evan, what the hell is going on?"

"Bomb," Evan wheezed. "There was a bomb."

"You were caught in an attack? And *walked* here? Shouldn't you be at the hospital?" Lai grabbed Evan under the arm.

Evan shook his head and pulled away. "I need the bots."

"The bots? What for? Shouldn't you go to the ER instead?"

"Not for me," Evan said. "For Marie."

Lai backed away. "She's in CDC isolation. They have the best people working on it, Evan."

Evan shook his head again, the full use of his lungs returning. "She's dying, Lai."

His boss sighed. "I'm so sorry, Evan. I am, really. I can't imagine what you're going through."

"I need the bots."

"Evan, they haven't been through clinical trials," Lai said, arms waving. "We're not even out of phase one yet. We have to look at optimal dosing, any adverse events, immune-mediated response, renal clearance for sure. Not to mention, so far *only you've* had a functional interface."

"It'll work," Evan said, already scanning the room for what he needed. "I can make it work."

Lai took a step toward Evan, right inside his personal space.

Under normal circumstances, Evan dealt well enough with such invasions. He'd always position himself such that a simple step backward or to the side would reestablish his perimeter, but today he was cornered. "I just want the rig and the bots," Evan replied. "Please, Lai."

Lai's face froze in annoying faux-empathy. An expression Evan knew well. Most people adopted it if he mentioned being on the spectrum and they had zero idea how to deal with the information. As if to them he immediately became less of a person and more something to pity or placate with fake condolences. Some even treated him like a child, and either talked slower or in simpler words. Lai did it whenever Evan talked about Marie, as if he didn't believe their marriage to be real. Marie had said Lai was jealous and possessive, and couldn't keep a boyfriend.

Marie.

Evan pushed past Lai, and headed to the refrigerator. He grabbed a Styrofoam box from the shelf and opened it. The dry ice inside released a waft of carbon dioxide into the warmer lab air. Evan turned his attention to the black panel embedded in the fridge. A quick tap of a code and thumb print ID, and the door popped open to reveal a rack holding six glass vials, each about the size of a rifle bullet, with metallic endcaps and a mercury-like liquid inside. He grabbed up all six, placed them in the Styrofoam box, and closed the lid.

Next was the gun—colloquially known as the Gatling Gun by his colleagues. Evan didn't care for the name. The bots needed to be introduced to the blood stream rapidly. While some patients could have a standard IV over several hours, the project brief had been to also create a rapid-fire mechanism that could be used in the field. The Gatling Gun had six chambers like a revolver, and a nauseating ten-gauge needle more than 3.5 millimeters wide. When fired, the gun would dump all six chambers into the blood vessel in quick succession.

Evan moved to the safe on the other side of the lab, placed the box next to the vacuum hood, and again began punching in his access code.

Lai stole the box of vials and clutched it to his chest. "You can't do this, Evan. It's not ethical. I'm sorry about Marie, but this is millions of dollars of technology and years of research. It's my career. If I let you take it, I'm done. If I turn a blind eye and you use the bots and something goes wrong, I'm done." He shook his head, lips mashed together in defiance.

Is Lai really putting his career above Marie's life?

Evan needed that box. It was Marie's only chance. He reached out to grab the container but knocked it from Lai's hands. The Styrofoam box hit the floor and spilled chunks of dry ice and the vials across the floor. Evan held his breath, watching the glass ampoules tumble end over end, praying to a god he didn't believe in they wouldn't break.

Thankfully, the end caps provided enough protection, and the vials rolled under his desk. Evan dropped to his hands and knees to gather them, but Lai stepped between him and his prize.

Evan's heartbeat became so loud in his ears almost nothing else was audible. Lai's words, muffled and garbled, lost all meaning. Not that it mattered, nothing Lai said would change Evan's mind.

"Lai, move," Evan said as he rose to his feet.

"I can't, Evan, I'm sorry."

"You're not sorry," Evan said. "It's Marie, Lai. My wife."

Lai seemed rooted to the spot; his expression unchanging.

"Please. She'll die." The lump in Evan's throat became so large he thought it might cut off his air.

Lai's face hardened. "And if you mess this up, thousands more may die, Evan. They'd never have access to our invention. Cancer patients."

"Soldiers," Evan spat back.

"Yes, soldiers too. It's how we got the funding. Don't be so naïve."

"I don't do this for soldiers."

"Spoken like a man who can never be called up," Lai snapped back.

Lai had never used Evan's diagnosis against him before. Never as an insult. Lai knew if it meant defending Marie and their way of life, Evan would be first to volunteer—he just wasn't allowed.

"I'm sorry, Evan that was—"

Evan shoved past his colleague. It was enough to knock Lai back and off balance. He stepped on a chunk of dry ice and slipped, his legs stabbing awkwardly at the floor. Evan didn't see it, but he heard the sickening crunch of Lai's skull making contact with the counter. With a thump, Lai slumped to the floor. Blood pooled around his head, and his eyes were wide and glassy.

Evan couldn't move. His legs and arms refused to work. The machinations of his own body, from a single shuddering gasp to the distant sour gurgle of stomach acid, were thunderous. *He must have slipped. Or did I do that?*

A muffled noise. Someone else in the room.

Evan snapped his attention to the doorway. It was Professor Dell, head of the department. The wiry woman, whose business attire seemed to hang from her bones, hung in the entrance shaking like a frightened chihuahua. "What's going on in here?" she snapped.

"I... I..." Evan stammered.

"What the hell, Evan! What happened?" Dell rushed over to Lai and placed two fingers on his neck. Her eyes widened. "He's got no vitals."

No words came from Evan. He covered his ears with his hands, just as he had done as a child when the world became too much. There in that moment he was five years old again, standing in the

66

kindergarten playground alone, counting away the minutes until it was time to go back to a quiet classroom.

"Evan!" Dell screamed at him.

Evan's stare met Dell's frightened and accusatory gaze. His world shuddered to a standstill. His vision narrowed and his hearing dimmed, as total vapor lock set in. *Breathe*, Evan told himself. All he needed was the damn bots. But if he took them now, he'd be hunted down. He was screwed. Which meant so was Marie. Would Dell understand? Would she let him take the bots and gun and headset and walk out?

He shook his head rapidly from side to side. His therapists used to call it stimming—figuring he was either under stimulated and needed something more intense, or overstimulated and needing to focus on just one thing. For him it was neither—it felt like he was shaking all the ideas in his head out through his ears so he could sift through them. As a child it used to help him think. He hadn't done it in so long, but right now it was all he had.

And then it happened. Evan's eyes snapped open.

An idea had shaken loose.

NeuroDelve. He had to go to NeuroDelve.

Evan started for the door, hands still over his ears.

Dell screamed something, but Evan didn't hear the words. "I'm sorry," he said. "I have to save Marie."

The professor's expression was slack.

Evan didn't wait for an answer, instead he ran along the corridor and into the square stairwell. On the last corner he tripped and fell into the wall. There he stayed, chest heaving, his brain on fire. How would he get to NeuroDelve, all the way up in Boston? He didn't have a car now. He'd been so intent on getting to the lab, he'd left it behind at the ruined checkpoint. And with a bomb attack, there would be even more blockades. Public transport might be his only way forward. The trains now had automated scanning points on their routes to detect bombs and weapons. But that also meant sitting with a lot of people for more than six hours and hoping his image wasn't fed to facial recognition cameras.

Evan's chest cramped again. *Get over it, Evan. You need to save your wife.*

Penn Station was about 1.6 miles from Johns Hopkins. He could walk that, keep to the smaller streets, and stay off the main routes. Evan was adept at utilizing the lesser trodden paths everywhere. Without the solitude of his car, quiet streets were the next best thing.

A clang of a door in the stairwell several floors above echoed down to him. Evan lurched into action again and made for the fire escape. No doubt Dell would have alerted security already. He couldn't risk being caught. The fire door burst open as he hit the brace bar, the alarm wailing in response. Evan thought he might vomit from the pressure of the shrieking noise, but the farther he ran the less it stabbed into his brain and the more he could focus. What came next was all that mattered. He had to get to Boston.

CHAPTER SEVEN

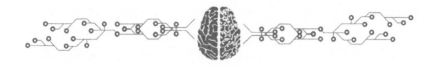

U.S. Army CID HQ, Quantico, Virginia

Wedged in a cramped parking space between a forgettable electric micro-car and an oversized orange truck with *Martinez* written in flowing script across the back glass, Billy sat drumming his fingers on the steering wheel of his automated Ford Explorer, feeling more than a little like the universe had drawn its plans against him. He pulled a small clear bottle from inside the console, squeezing a dime-sized amount of aloe scented hand sanitizer into his palm. He rubbed at his hands and fingers as if scrubbing a cooking pan laden with burnt residue.

"I mean, does that make sense to you?" The voice of his wife filtered through the Bluetooth-linked car stereo. "I just want you to understand what I'm feeling right now."

Billy waved his hands to finish the drying process. He leaned his head back against the headrest. "Yes, I understand. It's hard on you guys when I get involved in a case like this."

"But it's not that, really. The boys are a little disappointed, but they'll be fine. I'm fine as well. I can handle it. You know I can." Rosie paused, the open line bleeding soft white noise into the interior of the car.

"But?" Billy said, with a little more of an irritated sigh than he meant.

Rosie mirrored with a sigh of her own. "It's just you... and I'm not trying to give you a hard time, because I know what you do is important, and you've been busy—but you disappear on us, Billy. I mean, completely disappear. We haven't seen you in two days, and with the way things are out there, it's disconcerting."

"I know, honey. I'm... I've had to drive up to Baltimore to follow up on some leads, and when I got back, I ended up crashing in my office. I've got a lot going on and I can't—"

"Come home to sleep?" Billy could feel the heat coming off Rosie's words. "We're fifteen minutes away from your office. Ten with no traffic."

"Rosie, I know, okay? Can you give me a break? I'm dealing with a lot right now. I don't need grief from you on top of it."

There was a longer pause filled with the muted wash of more white noise.

"I love you, Billy," she said, her voice low. "I always will. Let us know when you can manage to squeeze in some time for your family."

Billy opened his mouth to respond when there was a peep from the vehicle's Bluetooth, the words *Call Ended* flashing across the digital dash.

"Dammit." Teeth clenched, fists balled, Billy could feel the days of pent-up emotion pooling in the center of his chest. For a second he thought he might explode. *Breathe through it, Billy*, he told himself. *Just like the shrink told you.* The fury seemed to ebb to a manageable level. He often wondered where all that emotion actually went—the storm of crushing fear, anger, and loss swirling inside him like a hurricane capable of laying waste to everything he'd worked so hard to build.

70

Part of Billy died in Syria, laid to rest alongside his brothers when they didn't return home from their last tour of duty. The crater blasted in his soul was now just a bottomless reservoir filled pain—the kind of hurt that binds with a person's very being. His wife often reminded him he was doing okay, compared with other guys who'd made it back. Post-traumatic stress manifested in many ways, and some couldn't harness the dangerous energy it pushed to the surface. Those guys disappeared into a bottle, got addicted to pills—or worse—took their own life leaving their family to pick up the pieces.

That wasn't Billy.

He understood his wounds could make him indomitable. That the scars of war, the pain and the fear of his own helplessness in the face of catastrophe, could drive him further than his will alone could take him. Rather than burden Rosie or his boys, Billy poured it into his work. Never coming up for air until the threat was over and the mission was accomplished. At night, when everyone else was at home watching TV or catching up on sleep, Billy worked. *Just two more hours*, he'd tell himself at three in the morning. But two more hours was never enough. Not until the mission was accomplished.

The phone rang, jolting Billy from his thoughts. He looked at the vehicle's display screen: *Unknown.* He didn't answer these calls, but the last few days had been anything but usual. Billy pressed the answer key. "Vick."

"Billy," a familiar voice said.

"Clarence?" Billy asked. "I didn't recognize the number. You calling from a masked line?"

"I am. They're encrypting all calls coming out of headquarters these days. What's up? I got your message."

71

Clarence was a good guy. Worked for the Bureau. He and Billy had been through a handful of forensic schools together. Billy tried to think how to best describe the mess he'd gotten himself into without creating a breach of classified information.

"You know anything about the reporter who flew into Dulles a few days ago on a military contracted flight?"

"Yeah, uh, Weyland, was it? A little bit. It was looked at by the FBI initially as a possible terrorist incident, but that notion was dismissed. She was sick and got quarantined. Everyone else was screened and released. CDC has operational control of the situation, which means it's not a law enforcement matter. We never officially opened a case on it."

"I see," Billy said.

"Why? Are you looking into that?"

"As a matter of fact, yeah. The Army may have a nexus."

"Something the reporter was into?" Clarence asked.

"Something like that."

"What do you need, Billy? I'll help if I can." Clarence sounded exhausted. "We're slammed right now. Just had another bombing, this one at the I-95/I-395 interchange."

"I was looking for more on the Weylands." Billy tapped the steering wheel with his palm. "Right now, the core of my investigation revolves around the woman, who is unconscious, and her husband, Evan Weyland, who is not cooperating."

"You can still detain him indefinitely with habeas corpus suspended."

"Yeah, I know..." Billy paused, not wanting to say too much. "I was hoping to not have to do that yet. I just need this guy to cooperate with my investigation. I know you said you guys didn't open a file on the Weylands, but do you know if your people

72

uncovered anything while looking into them?"

"Not to my knowledge, but I'll double check for you." Clarence said, then seemed to debate on whether to say more. "One thing did flag—but it was legit. Turns out he's employed by Johns Hopkins. He's been working on some high-speed research project. Real hush hush."

"Really?" Billy sat forward. "What sort of research?"

"Aggressive cancer therapy. Cutting edge medical stuff that sounds more like science fiction to me."

"Interesting."

"Yeah, I thought so, too," Clarence said. "But that's all I know. When we asked, the university politely told us to get lost."

Billy's attention turned to several stoic-faced personnel moving from their vehicles to the secure front entrance of the Russel-Knox building.

"Hey, man," Clarence said. "Sorry, but I'm heading out to the scene of this bombing. I'll have to catch you later."

"Sure. Thanks, Clarence," Billy said, touching the *End Call* button on the screen.

Even if Evan Weyland is working on something for the university, that doesn't mean anything to this investigation. Does it? Billy shook his head. Nothing about this damn case so far added up to anything worth talking about. He rattled through his contacts and found Adam's number. He pressed it and waited.

The line hummed for a full thirty seconds before Adam answered.

"Cap?"

"Kurkowski, I'm drowning here," Billy said. "Tell me you have something?"

"Of any relevance?" Kurkowski said.

"A guy can hope, can't he?" Billy said.

"Sorry, Cap. Nothing glaring so far. Just the Weyland lady's illness and the dodgy circumstances surrounding it. I'll keep digging."

"Okay, keep me posted."

Billy quit the call and let out a loaded sigh. He had no choice. He'd have to take this mess—all conjecture and theories—to the Major.

Minutes later, outside the unit commander's frosted glass door, Billy took a moment to straighten his tie and brush the lapels of his suit. He composed himself, then knocked on the door frame.

"Come in, Captain," Major Barclay called through the door. Billy entered, gave a crisp salute, and stood at attention. The Major's office was spartan, beset with a clean, militaristic order. Every single item, from the files on his desk to the simple but well-framed plaques and diplomas adorning the walls, had its place. *I bet the damn dust asks for permission to land in here*, Billy thought.

"You have something for me?" the Major asked.

"I do, sir."

"Have a seat," the Major said, leaning back and interlacing his fingers across his chest.

Where to start? Billy made his way around the front of an uncushioned wooden chair—the sort all commanders and supervisors seemed to have in their office to keep subordinates from getting too comfortable—and took a seat.

"So?" the Major said.

Billy felt an anxious prickle crawl down his spine. He looked up to meet the stern gaze of his CID unit commander.

"You had a look at the file I sent over, sir?" Billy said.

"I did." Barclay adjusted his bulk. "What of it?"

"Then you're aware of the circumstances involving a war correspondent by the name of Marie Weyland and how she boarded a military contracted flight out of Damascus, bringing an as of yet unidentified pathogen stateside?"

"I'm aware it's a CDC containment problem. What about this requires CID involvement, or any enforcement, for that matter?"

"I've got my people looking into what came before," Billy said, swiping open high-resolution photographs on his tablet before handing it to the Major. "Just this morning, I confirmed via this satellite imagery, a woman fleeing from a terrorist camp in Northwestern Syria just moments before it was hit with incendiaries."

The Major looked at the still photos and handed the tablet back. "Okay."

"That woman was Marie Weyland, our sick correspondent. The intel is limited, but I have reason to believe the village wasn't a clean target and the army called in an airstrike anyway."

"Not a clean target?" The Major stiffened. "What makes you think that?"

"Information we've dug up indicates the high possibility of hundreds, maybe even a thousand, Syrian refugees in this town at the time of the airstrike."

The Major's face darkened. "Collateral damage is an unfortunate part of our business sometimes, Captain."

"Sir, I'm not talking about a little collateral damage. I'm talking about the Army knowing families were in that town—and we called in the strike anyway." Billy let that sink in for a moment. "Sir, I want to know why. Marie Weyland knows. It's not a coincidence she's infected with an unidentified pathogen after fleeing the target location."

The Major leaned forward, placing his forearms on the desktop, his eyes narrowed. A moment of silence passed between the two men as the Major looked Billy over like a lion eyeing its prey. "You can't be insinuating what I think you are. That mess last year nearly destroyed both of our careers."

"Sir, I stand by my decision to go after and shut down Project Omega. It was un-American. If there's any chance this is even remotely relat—"

"That's neither here nor there." Barclay waved his hand as if something in the room stunk. "What I'm saying to you is neither of us will go down that road again. It's best if you drop this one."

"Drop…" The word seemed to fall from Billy's mouth. "The case? Sir?"

"The world is falling apart. Nobody cares about a bunch of Syrian refugees and the business with Marie and Evan Weyland is already being looked into. I got the call this morning. Drop it."

Billy's mind spun, reeling from the unexpected news. "I don't understand this. Under martial law, the Army has directives to detain and interrogate any suspicious persons in the interest of national security, and you want me to just drop the case?"

"Listen to the words that I'm saying to you." The Major leaned back into his chair. "Drop it. I've got a high-profile theft case I want your unit to look into instead. Happened on base. Brigadier General's nephew."

"A theft case? Now?" Billy balked. "But sir—"

"You're going to have to live with the answer being no, Captain. That's an order. I've got the Weyland thing covered. The lady *and* her husband. We clear?"

Billy's brain crackled as if struck by lightning. He'd not once mentioned Evan Weyland in this briefing, and yet, the Major had now done it *twice*. His superior knew much more than he had disclosed. Not uncommon in the military, but more and more this case just felt off. An empty chill spread in Billy's chest, but he sat unmoving, his eyes fixed straight ahead. "Crystal clear, sir."

"Now," the Major continued, "if your team has come across anything of interest already, it comes through me first. Understand? Outside of that, let me give you a strong word of caution—you need to learn when to let sleeping dogs lie and this isn't something we need to get involved in."

Billy gave a slow nod. "I'll keep that in mind, sir."

"Good. That will be all, Captain," the Major said, turning his attention back to the digital files on his desk.

Billy stood, saluted, and exited left. In the hallway he took what felt like the first breath since he'd entered the Major's office. He gathered himself and straightened his suit, then marched with purpose toward the orderly rows of stamped-out cubicles. Striding past his sparsely furnished office, he made a beeline straight to Kurkowski's desk. The First Sergeant was busy digging through intelligence reports. Billy felt the eyes of his people on him, watching in silent anticipation from their work stations.

"Kurkowski," Billy said, his voice low.

"Sir?"

"I want everyone focused on the airstrike. Full court press, but make sure they know to keep a tight lid on it. Nothing goes higher than me for now. You read me?"

Kurkowski stood, his voice little more than a whisper. "Everything okay?"

"No," Billy said. "Everything is definitely not okay. Watch yourself on this one. If you uncover anything, I want to know about it right away."

"Roger that." Kurkowski paused. "And the Weyland angle?"

"I got it."

"By yourself? You sure?" Kurkowski said.

"Yeah," Billy said, his hand on Kurkowski's shoulder. "I'll be in touch."

A sour feeling in the pit of his gut, Billy took a brisk pace and headed for the exit. He'd never had a superior officer give him orders to stand down on a case before. Something, maybe everything, was wrong with this, and though he had to, he wasn't so sure he wanted to get to the bottom of it anymore.

CHAPTER EIGHT

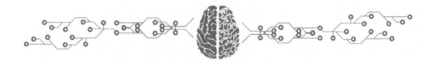

U.S. Army CID HQ, Quantico, Virginia

Major Ronaldo Barclay was a man of strict principle and unwavering conviction. Honor, duty, and country were everything. At least, that's what he told himself. He looked at the family photograph sitting on the corner of his desk, sandwiched between an orderly stack of unchecked case files and a bin that concealed to-do memos arranged by priority. He pursed his lips, studying the faces of his son and daughter, each with their families, surrounding him and his wife. They all looked so happy, so oblivious to the cruel designs of men. In the photo, even the Major appeared the ideal family man, complete with a plastic smile.

Do they still think of me as a good man? Do they know the machine grinds everyone within the churning gears of power and progress?

A knock at the door jarred him from his introspection. He cleared his throat. "Come in."

A trio of men wearing civilian clothes, though carrying themselves with a military swagger, entered. The first, bigger than the rest, had a lumberjack beard and muscular shoulders stacked like a rock-slide scarcely concealed beneath a hunter-green flannel. The second, a shorter man in a black hoodie and wind pants, had a shaved head and a heavy scar that ran horizontal beneath his hairline like he'd lived through an attempted scalping. But it was the final man who caught Barclay's attention. Dressed in a form-fitting navy polo, jeans, and trail-ready sneakers, the guy had an intensity that rivaled a hungry jungle cat. The man checked the hall, then shut the door. He stepped forward his hands clasped behind his back at parade rest. No salutes. No introductions.

"Can I help you gentlemen?" Major Barclay asked, glancing at the space between them and him, while gauging how best to reduce the damage of whatever conflict was brewing.

"Forgive the lack of formality," the front man said. "We have directives to minimize our presence and only answer up our direct chain."

"And who exactly is your chain of command?" Barclay asked.

"You can call me Ryder." The man said, then motioned to his stoic colleagues. "This is my team. We've been tasked with understanding and solving our mutual problem."

Barclay remembered the dressing down he'd taken over the phone from the Pentagon just that morning. They'd instructed him to keep his people out of anything to do with covert ops in Syria. Terrifying how fast things moved when the higher-ups in Washington got involved. "Well, that was quick. They said they might send somebody to look into the situation, but I wasn't expecting…"

A thin smile stretched across Ryder's face.

Never in all Barclay's years had he seen covert government assets deployed to assist with army business on U.S. soil. To his knowledge there wasn't any precedent for this. And yet here they were, standing in his office, sent from D.C. to clean up Vick's mess. He could only guess what alphabet agency they might belong to.

Barclay made a show of rummaging around his desk. "I didn't

receive any official orders."

"Nor will you," Ryder said, his tone cool and low. "This op isn't on the books. There won't be any memos, orders, or records generated by anybody, including you, sir. We have everything we need, case files on our targets, locations, our immediate directives. It's all very fluid and situationally dependent. Anything to do with Omega, even a rumor, is sensitive. I'm sure you understand."

Barclay's mind reeled as he tried to discern how this mess had become *his* mess. It started with Billy Vick a year ago when he'd gone after Project Omega and seen it shut down. Barclay even signed off on the investigation. After all, Vick was an excellent senior agent, a man of conviction and purpose whose team always developed good cases. Barclay had no reason to doubt him. That was before the hammer dropped on them both and entities, dark and powerful, started to pull at his strings.

The whole thing should have slipped by undetected, nice and quiet, a much-needed remedy to the global war on terror. When Vick exposed what it really was, what Project Omega planned to do—to American citizens, no less—he was compelled to act. *And why wouldn't he?* Barclay thought. They'd all taken an oath to defend the nation from enemies both foreign and domestic. Vick had done his duty, and in the process it almost sabotaged both their careers. Omega was put to rest, deep sixed alongside all the other military black box projects that never made it off the ground. Vick was allowed to continue doing his duty. He'd done what was right, and the rule of law, the Constitution of the United States protected him for it.

But this was different. Somehow, it seemed, Omega went forward anyway. Maybe not the way it was intended, through official channels in the United States, but it went forward nonetheless. How, and in partnership with whom, was the question—a question that was downright terrifying. As this thing reared its ugly head a second time, Captain Billy Vick was at the center of it again. This time, the higher ups had sent in a clean-up crew.

"Major Barclay?" Ryder shifted trying to meet the Major's distant gaze. "I said, do we have an understanding?"

"Understanding? You haven't said what you're here for," Barclay said, his stomach roiling.

Ryder eyed the Major for a moment, glanced at his men, then back again. "Intel, for now. I need to know what others, such as Mr. Weyland and his wife, know. And anyone else for that matter."

Barclay swallowed. *He meant Vick.*

"Major, my squad does things differently than you're accustomed," Ryder continued. "We are here to ensure things don't spiral further out of control. We don't work for you, and we don't answer to you. Now, as I understand it, your unit has an open investigation into an airstrike in Syria that may have connections that affect how we do what we do. Is that correct?"

"I gave my assurances over the phone to—"

Ryder held up a hand and shook his head. "Yes or no."

Barclay swallowed back the swelling sense of nausea that crawled its way up his throat. "Yes."

"Just as you were told on the phone, you are to shut this investigation down. Any of your people involved need to stand down so we can deconflict this op as quickly as possible. I don't need good American patriots in our way when it's time for us to go to work."

"In your way," Barclay repeated.

Ryder's eyes seemed to glitter, cold like splinters of ice.

Barclay blinked a few times. Nervous fingers brushed at the outer folds of his suit jacket.

"Major," Ryder's patience appeared to wane. "Do you have people who will be in the way or not?"

Barclay chewed at the inside of his gums. He'd told Vick to drop it, but the notion tickled at the back of his mind. *When was the last time Billy Vick ever gave up on anything?*

"Anyone we need to be aware of?" Ryder continued, a sigh buried in his words.

Barclay continued to blink, dots of perspiration forming on his brow. "No, there's no one."

"We'll be in touch," Ryder said, the three men slipping from the room like apparitions.

Major Barclay waited until the door to his office clicked shut before he collapsed into his chair, his posture sagging like a deflated balloon. With great effort, his eyes scanned the perfect order of his office, walls decorated with awards of a proud soldier. He'd been a man of such duty and principle, once. None of that mattered any longer. He needed this whole stinking mess to go away. If Billy did as he was told, it would be fine. If he didn't, then he'd be removed from the situation. And there wasn't a damn thing Barclay could do about it.

CHAPTER NINE

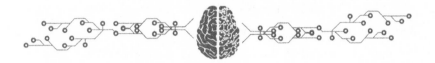

Train en route to Boston

Afar cry from Evan's childhood memories of Thomas the Tank Engine and constructing elaborate tracks that circumnavigated his home, real life trains were horrible metal tubes, crammed with more humans than ethically reasonable, each breathing in the other's fumes—bad breath, bacteria-infested sneezes, flatulence. And then there were bodily noises. Worse than conversation, which Evan had practiced being able to tune out, trains were awkward, voiceless vehicles where the sound of every tap on a smart device, clearing of a throat, and shuffle in a seat seemed amplified. Evan's stomach roiled. He scrunched himself into a tight ball in the corner seat at the very end of one car.

Mercifully, the train wasn't as busy today. Bomb explosions had the effect of driving most people into their homes like prairie dogs hiding from circling eagles. Still, in his car there were fifteen other people. He'd counted them on the way in. An elderly couple, a young family of four, a group of seven friends somewhere in their twenties, a middle-aged businessman, and a woman in her early thirties reading a paperback—*Crossroads* by Mary Ting.

Evan pulled headphones over his ears—he didn't like the in-ear ones, they felt invasive—and opened his news app. The tooth-filled smile of a peroxide blonde reporter appeared. She talked quickly, in that odd diction only reporters used, explaining yet another company takeover by the government, though this one was different. It seemed the U.S. made an attempt to confiscate a robotics program from Japan, and Japan was fighting it. A Dr. Ishiguro had created robots with an uncanny likeness to humans. The U.S. wanted to take the program and combine it with the research they had recently seized from Boston Dynamics, which was the most advanced robotics company in the world—at least for perception, navigation, and intelligence. *Super soldiers*, Evan thought. Whatever it was, he felt bad for BD. They were a competitor for Evan's program.

A man, tall and broad, in camouflage fatigues wielding an M16 rifle, entered the car. The officer stalked the walkway between the seats, scanning each and every passenger. Heavy footfalls pounded out, arrogant and foreboding. Under the current law, basic civil rights had more or less been rescinded. If one was suspected of having terrorist involvements in any fashion, they could be held and interrogated for as long as the government deemed necessary. The local police, once considered protectors of the people, had for the most part been overshadowed by these enforcers of a militant government. At least that's what Marie said. According to his wife, the U.S.A. was no longer any different to Afghanistan.

The footsteps stopped at the seat just in front of Evan, whose heart was now lodged in his throat beating out a powerful legato. The officer's boots shifted on the gray carpet of the carriage floor, scraping the short, rough fibers. *They know*, Evan thought. *They know about Lai.* For most people, instinct took over in such situations: fight or flight. The choice wasn't even conscious. For Evan, the decision was very much front of mind, his brain locked

85

in an endless feedback loop trying to decide whether to sprint for the door or try to wrestle the rifle from the soldier. Both were beyond foolish.

Evan licked his dry lips.

The officer hadn't moved. He must have been studying Evan, waiting for him to meet his gaze—to see if he matched the description of the BOLO that was surely out by now. Still paralyzed, Evan studied the reflection of the seats and his own face in the soldier's glass-like boot toe caps, then moved his gaze up the combat fatigue-covered legs to the duty belt, body armor, and finally the man's clean shaven, square jaw.

But the officer wasn't looking at Evan at all. He was instead fixated on the olive-skinned business man two rows ahead next to the opposite window. Evan breathed a sigh of relief, his chest emptying of trepidation.

"You have identification?" the officer said.

The jittery business man rifled through his pockets and then his bag.

This interaction was already on a downward slope. There were two types of military police officers: those who said please, and those who didn't. The one at the checkpoint earlier had said please, despite pointing a gun at Evan. He was young and scared of someone coming from the quarantine area of the CDC facility.

This guy was a douchebag.

Maybe these soldiers relished the new powers bestowed upon them. Maybe they were racist. Maybe they believed persecution was the only way to keep America safe. Whatever the motive, the outcome was always the same.

"I can't seem to find it," the business man said, his face panic-stricken.

The soldier's fingers curled against the foregrip of the rifle. "Can't find it, or don't have it?"

The train's brakes applied and a voice blasted over the speakers above, "Next stop, New Haven Union Station."

"I know I had it this morning, on the breakfast counter," the man stammered. "My wife may have moved it. My name is Fady Halabi. I work for United Health Group. I travel on this train every day."

The officer shifted his rifle to a more ready position. "You're going to need to get off at this stop with me."

The business man didn't fight. No scuffle or protest. Mr. Halabi was intelligent enough to know if he tried the MP could legally, shoot him on the spot.

The passengers huddled in their little groups, heads down. The continuous squeal of the brakes as the train approached the station filled the void until, at last, it stopped. A loud humming as the bomb and weapon detection drone whizzed down the length of the train. A peep signaled permission to disembark. The automatic doors shunted open.

The deflated Mr. Halabi gathered his briefcase and shuffled out of the car and onto the platform, a rifle barrel hovering about his spine. For a brief moment, the businessman looked back at the train and met Evan's stare through the grimy window.

Mr. Halabi had done nothing wrong, but was hauled away. Evan, on the other hand, had been involved in an accident that resulted in the death of a person, and somehow had been left on the train without so much as a sideways glance from the authorities. He fiddled with the buttons on his shirt. *Stay focused*, he thought. *Marie is all that matters.* The train pulled away from the station and Evan shrank farther down into his seat. *Still several hours to go.*

Evan liked Boston. It was the most European of the East Coast cities. Small and quaint, like Amsterdam or Manchester, central Boston was leafy and red bricked, with a colonial feel—remnants of civilization from across the Atlantic still very much part of the architecture. This was especially true of the Cambridge area, a tiny little square where most of the biotech companies headquartered their businesses.

Career opportunities in Cambridge were endless and it seemed many of Evan's colleagues had hopped on the corporate merry-go-round, changing jobs like their underwear and only having to cross the courtyard to do so. He'd been offered a job up here many times, but always refused. Boston was six hours away by train from Baltimore, and Marie was not going to leave her life there—or at least her home base. So Evan didn't leave either.

NeuroDelve's CEO Sharmila Vashi had made Evan one lucrative offer after another over the last few years. Of course, her company was also the rival for Evan's work at Johns Hopkins and the Endobot program. Evan was loyal and would never have joined Sharmila. And after he'd heard about the ethical nightmare they'd pitched to the DOD, he'd been glad of his choice. But now, the moral high ground seemed unimportant versus the life of his wife. So, on a bitterly cold afternoon in November, Evan stood at the large glass doors to the building that housed NeuroDelve.

Two armed guards eyed him.

Evan marched in as confident as possible, stopped at the receptionist desk, and fixed his stare on the nose of the young man manning the station.

"I'm here to see Ms. Vashi," Evan said.

The young African-American man looked up, taken aback by Evan's abrupt introduction. "Oh, good afternoon. Sure, what's your name so I can find you in the schedule."

"I don't have an appointment."

"Oh," the receptionist said. He stood, trying to meet Evan's eyes. "I'm sorry, but Ms. Vashi is extraordinarily busy. Without an appoint—"

"Tell her it's Evan Weyland."

"I'd have to interrupt—"

"Then interrupt her," Evan blurted out.

The receptionist hovered for a moment, then sat down. "Take a seat, Mr. Weyland, I'll see what I can do."

Evan duly sat on a nearby cushioned seat.

The interior of the twenty-story building was hollow. Evan figured it was meant to denote a blood vessel, the rooms lining the tube representing the cells of the vessel wall, while people, like corpuscles, roamed about on the inside. He shut one eye and leaned his head back to peer up through the center to the very top, imagining he were inside a giant, able to roam about the arteries and veins—a humongous biological maze. His monocular vision, staring way up, elicited vertigo, which immediately made him nauseated. It was a familiar feeling. As a kid he'd run around in tight circles trying to look out of the corner of his eye. Evan smiled to himself, then regretted it. Now was not the time.

"Mr. Weyland?"

Evan snapped back to reality and to the receptionist, standing a little too close.

"S-sorry," Evan said.

"Ms. Vashi will see you now."

"Oh, thank you."

"Can you please sign in?" the receptionist asked. "I'll give you a badge. You have a photo ID?"

Evan followed the receptionist back to the desk, fiddling with his old leather wallet. He opened it up to pull out his driver's license, only to have a faded picture of Marie staring back at him. His hearted faltered. Yes, he had pictures of her on his phone and social media accounts, and they now sold those new intelli-wallets, but they all felt cold and somehow impersonal. Marie had bought him this wallet and placed her picture inside. It was as if he carried a piece of her with him always.

"Mr. Weyland?" the receptionist said, the professional and patient tone fading fast.

"Yes, sorry." Evan handed over his ID.

"Thank you."

The man tapped away at his computer, then handed Evan a white card, with *Visitor* printed on it, attached to a cotton lanyard. Evan slipped it over his head.

"I'll give your license back when you return the visitor's badge. Top floor, first office."

"Thanks," Evan said, already heading for the elevator. "I know my way."

Twenty seconds later, the elevator doors pinged open and Evan was in front of Sharmila's office door. He inhaled and rapped on the glass.

"Come in," came the muted voice from inside.

Evan pushed the door open. It was a sparse room, with little in the way of comforts. Stark walls and a lone desk with two chairs and a high-end computer perched on top. A solitary spider plant sat in the corner, withered and dry.

Sharmila on the other hand was a picture of professional perfection. Hair tied up in a tight bun, makeup flawless, and dressed in a dark crisp skirt suit. Polished designer pumps of a respectable heel height adorned her feet. She stepped from behind her desk, and offered Evan her hand.

"This is a pleasant surprise, Evan," she said, her Delhi accent still lingering despite thirty years in the U.S.A.

"I'm sorry I didn't call before, but it's important," Evan said.

Sharmila sat behind her desk and gestured to the vacant chair nearest Evan. "How can I help you? Has the DOD finally realized their mistake?" She offered a jovial, but possibly fake, smile.

Evan had a hard time reading her. He didn't like sarcasm or veiled meanings. They were so hard to decipher sometimes.

"No, it's not like that," Evan said. "It's Marie, she's sick."

"Oh, I'm sorry," Sharmila said, leaning in. "What's wrong?"

"She came back from the Middle East. She's been infected with something, a bacteria, and it's resistant to everything. The CDC have her in isolation and are just waiting for her to die."

"Oh, Evan, I really am sorry. Truly."

She sounds genuine, Evan thought.

"But I have to say, I'm unclear on why that would bring you to me," Sharmila said. "Especially now. Shouldn't you be with her?"

Why *was* he here? It was possibly the stupidest idea he'd ever had, but right now it was the *only* idea. Marie would die if he didn't do something. Sharmila could help him.

"Is your Endobot program still running?" Evan asked, trying his best to meet the woman's pained gaze.

Sharmila leaned back in her seat, eyes now narrowed in shrewd analysis. "Why?"

"I need to use it," he said plainly.

"Use it? To what?"

"Go after the bacteria, hunt it down."

Sharmila's eye's widened in realization. She pursed her lips. "Your team won the bid, Evan. Why aren't you using your bots for this?"

Evan shuffled in his seat. He would have to lie now. She couldn't know what happened to Lai, or she'd never agree. Evan hated lying, but what choice did he have? Marie would call it withholding details. Sharmila hadn't asked what had happened specifically. He should only tell her what she needed to know.

"Evan?"

"It's not ready," he said finally. "We're not out of phase one yet. Maybe if it were in phase two. But we don't have enough safety data yet and—"

A smile spread across Sharmila's lips. "I see."

"Did you make it to phase three?"

Sharmila shifted in her seat, recrossed her legs, and tented her fingertips. "Ethics committees are difficult. The EMA rejected our proposals, so we are exploring other options."

Evan frowned. "So, that's a no."

"Actually, we've not moved past phase one, the patient and pilot sample is too small. We need more data to be able to progress to an accelerated phase two—three program. You know these bureaucrats, afraid of their own shadow. We'll have data soon enough."

Often the European Medicines Agency and its member states would deny specific clinical trials based on what they considered unethical standards. In the past few decades new drugs were harder and harder to approve because they were pitted against the current standard of care. Drug A had to be more efficacious than Drug B. But, during a trial if the doctor saw no benefit from Drug A, patients were often switched to Drug B, making it difficult to tease apart the effects of each treatment. Placebo-controlled trials were much cleaner—but how could a doctor justify giving a patient a placebo when an approved and effective drug was available for their disease? In these instances, sometimes pharma companies would need to seek out countries that had different views. Evan surmised Sharmila had liaised with such countries for her Endobot program.

"You've gone east?" Evan asked.

Sharmila nodded. "Something like that."

"Let me help. Give me access to your Endobots. You can have all the data."

"Wait," she said, now leaning back on the desk. "What's to stop the DOD just taking my program? Under the new laws, anything considered to be used in the fight against terrorism can be taken, unless iron-clad contracts are in place. We're talking agreed upon at the highest level." Sharmila shook her head. "It sounds like you don't have time for that, Evan."

Evan remained silent.

Sharmila's dark, shrewd eyes studied every inch of Evan's person. "They don't know you're here, do they?"

"No."

"See, Evan, I thought you'd come here because they couldn't justify using your program, but could possibly use ours. Contracts could be put into place. Maybe. But this? It's illegal."

Evan chewed the inside of his mouth and stared at his shoes. "It's Marie. I'm desperate, Sharmila. Think of the data you could collect."

"Evan, data on one patient and one pilot won't move the statistical needle on a program like this. You know that."

Evan rubbed his hair, a cold sweat on his brow. Giving away this next piece of information would likely be the nail in the coffin for his own research. He sucked in a breath, but didn't look up. "What if I told you I'm not a typical pilot? That data from me would change your program forever."

Sharmila cocked her head. "Go on," she said.

Evan stood up and moved around to Sharmila's side of the desk. She backed off slightly, perhaps afraid of what he might do, and waited. Evan pulled a smart phone from his pocket, tapped through a couple of folders, and then held it in front of Sharmila. The video recording was amateur and shaky, but clear enough.

On screen was Lai, wearing the nanobot head gear and gloves. Just in front of him, a drone hovered mid-air at the entrance to the assault course. Offscreen, Evan could be heard to say, "Ready." Lai shuffled into position and the test began.

On screen, the tiny drone zipped along, banking and turning—if not a little clumsily—before making a final run through a valley. It ripped through a thin membrane at the other end. Lai cursed, pulled off the headset, and pretended to throw it against a wall.

Evan felt Sharmila look up at him, but he focused on finding a new video. "Wait," he said, anticipating a question or twelve.

The next video popped up. This time it was Evan on screen, with Lai filming. Guided by the same headgear and the same gloves, the drone glided gracefully through the air, making barrel turns, U-turns and loops to navigate the course with ease. Down the same straight valley at high speed, the drone stopped short of the membrane and banked hard left to make it through a gap little

94

wider than the machine's body, then came to a halt in a circular, pool-like area.

Sharmila turned to face Evan, her mouth open.

Evan forced himself to look down and make eye contact for as long as he could stand to hold it. He tapped on his head and said, "Whatever is different up here… lets me do that. We can't replicate it with anyone else. *I'm* the reason why we got the contract."

Sharmila averted her gaze as she processed this new information.

"And I know why you *didn't* get the contract," Evan continued.

The NeuroDelve CEO glanced up.

Evan forced a smile. "Imagine what your interface could do if it were attached to me."

CHAPTER TEN

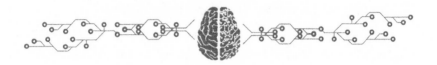

Fells Point, Baltimore, Maryland

Though old, the rough, gray stonework of the Weylands' townhouse appeared in good shape. The shaded window frames needed a fresh coat of cream-colored paint, and the pale blue wooden front door was a little worn and adorned with a wreath of fall colored leaves. A welcoming home in a good neighborhood.

In the Ford Explorer's cup holder, Billy's phone buzzed. He reached down and flipped it over to see a message from Kurkowski: *Call me when you get a chance.* Moments later, the sound of Kurkowski's voice, tired but still carrying a touch of optimism, filled the speakers of Billy's SUV.

"Hey, Cap."

"What's up?" Billy said.

"All right, I'm minding my own business here. Working on the airstrike angle. But I just saw a news report that one of the researchers at Johns Hopkins was found dead with a major head injury. Police suspect foul play."

"Johns Hopkins?" Billy said.

"Yeah, as in where Evan Weyland works. Too much coincidence if you ask me. Thought you'd want to know while

96

you're up that way."

"Thanks, Adam."

"Right. Later," Adam said, then terminated the call.

Billy held the phone in his hand, his wheels spinning in mad circles. He glanced up toward the Weylands' simple residence down the street and absently watched an old woman with white beehive hair cross up ahead with her Pomeranian tucked under her arm. She set the dog down in a bundle of grass and stroked his head. *Can't let poor Snookums dirty his feet*, Billy thought. He looked down at his phone again, searched for a number, and hit *Send*. It rang once.

"Janowick."

"Phil, it's Billy Vick."

"Captain Vick, no shit. Where you been, man? We missed you at the tournament this year."

"Not a whole lot of time for bowling lately, Phil. Work's been crazy."

Phil hocked a gooey laugh, a sound that must have navigated around a mouthful of cheeseburger. "Yeah, tell me about it. We've had two more terrorist-related bombings this month alone, and now the PD just opened another case on that bum killer. Makes six this year. I got paperwork coming out of my ears."

"Baltimore's finest haven't caught that psycho yet?" Billy asked.

Another wet laugh filled Billy's speakers. Phil was an admin Captain with Baltimore PD and a regular at the bowling alley. Not a bad guy, if a bit of a slob. Phil was a talker, and though Billy hated small talk, sometimes there was no way around it. In the world of favors, it was the lubricant that greased the wheels of information.

"Look, Billy," Phil said. "We can't all be CID."

"This is true."

"What can I do for you, bro," Phil said with a grunt.

"Yeah, so I know you guys are busy, just wanted to see if you knew anything about the incident at Johns Hopkins?"

"The downed person in the advanced biotechnology lab? Yeah. Not an official homicide at this point but still big time fishy if you ask me," Phil said, now drinking something.

"Why's that?" Billy squinted, turning the volume lower to make Phil's slurping manageable.

"Some guy fled the scene. And I mean, fled the scene as in running. My guys are looking for him now. What's your interest?"

Billy would have to give something up if he wanted Phil to keep talking. "I'm looking into a case, routine sort of stuff, but as it turns out the guy who I'm looking at is a researcher at Johns Hopkins." Billy forced out a manufactured chuckle. "Wanted to make sure he wasn't dead on the floor."

"Oh yeah, I get it," Phil said. "I'm not on scene obviously, which means I don't know a lot of details, but I do know the stiff is an Asian guy."

"Huh. Interesting," Billy said. "And the guy who ran?"

He heard a shuffling sound of movement on Phil's end, his voice pulling away from the phone.

"Hey Frank, what's the name of the guy our people are looking for over at Johns Hopkins?"

The response was muffled, distant.

"Weeland? That name ring any bells?" Phil said.

An electric tingle peeled across Billy's scalp. He worked to keep his voice neutral. "Nah, not my guy. I appreciate it though, Phil."

"No problem, Agent Vick," Phil said with dramatic flair.

"Hey," Billy said.

"Yeah."

"Beers on me when I see you at the lanes next time."

"You say that every time and don't deliver, ya jerk." Phil laughed.

"Fair enough. Thanks, Phil. Catch you later."

"Later."

Billy set the phone down and looked up at the Weylands' pale blue door. His original suspicions were confirmed. Evan was in over his head and had now killed a man. But why and what could it have to do with a possible Omega situation? Was it possible he'd be stupid enough to come back here? Billy dropped the car in gear and eased from the parking spot. Passing in front of the house, nothing appeared out of order. The shades were drawn, the house quiet. Billy made the block and cut down the alley behind the row of pleasant looking homes.

A neighborhood dog looked up from an overturned trash bin, a dirty sandwich wrapper hanging from its mouth as Billy eased the Explorer into the narrow lane. Forgoing the rest of its scavenged meal, the animal fled, disappearing into the wilted weeds of the adjoining lot.

Slowing the Explorer, Billy counted the back doors, looking for the right one. He stopped. His phone tumbled onto the floorboard with the abrupt mash of the brakes. Well inoculated to stress, Billy didn't sweat confrontation, but in this moment his heart picked up speed.

Ahead, the rear door to the Weyland residence was ajar, the frame splintered from force. *Had Evan returned home? But why would he break his own door?* Billy fumbled with his phone, and considered calling a local marked unit to investigate further. But

99

no, if Evan was on scene, they'd have him for the homicide investigation and Billy would lose the first-contact advantage.

"Damn," Billy muttered. He opened the car door and stepped out, scanning the alley. Satisfied all was clear, he made his approach along the wall. As he moved, he pulled his jacket back and drew the modular Sig P320 from the concealment holster on his side.

Angling out he cleared the threshold, completing an initial assessment of the entry point. The wooden frame near the bolt, splayed open, splintered fragments stabbing at the air. Beneath it a large crack ran the length of the frame. Someone had hit this door with something, and they'd hit it hard.

Billy crept up the three steps to the landing and called out into the darkened interior.

"Federal agent! If anyone is inside, announce your presence, now."

He waited, listening. The house beckoned, silent and dark.

Taking one step inside, Billy cleared the left corner, swept his muzzle hard right, and collapsed his sector of fire to the opposite corner. From the fractured, yawning door behind him, a gust of cold air blustered in carrying a few stray leaves with it. He held his position, scanning for threats. On the nearby wall, the alarm was green and inactivated. Billy moved through the kitchen, his shoes crunched on bits of wood and chipped paint. The cooking space lay dormant and undisturbed. Evan Weyland hadn't been here in at least twelve hours, maybe longer.

"Federal agent, hello," Billy called out again as he approached the living room. "I don't want any surprises. If you're in here, step out slowly and show your hands."

The muted sound of voices emanated from somewhere deeper in the structure. Cautious, Billy moved forward, his weapon swiveling with his body at the high ready. All around, furniture lay tossed on its sides, drawers and cabinet doors hung open, their contents rifled through. Scores of papers and tabletop items were strewn across the floor like the remnants of a recent parade. Billy shook his head, a tingle deep in the center of his chest. Somebody else wanted the same information he did, and they wanted it first.

Moving toward the sound of the voices, Billy scanned the interior of the ransacked place, one room at a time. He took a moment to side step an old soft couch and the hardwood coffee table in front of it. Nearing the sound of muffled conversation, coming from what appeared to be a home office, he slowed. Taking a knee to change his elevation, he leaned out to scan the small room.

The space was dark except for a computer monitor littered with images and scrolling data. Papers, hand scrawled notes, news articles, and a few photographs of the Weylands' vacationing adorned the desk and walls. Billy stood and cautiously approached the desk. Across the monitor screen a script of files flickered, uploading to some hidden drive. Billy leaned in to listen to an audio file as it played.

"It's classified. I'm not cleared to know why," a man said, an edge to his voice.

"Then how do you know at all?" a woman's voice asked.

"I'm flying the mission."

"It's not a drone hit?" she said.

"No," the man's voice seemed to waver. "We have orders to blanket the area with Mark-77Cs. We have to record mission specs for our flight, but they can be… adjusted."

As Billy listened to the recording, he studied the photographs on the screen. Images of data and reports, maps and charts of

Northwest Syria, the bases and military outposts circled. His gaze fell on a photograph on the bottom right side of the screen: a metal case, its lid hinging open on hydraulic pistons to reveal a canister inside. Even labeled in Russian, it was all too familiar.

"Oh my God," Billy said, the grip of his weapon suddenly damp with sweat.

The silhouette of a man, emerged like a wraith from the wall behind him. The muzzle of a pistol suppressor pressed firm behind Billy's left ear.

"Empty your weapon and show clear, then disassemble it and toss it in the corner," the voice whispered from the darkness. "Nice and slow."

Billy straightened. Gone was the fear he'd felt just moments before, burned away in a flash of adrenaline. "I'm Law Enforcement. Hurting me would be a mistake."

"I don't care. Do what you're told."

Billy raised the Sig and tabbed the release with his thumb, ejecting the magazine onto the floor. With his other hand he racked the slide to the rear, ejecting a single nine millimeter round that bounced off a cluttered bookshelf.

"Good," the voice whispered. "Now break it down and throw it in the corner." The suppressor nudged against Billy's skull.

Without a word, Billy did as he was instructed, disassembling his weapon and tossing each component into the corner of the room. He looked down, for the first time seeing the portable drive buzzing as it captured data from the computer. He listened for anything, any sign that might tell him more about his adversary. There was nothing. This man was here to steal the information Marie Weyland had uncovered, and Billy had blundered into the middle of it. If the guy got what he wanted, he might let Billy go—

or he might kill him.

"Just take it easy. I'll cooperate," Billy said, his voice calm.

"That's a good boy," the man said. "Now get down on your—"

Billy whirled into the man and forced his opponent's weapon up toward the ceiling. The gun fired, the suppressor allowing only a soft *crack*.

Powdered drywall and plaster sprinkled down over the shoulders of the struggling men. Billy clamped down on the man's suppressed Glock. Together, they crashed into one wall, then into the opposite bookshelf, books bumping and flapping as they fell from the shelves. Billy struggled against the power of the attacker—hardened, explosive, like a coiled spring.

With a groan, Billy reared back, then pitched forward with a vicious headbutt. The dull smack of bone-on-bone contact. The man wailed. With a groan, Billy pushed hard, forcing the Glock clenched in their hands toward the floor. They fell backward through the doorway of the office. Billy slammed the back of his attacker's hands against the doorframe, knocking the Glock from his grasp.

Billy took a hard punch to the ribs, then a second to the side of his head. The figure shifted, dropped his weight, and harnessed Billy's momentum. In an instant, Billy left the floor. Pitched through the air by a well-timed hip toss, he sailed over a nearby couch and crashed into the broad coffee table in front of it.

Stunned, the air knocked from his lungs, Billy sat there in the dark. The rapid sound of a magazine tap, followed by the pistol's slide racking to the rear—the clearance of a malfunction—brought him rocketing to his senses.

Billy heaved himself from the floor and fell over the other side of the toppled hardwood coffee table. A muffled snap and a hole punched through the wood where his head had been moments before. Two more shots followed in rapid succession, the rounds stitching their way through the table as Billy crawled for cover.

The repetitive snapping of the suppressed pistol faded, and Billy was *there* again, belly in the sand, listening to the crackle of fire and the distant boom of munitions, the screams of the dead and dying, all of it lost beneath the thunderous metallic rattle of an M240 Lima. Billy crawled through the sand and blood and over the lifeless corpses of men whose kids' names he knew.

"Billy!"

"I'm here, Pete! I'm here." Billy crawled up next to the flayed body of his friend.

"Billy," Pete whispered. "They killed me, Billy."

"I know, brother."

"They killed me." Pete's one good eye grew wide. "Tell Kristy and my kids—"

Another rocket propelled grenade exploded nearby rending the air with more screams.

"Shhh. I got you brother. I've got you." Billy wept, his blood soaked hands holding together the shattered skull of his friend.

"Sit up," a voice said to Billy, cold and distant.

The sand and burning sun faded and once again Billy was in Evan Weyland's home. He squeezed his eyes shut and opened them again. Sunspots distorted the cool darkness of the room.

He pushed to his knees and leaned back against the kitchen cabinetry, the sounds of war slipping away as the world drew back into focus. His lungs swelled in his chest. He raised his eyes to see a dark central figure flanked by two others. Billy tried to swallow, his mouth as dry as the desert hell he couldn't seem to escape.

"Did you see all that, Ryder?" the big man with the lumberjack beard said. "For a minute, he wasn't here, he was somewhere else."

"I saw it. He's a combat vet," the man up front said, kneeling to look Billy in the face. "Were you in the war?"

Billy shook his head, anger and embarrassment swelling inside as he stared into the electric blue eyes of this *Ryder*—if that was even his real name.

"You already shot the whole fucking place apart, pal. What difference does it make now?" Ryder asked.

"Ah, that wasn't me. That would be scar face over here." Billy nodded to a compact man with a pronounced scar across his forehead, visible even in the dimness of the room.

The scar-faced man offered a malicious scowl.

"If you're going to execute an unarmed man—then go ahead and do it," Billy said.

"We're not going to execute you," Ryder said, still kneeling.

"Really? Could've fooled me."

"Who are you with?" Ryder asked, again. "What organization?"

"I'd like to ask you the same question."

"But you're not asking the questions. We are." Ryder said.

Billy leaned back with a sigh and touched beneath his nostrils to see if they were bleeding. "Captain Billy Vick, United States Army, Criminal Investigation Command."

"Before you traded your fatigues for a suit, you ever deploy?" The scar-faced man asked.

"Yeah. 75th Rangers. Two tours. Syria."

A glance passed between the men in black.

"This op was supposed to be de-conflicted," the lumberjack said.

"It was," Ryder said. "He's not supposed to be here, are you, Captain?"

"I'm doing my job," Billy said.

"CID cannibal duty?" Scar waved the pistol at Billy. "How's that going for you, desk jockey?"

"Stow it," Ryder said with a sharp glance. He turned back to Billy.

Billy sized the men up. Each of them were decked out in unmarked minimalist tactical clothing and armor, black on black. These men were highly trained covert assets. Maybe former Delta now working government black ops. But why were they here? Poking the bear was dangerous, but it might also get him some answers.

"Yeah, cannibal duty," Billy said. "You know what drove me toward the military police, toward having to investigate my own?"

The men waited.

"It was seeing a few bad eggs with American flags on their shoulders doing things on foreign soil that were un-American. Some good examples of that might be…" Billy paused for effect. "I don't know, maybe breaking into a civilian's residence with the intent to steal something, or the attempted murder of a fellow soldier."

"You weaselly mother f—" the scarred man with the pistol started forward.

Ryder stood, shoving Scar back with a growl. "I said, lock it down. This isn't the time or the place."

Scar smoldered, touched at his bruised cheek.

Ryder turned back to face Billy and after a moment of deliberation extended his left hand out to the side. The lumberjack placed Billy's reassembled Sig in his palm. The squad leader held it out to Billy. "It's empty. You may re-holster your weapon, sir."

Billy took the weapon and did as he was asked. "It's *sir* now?"

"When asked to back off an investigation in the future, it would be in your best interest to do so," Ryder said. "You can get up."

Billy stood, smoothing his rumpled suit. "Funny, you somehow know I was asked to stand down, don't you think?"

The men stared at him, their silence speaking volumes. Ryder's eyes narrowed.

Billy pressed on, "Now you've stolen the information Marie Weyland came across. I saw the images. You idiots might be high speed, but you have no idea what you're dealing with."

"That's enough," Ryder said. "We're trying to be respectful, Captain Vick. You should stop talking if you know what's good for you."

"What's good for me?" Billy said. "Why stop with threats? Your man here already unloaded a mag at me."

Ryder said nothing. Behind him, the scar-faced man seemed to squirm with the desire to hurt Billy.

"What do you want with Evan Weyland?" Billy said. "You plan to make him disappear, don't you?"

"Some things are better for you to not know, Captain Vick. Forget we ever met."

"My command will hear about this," Billy said.

"Don't waste your time." The squad leader looked to his team. "Let's go."

Billy watched as one by one the men filed through the back door.

Short of exiting, the scarred man with the pistol glared at Billy. "Get in our way again and, uniform or not, I'll smoke check you myself."

Billy composed himself, the chill of the wind through the open back door biting at the exposed flesh of his neck. He went to the sink and washed his hands, squeezing his fists until the tremors faded. He took a long drink from the faucet and splashed his face, then dried his hands and face on a kitchen towel before making his way through the ransacked house, back to Marie's home office.

With a sigh of resignation Billy noted the bullet holes peppering the computer screen and hard drive. This mess was spinning out of control, the dark entities that began this dangerous game, now desperate to cover up something they didn't fully understand. Evan Weyland, the only person left who might know more, would be silenced by a hit squad. A lot of innocent people might die. That wasn't going to happen on Billy's watch. He had to get to Evan first, and bring him in alive.

CHAPTER ELEVEN

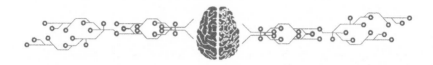

Fells Point, Baltimore, Maryland

Ryder stopped at the rear bumper of the ash gray Dodge Ram truck with blacked out windows and, blending into the cool blue shadows of an overcast November afternoon, took another glance at the breached rear door of the Weyland's residence. His team almost hadn't enough time to execute the op. Damn interference. He set his jaw, the taste of near operational catastrophe, bitter. But it wasn't random interference. It was a good combat vet doing his job, a man who should have had his leash jerked by now.

"Barclay," Ryder muttered.

That weasel of a Major assured him there would be no problems, that his people were out of the way and the situation was deconflicted. And now Ryder had this Captain Vick to contend with. Another obstacle between Ryder and the ends that justified these means. The Captain seemed like a bulldog, too. Would he let it go? Ryder watched a shadow move across the threshold of the shattered door. *Not likely.* Vick was still inside, poking around for evidence. Might even call Baltimore PD.

Ryder's blood boiled. *This could all have been avoided, but no, Barclay had to play his games.* He rapped on the rear passenger window of the truck which rolled down to reveal the bearded face of Duke, his tech operator, and the scarred face of Frank, his specialist.

"Yeah, boss?" Duke said.

"You got the scrambler handy?" Ryder asked, his stare still focused on the Weyland's open rear door.

"Right here." Duke laid a hand on a coal-black Pelican briefcase next to him.

"Activate it."

"We can do that from the road." Frank sat in the driver's seat, twisted around. He rubbed at the long horizontal scar on his forehead with irritation. "There's no reason for us to wait around here and risk being engaged by a BPD response."

Duke nodded. "He's right, I can tether in from the road. Proximity isn't required for this."

Ryder shifted his gaze to lock on his men. "Shut the fuck up and activate it. We have a job to do. Mine is to lead this team. Yours is to follow orders. Stay in your lane and stay the hell out of mine. We clear?"

"Crystal." Frank faced forward.

"Yes sir." Duke pulled the case into his lap.

With a flick of his thumbs, Duke released both latches. The device inside, smooth and black, resembled a painted series of lead bricks more than anything. Duke found the master switch and with a snap, sent the device humming. A small screen inside the briefcase lid winked on, WI-FI connections within a three block radius were identified and hijacked one by one. Ryder made note as the Weyland's connection alongside that of their neighbors ticked past.

"Just another few seconds and we'll have full engagement," Duke said.

Ryder watched through the truck window as Billy Vick stepped from the shadows of the splintered door and into the gray, sunless afternoon. Ryder touched his jaw, working it back and forth, a frown creased into his face. *Guy definitely isn't giving it up.*

Ryder glanced at the pharaoh tactical 300 blackout suppressed rifle nestled in its hard case. Then back to Billy Vick pacing back and forth beside his government issue Ford Explorer. It would be so easy to wrap this all up right now. Leave Vick dead in the alley behind an unsolvable burglary and the Baltimore police with more questions than answers. But that was the easy road and the easy road and the high road weren't always the same. There were other ways to dissuade Vick from probing deeper. The man was a fellow war vet and if he'd honorably served his country in combat overseas, he'd earned that much respect at least, no matter the thorn he might be in Ryder's operation. Ryder knew what the bosses would say, but the bosses weren't here. Right now it was his call.

"We're ready," Duke said. "Got full lock on a three-block radius. No stragglers in the vicinity."

"Throw it," Ryder said.

Duke depressed the activation switch. The device in the case made a sequential series of rapid clicks. With an abrupt *clunk*, the humming stopped.

"That's it," Duke said with a glance at Ryder. "Any surveillance in the area just got whacked. We're ghosts."

"Good," Ryder said. "Lock it up. Let's go."

The fake sound of an engine rumbling to life filled the cab. A feeling of loathing at that sound came over Ryder. *A fake engine rumble in an electric truck. Is there anything more disgusting?* From his coat pocket he pulled a can of dip and popped the seal. Pinching

111

out half of the can, Ryder stuffed the moist wintergreen flavored tobacco into the space between his teeth and lower lip.

The truck eased from the shadowed lane and out onto an unmarked side street.

"Where you wanna go?" Frank asked.

"Just get out of the area. I need a minute to think." Ryder let out a sigh and half turned to Duke in the back seat. "Everything is good on the data package we pulled from the Weyland's place?"

Duke nodded, his face aglow with light from an open laptop. "Yep. We're secure. Sending it via code uplink to Sweetie now."

"I'll call," Ryder said.

"I'm glad you're the one calling her. The required dialogue chains weird me out," Frank said.

Ryder pulled out his phone and held it up for facial recognition. The screen winked to life, the seal of the United States Government over a carbon gray background. "Call Sweetie."

"Calling Sweetie," the phone repeated.

It didn't even ring.

"Hello darling." A deep pause. "When are you coming home?"

If oaked whiskey with a touch of vanilla had a voice, this was its sound.

"There's a package coming, dear," Ryder said. "Can you get it off the doorstep for me? I'll need it unpacked straight away."

Silence. "That'll take time," Sweetie said.

"I'm afraid I'm in a rush. You know how important this is to me, dear," Ryder said. "I need to know everything that's in it. Everything." Ryder paused. "And one more thing, my love."

Ryder spit brown into an old fast food cup.

"There's more?" Sweetie asked. She no longer sounded amused.

"Put in an order for take-out. I want it flown in this time. My friend Billy Vick highly recommends this place. Best in the Baltimore area. I'll send you the info when I have it. Make sure you track the order at three-minute intervals, so we don't lose our food this time. Can you do that for me, honey? You can send the updates direct to my device."

"I can manage," Sweetie said. "I love you," the line disconnected with a click.

Ryder lowered his phone. Looked at it with a frown. "She never waits for me to reciprocate. It's hurtful."

"True that," Duke grunted, his fingers tapping against the keyboard.

Frank shook his head, rubbing at the scarred stripe of flesh across his forehead.

Ryder spit again. "Why are you always rubbing at that? You didn't just have the surgery. It was six years ago." Ryder held up the cup and spit a flake of tobacco off the end of his tongue.

"Hey, fuck you, Ryder," Frank said. "Don't act like you know my problems. It aches, okay?"

Duke chuckled.

Frank glared in the rearview. "And fuck *you*, too."

Duke laughed some more.

Ryder watched the near empty streets pass, cars parked in nice even rows along the curb, like driving through a fake, movie set town.

"And another thing." Ryder looked to Frank. "What was your problem back there?"

"My problem? That Vick guy attacked me."

"After you put a gun to his head," Ryder said. "Don't get emotional, just do the job. Intel gathering, that's the op. This isn't the wild west. Until we're greenlit, keep your damn gun in your holster. You understand?"

"I did the job, Ryder. We got the intel." Frank shook his head, focused on the road. "I don't know why you're up my ass about it."

Ryder spit. "Because I want you to cool out and act like a professional. Not everything is personal. That guy is a combat vet just like us. He's not some POG you can disrespect. He earned his place at the table."

"How d'ya know?" Frank asked.

"Just do." Ryder raised his phone and redialed Major Barclay's number. "Everybody shut up for a minute." Ryder dug the dip from his lip and flung it out an open window. He swished a mouthful of water and spit it out the window, too.

The phone rang a few times, then after a shuffling sound, the Major's voice was on the other end. "Barclay."

"Your personal phone will ring in ten seconds. Pick it up," Ryder wiped a drip of water from his chin. With a swipe he put the Major on hold and transferred the call. Another click.

"How did you get this number?" The Major asked. He sounded like he'd just run a sprint.

"I do my research. Turns out there are a lot of things I know about you, Major."

"Like wha—"

"Listen to me closely," Ryder said. "My team hasn't even been here twenty-four hours and you're already screwing things up."

Ryder let the words linger. The Major cleared his throat.

"I'm sure there's—" Barclay started.

"No," Ryder interrupted again. "I talk, you listen." The Major's labored breathing wheezed in and out like a punctured

114

bike tire on the other end of the line. "Now, I thought we'd deconflicted this operation. You gave me your assurances, but on our very first outing what happens? We clash with one of your people. A Captain Billy Vick was snooping around our first objective. Did you know about this?"

"No, I—"

"No?" Ryder pressed. "You're saying you don't have control of your unit?"

"I'm trying to answer you," the Major blurted.

"Get your house in order, Barclay. If you don't, we'll do it for you, and I promise you that's not what you want." Ryder terminated the call with a blade-like swipe of his hand.

CHAPTER TWELVE

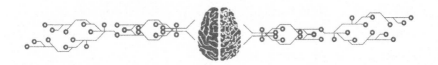

NeuroDelve HQ, Boston, Massachusetts

"Did you watch it?" Sharmila asked.

"Yes," came the man's voice.

"And?"

"Results," he replied.

Sharmila pressed her teeth together. Her business partner was a man of few words. Most of the time it was a helpful trait. Even if some government agency were listening, they'd never be able to glean anything useful. Still, here and now she needed more. Evan Weyland's video demonstrated a level of drone control no one had seen—and that was done with an EEP rig. With NeuroDelve's interface, the possibilities were endless.

"Yes, I understand that. And you'll get them," Sharmila said. "We have a phase two protocol being set up. Evan will be first pilot in. But then I need... more."

"Run pilot one. Then we'll talk."

The line clicked off.

Sharmila stood in her office, the silent phone still glued to her ear—her irritation growing. This is not how she'd intended her life's work to pan out. She'd built NeuroDelve from the ground up, on her own. Rather than finish medical school and go on to examine old ladies' bunions or children's chesty coughs for the next thirty years, Sharmila had turned her eye to the future. A PhD in biomechanics and an MBA from Harvard had provided her the tools to start her company—one designed to extend human life. Endobots—tiny, bacteria-sized machines engineered to repair specific tissue damage and seek out malignant cells or even foreign invaders like viruses—were her brainchild. How could she know back then that this was where her research would lead—dealing with unsavory characters in North Korea?

Of course, Lai Sim, who worked out of Johns Hopkins, had a similar idea. He called his creations *nanobots*. It was a two-horse race for U.S. government funding. Both she and Lai had understood the need for surgical control of their microscopic machines. Loosing something into the human body with no means of regulation from the outside—precision governance—would be dangerous. Both Lai and she had decided on creating a lead machine that could be controlled by humans, a tiny commander inside the body that would lead hundreds of other drones. But this is where her and Lai's research had diverged.

Lai had taken the safe route, as he always did, opting for a safer, non-invasive neural link. Head gear that could be put on or removed by anyone. The gear had to be configured for each person, which took hours, and if Evan was to be believed, it was also pathetic at registering commands. Sharmila's interface required a single surgery to tie control directly into the visual, sensory, and motor control areas of the brain. When the individual was connected to a full virtual reality rig, the degree of control was theoretically as fluid as any other physical activity a human might undertake. The command Endobot could be piloted as if the driver themselves were inside the patient's body.

The DOD, FDA, and EMA hadn't agreed.

The direct neural link had been deemed too high risk. Not because of the surgery itself—biomechanics were more and more commonplace—but because coming out of the DNL was tricky, and if done wrong the pilot could suffer brain damage. In fact, the primary concern was that if the command Endobot was destroyed *in vivo*, the pilot's brain would register the incident as actual death and cease all function. The pilot would die. A calculated risk Sharmila had been willing to take for the sake of great control of the Endobots.

"Sharmila?" Evan said.

NeuroDelve's CEO slipped the cell phone into her pocket and turned to face Evan, who was standing in the doorway, his gaze fixed just left of her. A small, pained smile graced her lips then faded away. She liked Evan very much. He was a straight arrow. A true scientist who followed the evidence and lived his life for the love of knowledge. A human computer who—if the subject matter interested him—could devour textbooks, manuals, lectures, podcasts, and any other available information to become an expert within a matter of months. Something that had taken her years. She'd wanted him for her own research, for this talent alone, but had underestimated one thing: he loved his wife even more than his work.

He'd declined her generous offers no less than six times.

It seemed ironic now that Marie's imminent demise would bring Evan to NeuroDelve. That his being on the spectrum might make him even more valuable than Sharmila had ever anticipated. But more than that, if any of the concerns of the medical agencies were justified, this experiment might kill him.

"Can we go?" Evan said, checking his watch.

"Of course, Evan. We should go."

Sharmila remained silent as she and Evan descended in the elevator into the bowels of the facility. The doors hissed open, revealing a positive pressure chamber—a waystation before entering the rest of the facility. The NeuroDelve CEO watched Evan's expression as he soaked in the transition from floors of offices, fax machines, and coffee dispensers above, to the sophisticated underground surgical laboratory. His face was white, all color drained. Sharmila gave him a reassuring nod and he was led away for preparation.

An hour later, Sharmila stood in the operating room, masked and gloved, two other surgeons and a nurse at her side. She eyed Evan on the table, head now half shaved to allow her to saw into his skull and implant the neural interface sensors. He looked up at her, bathed in the spotlights, eyes glassy.

Sharmila offered a sympathetic smile, then realized he couldn't see past her mask. She slipped on the protective glasses. "Count back from one hundred for me, Evan," she said, voice muffled.

Evan began counting, but never made it past ninety as the anesthesia took hold.

Sharmila picked up the circular bone saw and tested it. The high-pitched whine of the circular blade pierced her eardrums She took a deep breath and nodded to her colleagues. They were really doing this.

Evan woke with a start, his heart thumping, head throbbing. The overhead lights would have been dim to the average person, but his dilated pupils took in every photon in the room, rendering everything white and amorphous. He lay back down on his cot and rubbed at his bandaged head.

In that first foggy moment, Evan hoped he'd dreamed it all and Marie would be at his side, holding onto his arm or her foot resting on his, just as she always did. Not too much contact, nothing to press on his nerves too hard, but enough to let him know he was safe. Of course, Evan was never one to lay in bed for too long and would get up almost immediately to make breakfast. Every time he'd make it to the bedroom door she'd call after him.

"Hey," she'd say.

Evan would turn and stand there in his boxers.

Marie would wait until the count of three, before saying, "I love you."

"I love you, too," he'd always reply.

But that was just it. He always forgot to say it first.

I need to tell her, Evan thought. *I have to save her.*

He shifted to the edge of the bed, but the world spun and his stomach roiled. Evan slipped from the mattress and crashed to the floor, his surgical cape tearing open, leaving him near naked. Alarms wailed and monitors squealed as the sensors tracking his vitals came loose.

Two of Sharmila's people surged into the room and hoisted Evan back to the bed. They prodded and poked and asked their questions. He couldn't answer, his mind awash with too many sounds, smells, sights. Evan clamped his hands over his ears and screwed his eyes shut.

Soft fingers slid over his own and pried his hands from his head. For a brief moment he thought it might be Marie, but as he looked up, he was greeted by Sharmila. Her normal hard business glare was replaced by a warm and caring gaze.

"Evan, you can't leave yet," she said.

"But Marie, I need to get to Marie," he protested.

"And we will, Evan. But if you aren't in the right condition all this will be for nothing. You know that. Take comfort in the fact that the procedure went smooth and as soon as you recover, we'll be in business."

Evan controlled his breathing and felt his heart slow. Sharmila was right, and he knew it. Now he had to get his head together. He refocused on his number one priority. "When can we test the connection?"

"I thought you may ask that," Sharmila said. "We came up with a portable test system, for the field. Without having to plug you into the full rig yet."

Through the doors to Evan's small recovery room, a man wheeled a large flat-screen monitor hooked up to a microscope. He stopped it at the foot of Evan's bed and switched it on. The screen came to life to reveal a fuzzy image of the petri dish beneath the microscope lens.

Sharmila handed Evan a small device that looked much like a pair of wraparound Bluetooth headphones.

"Put this on," she said, then stepped to the microscope to adjust the focus.

Evan complied, setting the contraption around his neck, over the ears, and onto his temples.

With a few expert adjustments, Sharmila tweaked the microscope's focus, the resulting image now crisp.

Evan studied the image on the monitor. The liquid in the Petri dish contained at least four different types of Endobot. He cocked his head, and squinted one eye, focusing on each one. While lay people might consider a bot to be a tiny metal robot, with arms and legs, in reality, to work at a cellular level, nanobots and Endobots were biological—engineered to have a function. Work at the cellular level was much like machinery at a macro level, physically moving things around or welding them together—except here the tasks were completed by proteins and ions and sub-cellular structures.

Each Endobot on the screen was the size of a single cell, perhaps a large bacterium, and had a single flagellum—a long whip-like structure that rotated like a propeller—at one end to enable unidirectional movement.

"How did you overcome the immune response?" Evan asked, without breaking his gaze.

"We utilized a trick from cancer," Sharmila said. "The Endobots present programmed cell death ligand 1 on their surface. T-cells that come looking for the Endobots *in vivo* register the ligand and think it to be a normal cell within the body."

"Clever," Evan said, then pointed to the screen. "I don't know what all these are? How many types of Endobot are there?"

Sharmila stared at him, her fingers twitched at the collar of her blouse. Whatever she was about to tell Evan, it made her uncomfortable. "Our new partner in the program had specific needs. We had to accommodate."

"Explain," Evan said.

Sharmila pointed to the screen and picked out a single Endobot. "Okay, so here you have the medi-bot. It's loaded with enzymes and RNA strands designed to accelerate cellular repair. Metal oxide nanostraws, less than one hundred nanometers across, can penetrate a human cell and transfer the RNA and enzymes over to trigger the healing process. We used *Xenpus* oocytes as the base

122

model."

Evan nodded. Those were what he was used to working with. They were also what he had intended to use on Marie, helping her to rebuild any cells at risk of being destroyed by the infection.

"But what our employer needed, and honestly what you need right now, is something to do damage." She placed her finger on a cone shape on the screen. "This is an infantry bot, designed for up close and personal combat with—well, anything you want. A foreign invader, a cancer cell, even a virus. It's based on a jellyfish nematocyte."

Evan raised his eyebrows. *A nematocyte?* That would mean it had an internal, spring-loaded nematocyst—a needle—that when triggered would explode out, pierce anything nearby, and inject toxins. Jellyfish used paralyzing agents, but here it could be anything the engineer desired.

"Then," Sharmila continued, "you have the artillery bots. Several types, all with an arsenal of cytokines and proteins, designed to stick to the enemy and tell the host's immune system to attack. It's like bringing in the big guns."

"That sounds like a shotgun approach. How do you define what is the enemy and what is friendly when launching such an attack?"

"That's your job," the CEO said, and traced her finger to the last type of cell—larger than the rest. "This is you. Your command Endobot modeled on *Stentor coeruleus*, but packed with some of the same features as your army. You have a nematocyst embedded, the ability release cellular regen RNA, fire an artillery, attach a tag to the enemy like a target—but most importantly this one releases command cytokines. It's how you control the others."

"And how do I see where I'm going?"

"Right now, you can't." Sharmila said. "That interface is the one that needs the full rig. The whole body of the Endobot acts like a lens, focusing light to a spot on the back wall near the flagellum. The image is fuzzy but using AI and your brain, it's enhanced to be able to see nearly crystal clear. The world's smallest camera."

NeuroDelve's program was impressive, and for a brief moment Evan regretted never having joined. But his thoughts were pulled back to his beloved wife now dying on a cot in Washington. That, and another nagging feeling in the back of his mind. Why the need for such an aggressive force inside the body? "These are set up like a you're going into battle."

"Actually, defense," Sharmila said.

"Defending against what?"

"Biological warfare," she said. "There's something specific in mind my investors are looking to fight. Something called Project Omega. Highly classified. Even I don't know what it is. I thought maybe you might."

Evan shook his head. "No."

Onscreen, Evan saw his command Endobot scuttle through the liquid, its flagellum rotating in frantic circles.

"Ah, the link is working."

Evan cocked his head, concentrating on the command Endobot, willing it to move. The tiny biological machine complied, flicking its miniscule tail.

"We've clocked them at one hundred micrometers per second. It doesn't sound that fast, but at that scale, it's a supercar."

"I know," Evan said, still focusing on the screen.

"Tell the others to come closer, to follow your lead," Sharmila said.

Evan thought about it, but instead of using words in his head he imagined the scene—envisioned the picture of what he wanted to happen. After a second or two, the army of Endobots began to gather around the leader.

"Bravo, Evan. The link works."

"That's very delayed," Evan said.

"Yes, this is only the test kit. Once you're in the virtual reality rig, it'll be a lot faster. The delay between you and the command Endobot is significantly shorter."

Evan chewed his lip. This was insane, and he could die trying to do this, but Marie would definitely die if he didn't.

CHAPTER THIRTEEN

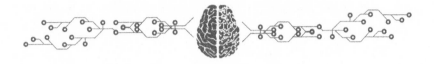

Fells Point, Baltimore

From the green pharmacy bottle with his name on it, Billy shook a single ovular blue pill into his palm. He tossed the pill into his mouth and chased it with a swig of coffee gone cold from sitting in the cup holder too long. He flipped his head back and swallowed. With a grunt of disgust, he dropped the bottle back into the center console. He never figured himself for the guy who'd have to take anti-anxiety meds just to get through the day, but here he was, popping pills to make the tightness in his chest subside. It wasn't a permanent condition. He'd get it worked out one day. That's what he told the man in the mirror, at least.

His interaction with the men in Evan's townhouse kept running in a continuous looped feed through his mind. The way they'd acted, intent on killing him too until they realized he was Army. Then came the little gestures of respect, the squad leader calling him *sir*, letting him preserve his dignity, giving him his weapon back. That was one soldier honoring another, even if on different sides of a conflict. He heard the words of the squad leader over and over in his head, a response to Billy's statement that he was going to his command about this.

Don't waste your time, sir.

Billy rubbed his sternum, the sensation of pinched tightness in his chest beginning to fade. Was it possible his command was in on this? A covert unit acting on orders to cover up this whole stinking mess? Was that why the Major had told him to drop the case?

From the concealment of his government-issued electric Ford Explorer, Billy watched as a Baltimore Police cruiser pulled into the alley behind the Weylands' residence. The patrolman exited and approached the shattered rear door with his service weapon drawn. BPD would have a hell of a time figuring that scene out. Billy had made the call, identified himself, and told them he discovered the break in. That would be enough to explain any of his DNA recovered from the scene. Outside of that, it wasn't his problem. He had to keep moving.

Johns Hopkins University was just a short fifteen-minute drive across town. The crime scene there would still be fresh and they'd likely still have witnesses on scene. Before he left back for Quantico, he needed to know what the people Evan worked with knew. In the wake of a possible murder, they'd be shaken up and might divulge more than usual. He had to strike while the iron was hot.

Deep in thought, Billy made his way down to the Interstate 83 on ramp headed north. Even in the middle of the day, downtown Baltimore was deserted of pedestrian foot traffic. Billy mused on what the constant threat of terrorism combined with the application of martial law did to a society. No longer did lovers take casual strolls down to the pier hand in hand, or children play with carefree screams of joy in a local park. The country was gripped in fear, her cities looking far more like a desperate ravaged Europe during the Second World War than the America Billy

knew and loved. As with all wars, the one happening at home could
be boiled down to three things: money, power, and religion. Pete,
the best man Billy had ever known, died years ago in a desert hell
for what now seemed like petty arguments played out on a global
scale. It was only getting worse. Billy sighed. Maybe in time the
ship would right itself and the America of his youth would return.
Maybe it wouldn't.

His phone rang. Billy looked down to see the number for the
Major's office light up on the screen. "Shit." He screwed up his
mouth. "That's not good." Definitely related to his earlier run in,
and this call only served to confirm his suspicions. He would get
his balls broken over disobeying a direct order. "Shit!" he yelled
again. *Are my own people against me now*, he thought. He reached
down and pushed the call to voicemail.

The smooth lines, and perfect shining plastic of his car interior
annoyed him. Nothing in life was like that. Life was messy,
convoluted, hard to swallow. Not this fake luxury. Maybe that's
why the auto manufacturers did it; they understood most people
didn't truly care about good things, only the luxury, the
appearance.

Billy watched the long line of cars ahead as they passed through
the checkpoint. He drummed his fingers on the steering wheel.
There wasn't time for this. He had to get to Johns Hopkins. He
reached down between the seats and retrieved the controller for his
vehicle's emergency equipment. Activating the lights but not the
siren, he eased out into the emergency lane and rolled up toward
the military chicane.

"Hey, hey, stop right there!" a young soldier at the barricade
shouted, stepping out into his lane, rifle raised.

Billy stopped the car, his window rolling down. "Army CID, I need to get through," he shouted back.

"Shut the car off and step out with your hands up," the soldier shouted.

"For fuck's sake." Billy gritted his teeth, forced the gearshift into park, and shut off the car. In a flash he was out of the SUV, his shield in his right hand. "Captain Vick, Army CID, on official business."

The young man looked left and right.

"What's the problem over there?" another soldier shouted.

"Sarge, this guy says he's CID." The nervous young man's voice squeaked. The kid looked to be fresh out of boot and still wet behind the ears.

A more confident man approached with chevrons on his sleeve and a crisp salute. "Sir?"

"Staff Sergeant." Billy saluted. "Captain Vick, attached to the Criminal Investigation Command out of Quantico. I'm following up on an active investigation and the clock is ticking. I know how it is and can appreciate the need for procedure, but I can't wait in this line."

The Staff Sergeant examined Billy's credentials. "Sorry, sir, our guys have been on edge. Just got upgraded to Defcon 2 after last week's incident. Guy in a stolen police vehicle blew himself up at a checkpoint out in Los Angeles."

"I understand all that, but you need to ring the water out of this one here. Not everyone is a threat and we all still live in a free country last time I checked."

"Yes, sir. I'll handle it." The Staff Sergeant pinched his lips and waved the nervous soldier from the lane.

After a quick scan of his ID and a cursory sweep of his vehicle, the soldiers manning the checkpoint stepped aside.

Billy climbed back into his car, powered it on, and accelerated slow into the curving path that snaked through the chicane of alternating concrete barriers. He passed the sergeant, now shouting and pointing with a knife-hand in the young soldier's face.

Billy huffed out a chuckle. Nothing like the good ol' knife-hand to get some POG's attention. Kid needed a dressing down. Billy couldn't see how these anxious young soldiers didn't accidently kill more citizens on a daily basis. He continued up the near empty ramp onto Interstate 83.

In minutes he'd arrived and turned off Wyman Park Drive onto the campus of Johns Hopkins. He navigated into the parking lot filled with an assortment of marked university police and Baltimore police cars, ambulances. The coroner was even on scene already, the grim-faced assistants busy loading a full body bag into the rear of their van.

Billy exited his vehicle with a groan. The twisting made his ribs radiate with pain and sitting still for the last twenty minutes seemed to make any movement worse. Clearing the door, he continued on with as much effort as he could muster toward the fluttering crime scene tape and the patrolman who now eyed him with suspicion.

"Captain Vick, U.S. Army Criminal Investigation Command." He flashed his badge for the patrolman to see.

"Yes, sir," the patrolman said.

"I'm working a case that may have a nexus with this incident. Who is the detective handling the case?"

The patrolman made note of Billy's information in his log and jerked his head in the direction of the door behind him. "That would be Groseman. He's inside." He lifted the crime tape.

"What's with all the cars?" Billy said as he ducked the tape.

"Homeland is here, too. They have some connection."

Billy nodded. "Any luck catching the guy that fled?"

"Not yet." The officer shook his head. "Trail's gone cold."

Billy opened the outer door, the sour musty smell of the enclosed stairwell filling his nose. He stopped at the sight of a handful of evidence techs combing the stairs for anything worth logging.

"Am I good to come through here?"

"Come on. Stay to the right. This is just a final sweep to make sure we didn't miss anything," said a technician wearing booties and gloves.

"Detective Groseman?"

"Top of the stairs," she replied, still scanning a handrail.

Billy eased past the techs and ascended the stairs. Exiting the stairwell, and feeling relieved the whole building didn't smell like the stairs, he identified Detective Groseman in short order. The man was an enormous figure, as tall as he was wide, and though he was covered in sweat and appeared to survive on copious amounts of gas station coffee and cheap takeout, Billy was also confident he wasn't the sort of man you wanted to lay hands on you in a fit of rage.

Beside Groseman, a woman maybe five years Billy's junior spoke in hushed tones. *Where have I seen her before?* Billy thought. She was short and compact, with a dark ponytail pulled tight and an athletic figure. She pointed to one side of the area, then the other, working something over with the detective. She was a professional, likely the representative from Homeland on scene. The look of the woman reminded Billy that just like C4, sometimes explosive things came in very small packages.

Billy turned his attention back to Groseman who seemed to deflect each person who approached him waving papers or asking questions. The detective looked like he was about to boil over, as if the ten thousand things he could be doing would get done if he didn't have to babysit everyone else who wanted to check in with the case agent.

Billy knew that feeling all too well, but he also needed access to witnesses. That was only going to happen with this man's approval. A different approach was in order.

He scanned the hallway and found what he wanted. After stepping into the break room, he re-emerged moments later with two black coffees, steam wafting from their thin Styrofoam cups. He approached Groseman.

"Gonna be a long one huh?" Billy said.

Groseman turned, sizing Billy up. "Yeah, especially when everyone has something they want to say to me."

The Homeland agent in a well-tailored navy suit, stared at Billy with eyes like carved jade, but said nothing, and that's when it hit him: she had pushed past him when he'd first met Evan at the CDC. But what was she doing there? Did she know?

Billy extended the coffee to Groseman. "Captain Billy Vick, Army CID."

Groseman took it and gave a murmur of satisfaction. "Groseman. Thanks." He shook Billy's hand.

"Billy," he said with a smile, extending the other coffee to the woman. "Can I offer you a coffee?"

"I can get my own." She bypassed the coffee and took his hand, surprising him with a vice-like grip. "Reinhardt. Homeland Security," she said. "You get in a fight?"

"Yeah, actually." Billy laughed and touched at his bruised cheek. "Just some jerk who didn't want to play ball with my investigation this morning. He's regretting that decision now."

Reinhardt raised an eyebrow. "What business do you have here?"

"I could ask you the same," Billy said, and took a sip of his coffee.

"We're not official here, but Homeland takes an interest in anything that may involve national security."

"National security?" Billy repeated, feigning ignorance.

"Yes." Reinhardt's tone was clipped.

Billy swallowed a witty response. Manufactured a smile.

"And what exactly is your involvement?" She locked him down with those green eyes.

Billy wasn't here to talk to this lady, but he already found himself respecting her directness. She knew something more, hell, she might even be aware of his angle. He resolved to proceed with caution. Law enforcement allegiances weren't what they used to be these days.

"I'm working a case that might indirectly involve your suspect, Detective," Billy said, turning back to Groseman.

"Weyland? You don't know where he is, do ya?" Groseman said.

"If I did, I wouldn't be here."

Groseman nodded and took a slurp of the coffee. "I got my hands full, Agent Vick. What can I do for you?"

"I need to have a word with any witnesses. Anyone who might know Weyland and what he was working on?" Billy said.

"I'd love to help you out but most of the witnesses have already been interviewed and cut loose. There's only one still here, but she's shell shocked in a bad way."

"Shell shocked?" Billy said.

"Totally non-responsive," Reinhardt said.

"Yeah," Groseman added. "She walked in on it. Immediately after she did, Weyland fled. She might be solid, maybe even our star witness, if she could say her own name."

"You mind if I have a crack at her?" Billy asked.

Groseman shrugged. "Knock yourself out. She's in the lounge over here with one of my uniforms. The paramedics are checking her out."

"Thanks, Detective," Billy said.

"I've got to check up on the progress with the crime scene. You'll keep me informed if she says anything?"

"Of course," Billy said.

"You don't mind if I tag along, do you?" Reinhardt asked.

"Be my guest," Billy said with just a touch of reluctance.

"Good. I'll show you where she is."

With Reinhardt in the lead, Billy headed down the hallway in the direction of the lounge. To his right a flurry of activity caught his eye. As he passed the lab, he watched evidence technicians snap photographs of little yellow placards marking vials scattered across the floor as well as other items of evidentiary interest. On the floor, undisturbed, a large congealed pool of clotted blood fanned out.

"You think Weyland murdered this other researcher?" Billy asked.

"BPD has to treat it that way for now, I'm sure. There was definitely a struggle of some sort," Reinhardt said, stopping and motioning to a pale yellow sitting room complete with a sink, coffee maker, microwave, and a mini fridge. "She's right here."

The uniformed officer stepped to the side to let them through. Billy thumbed the micro-recorder in his jacket pocket to the ON position.

Just inside sat an extraordinarily thin woman with stick-like limbs and drawn, pinched features. Little spots and smudges of blood adorned her clothes, a sign that she may have tried to help the victim. Her lip quivered and she bit it. She stared at the opposite wall.

The paramedic stood up and removed the blood pressure cuff and stethoscope from the woman's arm. He turned to Reinhardt. "She's fine. Slightly shocked, and her blood pressure isn't where it should be, but that's understandable considering what she's been through. Everything else checks out." The paramedic shrugged. "She refused medical transport, so I'm outta here."

"Don't go anywhere just yet," Billy said as the paramedic passed him.

The man paused for a moment, then gave a nod.

"Thanks," Reinhardt said, stepping to the side so the paramedic could get by. She stooped to try and catch the thin woman's eyes. "Professor Dell?"

The woman gave a little shake of her head, her gaze fixed on the opposite wall. A tear streaked down her cheek and fell into her lap.

Reinhardt gave Billy a look that said, *told you so.*

Billy nodded.

"Professor Dell?" Billy said, grabbing a chair and pulling it over. "I know you've been through a lot today and I understand if you don't want to talk." Billy offered a smile and sat down. "But we've got a mess here and we could use your help."

Professor Dell chewed her lip.

"I know it's hard," Billy continued. "Not something you want to go over again. But speaking with us could really help us, and might even help you process what you've been through. Put words to this tragedy." Billy paused. "Professor Dell, is there anything you can tell us?" A moment passed. Billy rested his hands in his lap, letting the silence build. "We can give you some more time if you need it." He eyed her one last time and moved to stand.

"Jeanine," the professor whispered.

"I'm sorry?" Billy said, sitting back down.

"My name's Jeanine," she said, her voice frail.

Billy leaned closer and briefly touched her shoulder. "Hi Jeanine, my name's Billy. I'd like to help you. Will you let me do that?"

Jeanine Dell nodded and wiped a tear from her chin.

Reinhardt straightened, her interest piqued. She met Billy's glance and nodded for him to continue.

"What happened to your face?" Dell said, staring at Billy's bruised mug.

Damn, Billy thought. *Is it that bad?* He forced another smile. "Guy punched me this morning."

"Why?"

Billy shrugged and let out a sigh. "Guess he didn't like my style." He met Professor Dell's eyes. "Say, if you decide to sock me, too, could you do this side and even me out?" Billy pointed to his opposite cheek and chuckled.

She smiled.

"See, look at that smile," Billy said. "You're going to be just fine, Jeanine."

Her smile faded back into a look of despair. "I'm not so sure."

Billy leaned forward. "Why's that?"

Dell looked up. "Is Lai... I mean, he's..." She swallowed, unable to finish her sentence.

Billy lowered his head and gave a little nod. "Yeah. He's gone." He paused, letting the gravity of the statement sink in. "Can you tell us what you saw?"

Dell shook her head again, a fresh batch of tears welling. "I just walked in to ask him a question about the project. I didn't even know Evan was there. There was so much blood. I tried to help but I didn't know what to do."

"What was Evan doing at this time?"

"He wasn't doing anything. He was frozen. He looked like a child that had broken something and was afraid to tell anyone." Dell sniffed and wiped her chin. "Is he in trouble?"

"Well, considering he may have killed somebody..." Reinhardt said.

Billy shot her a glance. Reinhardt folded her arms and leaned back against the wall.

"My God, but it's Evan. He wouldn't try to hurt Lai. They were friends."

"You sure?" Billy said.

"Yes. I mean, *it's Evan.*"

Billy leaned in more. "What does that mean when you say, '*it's Evan*'?"

Dell looked from Billy to Reinhardt and back to Billy. "You don't know about him?"

"Know what?" Billy said.

"He's on the spectrum. Autistic, I mean. Incredibly intelligent, I mean, no one can do what he does, he's just sort of socially awkward sometimes. But it's Evan. I mean, he would never hurt someone intentionally. It's just not in him. The only one who he gets close to is Marie."

Billy sat back, the wheels in his head spinning. *Autistic.* How had he not realized this before? Of course the guy was on the spectrum. It all made sense now—the meticulous order, the reason

137

he'd been so difficult when Billy interviewed him. A sense of shame poured over Billy. He'd been a real asshole and totally mishandled that first contact. The guy just wanted to save his wife's life. But the questions still remained. What did Evan know that Billy didn't? Where was he going now and why? Did it matter? Was Billy chasing his tail? Marie was the one infected, what did it matter if they found Evan or not? *Unless...*

"Jeanine," Billy said, his voice as calm as an undisturbed pool. "What was the nature of Evan and Lai's work here?"

She gave a sheepish shrug. "We're not supposed to talk about it. Signed a non-disclosure agreement and everything."

"Sure, and I appreciate your wanting to honor that, but here we're dealing with some unique circumstances. Evan is now wanted in connection with a homicide. We don't have any choice but to look at it that way... unless you can convince us otherwise?"

Professor Dell wrung the life from her hands over and again, fingertips blanched white.

"Nobody's going to say anything," Billy added. "You've got completely valid reasons to disclose."

"We're working on a vital medical research project." Dell shifted and looked over her shoulder. "Microscopic drone technology. I'm talking about repair on a cellular level here. It's incredibly experimental. Some think it could lead to the cure for cancer, all cancers. Lai and Evan are the project leads, but... Evan is the only one who could successfully pilot the nanos."

Billy flicked his gaze at Reinhardt, who seemed to have perked up, and turned back to Professor Dell. "Nanos?"

"Nanobots."

"That's like, what? Little machines engineered to perform a task?"

Dell sighed. "Yes, but it's a bit more complicated than that."

"Of course," Billy said. "Can you explain it to me?"

"They do work autonomously, to a degree, but the team of nanos needs a principal; a piloted micro drone that has the ability to control the others."

"A pilot? For a tiny cell-sized machine?" Billy rubbed his chin. "What sort of real world applications would this have?"

Dell leaned in, a youthful excitement filling her thin features. "Think about it. An army of nanobot machines, injected into the bloodstream and given a task like clotting assistance, or tissue repair on a cellular level. We're talking about real time microsurgery here. Like I said, maybe an eventual cure for the uncurable."

"So, the pilot would be able to… see and navigate a tiny nano machine inside a human body?" Billy tried to keep his expression neutral. *What the hell is this sci-fi bullshit?* "How is that even possible? A radio transmitter alone would be bigger than a cell."

Dell nodded. "I told you it's complicated. But at that scale we can use quantum entanglement—manipulate the atoms of the nano to do what we want by manipulating other atoms that are connected like a remote control."

Billy just stared, brow creased.

"Anyway, we could destroy cancer or diseases. And think about other applications. There's no telling what sort of leaps forward humankind could make with this technology. This project is the tip of the spear, and Evan was the only one who could pilot it. I think that's why he wanted it so bad."

"Wanted it?" Billy said, his eyes narrowing.

"Yeah," Dell said. The look of nervousness had returned. "I think he was trying to take it when I walked in. He must've shoved past Lai to get to it, and… I'm sure was an accident."

Billy's face went slack, the obviousness of it all like a punch to the gut.

Reinhardt took a step forward. "What would cause him to be so desperate to have it?"

Dell looked flabbergasted. "His wife is sick. I heard the doctors don't know what it is. Evan has a singular focus on everyday tasks, but with his wife it's tenfold. There's nothing that will stop him from trying to help her."

"Even if that means stealing his own project and using it to go inside his wife's body to destroy the disease," Billy said, standing from his chair.

"That's right," Dell said with a nod.

"But if he didn't get it, where would he go?" Billy said.

"I don't know." Dell began to massage her fingertips again. "As far as I know we're light years ahead of the competition. The only other contender was considered unethical and—"

"Who are they?" Billy interrupted.

"NeuroDelve, up in Boston, but Evan wouldn't..." Dell's voice trailed away as Billy punched the record-stop button on his micro recorder.

"Thank you for your time, Jeanine," Billy said with a reassuring wink. "You're going to be okay." He exited the room with Reinhardt in tow.

"Agent Vick," Reinhardt said, stopping Billy in the hall.

He turned to face her, palming the micro recorder. "What?"

"What do you know that I don't?" Reinhardt said, searching his face.

"As far as this goes? Probably a lot," Billy said, handing her a micro data card from the recorder.

Billy's phone buzzed in his pocket. *Maybe Adam with an*

update. Billy fished out his device to see a text from an unidentified number. He pressed on the icon. *What are you doing?* The message read. Billy frowned. A new message pinged in. *I thought we'd agreed you'd leave this alone. Think about your family and don't be a fool, Vick.*

Billy looked up to the waiting face of Reinhardt.

"Agent Vick?" Reinhardt pressed.

Another message. This time a picture of the front of Billy's house.

Billy's heart hammered. He typed out *who is this?* And thumbed send. A message came back as undeliverable to a bad number. *Shit. Rosie.*

"Do me a favor and give this to Groseman," Billy said. "He's going to want that interview. I gotta go."

"Homeland can help, you know," Reinhardt said.

"Maybe," Billy replied, "but I don't think you or your people want any part of this, Agent."

"Don't assume that for me," Reinhardt said, her jaw set. "Where are you going now?"

"To figure out how to stop this before we all end up dead." Billy turned, headed off at a march down the hallway and disappeared into the stairwell.

Billy stood before the door to his residence. No forced entry. No signs of violence. He thumbed the scanner and the door popped open. He dropped his duffel in the darkened foyer and closed the door, the entrance and stairway dark.

"Rosie?"

The house was still, dark and silent.

"Rosie?" Billy's voice raised, his heart picking up speed as the most terrible things he could imagine sprang to life.

He half ran, half stumbled through the foyer, the sound of a spoon clinking against ceramic as he rounded the corner. Surging into the low light of the kitchen, Billy stopped. A wave of relief crashed over him. Rosie glanced up and made the shush gesture with her finger to her lips. She removed her earbuds.

"Why are you shouting?" she asked.

"I just, um…" Billy swallowed, rubbing his chest. "Had a scare that's all. Are you guys okay? Where are the boys?"

Rosie frowned. "They're asleep, Billy. What's gotten into you?"

"What do you mean?" Billy said, his heart slowing.

"You've been totally MIA the last few days and then just blow in here at nine thirty at night shouting and wondering where the boys are."

He sighed. "I'm sorry, baby. I couldn't reach you on the phone. Are you guys okay? Nothing strange going on?"

Rosie softened, raised her mug and took a tiny sip of her hot beverage. "Who are you, again? I have a husband, but he's not crazy."

Billy sagged and leaned against the door to the kitchen. "I know, I just got wrapped up in something big and, I guess I got a little paranoid when I couldn't reach you…"

"Uh huh." She paused to take another sip. "Yes, we're okay, sweetie. The lockdown is a little scary for the boys sometimes, and it would be helpful if you were here to explain things to them, but yes, everybody is fine. Honestly, it's you we're worried about." Her face darkened as her gaze found bruises on his forehead and cheek.

She set down her steaming mug and approached to touch his face.

Billy closed his eyes and sighed at the gentle caress of the woman he loved. He reached out and embraced her, but winced when she put her arms around his midsection.

"Billy?" She pulled away, then reached down and lifted his shirt. A gasp escaped her lips when she saw the large purple bruise across his ribs. Her stare cut right through him. "Billy Vick, you tell me what's going on."

Billy lowered his gaze. "I can't tell you. You know how it goes."

Rosie's angry expression faded into pained sympathy. "Then how am I supposed to help?" she asked.

"I don't know." Billy shook his head, perhaps hoping it would jar his thoughts into a discernible order. "You ever question why you're doing something? Ever lose your way in something that feels out of your control?"

"Yes," Rosie said. "Is that what you're feeling?"

Billy nodded and rubbed his hands.

"What is it?" Rosie pressed, gently.

Billy chewed the inside of his lip. "Something bad is happening and… well, I don't know if I'm making it worse by trying to stop it."

Rosie sidled closer, took his hands and squeezed them. "Billy, you're a good man and I love your heart, even if you're a little crazy sometimes." She smirked.

Billy gave a good natured chuckle, "Yeah, I know."

"Listen," Rosie said. "If you do what you know is right, if you choose the way that is noble and honorable, it's never the wrong thing—even when it seems to make things worse."

"Okay, baby," he whispered, then leaned forward to embrace his wife.

"You'll stay here tonight," she said.

"No, I've got a lot to—"

Rosie pulled back and fixed her dark-eyed stare on him. "I wasn't asking. Whatever it is can wait. You'll rest and let me take care of you tonight. Whatever is ahead of you will still be there first thing in the morning. Agreed?"

Billy thought about the text message. Somebody outside his house. He smiled and gave his wife a kiss. "Yes, ma'am."

She gave him a pat on the back. "Go wash up and I'll be up in a bit."

He turned and made his way to the stairs, grabbing the duffel of clothes on the way. At the top of the stairs, he entered his room, dumped the contents of the duffel into the laundry hamper, and took off his suit jacket.

Starting youngest to oldest, he went from room to room kissing each of the sleeping boys and smoothing their hair, ensuring they were well tucked in before making his way to the shower. Billy cranked the faucet open, which quickly filled the room in comforting warm steam. He pulled off his shirt, baring his teeth at the pain of raising his arms. Stepping into the shower, Billy let the scalding hot water run over his skin. A blistering hot shower after work was a ritual tied more to a mental and emotional cleansing than anything else: a divider between work and home. The sensation of washing away the ugliness of the world. Though tonight, even when he turned the faucet so hot he thought it might actually scald him, he couldn't escape the feeling that the worst sort of clinging filth remained.

CHAPTER FOURTEEN

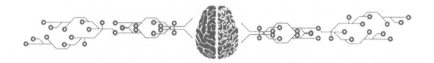

Undisclosed Location Near Dulles International Airport

E van yawned and checked his watch: 4:03 a.m. Securely buckled into his seat, his gaze wandering about the interior space of the enormous Freightliner trailer, retrofitted to be a mobile operations base for NeuroDelve's virtual reality rig. An array of monitors lined the walls touching edge to edge. Before them, two of Sharmila's staff manned keyboards. Some stations supervised the link to the Endobots, while others assessed the health status of the pilot. At least two were designed to show the environment as the command Endobot—and thus the pilot—saw the world inside a patient's body.

At one end of the trailer was the only door in and out, while at the other end was the immersion rig, which Sharmila referred to as *the Sphere*. A silver ball eight feet in diameter, it allowed the pilot to float inside with the aid of electromagnets and a special suit. Evan stared at it and cocked his head.

Curiosity overcame him.

He unbuckled himself and sauntered over to the Sphere, careful not to trip as the Freightliner rumbled over yet another patch of gravel. The Sphere had to be within a certain proximity to the target subject—his wife—in order for the tech to link up,

145

thus the need for a mobile command post. Couldn't get too close to the CDC facility, though; according to Sharmila, the building was crawling with government agents and straying too near would draw suspicion.

Evan ran his fingers over the smooth surface of the Sphere. A light crackling sound followed, like the static electricity from a pulled sweater. As his hand passed over an embedded control panel, a human-sized rectangular piece of the Sphere's wall popped open with a hiss and slid away on specialized hinges.

Evan stepped inside for a better view.

Though gloomy inside, light cast through the open doorway revealed a glassy jet-black interior. The entire internal surface of the Sphere comprised a continuous screen. No seems or joints. The patient's internal environment would be projected onto the inside of the Sphere's walls, making the pilot feel as if they were inside the body. This allowed complete engagement; a VR-style experience, providing total isolation from the outside world. The pilot—linked to the Endobot—would see, hear and feel as if they themselves were floating inside the patient's body.

Of course, Sharmila's team had to get a dose of Endobots into Marie's system first.

Sharmila's voice grew loud.

Evan emerged from the Sphere and caught the end of Sharmila's heated phone call.

"I'm sorry, did you ask if you're off the hook? There is no hook, it's a spear." Sharmila switched the phone from one hand to the other. "And you're impaled on the end of it. I'm merely helping you stay alive one more day by giving you an opportunity to show you might still have value. The people you and I... work with ... do not take lightly to their money being gambled away on a bender in Vegas. You owe them. Surely you understand this?" She waved for a monitor to be initiated.

A blank screen sprang to life.

"Good," Sharmila continued. "I trust you have the micro camera activated? Make sure, right now, that it's secure on the hood of your face shield."

The screen opposite Evan flickered to life, revealing an awkward view of the CDC isolation facility. He cocked his head to straighten the image. A moment later the image shifted upright.

"Good. Now don't screw it up, or it's your ass." Sharmila clicked off the call.

"Who was that?" Evan asked, without breaking his gaze.

"A doctor, a mole, with a penchant for high stakes poker and expensive prostitutes." Sharmila stood in front of the monitor, half blocking Evan's view.

Evan shuffled to get a better line of sight.

The onscreen view wobbled with the gait of Sharmila's spy, like a bad first-person shooter video game.

"No microphone?" Evan asked.

"There should be sound." Sharmila threw an irritated glance at one of her minions.

The station operator tapped and clicked at menus and systems but Sharmila's team were still deaf to the inside of the CDC facility.

"There must be a malfunction," the employee said.

"Reassuring," Evan said.

Sharmila scowled, but her attention fixed back on the screen. Her mole was on the move. The point of view teetered down the corridor. Each time a CDC worker passed, the forward movement slowed, as Sharmila's mole seemed to waver, maybe nervous he'd be discovered. Evan had a certain empathy, knowing all too well the fear of impending human interaction each time someone came close.

Through several security doors with a swipe of an ID card, the mole-cam passed with ease through the facility, until reaching the glass window to Marie's isolation room.

Evan's gut clenched tight. His wife's skin was gray and sunken, her body frail. In a matter of days, she had wasted away. He'd taken too long.

A security guard outside the room half looked up from his phone at the approach of Sharmila's man. The camera dipped as the mole must have given a brief nod. The guard said something, but Evan couldn't read his lips. Then there was another swipe of the ID card and the spy pushed through into Marie's room.

Once inside, the doctor's shaky hands pulled the injection device from his lab coat pocket. It was smaller, sleeker, than the one Evan's team had developed. Not a Gatling gun, but more like a pistol with a silencer screwed into the barrel. The fingers struggled to get a glass vial full of a silvery liquid into the top of the gun-injector. A hand pulled back the bedsheet and lifted Marie's shirt, exposing her upper abdomen.

"Wait, what is he doing?" Evan blurted out.

"What?" Sharmila asked.

"The infection is localized in the brain," Evan said. "If he injects into the peritoneum, it'll take forever for the Endobots to migrate."

Sharmila's face slackened.

"Can we speak with him?" Evan asked.

Sharmila shook her head.

The mole pressed the injector-gun to Marie's solar plexus, his breathing loud and rapid over the speakers.

Evan's chest tightened. *This idiot should have injected the Endobots closer to the infection.* Now, before Evan could tackle the actual ailment, he'd have to guide Sharmila's bacteria-sized army across what would seem like miles of internal organs by the fastest route to his wife's brain. But which way? He closed his eyes and imagined the vascular system of the human body. The network of vessels to and from the heart formed in his mind; an ordered web of endless bifurcations radiating out from the center mass. But his path was clear. He'd memorized the entire network for the day he would have to pilot his own nanobots. Evan surmised he'd need to infiltrate the inferior vena cava, then into the superior vena cava, somehow fight the flow from the head back to the heart, skip across to the carotid artery—the equivalent of battling a rushing river to reach the shore, breaking through two walls, then jumping into an even faster river. After that, he figured navigating through the vertebral and basal arteries would be a breeze compared with not getting destroyed by the immune system or sucked into the heart or lungs along the way.

"Evan?" Sharmila's voice was muffled behind Evan's thoughts.

"Wait," he said, searing the vascular road map into his visual memory. Evan opened his eyes. "Yes?"

"It's done," Sharmila said.

Evan turned his attention to the mole-cam, but the screen had gone dark.

"You need to get into the Sphere," Sharmila said.

There was no need to ask Evan twice. He pulled off his shirt and dropped his pants. The techs flinched and turned away.

"Damn, man," one of them said. "I was going to hold up a sheet for you."

Sharmila averted her gaze, an amused smile on her face.

Evan stood nude, waiting to be handed the specialized rig outfit. The tech reached out to him, head turned, his fist grasping a black one-piece with a few dozen metallic nodes spread all over it. Evan took the suit and gave it a once over. He had seen something similar used in the movies—motion capture suits. He slid it on, ensuring a good fit for the built-in booties and gloves, then zipped it up to his neck.

"Now for the cranial rig," Sharmila said, then nodded to her team.

Two men carried over a metallic ring that resembled a crown of barbed wire—all edges, blinking lights, and cables. They lifted it with care and placed it over Evan's head, setting it down gently into position. A *fizz* and a *clunk* and the crown engaged with the connection points protruding a few millimeters from Evan's scalp. Immediately his vision blurred, and the world spun. He crumpled to his knees, vomit spilling from his mouth onto the metal floor.

Sharmila put a hand on his shoulder. "It's okay, that's be expected. It'll pass. Give it a moment."

Evan panted, staring at the fuzzy raised pattern of the metallic panels under his palms. He closed one eye and focused on a single raised fleck, allowing it to occupy his entire field of vision. *Breathe, Evan, breathe.* The spinning slowed and the pattern became crisp again. Evan climbed to his feet and wiped his mouth.

"I'm ready," he said.

The small door in the Sphere slid open. Evan took a step inside, then paused. Without turning, he said: "I'm assuming I cross cell layers by forcing myself through intercellular junctions?"

"Yes," Sharmila said. "We looked into transcytosis—moving through a human cell—but the Endobots are too large. You'll have to ram-raid the joints between the cells in a membrane. You have the ability to release vesicles loaded with ions to initiate loosening of the cellular adhesion. Hopefully it'll be enough to widen a gap between cells for you to slip through."

Evan just nodded.

The door closed behind him, a hiss signaling the seal. A low hum filled the space, reverberating off the concave, glassy walls. Evan became weightless, his feet lifting from the floor. An odd, exhilarating sensation. As a child he'd strip down then run and jump and spin, searching for that endless feeling of floating, of having nothing to overload his senses, nothing to touch his skin— not his clothes, nor the ground. Here, now, this was as close as he could get. Even the suit felt ethereal, just like mithril armor described in so many of his fantasy books. Evan allowed himself a guilty smile. He hovered, arms and legs wafting. The suit provided haptic feedback, pushing back on his muscles as if he were swimming against the liquid in Marie's peritoneum and not the air in the Sphere.

The internal surface of the Sphere pinged to life all at once, filling the space in a harsh white light. Evan blinked and refocused. A readout appeared on the curved wall to his right. A neon green outline of a human body, which he assumed was meant to equate to Marie's anatomy. A pulsating red dot in the center was meant to represent him. To his left, another readout glowed electric blue. Metrics on his army, artillery reserves, number of Endobots still functional—by type—and a plethora of information he'd have to figure out on the fly.

A large number three appeared on the wall in front of him. Then two, one.

Evan's brain overloaded, every neuron firing at once. He

scrunched his eyes shut and clenched his jaw, breathing through the pain. And, as quick as it came, the agony left. He opened his eyes. As he swiveled his head, the picture on the concave wall filled—the environment constructed onscreen as the command Endobot experienced it. He shifted his gaze up, down, left and right. The picture on the wall formed, group of pixels by group of pixels. The AI completed the missing pieces and crystalized the fuzzy, jittery image. Particles like dust motes sailed past his field of view. White connective tissue with a dark reddish-brown mass behind it was straight ahead, all bathed in the greenish glow emanating from Evan's Endobot.

"Bioluminescence is active," Evan said. An ingenious idea he'd come up with, too. Biological headlights to see in the pitch dark of the human body. "It's working surprisingly well."

"At the nanometer level that's pretty damn bright," came Sharmila's voice in his ear.

"It uses up a lot of energy, though. Since it's a chemical reaction, it only lasts about twelve hours. Then, it's lights out."

"What?" Evan said. "You don't draw on the host body to refuel the chemical reaction?"

Silence.

"Sharmila?"

"A note for later, Evan," she replied.

The green anatomical image to his right expanded and zoomed in on the abdominal area, then farther still until Marie's thorax was now a clear map, as if he were looking at the state of Washington. If he was correct, he—or at least his Endobot—now floated in the parietal peritoneal space not far from the liver. His destination, the inferior vena cava, was located near the spine, behind the peritoneum. Evan imagined being there at the vessel wall. The thought was interpreted by the command Endobot, which began twirling its flagellum—propelling itself through the serosa fluid in Marie's peritoneal space. Evan felt the pressure on his suit, as if swimming himself. The red dots representing his army darted forward on the virtual map of Marie.

Evan cocked his head. "Why do I hear the sound of rushing water when I move?"

"It's the AI filling in for that sense. It's disconcerting to not hear at all."

It's a nice touch, Evan thought. *I should have thought of that.*

"Everything looks good, Evan, all systems are green. You have navigational control. The system will alert you when you reach junctions in the path."

"Okay," was all Evan could say, his gaze fixated on the innards of his wife. So odd to know he was exploring Marie's body. Evan found himself fascinated by the scale—how the organs looked huge and the peritoneal space itself, only millimeters and filled with less than 50mL of fluid, felt like a cavern. Protein structures floated by—microscopic tumbleweed in the vast chasm of this alien microcosm.

"Evan, the clock is ticking. You have to get moving," Sharmila said.

Evan snapped from his train of thought, glanced at the map to orient himself, then commanded his Endobot army to begin the arduous journey to the retro-peritoneal wall and into the inferior *vena cava*—a raging river of deoxygenated blood packed full of monstrous beasts, the immune response, sent to devour him.

If I die in here, I die out there, Evan thought. *Don't stop now.*

CHAPTER FIFTEEN

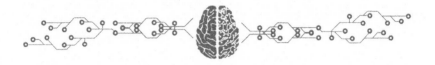

Quantico, Virginia

T he thumping sound of a fist banging on the front door roused Billy from a fitful sleep. Dust and smoke mixed with the coppery scent of blood, filled his nostrils. It was dark and his heart hammered in his chest. Billy fumbled to check Rosie was still at his side—to confirm that making it home wasn't some beautiful dream and he wasn't in fact still pinned down by enemy fire, reliving his best friend's final moments in the longest six hours of his life.

Billy exhaled long and loud as his fingers found his wife's shoulder in the dark.

More banging snapped Billy from his sleepy trance. He scrambled out of bed, stumbled through the bathroom to the closet, and placed his thumb against the biometric scanner. A *clunk* followed. He reached into the steel drawer, retrieved his Sig, and angled back for the bedroom.

"Billy? What is it?" Rosie said, her croaky voice thick with sleep.

Billy jerked on a pair of sweatpants. "Somebody's at the front door."

"What?" Rosie sat up. "It's four in the morning."

Billy didn't respond, instead moved shirtless into the narrow upper hallway of their two-story home. He took an angle on the stairs from where he could see the front door and the shadow of a man through the glass. Another series of thumps echoed in the entranceway, followed by the sound of a voice.

"Captain Vick. Come to the door, please."

Billy knew that voice. It was Adam Kurkowski. What the hell was he doing on Billy's doorstep at four in the morning? He couldn't have called? Billy descended the stairs two at a time and placed the Sig on the side table next to a family picture.

He clicked the dead bolt back and swung the door open. "Adam, what the hell—"

Adam's face had no color. He looked as though he'd been forced to swallow cyanide. At his side was half a dozen grim-faced MPs. Behind them, the passenger door opened on the first of several coyote tan Humvees parked on the curb in convoy formation. Major Barclay exited the vehicle and stood straight, arms across his chest, his expression stormy.

Adam swallowed and shook his head. "I'm sorry, sir."

Billy turned to Kurkowski, his voice low but furious. "What the hell is this?"

"You have to come with us," Kurkowski said. "Major's orders."

"Am I being arrested?" A swarm of heat enveloped Billy's skull.

"Do you think you should be, Captain Vick?" The Major stepped forward. "You disobeyed a direct order, have been in dereliction of your duty, even planned to go AWOL. It's time for you to come in."

"I convinced the Major to let it be me who talked to you," Kurkowski said. "Come in and we'll work this out."

"You know something is going on here, Kurkowski. You know.

155

Why are you doing this?" Billy gnashed his teeth.

"I don't have any choice." Kurkowski seemed to squirm in his own skin. "Command has ordered you to come in."

Billy's muscles tightened. "And if I say no?" He glanced at the Sig on the side table by the door.

"Don't. Please don't." Kurkowski's words were little more than a whisper.

"Billy?" Rosie said, standing on the stairs behind him. "What's going on?"

In an instant, the irrational anger mounting inside him drained away along with his will to resist. Rosie or his boys might get hurt. *Not here, not now.* Billy turned and looked at Rosie. "It's okay, baby. I just have to go handle something."

"Right now?" She descended the stairs and walked up to Billy's side. "Like this? I mean, what the hell is going on?"

"He's not under arrest or anything like that, Mrs. Vick," Kurkowski said. "It's just important that he come back to the office with us to get a few things straightened out."

"I should think so—" Rosie started, but stopped short when Billy squeezed her hand.

"I'll take care of this. Don't worry, okay? I haven't done anything wrong."

"That remains to be determined, Captain," the Major said, skulking from behind the strength of his men. "Time is of the essence. Let's go."

Rosie balked. "He can't get some shoes? Put a shirt and jacket on?"

"Honey—" Billy squeezed her arm.

"No," Rosie said, her eyes boring holes in the Major. "I don't care who you are out there. In our house, you'll treat my husband with a little respect, *sir.*"

"A jacket, sir?" Kurkowski asked looking to the Major, "and some shoes?"

Barclay shook his head. "If the Captain wanted shoes and a jacket, he should have done as he was told."

Billy could feel the heat coming off his little five foot nothing wife. He knew what was coming. "He's being a prick. It's fine, baby," Billy whispered, kissing Rosie on the cheek. "I love you. I'll call when I can. Don't worry."

Billy exited the front door, the cold brick stairs stinging the soles of his feet as he descended between the gathered men. Behind him Rosie stood at the open door, tears streaming down her cheeks.

"Sorry, sir," one of the men mumbled as he passed.

Billy's heart went out to these guys. They didn't want to be here any more than he did, the idea of detaining one of your own a bitter pill to swallow. He reached the bottom of the stairs and walked, feet numb, toward the Major. As Billy approached, two young MPs stepped up, flanking their commanding officer.

Billy stopped, but said nothing.

The Major shook his head. "I'm disappointed in you, Billy."

"Just doing my duty, sir," Billy said, chin high.

"No." The Major's eyes narrowed. "You're making this about *you* and what *you* want."

"Sir, respectfully, you have no idea what you're dealing with here. You can't just make this go away. By ignoring it, a lot of people could die. You need to let me do my job."

"I've heard your conspiracy theories. You were told to stand down on the Weyland case, Captain, and now you've made a mess of it. I told you I had people working that angle."

"Yeah," Billy said, pressing his teeth together. "I ran into *your people.* They almost killed me."

"Get him out of my face," the Major said, turning away.

MPs surrounded Billy, ushering him to the second to last Humvee. An MP pulled the door open. Billy stepped up and into the large, spacious interior, then made room for the MPs who climbed in and sat on either side of him. Billy watched as Adam climbed into the front passenger seat.

"Get us out of here," Adam said, his face screwed up in a bitter grimace. "We're not going to sit here and make any more of a scene in front of the Captain's family and neighbors."

"Yes, sir," the MP behind the wheel said. The convoy of three Humvees eased from the curb, the Major's vehicle leading the way.

"I'm sorry, Adam," Billy said. "I hate that you got stuck in the middle of this."

Kurkowski seemed to clench his teeth, jaw flexing, eyes fixed straight ahead.

Billy sat, inhaling shallow breaths as the convoy picked up speed. If the Major didn't have official paperwork, he would soon. At best Billy would be disgraced, busted down in rank, or dishonorably discharged. At worst, he'd be court martialed and thrown in prison. They could pin whatever they wanted on him. Under martial law, who would stop them?

Billy swallowed. The founding fathers would be rolling over in their graves right now if they knew what had happened to this country. Not that any of it would matter if Evan started tampering with some variant of Omega.

Looking past the stony faced young man to his left, Billy gazed out the window at the concrete divider whipping past as the convoy accelerated up the interstate on ramp. *How could this have gone so wrong?* Billy thought.

The Humvee groaned and the tires whined as the lumbering vehicle picked up speed and emerged out onto the empty interstate. This early, and with curfew still in effect, Quantico was a ghost town. But a shadow flicked past, followed by a second. Billy blinked, shaken from his trance. He shifted his position to get a better look as a third shadow flitted past.

"Sarge, we may have a problem," the driver said, glancing at Kurkowski.

"Stand ready, people," Kurkowski replied, his head on a swivel.

The cab of the Humvee filled with strobing blue light. Outside, a convoy of armored Suburbans flanked the left side of the Major's Humvees. The Suburbans pressed in, lights flashing, forcing the military convoy closer to the concrete barrier on the right. With a jerk, the Humvee came to a stop, and the MPs scrambled for their pistols.

"Police?" the driver shouted.

"Relax," Kurkowski said. "Everyone just relax. Hold what you've got."

Billy watched through the window as agents in black body armor took cover behind their dark Suburbans, rifles trained on the military convoy. A familiar woman exited the passenger side of one of the oversized SUVs. She was dressed in midnight tactical clothing, a black plate carrier strapped across her chest. From behind the cover of the Suburban's armored door she raised a mic to her lips. The Suburban's PA system activated with a squelch of noise.

Billy shook his head. "Reinhardt?"

"This is Special Agent in Charge, Reinhardt with the Department of Homeland Security, Anti-Terrorism Task Force. We have obtained felony warrants for the arrest of Billy Vick." In her free hand she held up a tri-folded bundle of papers.

"What the hell is *this*?" Adam said, wide eyed.

"Release him to us now," Reinhardt said. "There is no need for a confrontation."

The radio in the Humvee crackled. "Hold your fire, get a perimeter, and stand your ground," the Major said, his words laced with profound irritation. "We are the United States Army. We don't surrender anything to anyone."

The Major's soldiers stepped out of the Humvees, most with their pistols already in hand. Billy stayed put as Adam and the other MPs exited his vehicle. Finally, the Major climbed out and adjusted his shirt as he walked around the rear of his transport to face the intense little woman three car lanes away. He came to a stop and with a wave of his hand two MPs flanked him, weapons at the low ready.

A tired smile spread across the Major's face. "What's this all about, honey?"

Reinhardt shifted and re-gripped the mic, her voice projected over the Suburban's PA. "As I told you, sir, we have felony warrants for the arrest of Billy Vick." She gave the bundle of papers a little shake.

"For what charge?" Major Barclay asked.

"Conspiracy to commit an act of terrorism."

Major Barclay hocked a laugh. "Conspiracy? Terrorism? Billy Vick is one of our finest senior agents. We are to escort him back to base for a debriefing. Now let us be on our way or you're about to have a bunch of dead DHS agents on your hands."

"Sir, are you threatening us?" Reinhardt said.

"Sweetheart." Barclay laughed. "You don't have the fire power to—"

Reinhardt held up her hand. The squall of tires burning against asphalt followed. Two additional Suburbans screeched up in reverse. In unison, their tinted back glass slid open to reveal stoic-faced agents anchored behind M134 Miniguns. With a whine the electric barrels began to rotate.

Fury poured from Major Barclay's face. He wiped at his forehead dotted with sweat despite the cold. "This is… you can't… we are the United States Army and under martial law—"

"Let me stop you right there," Reinhardt said, her words amplified by the megaphone. "This country is still ruled by a civilian government, not a military dictatorship. Martial law or not, it is federal law enforcement's job to enforce the laws of this land and we carry the authority of the highest levels of government when we do so. Failing to release this man to us is a criminal act."

Billy released an incredulous laugh.

Reinhardt continued, shaking the folded warrant in Barclay's direction. "Directing force upon us will get you and the soldiers under your command killed. We are not overseas or on your base, sir. You are in my world right now. Do I make myself clear?"

Billy, looked from Reinhardt back to the Major who quivered with rage, a throbbing purple vein standing out from his neck.

"Release him," Adam Kurkowski said, jerking his head at Billy.

"But sir," a pale-faced young soldier said, pawing at the door with jittery fingers. "The Major."

"Let me worry about the Major. Release Captain Vick, now."

The MP opened the door and motioned for Billy to get out. Sliding to the edge of the seat, still shoeless and wearing sweatpants, Billy stepped out onto the interstate. He watched his breath float from his mouth in steaming white puffs, the deep moist chill in the air soaking into his bare skin and stinging his feet.

Kurkowski turned to Billy. "Is this legit, Cap?" His eyes searched the face of his team leader. "The conspiracy charge, I mean."

"I don't know what they have on me, but I haven't committed conspiracy. Everything I've done, you knew about. I just want the truth."

"Roger that," Kurkowski said, casting a sideways glance at the Major, who was still fixed on Reinhardt.

Kurkowski looked around. "Cap, listen to me. We're compromised. The whole unit is shut down. The investigation into the bombing in Syria is closed. I don't know what the brass is trying to hide with Marie Weyland, but they're looking to wipe this whole thing out."

Billy nodded.

Kurkowski extended his hand. "I don't know if you can do anything by cooperating with Homeland, but this may be our only shot. Make it count, sir."

"You going to be all right, Sarge?" Billy took his friend's hand and gave it a firm squeeze.

Kurkowski pressed his lips into a thin line. "Time will tell, sir." He tilted his head toward Reinhardt. "If I'm not in shackles myself, I'll keep an eye on Rosie and the boys until you get back. Take care of yourself."

"Thank you," Billy said. With slow deliberate steps, he raised his hands in the air and walked toward Reinhardt.

"First Sergeant!" the Major shouted. "What the *fuck* are you doing?"

A wild barrage of curses spilled from the Major as he stomped toward Adam Kurkowski. Billy quickened his pace crossing to Reinhardt, who stood behind the door of the up-armored

162

Suburban.

"Get behind me," she said to Billy, then turned to one of her agents. "Load up."

"Yes, ma'am," Billy said.

Billy climbed into the rear seat of the large armored SUV and slid to the far side. An agent with a Hollywood cleft in his chin, climbed in behind him and shut the door. A moment later they were joined by Reinhardt and the driver. In seconds, the Homeland convoy stacked in unison, shot off into the early morning dark leaving the Barclay's entourage behind.

The chin-cleft agent on Billy's right turned to him and stuck out his hand. "Glad you're okay."

Surprised, Billy shook the man's hand. "Thanks, I guess…"

Reinhardt swiveled in her seat, intermittent streetlamps spotlighting the scowl on her face.

"Your commander couldn't even let you get shoes and a shirt when he kidnaps you from your house at four in the morning?"

Billy shrugged, the bare flesh of his chest prickled from the cold. "I suppose not."

"Sounds like a guy who takes good care of his people." She paused, looking over his disheveled, half-dressed appearance. "What is going on with you, anyway?"

Billy stared at Reinhardt. "You tell me, *Special Agent in Charge*. Sort of an important detail you left out yesterday. I was under the impression…"

"What? That because I'm a woman, I couldn't hold a position of any importance?" She glared at him.

"Now, hold on. That's not what I said."

"It's not?"

Billy blew out a stream of air from between pinched lips. "Can

163

someone please tell me what the hell is going on here? Were you following me?"

"I didn't like how things went down yesterday so I had someone tail you to your residence and hold surveillance to see where you'd go today," Reinhardt said. "When your people picked you up, I activated my team."

"Am I under arrest?" Billy asked.

"No." Reinhard tossed the tri-folded bundle of paper on the dash.

"No? Then what are those papers?" Billy asked.

The angry façade cracked, a little smirk forming on Reinhardt's face. "My car's last battery core service."

"You almost started a shootout with a military convoy over battery service paperwork? Are you crazy, lady?"

"You have no idea what was about to happen to you, do you, Billy Vick?" Reinhardt locked him down with those hard green eyes. "You were going to be silenced. That's what the military does to people who stand against its interests."

"No, come on..." Billy started, stopping when he saw the look on Reinhardt's face. "You can't be serious."

"I'm deadly serious," she said, lowering her voice. "Do you know how many people have disappeared across the country over the last year since we've been under martial law?"

Billy shook his head.

"Almost four thousand." Reinhardt jabbed the console with her index finger. "That's a drop in the bucket compared to the population, easily written off as accidents, missing persons, and the results of criminal activity. But do you know how many people disappeared the year before? Half that. The legitimate, never show up again, missing persons cases *doubled* in the year since martial law went into effect. Does that seem like a coincidence to you?"

All he could do was shrug.

"Take the soldiers who were on the jet with Marie Weyland," Reinhardt said. "All released. Now all missing or dead in a matter of days. Car accident. Accidental overdose. The list goes on."

"How is that possible?" Billy said.

"Nobody cares, Billy," Reinhardt said. "Everyone is so warped by the threat of terrorism, they've traded their freedom for what they think is security. It's not. We're becoming the next military dictatorship."

"This crap just gets better and better," Billy said, leaning back.

"Exactly," Reinhardt said. "Now, the military appears to be hiding something in regard to this infected woman—a case that very well could be some sort of bio-terrorism. I want to know why they're trying to cover it up."

Billy held her penetrating gaze.

"You're the only one over there who seems to care about the truth," Reinhardt said. "I think it's because you know more about this than you've let on." She leaned toward him, her voice a growl. "Before you walked away yesterday at Johns Hopkins, you said you had to put a stop to this before we all ended up dead. Why would you say that?"

"It's a long story, Reinhardt."

"It's a long drive, Vick," she said, and tapped *Record* on her phone, setting it on the console in front of him.

CHAPTER SIXTEEN

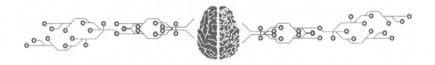

Quantico, Virginia

Ryder straightened; the muzzle of the pharaoh tactical 300 blackout rifle angled up toward the early morning sky ringed with fading stars. He watched as the convoy of black Suburban's sped away north along the I-95 interstate, leaving the Major to hurl impotent threats at his men. The only detail Ryder gleaned through his scope as this unmarked armored convoy dismantled the Major's feeble efforts to contain Billy Vick, were the placards on the black armor carriers: *Homeland.*

He let a steam laden hiss of frustration pass his lips. "Well here we go." *Shit just got real.*

It was the second time he'd had the chance to snuff Captain Billy Vick. With a single pull of a two and a half pound trigger he could have ended this branching set of dilemmas, a mess that was proving harder and harder for his team to mitigate. But Ryder didn't like the idea of being a faceless assassin. Just like tracking big game through the mountains out west; when the time came for the kill, he wanted his quarry to know it was him. Up close and personal. A duel of honor. As a fellow warfighter, Vick deserved that far more than a copper-jacketed ball of lead traveling at 2,900 feet per second. That one choice made everything more difficult for Ryder, but holding to it was what his gut told him to do, and his gut was never wrong.

Ryder rolled onto his shoulder to reach the phone in his pocket. Frosted blades of grass tickled his earlobe. He held the device up and after a moment of auto analyzing his facial profile, the screen brightened. Ryder selected the top number in recent calls and held it to his ear, turning his attention back to the Major's convoy.

"Go," Frank said on the other end.

"Bring the truck around."

"What happened with it?"

"Just bring the truck around." Ryder hung up and secured the phone.

The stars glittered in their heavenly perches, shimmering specks of ice-colored fire that reached out to him from across the galaxy. A whisp of cloud concealed and then revealed them again. Another steamed breath pushed slow across Ryder's numbed lips, and for just a moment, he was back in Montana with a warm cup of coffee between his fingers, enjoying the cold night sky with old Buck curled up on the porch next to him.

Those days back on the ranch were good days. Not like this. This was going to be hell, and he could feel the deep ugliness of it in the marrow of his bones. A baleful frozen wind bit at the nape of his neck, the sensation as bitter as this unfortunate shift in events.

Ryder produced another can of dip and popped it open with his thumb. He pinched up half the can between forefinger and thumb and wedged it deep in his bottom lip. Everyone wanted to stick their noses in this damn op. It was only a matter of time before his end of this mess turned from intel gathering to clean up.

He plucked up his binoculars and dialed them in. Through the lenses he watched the interstate, strange and silent amidst the enforced curfew, and turned his focus back to Barclay's convoy. Now the Major was in the first sergeant's face, the guy named Kurkowski. The sarge was taking his dressing down like a man, too. Eyes forward, face stoic, he didn't appear to be the type to be rattled by a little scream-flung spittle, least of all from that doughy sack of hot garbage.

The Major gave a sharp jab of his finger in Kurkowski's chest. Ryder felt sure only a thread of militaristic order kept the fit redheaded sergeant from punching his superior officer's lights out. But the first sergeant seemed a good soldier, a dutiful soldier. And he'd let Vick go. Why? It was time for Ryder to find out.

He packed up his gear, grabbed his rifle, and headed back down the far hillside toward the waiting truck. Damn thing didn't make a sound, it just sat there not-idling. Ryder spat in disgust, a string of tobacco juice clinging to his lower lip. What he wouldn't give to hear the groaning thump of an actual fume-chugging combustion engine.

Ryder jerked the passenger side door open and swung his ultra-trek stealth backpack into the rear seat alongside the rifle. "Fuck this car."

Duke frowned, looked up from his laptop in the back seat. "It's a truck."

"The hell it is," Ryder scoffed. "This ugly piece of garbage is an imposter, an insult to its American heritage. Wanna fight about it?"

Frank smirked. "Tell us how you really feel."

"Just did." Ryder cast a look at Duke. "Tell me you've got something else on Vick. You able lift his records?"

"You're not going to like it," Duke said.

"I don't like jack about this op already. What is it? Keep it brief."

"Okay," Duke said. "Your guy's a mustang. Enlisted when he was eighteen. Went infantry and was later assigned to the 75th Ranger Regiment. Served eight years in various combat zones around the world including two tours in Syria, the second was Operation Ground Clear and the retaking of Aleppo."

"Dude." Frank glanced at Ryder. "The real deal. That push was the worst of the war."

"What did I tell you?" Ryder said, nodded to Duke. "Continue."

Duke sighed. "Tried to go Delta twice. Medical drop out both times due to unreconcilable injury. Awarded the silver star for valor when a bunch of his squad got wiped and he and two others held off a force of thirty-five Syrian-Iraqi fighters. After that he moved around and ended up in Belarus on an advance border protection team flying micro drones. That's where he met his wife. Brought her to the states, they married, three kids, blah, blah, blah, happy American family."

"Oh yeah," Frank said. "Good looking family. Especially the wife. Got the pictures to prove it, too."

"You said he was a mustang. What about that?" Ryder pressed.

"Yeah, came back and went OCS. Lateralled into his current MP company and CID. Been there a few years. Submitted a letter requesting that he not be promoted further."

"Because he likes mud on his boots," Ryder said. "The kind of guy who gets the job done. I can respect that."

Ryder's phone chimed. He pulled the device from his pocket and saw that he'd missed the first alert. With a tap he displayed the message sent from an encrypted number. An auto scrub timer began ticking down at the top of the message.

Asset confirmed. Time is short. Advance the ball down the field. Now.

Ryder rubbed at his face. "Whatever we pulled from Weyland's computer, Sweetie reckons it confirms Omega on U.S. soil. You boys ready for some real work?"

The timer above the anonymous text hit zero, the message flashed and disappeared.

"Hell yeah, boss. What's up?" Frank asked.

"This mission just turned into tying off loose ends." Ryder surveyed his men. "For a guy with issues, Evan Weyland disappeared like a champ. We know where his wife is but she's under such scrutiny right now, we'll be hard pressed to get to her discretely. Billy Vick wasn't even on the radar, but now he's made himself a problem—one we need to rectify. All three need to be zipped up."

"Vick will come straight at us. We could leverage his kids." Frank spoke with a gleam in his eye.

"Nobody touches his family." Ryder starred Frank down. "The man deserves more respect than that. You leave him to me. The shot callers want us to advance the ball. We'll do that, and we'll use all the muscle Barclay can bring to bear to get it done. That means we'll have to break a few eggs."

"Frank and I can work on running Weyland down and develop contingencies for accessing the wife," Duke said.

"Good, do it," Ryder said.

"What about you?" Frank asked.

Ryder sat back, a smug look of satisfaction on his face. "I think it's time I get the Major's house in order."

CHAPTER SEVENTEEN

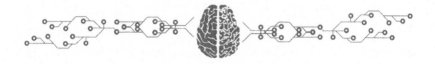

Inferior Vena Cava, Marie Weyland's Body

Evan's command Endobot hovered in front of the epithelial cells making up the wall to the inferior *vena cava*. He stared at the image of the wall made up of huge bricks—but instead of solid cement, these bricks were cells. The biological barrier loomed before him and seemed to grow in size as he tilted his head back to take it all in. Inside Marie's body lived another universe, a place of walls and turrets and monsters and heroes. A fairytale played out at a microscopic level. Evan's chest heaved, his eyes locked wide open. Only his nagging conscience, reminding him to save Marie, prevented his wandering off on a fantastic voyage through a real human body.

Concentrate, Evan. He checked his readout; his connection was good and the army of Endobots floated nearby in the detritus-filled fluid. He scanned the biological barrier ahead, examining its structure in the greenish luminescence given off by his command Endobot. *The joints between cells—that's where I have to squeeze through.*

First, Evan needed to loosen the cellular adhesion—make the joints between cells looser—then push between the space and into the lumen of the inferior *vena cava* full of deoxygenated blood rushing back to the heart. To achieve that, he'd need to release a barrage of vesicles—tiny packages—with chemicals that would in turn tell ion channels—miniscule faucets in the cell surface—to dump a lot of the intracellular calcium. The proteins and structures, like screws and rivets binding the cells together, would then come loose.

Easy enough, Evan thought.

But damaging the cell wall would trigger an immune response. He might as well sound an alarm, alerting T-cells, macrophages, and antibodies to his location.

"Evan?"

That was Sharmila's shrill voice. Evan had almost forgotten she was on the other side of the Sphere, watching everything on her monitors and expecting results for her questionable benefactors.

"We're monitoring your progress," Sharmila continued. "You've been stalled at the inferior *vena cava* for a while. Is everything okay?"

He'd stalled? How long had he been staring at the cell wall? Evan was known to drift off into thought, but it was never more than a few seconds. "How long?"

"Forty-three minutes," Sharmila said.

Forty-three minutes? How is that possible?

"Time is a tricky thing while in the Sphere, Evan."

"Tricky how?" Evan asked.

"It's important you don't feel claustrophobic or trapped while in there," Sharmila said, her tone a touch sheepish. "Removing someone from the Sphere takes time, unless you want to cause permanent brain damage. So, to avoid a pilot panicking and pulling the plug, the surgery you had also altered the neural network for how you perceive time."

"You altered my perception of time?" Evan said, his voice little more than a hoarse squeak.

Time had been a tricky thing growing up. *Not now*, *later*, and *tomorrow*, had been words thrown at him by his parents but so very difficult to assign any meaning. His teachers at school were kind enough to set up a visual system to help—a board with *today* and *tomorrow* columns, and stickers to be moved from one to the other. A pencil sticker meant he'd be writing. At the end of one day it would live in the *tomorrow* column. The next morning, it would move to *today* and writing was the task that morning. Once he'd grasped the concept of time, it became a cornerstone of his existence. A roadmap on which to place important events—like Marie calling him or coming home. To now know Sharmila had messed with his brain, tweaked how he felt the passage of time, made Evan's stomach cramp and his mind burn with a thousand thoughts all at once.

"How is that achieved?" he said, at length. Perhaps knowing would help, give him back control.

"Clock is ticking. Is that important now, Evan?" Sharmila asked.

"Yes," he said. "Please."

Sharmila sighed. "For things humans enjoy, time seems to pass quickly, while for things they don't, time goes slower. It sounds obvious, but it's been shown to be an actual phenomenon. We altered the neural pathways to make every experience in there more… enjoyable. You don't know how long you've been in there, and you're happy to be there." After a long pause, she added, "A happy pilot is a more effective pilot."

Evan wasn't *really* experiencing the awe coursing through him. It was manufactured to stop him from freaking out. A brief flash of inspiration to use this methodology in order to help people like him—people on the spectrum—burned bright in his mind, before fizzling out like an extinguished torch. This was no time to be selfish, he had to focus on Marie.

"Releasing vesicles now," Evan said, then directed his command bot to release the chemical packages that would loosen the wall.

Instantly, miniscule spheres bubbled up around him and powered forward with surprising speed. They hurtled out toward the epithelial wall, before exploding like tiny bombs. The chemicals inside dissipated into the peritoneal fluid. A moment passed, only a manufactured sloshing sound filling the silence. Then it happened. The cellular bricks of the epithelium began to separate. To Evan it looked like pulling cheesy bread apart—two hunks of a French loaf connected by many long stringy strands.

Evan centered his concentration on heading for the gap between the cells. Sure enough, his command bot powered forward, the army in tow, and fought against the rushing plasma leaking from the damaged blood vessel. Evan began swimming— an instinctive waving of his arms and kicking of his legs in mid-air—in hopes it might aid his Endobot's struggle. The added mechanics worked a little, the tiny biological machine moving just a little faster, but Evan's muscles rapidly tired and after a few minutes he had to stop, exhausted.

The gaping maw between the cells began to close, the effect of his chemical packages now dwindling. He had to make it through, or risk being trapped—even crushed—between the biological bricks. Evan imagined passing through the other side, willing his army to follow him through the breach.

A tremendous pressure clamped down around Evan's whole

body as the command bot squeezed between the cells of the wall. Devoid of oxygen, Evan lungs refused to inflate. His vision darkened and his bones felt as if they might break under the incredible weight.

The pressure stopped and Evan's bot—and a good portion of his troops—popped through the vessel wall. Inside the Sphere, Evan sucked at the air but the relief lasted only a moment. The rushing channel of blood dragged his bot tumbling and spinning up, up, up, toward the superior *vena cava*. Toward the heart, and his imminent destruction. Vomit rose up into Evan's mouth as he gyrated in uncontrollable loops in the Sphere. The rollercoaster-like motion pulled him in and out of the immersive experience— one second watching his reflection in the curved glass inner wall of the Sphere, the next focused on the pain of a corpuscle crashing into his command Endobot.

"Evan? Evan? Can you hear me?" Sharmila's voice seemed so far away.

The sounds of Evan's own heart and the simulated rushing of blood plasma in the superior *vena cava* filled his ears. *Blood takes forty-five seconds to make a complete circuit of the human body*, he thought. From his position, he had at best ten seconds to act. Evan's mind numbed and his body stiffened. In the real world he would cover his ears and scrunch into a ball to block out all stimuli, but here in the Sphere, connected to the command Endobot, everything was fed direct into his brain—no way to stifle the onslaught, to protect himself. Evan cried out in pain.

"Evan, you have to listen to me," Sharmila pressed. "If you're sucked into Marie's heart you'll be crushed by a valve or—if you miraculously make it through—be forced into the alveolar space in the lungs and glued there by mucous. Either way, if that happens, your Endobot is shitcanned and so are you."

Evan threw up, spraying the inner curved glass of the Sphere with vomit.

"Evan, you have seconds before you're at the heart," Sharmila shouted. "We planned for this. You have to engage the adhesins. Do it!"

Evan screwed his eyes closed and imagined clinging to the vessel wall with his fingernails, clawing and gripping with all he had.

The spinning jerked to a stop.

Evan eased open his eyes, frozen in an awkward pose as if hanging from an indoor climbing wall. Fluid rushed past, vibrating the image before him. On the Sphere screen, he saw his army of Endobots stuck to the inner wall of the superior vena cava. The deep thrumming of Marie's heart pulsed in his ears. He was at the juncture between the inferior and superior *vena cava*, emptying into the right atrium of the heart.

The adhesins worked. Tiny claw-like chains of amino acids used by normal bacteria to gain a foot hold on host cells. Here he could use them to cling to the wall of the blood vessel and also as a sort of primitive walking apparatus. He could tread a slow path against the blood flow through the superior *vena cava* up into to the brachiocephalic vein and then bust through and across to the carotid artery.

Evan swallowed away the acidic taste in his mouth and centered his focus on his Endobots. He'd lost too many—maybe thirty percent along the way—and from here on in he had to be vigilant. He'd need this army once he made it to the brain stem.

If he made it.

Sharmila unclenched her fists, the dig marks in her palm white. She blew out an anxious breath, long and purposeful. She glanced over at the Sphere, imagining Evan inside, exhausted and fragile. "How's his heart rate?"

"Returning to normal," the technician answered. "Thought his heart was going to explode at one point. The stress is greater than we expected, even with the neuronal control."

"We need to up the endorphins and adrenaline," Sharmila said. "Keep him alert, but happy."

The tech turned to face her, peering over thick-rimmed glasses. "Increase? But his heart—"

"If he doesn't complete this, his wife dies, and our research with her."

The tech nodded, his lips pressed together.

Sharmila surveyed the neurolink readout displaying a plethora of data regarding the rate of information exchange back and forth between Evan's brain and the Endobots. The sheer volume of particles in sustained quantum entanglement was greater than she'd ever seen. Millions of particles, with entanglements milliseconds long, before breaking then re-establishing—in subatomic terms, a veritable lifetime. Did Evan's brain somehow function differently in this respect? Is that how autism spectrum disorder worked? Were these individuals linked to the very environment, the universe around them on a subatomic level? Is that why Evan and people like him experienced stimulus overload?

The academic implications were enormous. Understanding biology in terms of quantum physics—she could unlock treatment

177

paradigms for people who suffer with ASD—if of course one could still consider it suffering? Maybe people on the spectrum were more advanced than the average human. Hell, such a thing could explain all kinds of phenomenon. Perhaps conditions like schizophrenia and multiple personality disorder were not illnesses but connections to other things and people? Were voices in people's heads and ghost sightings, often attributed to a damaged mind, one human connecting to another at the quantum level? Had medical science wrongly incarcerated and medicated so many people? Armed with such information a cure, or even more advanced communication technology, could be envisioned.

Sharmila pinched her lips and shook off such thoughts. Long ago, she was an academic. Now, she was a businessperson—one in debt to terrible people—and could no longer afford to follow such philosophical whimsies for the sake of furthering human knowledge. The almighty dollar ruled. Evan was both her meal ticket and her survival. Failure was unacceptable.

"Dr. Vashi?"

"Yes?" Sharmila pulled her gaze from the data flow onscreen, now aware the freightliner had stopped moving.

Her head of security, a mercenary for hire brought along as insurance should the worst happen, stood in the open door, his face stoic, a large rifle in one hand. Sharmila had never learned his name, never wanted to. Distance meant deniability.

"The facility is crawling with agents. Your... associate. The one inside the CDC. He may be compromised. We have to assume they know about him, and what we're doing here." He pulled the door shut and scratched at his short beard.

Sharmila pulled her phone from her pocket and speed dialed the mole. The ringer hummed and hummed, then, unable to connect, clicked off. "No answer."

The merc nodded. "Just as I thought."

"Recommendations?" Sharmila asked.

"We call in a chopper," he said, now cradling his rifle, "have it ready for an emergency extraction if necessary, but keep this facility moving. I'll send in a team, ready to cause a little distraction should we need it."

"Agreed," Sharmila said, with a curt nod. While quantum entanglement could theoretically occur over vast distances, Sharmila's researchers had found proximity still helped the pilot maintain control. "But extraction is the final option. I can't afford to screw this up." She needed as much data as possible. Record all information up until the last possible second. Perhaps then her associates would allow her to live, and maybe even pay the sums promised. Why think about money now? Because that was the point of dealing with a shady benefactor hiding in a bunker somewhere outside of Pyongyang. To get rich. Sharmila had to admit, exchanging her Casio for a Rolex, and her studio apartment for a penthouse suite, almost made up for selling her soul. Almost.

"We'll head out," the merc said. "You shouldn't contact us. Observe total radio silence. If I feel you need the chopper, I'll send it. No questions asked."

Sharmila nodded.

The merc opened the rear door, jumped out and closed it again.

The converted Freightliner rumbled to life and lurched forward to once again circle the network of interlocking streets and side roads surrounding the CDC facility. Sharmila watched the truck's external camera feed, tracking the merc's strike team darting away. As the truck turned a corner and the camera's view shifted, she caught sight of two, maybe three, shadows—armed shadows— who ducked behind a BMW parked on the side of the street. *Who the hell is that?* Had the Koreans sent in their own team? Perhaps some back up? *Can't worry about it now,* she thought. *Clock is ticking.*

CHAPTER EIGHTEEN

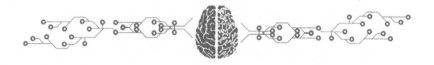

Undisclosed Location, Quantico

"Yes sir, I'll take care of it," Major Barclay said into the phone wedged against the clammy flesh of his face. His stomach gurgled, tightening. He clawed at his lower abdomen hoping the pain would subside, that he wouldn't end up on the crapper for a fourth time this morning. *What a fucking nightmare.* "No sir," he said, the perspiration on his forehead building. "I assure you, I have it under control." He flinched at the sworn threat of death. The cold silence of a dead line followed. He licked his lips, looked at the screen one last time to ensure the call had terminated, and slipped the phone into his pocket. Another gurgle from his stomach.

"God help me." The Major grimaced, pulled a handkerchief from his pocket, and blotted his forehead. He turned back to the empty room stinking of mold and rot, the carpet squishing wet beneath his boots. Sparse, water-stained ceiling tiles hung broken and disjointed, marking years of neglect. A segment of electrical wiring dangled through one of the missing tiles. In the center of the decrepit windowless space, Staff Sergeant Adam Kurkowski sat handcuffed to a metal chair, clothes torn, head down. Nearby, on an uneven three-legged table, a propane lantern sputtered stale, piss-colored light.

Major Barclay looked to the two grim-faced MPs standing guard by the door. "That will be all for now."

"Sir?" one of the MPs asked.

"Take a break. Wait outside."

The young men looked at each other, fear in their eyes. "Yes sir."

Barclay waited until the MPs filed out of the room. He and Kurkowski were alone. The smell of mildew, like sour cheese, and the distant sound of dripping, only served to emphasize the dank, morose nature of this long decommissioned section of the base. Perfect for undocumented interrogation. Barclay stood with his hands clasped behind his back, his gaze burning holes through the wilted Staff Sergeant.

"Going to have all your subordinates arrested and beaten, Major?" Kurkowski raised his bruised face and huffed out a laugh. "Your qualities as a leader know no end, *sir*."

The Major clenched his jaw as another gas pain knifed him in the belly. "Staff Sergeant, do you realize you and Captain Vick can be charged with conspiracy to commit treason?" The Major began to pace, his arms still behind his back. "An unfitting end to an otherwise exemplary, if short, military career."

"That's a load of shit and you know it!" Kurkowski spat. "I don't have to answer your questions."

Barclay nodded to the dark. Layered ink-like shadows concealed everything beyond the meager pool of pale yellow light. Kurkowski squinted, searching the black. A figure stepped forward from the gloom, working his hands into a pair of leather gloves. They made a tinkling sound as the sewed-in pocket of lead shot adjusted around his knuckles. He grinned, the broad scar across his hairline pulled tight.

Kurkowski swallowed. He looked from the scarred man back to the Major. "Sir, we haven't committed treason."

"That's what we're here to find out," the Major said. "You chose to release Vick to Homeland. Now you get to answer my questions."

"Or wha—"

Scar's lead-knuckled punch rocked Kurkowski's head back.

The stunned Sergeant opened his mouth, blood weeping from a busted lip. "Shit, man…"

"Well?" the Major said. "I want to know everything you and Captain Vick were up to. Everything."

Kurkowski sniffed. "We were just doing our job, *sir.*"

Another punch, this time a sharp right hook, snapped against the side of Kurkowski's jaw. His head twisted and a moan of pain seeped from his lips.

"Staff Sergeant, you should choose your next words very carefully," the Major said. "If not, I'll make sure you spend the best years of your life in a military prison. Tell me what I want to know."

Kurkowski's expression frosted over. He ducked his chin and touched the drop of blood hanging from his lip to the cloth of his shirt at the shoulder. "I guess you'll have to beat it out of me."

The words weren't out of Kurkowski's mouth when Scar hit him with a brutal uppercut, clacking his teeth together. A second punch landed dead center mass, the solar plexus. Kurkowski doubled forward and hung there, straining the ropes that held him fast.

"I don't like your attitude, First Sergeant. If you just tell me what you know I can make this all stop."

Kurkowski leaned back. A read smear across his face, he looked long and hard at the Major, as if searching for truth in his words.

The Major nodded. *Every man has his limit.*

"It's Omega," Kurkowski said. He lowered his head again. "Marie Weyland is infected with Omega."

Barclay already knew that, so said nothing and waited for the rest of the bombshell to drop.

"I don't know who's behind it, but it has all the trappings."

"Go on," the Major said.

"Go on what?" spat Kurkowski. "Omega on U.S. soil! The Army Biological Warfare Division's end solution? Their answer to the threat of Middle Eastern terrorism. Take them all out in one fell swoop. Ring any bells?"

"I know about Omega. I was there, too." Barclay pinched his lips, fighting back another spike of abdominal pain. "Tell me something I *don't know*. I told Vick to leave it alone. Why didn't he?"

"Why?" Kurkowski screwed up his face. "Marie Weyland was almost killed by a US Army orchestrated firebombing of a civilian settlement in Syria and arrives back in the USA sick with what looks like Omega. Connect the dots, *Major*. Someone moved Omega forward even after we shut it down. Whether it was us or someone else, our government decided to wipe out a non-military village to presumably destroy a sample of the damn weapon or maybe prevent someone else from having it." Kurkowski let his words hang in the air. "Hundreds of civilians died. Women, children. That's a *war crime*, Major. That's why Vick couldn't leave it. Not to mention Omega is now stateside, there's a potential containment problem and Evan Weyland is trying to use his experience with nanobot tech to save his wife's life. That's what *I* know. And *you* know what'll happen if Weyland messes with Omega."

The Major clutched at his belly, now roiling with gas pain and pure dread. Weyland could make this all a thousand times worse.

"Dirty business, to get involved in a cover up, don't you think, sir?" Kurkowski said. "What do you know about it? Who did the Army collaborate with to do this behind our backs? North Korea? The Russians—?"

A snap pierced the air.

Barclay flinched, an awkward cry in his throat, his face peppered with a sheen of red mist.

Adam Kurkowski's head lolled back, a trickle of blood streaking from the perfect hole in his forehead. It dribbled down the bridge of his nose and splattered maroon ink blots on the breast of his shirt.

"My God," Major Barclay gasped. "He's... you..."

From the shadowed corner of the room, Ryder stepped forward, unscrewing a suppressor from the end of a Sig Sauer pistol. He slipped the suppressor into a pouch at his belt and re-holstered his weapon. "Wipe your face, Major."

Major Barclay touched his face, the tips of his fingers wet with Adam's blood. He quivered with disgust. "You said you were here to deconflict. This wasn't part of our arrangement. You can't just go around—"

"Stop your whining." Ryder wiped his hands. "It doesn't suit a man of your position. And wolves don't make arrangements with sheep."

"We're on base—and you just killed one of my men," Barclay said, his extremities shuddering like a leaf in a gale.

Ryder took a step closer, his eyes narrowing. "Pull yourself together, *Major*. He knew too much. You know he did. The mission is to scrub everything. If you don't want the same

185

treatment, you'll shut your mouth and start doing what's expected of you. I'm not here to babysit." Ryder looked from the shaken Major back to Kurkowski, whose glassy, open-mouthed stare remained fixed on the moldy ceiling above. A light pitter-patter filled the silence as blood and brain smacked and puddled against the concrete behind the chair.

The Major gulped at the stale air. The sour taste of it, dank with mold and coppery with blood, brought on the need to wretch. Too long behind a desk now, having not seen combat in decades, he gagged, choking on his own welling saliva.

Ryder crossed his arms, looking on with disapproval. He nodded to Scar who went to work cutting Kurkowski's corpse free from the metal chair. "My team will dispose of the body and clean up here. You locate Billy Vick. I'll contact you and, assuming you've found him, my team will escort you to pick him up."

"Then what?" Major Barclay felt his abdomen tighten, the sensation so strong he believed his bowels might release right there into his pants. He struggled to contain it, his face pale with sweat.

"Then we make this all go away, Major." Ryder offered a shark-like smile, his face glowing in the low light of the room. "And if you're a good little soldier, you won't go away with it."

Major Barclay couldn't contain his rising terror, the ugliness of a situation grown so monstrous he had no choice but to let it consume him. He had to get out. Pulling a handkerchief from his breast pocket, he wiped the speckled blood from his face and jacket and turned toward the door and his Humvee waiting outside. *We're all going to burn for this.*

"Oh, and Major," Ryder said, waiting for Barclay to stop and meet his gaze. "It would benefit you to keep in mind—those we report to do not suffer the failures of fools."

CHAPTER NINETEEN

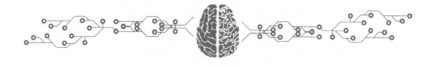

I-495 En Route to Dulles CDC Quarantine

Outside the cold glass of the police package Chevy Suburban, a frosty gray dawn lit the horizon and gave definition to the rolling hills. Inside, Reinhardt listened as Billy recounted his story, what he knew about the Army's Project Omega, and how his unit had been responsible for the investigation that buried it. She sat with her arms crossed, skepticism pouring from her features.

"So, what you're telling me is the Army's Bio Warfare Division proposed the development of a smart biological organism?" Reinhardt said.

Billy nodded. "A bacteria. They called it the Omega Variant."

"Why?"

"It was the easy button, the final solution—a *bona fide* end to the unstoppable plague of Middle Eastern terrorism and jihad."

"Doesn't sound so bad to me," Reinhardt said.

"You're right, it doesn't, on the surface." Billy rubbed the still cold tips of his fingers together. "Until you realize how many innocent men, women, and children—how many Americans— were going to die if it was implemented." He stuck his fingers beneath his bare armpits and pinched his arms down.

Reinhardt frowned. "Explain to me how it works."

Billy released a sigh. "Look, I'm not a scientist—"

"Clearly. Just tell me what you know." Reinhardt waited, her gaze roving over Billy's athletic silhouette, a man to whom she found herself drawn. Was it the mystery surrounding him and this Omega Project? Or was it something else? *Stupid, girlish thoughts,* she chided herself. *Stay on task.* "Well? Spill it."

Billy scrutinized her face, as though he were judging her merit.

"It's like this," he started. "The bacteria is not natural—it's augmented, weaponized. It's been developed to attack targets with a specific genetic blueprint."

"People of Arab descent?" Reinhardt said, her heart cramping.

"Right. A specific marker in their genetic makeup. I'm talking total biological system shutdown. It's an off switch. I don't know the ins and outs, but I do know the farther away someone is genetically, the less important this marker is. In lay terms, if your granddaddy was from Iraq you're screwed."

"And everyone else?"

"Carriers," Billy said. "My background, for example, is Scandinavian and German, with just a touch of Portuguese. If there are any Arab genetics in my family tree, they are miniscule. I wouldn't show symptoms or be impaired in any way by this disease. Hell, I wouldn't even know I had it, but I could carry it and pass it on to my elderly neighbor from Iraq."

"Holy shit," Reinhardt said. "You're talking genocide."

Billy nodded slow. "Highly effective—"

"At what?" Reinhardt shot back, her face flush. "Wiping out an entire people you'd like to conveniently blame for everything."

"Not everything," Billy huffed. "But look at the damn news. It's a global problem." He paused and met Reinhardt's gaze. "This war with guerilla forces we can't fight toe-to-toe has gone on long enough. The higher ups want it over, and they're willing to sacrifice a lot of innocent human lives to see that achieved."

Silence, long and cold, descended on the passengers of the Suburban. Reinhardt shifted, uncomfortable in her plush leather seat, as she tried to process the implications of such a thing. She looked up through the sunroof to see the sky blue and orange and gray, brightening with the dawning of a new day. *Elena*, she thought. *If this thing isn't stopped, how many sunrises does she have left?*

"How could you contain something like that, if it hit a civilian population?" Reinhardt said, her face pale.

"You can't. That's the whole point. It's a windswept wildfire."

"But the program you shut down was never green lit?"

"Of course not. That was the whole point of my investigation."

"Then how the hell did Marie Weyland get infected? Give me something. No more stories, Vick."

Billy shook his head. "Marie had photos of a broken cannister. At some point she was in direct contact with this thing. Add to the mix she also happens to have a grandfather from Iran."

"Tell me about the cannister. Where did it come from?"

"No clue, but whoever created this thing, they did it utilizing specs and data stolen from the project I shut down."

"Stolen," Reinhardt said. "Or purchased? Or maybe it was a collaboration between two or more governments with the same problems, in need of a drastic solution?"

"Damn, Reinhardt," Billy said.

"It's possible. Hell, it's more than possible, it's plausible. Whoever developed it sent it in transit to God knows where—a buyer, maybe? Somehow, terrorists captured the sample—"

189

"That Russian plane that was shot down over Syria," Billy said, his eyes widening. "That's it. When the Army got intel of what the terrorists may have captured, they destroyed a whole village of innocents."

"To clean up their mess," Reinhardt said. "If Marie Weyland hadn't been there, we wouldn't even know."

Billy huffed. "And we also wouldn't have a potential pandemic on our hands."

Reinhardt leaned toward the back seat, her gaze fixed on Billy. "How do we stop it?"

Billy made a helpless gesture. "Stop it? If Marie is contained and she's patient zero, shouldn't it be considered stopped?"

"Maybe," Reinhardt said. "The soldiers on her flight are all missing or dead. In line with this cover up."

Billy hunched forward and rubbed his face. "But we can't rule out exposure."

Reinhardt nodded. "I need a vaccine, Agent Vick."

"A vaccine can't be develop—"

"We've got to try!" Reinhardt said, her voice rising with an unintended flare of emotion. She blushed and turned forward in her seat, her teeth biting into her lower lip.

"It's personal for you," Billy said, breaking the silence, "isn't it? Who is this going to affect? Someone you care for?"

A moment passed, the only sound a symphony of humming tires and jostling shocks.

"Like you said," Reinhardt replied, an icy edge to her voice. "It's personal."

Billy pinched his lips into a line and sat back.

"Which is why," Reinhardt continued, looking out the front windshield toward the brightening horizon, "I'm going to send a

security contingent to lock down Marie Weyland. We will protect
her while CDC researchers work on understanding this bacteria
and how to fight it."

Billy shook his head. "There's no vaccine. No cure for this
thing."

"And why's that?"

"Because it is designed to fight back."

Reinhardt starred Billy down. "What the hell does that mean?"

"It can change, alter itself, to not only make it invulnerable,
but also destroy whatever you send in to kill it. That could create
an even more aggressive bacteria—one that won't care about
ethnicity."

"You can't throw all this doom and gloom at me and not offer
solutions," Reinhardt said, then sat in silence for a beat. "There has
to be a way."

"Maybe, but we have no time," Billy said, shaking his head.
"Evan's ahead of us."

"Weyland?"

Billy nodded. "Look, Dell told me that Evan wanted the
nanomachines he'd developed to fight cancer. He didn't get them,
so he went to NeuroDelve, presumably because they have their
own nanotech."

Reinhardt nodded. That made a lot of sense. After the
interview with Professor Dell they'd parted ways back at Johns
Hopkins, and she'd put her entire intelligence team on uncovering
everything they could find on NeuroDelve. As it turned out, the
company was on several federal watchlists for less than reputable
industry contacts, under-the-table dealings, and even possible ties
to North Korea.

"I did some digging on NeuroDelve. I've seen a lot, and this company takes the cake," Reinhardt said. "The FBI has an ongoing investigation into their CEO, Sharmila Vashi. Though the Feds are reluctant to share details, the case has been ongoing for years. It doesn't appear they have anything actionable as of now."

Billy rubbed his stubbled chin with the back of his hand. "Have your people tried to make contact with this Vashi?"

"I've got agents surveilling the NeuroDelve HQ in Boston as we speak. The place has gone dark. They're denying us entry and we're waiting on a search warrant before forcing entry."

"Don't we have to assume Vashi is now helping Evan?" Billy said.

Reinhardt sat still, her mind racing. This was an absolute dumpster fire. If Weyland was allowed to get nanobots into his wife's body, he'd trigger Omega to fight back and become something worse. Much worse. *Triage*, she thought. *First, we have to stop, Evan. Second, we track down anyone Marie came into contact with. Then find a way to beat this thing.* Reinhardt pulled out her phone.

"What are you thinking?" Billy asked, arms clinched across his bare chest.

"I'm thinking we need to head Evan off and stop him from making this mess worse."

"Yeah, stop him before he can get those nanos into his wife," Billy said, nodding.

"Or if we missed the boat, we head him off inside her body."

Billy's face screwed up. "Inside? As in…? What kind of silly shit is that?"

Reinhardt bored holes into Vick. Then turned to the agent with the heavy cleft in his chin. "Contact the team, double up the protective detail on Marie Weyland. No mistakes."

The agent nodded and made a call. Reinhardt dialed her phone as well.

"Inside her body?" Billy said, an incredulous look plastered across his face. He stared in total confusion at Reinhardt, who wasn't listening. "You're joking, right? Hello?"

The call connected and Reinhardt held up a finger to silence Billy. "Dr. Dell? Yes, it's Agent Reinhardt. Yeah, looks like we're going to need your help, and fast."

The caravan of Suburbans pulled to the secure rear of the CDC facility. It was a massive structure, stark white with, large dark windows and high reinforced stone walls that secured both the perimeter and the rear lot. Childhood fantasies of medieval fortresses with towering parapets and archers spread along the walls filled Billy's mind. If a more secure a place existed, Billy hadn't seen it. The drivers checked in with the guard on duty. The CDC's typical security was replaced by Homeland agents in full urban gray tactical gear, rifles slung across their chests.

"Your boys?" Billy said, taking stock of the paramilitary force assembled at the facility.

"A mutually beneficial arrangement," Reinhardt said. "We need the CDC to do what they do, liaise with Atlanta, and find us a vaccine for Omega. They need us to beef up security and protect Marie Weyland, a woman who now has more or less become a living bioweapon."

"Because whoever is trying to cover this up will just kill her," Billy said.

Reinhardt nodded. "That would be the fastest way to stop the disease and cover up its origins, don't you agree?"

"I have to admit, it's a tough dilemma," Billy said. "In the military we're trained to consider what level of losses are acceptable in order to achieve mission success. If only one person has to die for this thing to be stopped, it could save the lives of millions, maybe even billions."

"That's true." Reinhardt studied Billy's face. "But this isn't a battlefield and Marie Weyland isn't a soldier. Is sacrificing even just one innocent person acceptable? Is that American? What does your heart tell you, Billy Vick?"

Billy let out a sigh and shook his head. "No, it's not. But I have a feeling my higher ups won't agree."

"Thus, the security enhancements," Reinhardt said with a curt nod.

The Suburban rolled to a stop along the curb. A trio of rough, capable looking men in urban gray tactical gear approached, the letters SRCAT stenciled in white on their chests.

"And who are these guys?" Billy asked.

"Members of Homeland's elite Special Response and Counter Assault Team," Reinhardt said. "I got approval to have them sent over to assist us. Everyone knows about FBI Hostage Rescue Team and The Marshals Special Operations Group. These guys are on the same level, the best of the best."

"And you know this how?"

Reinhardt flashed a smile at Billy as she exited the vehicle. "I was one of them."

Billy watched as the Special Agent in Charge strode forward with a Cheshire grin and gave the SRCAT team leader a hug. She laughed and knocked fists with the other two men.

"Of course you were." Billy shook his head with a smirk. *This woman is full of surprises.*

Billy climbed from the Suburban as the Agent with the huge chin cleft held the door for him.

"Thanks." Billy straightened, placed his bare feet on the concrete, and stepped out.

The SRCAT guys looked in his direction, grins on their faces.

"Gentlemen," Reinhard said. "This is Captain Billy Vick, he's with the United States Army's Criminal Investigation Command. He is here as a special liaison to assist with our operation."

Billy shook hands with the stoic men, a chill wind prickling his skin.

"Captain Vick," the team leader said. "I'm Mike Barrett. It's good to have you with us." He motioned to Reinhardt. "How do you guys know each other?"

"Guess you could say we have mutual interests," Billy said.

Barrett raised an eyebrow. "Well, watch out. She's a live wire, this one."

"I can tell," Billy said.

Reinhardt frowned. "A live wire? I don't recall being the one who drove a Bearcat armored vehicle through a concrete block wall when the team was pinned down on Operation Pitchfork, *Mike.*"

"Well." Barrett chuckled. "If you want to be SRCAT, you got to be a little different."

Billy nodded approvingly. "I can get down with that."

"So, Vick," Barrett said with a wry smile. "Are you allowed to wear clothes?"

"On occasion," Billy replied.

"Good. I've got an extra set in my truck. We can rustle you up a pair of boots as well." He glanced at Billy's bare feet. "Size eleven?"

"Ten."

"We'll get you taken care of."

"I appreciate that," Billy said.

"Hey boss!" The group turned to see another agent, this one petite with tight brown curls that bobbed as she moved. She crossed the parking lot at a jog, her dark suit jacket flapping. "We couldn't reach you by phone. There's been a development. You're going to want to see this."

Reinhardt straightened. "What kind of development?"

"The bad kind." The agent waved them on. "I'll brief you on the way."

Reinhardt set off at a trot after the agent with Billy in tow, having completely forgotten about getting clothes. The other agents followed.

The group passed through several keycard locked doors inset with bulletproof glass and reinforced steel. Billy listened as the curly-haired agent filled Reinhardt in on the bad news.

"Guy must have gotten access to the patient before we could get the place locked down." The young agent said, "He's a doctor, had CDC credentials and everything. If they're forged, they're high quality fakes with keycard access."

Reinhardt followed the agent through another secure series of rooms as the facility opened up into a labyrinth of intersecting corridors connecting labs, isolation units, and office space.

"You said he was able to get access to the patient," she said. "What the hell does that mean? Did he do something to her?"

"Yes, ma'am," the curly-haired agent pinched her lips. "He gave her some sort of injection in the middle of her torso."

"Something lethal?" Billy said, following the others into a

196

white-walled observation room with long thick glass windows looking out into Marie's isolation chamber. Inside, two CDC doctors in full level-A hazmat protective gear, assessed Marie's condition. Billy leaned closer to the glass. The poor woman looked like a corpse. Pale olive skin, limp brown hair strewn about her pillow. He tried to count the number of tubes and wires going to and from her body. She was now just a shadow, a shell of the vibrant woman he'd seen in photographs scattered around Evan Weyland's residence.

The agent shook her head. "Here's the thing, she's shown no sign of toxicity or poisoning. The attending doc says she's still stable on life support, for now."

Billy looked to Reinhardt. "Evan. They got someone to her."

"Tell me you got the damn guy?" Reinhardt asked, a flare of anger in her voice. "Who's he working for?"

"Yes, ma'am. We got him." The agent pointed across the way to another door. She stopped at a terminal and pulled up the camera for the holding room beyond. "We put a little pressure on him and he cracked. He's still in there, spilling his guts."

"About?" Reinhardt said, and gestured for the agent to activate the room's audio.

"See for yourself," the curly-haired agent clicked the microphone button in the corner of the image.

"This whole thing is a trumped-up crock of shit," the odd, balding, anxious fellow on the screen said, as he rocked his body weight back and forth. Across from the mole, one of Reinhardt's agents sat forward in his seat. The mole mumbled something incomprehensible, then continued. "I had assurances, ya know? Yeah, okay, so I fucked up and blew the money in Vegas. My mistake. How was I supposed to know the funding came from the

Koreans? I mean, they're probably going to kill me for this."

"You think the Koreans are going to kill you?" the interviewing agent asked.

"Fuck yeah, they are, I mean, it's North Korea, for God's sake! And I took their money!" the mole whined.

"He's crazy," Billy said. "Just look at him."

"Wait," Reinhardt said, holding up a finger.

"I was set up from the start, see?" The mole rubbed at his comb over. "Sharmila Vashi set this whole thing up. It's her baby and she needed someone to take the fall. I was in a pinch after Vegas, so what choice did I have? I'm fucked either way."

"The Koreans financed NeuroDelve," Billy said. "Vashi definitely got Evan in there."

"Dr. Dilarney, we've been around and around with this. Listen to me carefully." The interviewing agent leaned in close. "I need to know what you injected into this lady and I need to know now."

Dilarney threw up his hands. "Fuck if I know, man. I'm just the fall guy."

"Guess," the interviewing agent said.

"Guess? Okay." The dumpy man bobbed his head. "Bots. I think it was some sort of bot army. I mean, that's the cornerstone of NeuroDelve's research, right? Do you know how hard it is to field test that sort of thing on a live subject—and do it legitimately?" Dilarney snorted. "Next to impossible."

"Damn," Reinhardt said, her eyes wide. "You're right, Vick. They've beat us to it. Evan is already in." She looked to the curly haired agent who'd escorted them inside. "Get Williams relieved in that interview room, I want a full briefing from him in ten minutes. I need to know everything this mole knows."

"I'll take care of it," the agent said, wheeling in the direction of the interview room.

Barrett entered through the secure access door carrying a loose folded pile of clothes topped with a pair of boots. "What'd I miss?" He handed the pile to Billy.

"The feces hitting the fan," Reinhardt said, marching across the room toward a makeshift operations center full of homeland personnel setting up computer monitors and arranging tables.

"Get dressed, Agent Vick. I want an all hands meeting in Ops in ten. Barrett, can you get all essential personnel rallied up?"

"Yes, ma'am," Barrett said.

Billy crossed the bustling makeshift operations center, shrugging into the HIS T-shirt as he went. The hubbub in the room seemed to Billy's ear like the noise before a rock concert. Computers and other electronic equipment he'd never seen before, powered on with blips and chimes. Murmurs filled the space, organized chaos as each person went about their assigned duty. Across the room someone laughed and was told to keep it down.

Billy walked to the corner of the room, and, never one to be modest, dropped his sweats to the floor. He kicked them to the side and, still in his undershorts, stepped into the tactical pants Barrett gave him. A little big but they'd do. He'd laced up one boot when Professor Jeanine Dell blustered over to Reinhardt, stick-like arms whirling.

"Shit, um… my guy just had a seizure." Dell sought to compose herself. "I don't know what happened. We were just testing the visor and he collapsed."

"Woah, slow down," Reinhardt said. "Is he okay?"

"No," Professor Dell's voice rose in pitch. "They're wheeling him off now. Said it might be previously undiagnosed epilepsy. He's out of it."

"Okay," Reinhardt couldn't conceal her irritation. She breathed in deep through her nose, exhaled. "Who else can go in?"

"That's just it," Dell put her hands against her face. "No one else is qualified, I mean, maybe I could, but I don't know if I have the constitution for that. Besides, who would do the system control out here?"

"This op is dead without a pilot, and we're short on time," Reinhardt frowned. "I'll do it. Just give me a crash course."

"No," Billy synched his second boot tight and stood. "You're vital to running the entire operation here. Your people need you present, fluid, trouble-shooting problems as they arise. Put me in, I'll do it."

Reinhardt and Dell stared back with blank expressions.

"You can't," Reinhardt said. "You're a consultant. I need you out here with me. We'll find someone else—"

"There is no one else. I don't know how to work that set up, but I'm a quick study. I've got combat experience, been trained in historical military tactics, and I've got two years of training and live ops under my belt operating micro surveillance drones via VR and joystick controls. How much different can it be?"

Dell's face took on a ghostly pallor. "Quite a bit different, actually."

Billy strode forward and stopped before the two women. "I've met Evan. He'll know me. I can try to talk him down. Besides, I have the best working knowledge of Omega in the room. That alone qualifies me. I'm the *only* one who should do this."

Dell turned to Reinhardt. "It could work. He'll have our AI construct to guide and assist him."

Reinhardt looked long and deep into Billy's resolute stare. Was that concern for him in her eyes? The noise in the room seemed to dim. People were watching.

What the hell are you doing, Billy?

"Vick," Reinhardt said, her words slow and measured. "There's a lot of risk with this. Are you sure?"

Billy smirked, a natural air of confidence shining through. It was all bluster. This wasn't a damn video game. This was high stakes poker and he'd just thrown all of his chips on the table over a shit hand of cards. He was out of his mind.

"Totally sure. I got this." The knot in Billy's stomach tightened.

CHAPTER TWENTY

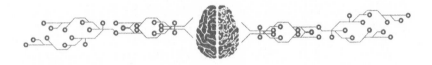

Brachiocephalic Vein, Marie Weyland's Body

The crawl along the inner wall of the superior *vena cava* seemed to take forever—even with Sharmila's neural trickery skewing how Evan experienced time. Pushing against the blood flow back to the heart felt like standing in storm, leaning forward into a hundred-mile-an-hour wind and taking one slow step at a time. Evan's arms and legs burned with lactic acid. He didn't need to move his limbs in order to shimmy the bots along, but it was so difficult to separate physical effort from mental will. Another side effect he hadn't considered in his research. He checked the holographic map floating in the air off to his right. Finally, he was in the brachiocephalic vein.

That meant he could force an exit through the wall of cells, track over to the carotid artery, force his way inside, and let the natural blood flow carry him up into the network of vessels surrounding the brain stem.

Evan commanded his bot army to stop crawling and took a moment to compose himself. He shook out his arms and legs, letting them recover from his marathon swim. A quick check of the environment. The light from his command Endobot lit the way just before him, after which lay a black void. He watched huge red blood cells, biconcave, spongey discs, as they rushed out from the dark and crashed past, bumping and jostling in the tight space. Hypnotizing, it reminded Evan of when as a child he'd rub his eyes hard causing colors to spill out of the dark. He'd always been afraid a monster might claw its way out of the gloom behind his eyelids.

Here, inside his wife's body, somewhere near the collar bone, a real monster emerged from the dim and prowled toward him—a neutrophil—the first responder of Marie's innate immune system, designed to swallow up and destroy foreign invaders. Like an investigator, the neutrophil would present fragments of the dead invader for the rest of the immune system, the search party, to recognize. Then it would be hunter-killer time. Marie's acquired immune system, now understanding what to look for, would send out the assault force—other white blood cells. This would all happen in a matter of hours. Evan had to hope the engineered antigens on the surface of his Endobots would trick the neutrophil into believing his army was meant to be there, hanging around in his wife's body.

The giant neutrophil cell, spherical and transparent, containing pink-purple granules and a lobed nucleus, made a beeline for one the Endobots. Evan held his breath, watching as the immune cell latched onto a medi-bot. It smothered his soldier, probing the outer surface. After a few seconds, it let go as if satisfied there was no threat. He watched as the neutrophil re-entered the flow and a moment later was gone.

Need to leave. He ordered his command Endobot to fire another package of vesicles and initiate loosening the wall of cells. Onscreen inside the Sphere, a net of bubbles fizzed out then popped, releasing their cargo. As the wash of chemicals dissipated, Evan caught sight of a squad of neutrophils barreling down the

STU JONES & GARETH WORTHINGTON

pipe out of the dark. Even though the first neutrophil had not decided to swallow up the medi-bot, sensing something out of order it had still called in the cavalry, perhaps already on high alert from the infection in Marie's brain. The newcomers swarmed Evan's Endobot army.

A gap in the wall of the brachiocephalic vein began to appear, but at a glacial pace.

Evan watched as another neutrophil sucked up a medi-bot.

"Oh no," he said aloud.

"Evan?" Sharmila's voice echoed in his head.

"Camouflage didn't work," Evan said.

"The immune system detected you?"

"Yes, they're all over the medi-bots."

"Fight back," Sharmila barked. "We sent you in with an army. Take them out, then get the hell out of there."

"Fight?" Evan said, his voice an octave higher than usual.

"Yes!" Sharmila shouted. "The same way you intend to fight the infection, Evan. Fight them!"

Evan imagined his infantry bots lancing the immune cells with their microscopic swords. On command they lined up in defensive regiments and struck out with their nematocysts, puncturing Marie's white blood cells. The fragile biological sacs burst, spilling their cloudy contents into the blood stream. Another flash of inspiration and Evan launched a barrage of antigens that adhered to the surface of Marie's own immune cells, resulting in them turning on each other. Captivated with the dance of death, he watched as they tumbled and fought with each other.

It was short lived. Something shifted in the atmosphere; they were learning. As if suddenly aware Evan called the shots, several white blood cells thrust toward his command Endobot. Evan's heart faltered and his limbs stiffened again as the microscopic monsters loomed down, green bioluminescence compounding the nightmarish vision. He ordered his remaining army to push through the intercellular gap in the vein wall, now wide enough to enter. An immense, bone-crushing pressure squeezed throughout his suit, an impression conveyed by the neural link. This time ready for it, Evan breathed through the agony, confident in his ability to endure—until a new pain came—a strange tugging sensation from behind. The AI interpreted the sensation as a pain in his legs. Something in Marie's body had hold of him. While Evan couldn't see behind his command Endobot, his instincts told him a neutrophil or monocyte had clamped onto him. It would attempt to absorb and destroy the biological drone, killing him in the real world.

A fresh wave of nausea hit, cold sweat forming on his brow. The simulated sound of sloshing, the manufactured pain of being eaten alive, and the fluorescent green hue in his eyes attacked Evan's brain.

"Evan, your heart rate is through the roof," Sharmila screamed. "You have to calm down. Evan, can you hear me? Evan!"

But Evan couldn't distinguish Sharmila's voice from the crash of waves and rushing fluid, as the pressure squeezed him to death. The love of his life—Marie's own body—was about to murder him, and there wasn't a damn thing he could do about it.

CHAPTER TWENTY-ONE

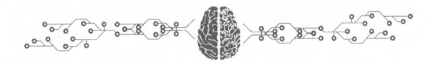

CDC Quarantine

Dressed in gray tactical pants, boots, and an HSI T-shirt, Billy took a chair amidst the bustling chaos of the makeshift operations center. Glaring florescent lights cast a sterile hue over the room. At the back, standing beside a bank of monitors, loomed a giant transparent booth housing a bizarre bright yellow industrial arm, with an open, multi-jointed claw at the end. It jutted upward from its anchored base and bent over like a hanging tree branch.

What the hell could that be used for? Billy thought.

The whole set up had an uncomfortable, hastily assembled appearance. Computer equipment and screens sat askew, cables and wires running in all directions as though the guts of the machines had taken on a life of their own, spilled forth, and attempted a coup.

Billy watched as Special Agent in Charge Reinhardt paced back and forth, her hands clasped together. All around, the hodge-podge, world-saving crew of Homeland agents in suits, geared down SRCAT members, CDC personnel, and Johns Hopkins researchers readied their stations and prepared for the brief.

"All right, everyone listen up," Reinhard said, clapping her hands twice. A hush fell over the group.

Billy smirked. *Woman knows how to wrangle a crowd.*

"If you're sitting in this room, you are now a part of a very special team group. Today, with minimum resources and little time, we will attempt something never before attempted. We will utilize experimental virtual reality technology to link with a team of nano-machines. These machines, piloted by Captain Billy Vick here," Reinhardt gestured to Billy, and offered a thin smile, "will be injected into the body of Marie Weyland in an attempt to stop a rogue force of similar machines already in vitro."

A cascade of mumbles rolled through the room.

Reinhardt held up her hands. "Suffice it to say, there are no guarantees of success, and this operation has a high level of danger, especially for Captain Vick."

Billy shifted with a growing discomfort in his plastic-backed seat.

"Now, I know you all have a million questions, but here's what you need to know: Marie Weyland is infected with a biological weapon. This weapon is dangerous enough in its own right, but if tampered with by this aforementioned rogue force, it could become something much worse. We must not allow that to happen. Billions of lives are at stake."

Reinhardt paused, surveying the group.

"Operational security is of the utmost importance here. I cannot have information leaking from an active mission and compromising our hard work. That means from here on out until this is done, I want no communications with the outside world. Maintaining OpSec is vital to success, and there will be consequences for not following strict protocols. No exceptions. That means no calls out to your spouse or lover or child, period. I know that's tough, but I'm serious about this."

Reinhardt padded across the front of the room, her posture straight, demeanor commanding, a lioness on the prowl.

"Here's what I need from each of you. Compartmentalize your work. You may not see or even understand the big picture or how you fit into the overall mission. Just know you play a critical part in our success. Understood?"

A chorus of acknowledgement rose up from Reinhardt's agents as well as Barrett and the members of SRCAT.

"Good. Let's get in position to make this happen. We're on the clock." She tapped her watch and turned as the group, some thirty-odd people jammed into a medium-sized observation room, broke into smaller groups to prepare their stations. "Let me get the core team over here."

Billy rose and joined the few of Reinhardt's team, as well as technical personnel and members of the Johns Hopkins team. *Evan's team*, he thought. *Hope these people don't have divided loyalties.* He met the glance of Professor Dell, who offered a genuine smile and a wave of her hand. Billy returned the gesture.

"Okay, guys," Reinhardt said. "We've got a lot of work to do and little time in which to do it. I'm going to turn it over to Professor Dell and she and the others are going to fill us in on the technology at play here."

"Right." Dell stepped forward clasping thin, bloodless hands. "It's good to see all of you. I wish it were under better circumstances." She managed a wan smile. "This is all quite irregular and, I must say, even under law enforcement supervision, illegal, without Marie Weyland's consent." She cleared her throat three times before continuing. "That said, desperate times call for desperate measures, and after the moral failures of my counterparts,

I feel obligated to help in whatever way I can."

"Professor Dell." Reinhardt motioned to get on with it.

"Of course, sorry," Dell said. "First let me introduce Doctor Hakagi." She gestured to a squat Asian man with eyes that magnified to anime character proportions through his coke-bottle lenses. "He will assist with keeping everything operational. We also have Nate Donner here with IT who's been a godsend in getting all the computers and tech networked." The portly IT specialist, belly jiggling, waved his hand with a nervous smile.

Dell touched a button and a monitor flickered to life with a PowerPoint image of a grouping of cellular machines shaped like tiny capsules with gangly hair-like arms.

"I'll make this quick," Professor Dell said. "What we're essentially looking at here is warfare at the cellular level. For anyone who hoped this might look like spaceships and phaser torpedoes, I'm afraid reality is far stranger than the average *Star Trek* episode." Dell laughed with a high-pitched, musical whinny and followed it with a little snort. A few polite chuckles rose from the small group.

Inwardly, Billy cringed. He glanced at Reinhardt who returned a smirk.

Dell composed herself and continued. "We designed this technology to assist in real time with battlefield trauma in soldiers, not to wage war against other biological nano machines. We will be using our assets to try and intercept other bots already inside the body of Marie Weyland, controlled by her husband Evan, our former lead researcher. Evan believes he's going to save her life. In reality, according to Captain Vick here, he could be about to make things much worse." Dell managed a smile. "Hardly what any of us expected for a maiden voyage."

Billy looked around the small core group of just half a dozen researchers and tech personnel. Judging the sour looks on their faces, several of them seemed to want to call bullshit. To their credit they kept their mouths shut.

Dell continued, "That said, just as these tiny machines are equipped to heal, they can also destroy. Think of how a surgeon's scalpel can also act as an instrument of death in the hands of a killer. You get my point."

"Can you unpack how that looks in action?" Reinhardt asked.

Dell clicked to another slide, this one showcasing a microscope-zoomed video on the cellular level. On screen, the bizarre, alien creature shifted, it's arms waving. From inside the thing, a barbed spear shot forth, then retracted again. "Mr. Vick will have access to a hundred of what we call medi-bots. Designed to heal, they are more or less wielding scalpels and syringes, to put it in layman's terms."

She played the video. "Here a medi-bot is injecting a damaged cell," Dell said. The group watched as a cell-like bot injected a damaged cell with a solution that, in time lapse, caused the cell to rebuild itself. "The injection is loaded with enzymes and RNA strands to accelerate cellular repair. Of course, as I already stated, the same process can be used to attack." Dell played a second video. "This time the repurposed medi-bot injects a toxin designed to cause cell death."

Billy watched as the affected cell broke down and dissolved in a cloud of hazy particulate before his eyes.

"And it's that simple," Dell said, turning to Billy. "You'll have one hundred bots to work with, fifty of them operating like standard healing or defensive medi-bots, the other fifty loaded with more offensive capabilities."

"What will Evan's bots look like? How will they function?"

Billy asked.

Dell shrugged. "They're the competition. Who knows what NeuroDelve has come up with? That said, we think he'll be working with a similar platform."

"And how do I control these… machines?" Billy asked.

"A fair question," Dell said. "You don't… well, you will have input, and the ability to issue commands via a neural link, but the actual maneuvering of the machines is done by an AI auto pilot."

"An auto pilot?"

"That's right, Billy. Evan is a prodigy with this stuff. No one in our group could hold a candle to him during trial runs. With no training or experience, you wouldn't stand a chance outmaneuvering him, all things being equal. So, with that in mind, we were able to compile and code a rudimentary AI based on Evan's previous test flights to help you. Trust me, when he realizes you've come to stop him, you'll need all the help you can get."

"But can I take full control if I need to?" Billy crossed his arms.

"It's not advised. The bots are notoriously difficult to pilot if you don't have extensive experience and, honestly, a gift for it, like Evan Weyland does."

Dell pulled up another slide detailing the specs of a larger bot nestled at the fore of the others. Billy watched as a tail-like rotor propelled the thing forward and shifted it side to side.

"This is the commander bot. Billy, you will be in direct control of this one, and will issue commands to the others. These orders will be done via the neural link. That means you think about what you want to accomplish, and the other medi-bots will follow your lead."

"Do I wear a VR headset or something?" Billy asked.

"Yes, but it's a bit more complicated—and dangerous than

211

that, I'm afraid," Dr. Hakagi said, stepping forward.

Billy glanced at Reinhardt, who crossed her arms possibly to keep her from wringing her hands.

"What are you saying?" Billy said.

"In a perfect world we'd have more time to develop a safer interface…" Hakagi said.

"Don't sugarcoat it for me, Doc." Billy interrupted. "Tell me straight. What's this going to involve."

Dr. Hakagi plied his pale fingers together. "We took the rig from Johns Hopkins, which uses an ErrP interface, but that won't suffice without training. To make this work, we had to jerry-rig the crane—to jack into your spinal column. The procedure itself could have major complications such as paralysis but the real risk lies in engaging Evan's forces.

Billy could feel his anxiety growing, looming, threatening to shut him down. He wished to hell he'd brought his medication.

"Each bot you lose will physically affect you," Hakagi continued. "Your brain will interpret the loss as one of your own limbs or muscle groups. Once jacked in, your mind won't be able to tell the difference."

"And if I lose too many bots?"

Dr. Hakagi shook his head.

"Yes, so," Dell broke in, "all of our models indicate catastrophic brain damage is possible, maybe even probable in the event of extreme loss."

The small group grew silent. All eyes focused on Billy.

"Vick?" Reinhardt said.

"Yeah, just…" Billy said, his thoughts returning to Rosie and his boys. He hadn't even said goodbye. "Just give me a second."

Time seemed to stall. Billy's thoughts, tangled with

information, detached from the present. The smell of dust and fire filled his nostrils. Pete's blood seeping between pinched fingers.

"Hang on, Pete. Medivac is en route. We're gonna get you outta here, brother. Just hang in there."

Pete's hand grabbed Billy's sleeve. "Why are we here, Billy?"

"I... I don't..." Billy clenched his teeth, his bare fingers cradling the shattered back of Pete's skull, the pieces scraping together beneath a thin layer of scalp like broken mismatched shards of pottery.

"They killed me, Billy." Pete's one good eye grew wide. *"Tell Kristy and my kids I..."*

Another rocket propelled grenade exploded nearby, rending the air with fire and more screams.

"Shhh. I got you, brother. I've got you. You'll make it."

"No, Billy," Pete whispered, his voice a low gurgle. *"Promise me you'll make it. Be there for your family. Don't die for nothin'..."*

"You didn't die for nothing, Pete," Billy whispered.

Reinhardt touched Billy's shoulder. "Hey."

Billy jerked back to the present and touched his chest, his heart banging beneath his fingers. He looked around the small group, his gaze that of the lost.

"You okay?" Reinhardt asked. "If you need some time..."

Billy didn't reply. He turned and exited the operations center.

From out in the empty white-walled CDC hallway, Reinhardt eyed Billy.

Should I leave him alone? she thought, assessing the gloomy look in his face. *Maybe not.*

She put on a smile and entered the deserted staff lounge—just a small kitchenette, a few plastic chairs and two round tables with scattered crumbs on them. The hostile fluorescent lights above strained the eyes and made the space feel more laboratory than breakroom. Reinhardt held up two warm, tightly wrapped, breakfast sandwiches.

"Biscuit?" she said.

Billy raised his gaze from the steaming paper cup of cheap coffee, to the grease-stained wrapper of Reinhardt's breakfast sandwich. "Thought we were supposed to be on the clock?"

"They tell me you shouldn't go in on an empty stomach—if you're still going."

"I don't think you're supposed to eat before surgery."

She offered a weak smile. "They're still warm. I've got sausage and egg or steak."

Billy looked into the oily cardboard box on the table. Only three biscuits remained.

"The crew picked them over pretty well before I got there," Reinhardt said.

Billy huffed. "I'm supposed to be on a thirty day no-carb challenge, but… in the face of certain doom, I guess that seems kind of stupid now. What the hell. Steak."

Reinhardt grabbed one and slid the wrapped biscuit across the table. "I didn't mean to interrupt."

"You're not interrupting anything," Billy said, unwrapping the biscuit. "Sit, if you'd like."

Reinhardt paused for a moment, then took a seat across from him, unwrapping the grease-soaked wrapper. She took a bite, her eyes narrowing in ecstasy. "Mmm." She swallowed. "I never eat these. But I guess operational food is what it is."

Billy took a bite. "Beats the hell out of an MRE," he said through a bolus of the sandwich.

They ate in silence. The warm butter flavor of the flaky biscuit and the salty breaded steak inside it, offering a measure of comfort.

Billy wiped his mouth. "Sorry for making a scene back there, right in the middle of Professor Dell's presentation. I just, ah… I guess in the moment, it was a lot to process."

"I'm the one who needs to apologize, Billy." Reinhardt set her biscuit down. "I accepted your volunteering before knowing just how dangerous it would be for you."

"That makes two of us," Billy said.

"I'm sorry. If it's too much, I understand. We can find someone else to run the op."

Billy sighed, then finished his biscuit. "It's not the risk. Life as a soldier, hell, even my induction into law enforcement, it's all been full of risk. On some level I guess I've become numb to it. Just part of the job."

Reinhard waited. "But?"

Billy shrugged. "I made a promise to my best friend once." Billy rubbed his hands, wiped a few crumbs from the counter as if deliberating on whether to continue. Reinhardt gave a patient nod.

"Long before I was a West Point grad or assigned to the 701st MP Group in Quantico, I was an airborne Ranger. The 75th Ranger Regiment, third battalion out of Fort Benning. Member of a rifleman company. Rangers lead the way and all that. Some of the best and… worst moments of my life." Billy glanced at Reinhardt. "We were part of the invasion into Syria, Operation Ground Clear. My company got tasked with taking an airfield that was of significant strategic importance to our push into the country. We'd seen our fair share of desert and mountain combat up to that point and we were hungry for more. Just stupid kids back then, I guess." Billy sucked air though his teeth. "Problem was the Syrian-Iraqi alliance, with Turkey backing them, didn't want to give it up that damn airfield and they had us out numbered three to one."

"What happened?" Reinhardt asked. *Do I want the answer?*

"One hell of a sustained fight. But we were Rangers. Surrender is not a Ranger word. We took the airfield. Significant losses, too. We were mopping up, taking cover in one of the central concrete buildings when we came across a pocket of fighters we'd somehow missed. Pete, my squad leader, saw the RPG first. I can still hear the sound of that damn thing flying at us, like the sound of a bedsheet tearing. Pete slammed into me. Son of a bitch saved my life. Shoved me down a flight of stairs, causing burst fractures to my spine at the L2 and L3 vertebrae."

"My God, Billy..." Reinhardt said, her voice soft.

"I didn't know it at the time, so much adrenaline and all." Billy pitched his biscuit wrapper into the nearby trash can. "Pete took the brunt of the blast. The fireball blew him out a two-story window. Me and my guys fought tooth and nail to kill the rest of those bastards. Afterwards, I couldn't walk, so I crawled my way to Pete. It was the damnedest thing. As messed up as he was, he could still talk, just like we're talking now. I went to help him sit up, and that's when I realized just how bad it was. Touching the back of his head was like..." Billy pressed his lips together. "Like palming a bag of broken glass."

Reinhardt winced.

"They couldn't get medivac to us because the LZ was too hot and in his condition, we couldn't move him. So, my squad set up a perimeter and I talked to him for hours until the swelling on his brain eventually caused him to pass out. One of the last things he said to me, before he stopped taking—he made me promise, if I made it back, that I'd live a good life, that I wouldn't die for something I didn't believe in."

Reinhardt gave a slow nod. "And we're asking you to take that risk."

Billy's throat moved. He looked down and away, shook his head. "I told you, it's not the risk. But I came home. I got to see my family again. I made it back, when Pete and a lot of other good people didn't. That means I get to live for them and they get to live on through me. Which makes this," Billy extended a hand, shaking with tremors, "and all the godforsaken nightmares, worth it." He looked at Reinhardt for a long moment. "I already know the answer to this," he said, surveying her face for a moment. "I guess I just need to hear you tell me how important this operation is."

"Billy," Reinhardt said, leaning forward, her arms on the table. "You said it yourself—we have to stop Evan. If we can control the environment, the disease, we have a chance at stopping this and preventing a lot of senseless death. But if Evan gets to it first and it mutates, any vaccine or cure for Omega will be useless. A lot of people will die, and…" Reinhardt stopped, an unexpected lump in her throat.

Say it. He should know, she thought. "And one of those people could be my little sister, Elena."

Billy leaned back, slow. "It *is* personal."

"Yes," Reinhardt said.

The plastic chair flexed. "Your sister? But not you?"

"Half-sister," Reinhardt gave a sober nod. "My step-father, married my mother when I was in high school. He's from Emirates."

"I see," Billy said. After a moment of deliberation, he stood from the table, the chair behind his knees squeaking across a waxed floor.

Reinhardt furrowed her brow. "What?"

"The clock is ticking, right?" Billy said with a reassuring wink. "Are we going do this thing, or what?"

Reinhardt stood, her eyes narrowing. "Don't do it for me, Billy Vick."

"Wouldn't dream of it," Billy said with a smirk as he disappeared into the hallway.

CHAPTER TWENTY-TWO

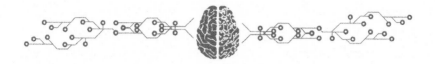

NeuroDelve Mobile Unit

"**E**van! Evan!" Sharmila screamed, her wild stare no longer on the monitor but on the silver spherical prison holding Evan.

The trailer fell silent, her techs unable to look at her, or each other, in the eye. Evan was clamped in the jaws of death inside Marie's body, all played out in vivid virtual reality inside the Sphere. His brain would tell him he's dying, and his body would oblige.

Sharmila had to act now.

"What do we do?" asked one of the techs.

"He's gone Condition Black, total lockup," Sharmila said. "We have to bring him out of it." Though, she had no idea how. For soldiers in the field, going Condition Black in a life-threatening situation was a death sentence.

A wing of her company had contracts with the DOD, working to improve soldiers' awareness in the field. One particular aspect ensured all soldiers were in a constant enhanced state of Condition Orange. According to a system the U.S. Marine Corps developed, five levels of awareness existed in any situation. White meant an individual was unaware and unprepared. If attacked in Condition

White, the only thing that may save the person is the inadequacy or ineptitude of the attacker. In the field, no self-respecting Marine allowed themselves to be in this state. The next step up, Condition Yellow, indicated a relaxed but alert nature. An awareness of the ever present danger even when walking down a street. Soldiers in Conditional Yellow continually watched their six.

Orange meant something in the immediate environment required attention. The soldier shifted primary focus to investigate further and determine the threat level. In Condition Orange, a soldier set a mental trigger: *If that person does "X," I'll have to do "Y."* Prolonged periods of time spent on high alert in Condition Orange can cause severe strain on the human mind and body, and this is where Sharmila's team came in. Biotechnological upgrades allowed soldiers in Condition Orange to have superhuman vision, hear a greater range of frequencies, and hold that level of mental acuity for extended periods.

Imminent danger presenting itself resulted in Condition Red where the human body's fight or flight response engaged—or in other words, X had happened and the fight was on.

Condition Black, however, meant the person was immobilized by panic or overwhelmed by fear. This occurred when a person was unprepared for extreme violence or terror, or got ambushed with critical stress while in Condition White. The result was a thumb-sucking mental shut down that left a person unable to act, to complete their mission, or to defend themselves or their squad. It cost many untested young soldiers their lives.

And it was about to cost Evan *his* life.

"I need to get in there," Sharmila said, marching toward the Sphere.

"You can't do that," the tech manning the quantum

connection said. "If you confuse his system with external physical stimuli it may overload him."

"He's already overloaded. We're not getting through to him. We have no choice." Sharmila stepped to the Sphere, ready to enter the hatch. "Open it."

"Dr. Vashi," the tech said. "This is really *not* a good idea."

"He's about to be devoured by her immune system and rendered brain dead. What do you suggest?"

"We have another problem," said another scientist posted at the station that monitored the connection between them and Evan inside the Sphere.

Sharmila clenched her jaw and stormed back to the monitor. "What is it?"

The scientist's brow creased and he scratched at his thinning hair. "I was looking for a way to maybe boost the signal to Evan, so your voice could be heard above everything—"

"Get to the point," Sharmila snapped, her glance flitting from him to the Sphere.

"Someone else is in there, or will be soon."

"In where? *Marie's body?*" Sharmila asked.

The nearby tech leaned in, studying the information onscreen. "I'll be damned. It's a signal, like ours, between a rig and control." He clicked a few buttons and two voices came over the speaker.

"Test complete, signal strength within tolerances," an unknown man's voice said over the speaker.

"Good. And quantum connection?" a woman said.

"Seems okay, but won't know 'til Vick is all buckled in," replied the man.

"Can't believe he's doing this."

"Poor bastard doesn't know what he's in for."

"Nope. Wandering around inside this poor lady?" the woman said. "I'd have killed her and been done with it long ago. Look at her. It'd be a mercy."

Sharmila's scientist muted the conversation.

Sharmila rubbed her hands together, eyes wide. Who were they? Who was Vick? Why would they go into Marie's body at all? Had she doomed her own company... or stumbled into an opportunity? Her backers wanted data. NeuroDelve had designed the Endobots for war. Now she would get one. A live battlefield test. She never could have constructed a trial like this with voluntary, contracted human subjects. If she won this—if Evan won it—there was no way she'd not be funded. Of course, if Evan failed, she'd lose everything. This was it. Do or die.

"Do they know we can hear them?" Sharmila asked.

"No, I don't believe so," the scientist replied.

"Can we talk to them?" Sharmila pressed.

"Talk to them?"

"Yes, reach out, communicate with them," Sharmila barked, miming a moving mouth with one hand. "Can we—can *Evan* talk to them?"

"I guess, maybe. Why?"

"It may be the motivation Evan needs," she said, then turned on her heel and ran to the Sphere.

Sharmila pressed her palm to the ink black panel and recited her CEO override code. The Sphere door popped open and she stepped inside where Evan hung limp in mid-air, twitching. The glassy walls were alive with activity—a gruesome, hyper realistic video game displaying monstrous grotesque cells attacking other ugly amorphous blobs. The medi-bots fended off Marie's immune system in the eerie green bioluminescence. A terrifying, dark, biological warzone. Evan's Endobot counter ticked downward. He was losing.

Sharmila stepped to Evan and placed a hand on his back. He stared down, his face twisted in pain—an expression intensified, no doubt, by his surprise to see Sharmila's form appear in Marie's superior *vena cava*.

"Evan, Evan, you have to listen to me. You have to fight through this. Someone else is coming for you. They're going to inject someone else into Marie. I don't know who it is but I think they're going to try and stop you. It could ruin your chances of saving your wife. You must destroy them first. Do you hear me?"

Evan didn't speak. His stare passed through Sharmila and off into some unknown space between the virtual and real.

Sharmila shoved him in the back, and Evan swiveled until the AI's electromagnets corrected his position. "Evan, get a hold of yourself! Someone is coming for you, and Marie will die." She turned and shouted through the open hatch. "Open the channel so he can hear them!"

"Are you sure?" the scientist asked.

"You heard me, do it."

Inside the Sphere, the audio transmission bounced off the singular curved wall.

"This woman is near death anyway, I'm telling you. All we'd have to do is shut down the ventilator," a man said.

"Reinhardt was clear that wasn't an option, unless Vick fails to take out this Evan guy." A woman replied. "Last resort only."

"Last resort? If what she said about this Omega bacteria is true, we could all die anyway."

"Well, just the Arabs," the woman said.

"Really? Did you actually just say that?"

Sharmila drew a flat hand across her neck.

The transmission ended.

"Evan, did you hear that?" Sharmila asked. "This guy Vick is coming for you, and they're talking about killing you and Marie. You're running out of time."

Evan's confused face hardened, his searching eyes filled with furious recognition.

He understood.

Evan's heart beat fast, the cloud fogging his mind, dissipating. Agent Vick—the man who had hounded him—now wanted to kill Marie. Evan clenched his jaw. Adrenaline pounded through his arms and legs. Somewhere in the periphery he heard the hatch to the Sphere snap shut, but he couldn't worry about that now. He turned his attention to the battle at hand—a battle he was losing.

The wall of the superior vena cava closed around his bot, the AI-transferred pressure on his body growing stronger. His command Endobot was still in the jaws of some determined white blood cell, tugging at him. Evan deployed his bot's nematocyst. Though, he couldn't see behind himself, the AI simulated the sound of a watery bag popping as his microscopic weapon lanced through the attacker. The clamping sensation eased, and cellular debris floated past—the guts of his aggressor. Evan turned his attention to squeezing through the gap in the vein wall, calling to his legion to retreat.

The cell-sized soldiers complied and followed him through the fissure into the space between the superior vena cava and a host of veins and arteries running through Marie's neck. He swiveled to see the wall seal shut behind them. Finally safe—for now.

"I'll head to the carotid artery," Evan said. "But I want to know where Agent Vick is. I want to talk to him." Evan tried his best to keep language to a minimum. But here, now, he wanted to confront Vick. Stop him. Hell, Evan would kill Vick if necessary. The thought made Evan's gut knot. Until the accident with Lai, he'd never hurt anyone—human, plant or animal—in his life. Now, though, his great love—his wife—was in imminent danger.

"I'm not sure who Vi—" Sharmila started.

"Army CID," Evan interrupted.

"CID? What does an investigator for the Army want with you?"

Evan ignored the question, gathered up the remains of his army once again, and headed to the carotid artery. The flagella of his troops twirled furiously, propelling a fleet of cellular submarines, each packed with weapons and going to war. Not only must he face whatever malevolent bacteria now infested Marie's brain, but also the man trying to stop him—Billy Vick.

"Thank God that had the desired effect," Sharmila said, pulling off her headset with a sigh.

Her techs shared a worried glance.

Before Sharmila could question them, her burner cell vibrated. She pulled it from her pocket and pressed *Answer*. "Yes?"

"We have a problem," her merc said.

"What problem? Where are you?"

"The place is crawling with Homeland Security," he replied.

"I already know this—"

"There's another group," he interjected. "I don't know who they are, but it isn't good. Did your benefactors send someone in?"

Sharmila shook her head. "No, they… I don't think so… why would they?"

"Well, we just spotted at least three soldiers on the move." Static washed over the merc's line. "No insignias. Don't seem to be in contact with the other agencies here. In fact, they don't look like they're with them at all. This is getting out of control."

"Well, get it back under control. That's what you do."

"Look, as long as we play by the rules, Homeland won't execute us, a private security firm, without cause," the merc said. "These new players could be assassins or foreign operatives for all we know. Mitigating threats on that level is not part of our agreement. I'm pulling my team out."

"Wait—"

The line clicked off.

"Shit!" Sharmila shouted. She threw her phone at the wall and the cheap device exploded in a shower of plastic and glass. "We need to finish this right now. I need Evan as alert as possible. He's got to be on point. You hear me? The Sphere has a stimulant system embedded in it, right? From the Condition Orange program?"

"Yeah, but we haven't meshed that with the Endobot program before," the scientist said, stumbling over his words. "There's no telling how that'll affect it. We're still experimenting with the formulas. I don't like—"

"Give him Hyper," Sharmila fired back. "I need him at full capacity. Every fucking neuron firing. Do it."

"That's not ethical… is it?" the tech asked, his voice a whine.

"None of this is ethical. Just do it."

Sharmila's scientist scrambled to the refrigerator and collected a glass vial with yellow liquid inside. He took it to the Sphere and dropped to his haunches. Exercising great care, he screwed the container of Hyper into a valve at the base of the Sphere. A click sounded, followed by hissing as the liquid vaporized and filled the Sphere.

Inside, Evan gasped.

CHAPTER TWENTY-THREE

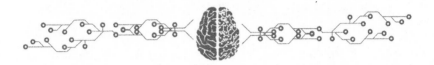

CDC Quarantine

Billy removed his shirt, and his skin prickled. He entered the Plexiglas sound-proof booth and stepped into the cradle of the robotic arm. Between his legs, a seat-like padded clamp rose with a soft whine and hooked up to his beltline. At the same time two more clamps lowered over his shoulders. They clenched down over his pectorals and connected with the lower piece, snapping together against his body like the closed fist of some giant robotic oppressor.

The energy in the room was palpable. Billy imagined this must be how NASA Mission Control must feel prior to a launch. Reinhardt's Homeland agents had secured posts that locked down all points of facility ingress and egress. Scientists and techs fluttered about, observing displays and conducting com checks.

Professor Dell continued her final mission briefing. "Our only godsend at this point is that our would-be saboteur, now in custody, injected Evan's bots into Marie's peritoneum. That means at this point, Evan will have endured a long, arduous microscopic journey in an attempt to reach the concentration of the bacteria at her brain stem. That's assuming some sort of colossal tech failure hasn't beset the NeuroDelve operation or Evan's nanobot force hasn't been destroyed by the host's body yet."

She turned her attention to Billy. "We are going to inject your bots at the site of the infection. That means all you have to do is set up a perimeter and wait. Remember: You think. They react. We will be there via commlink to walk you through everything."

"Got it," Billy said. The back of the arm-cradle pushed flat against his back, curving with the bend of his spine.

From across the room, Reinhardt offered Billy a smile and a thumbs up.

He returned the gesture.

Dell approached and slipped a VR headset over Billy's forehead. She then handed him two analog joystick controllers, one for each hand. "It will feel a little like a video game in the first-person perspective. Controls are similar, too. While you can think your bots to move, having the physical controls helps."

"I have some experience with this sort of thing. Micro surveillance drones, at least."

"Yes," Dell said. "That's perfect. So, you feel confident with this type of control scheme?"

"Yeah, but..." Billy chuffed. "It's been years now and this looks way different."

"It's okay. That's what the AI is there to help you with," Dell said. "The left stick will move your commander forward, backward, and strafe right and left. The right stick will assist your visor with three-hundred-sixty-degree directional rotation, or your camera view, so to speak."

"Okay," Billy said.

"Billy." Professor Dell touched her spidery fingers to his forearm. "You were kind to me yesterday at the lab when... when I needed some kindness." She smiled. "We are with *you*, not Evan.

We're going to take care of you out here."

"Thank you, Jeanine," Billy said, the arm lifting him suspended above the platform. He pulled the headset down over his face and inserted the earbuds. The screen, his whole plane of vision, held a soft blue glow, the word *Standby* flashing in the middle.

"Remember, in here, you won't be able to hear us, and we won't be able to hear you, except over the radio," Dell continued. "The isolation is important. It helps your brain disconnect from the real world and work on a more efficient level. There's also very little ambient sound. It will feel like scuba diving, to a degree. Think of it as a training simulation."

A training simulation where I die or end up a vegetable if my forces lose. He found himself wishing he'd been able to call Rosie and his boys, maybe for the last time. *Not helpful, Vick*, he thought. *Time to screw yourself down. Mission first.*

"Are we ready, Captain Vick?" Dr. Hakagi called out from his terminal.

"As ready as I'm gonna be," Billy said.

Dell and a medical technician pushed the heavy door to the soundproof room closed.

"Our people are with Marie, standing by with the injection," Hakagi continued now via Billy's earbuds. "Once you get the commander bot oriented inside the syringe, we will inject your team into Marie's body at the site of the infection."

"Copy," Billy said. He licked his lips. "Let's do this, already."

"Okay," Hakagi said, his voice tinny in Billy's ear. "Standby to initiate neural interface in three, two, one."

"This is crazy. I must be crazy," Billy muttered.

A peep sounded in the room, followed by a mechanical snap as the cradle meshed with his spinal column. The blow came hard and fast, a knife handled by an expert assassin. He felt it plunge deep into his back between his shoulder blades, sinking deeper and deeper. The air expelled from his lungs with an agonized groan. Billy's eyes stretched wide; his teeth bared in an awful grimace. He tried to call out for it to stop, that he wanted out, but he could only make a terrible *unnng unnng* grunt between the quick gasps of each half-breath.

"Is he okay?" Reinhardt called out, her voice distant, dreamlike.

"Just another second!" Dell said.

The colors on Billy's visor screen turned pale yellow, blurring with the involuntary watering of his eyes. And then, as quick as it came, the agony was gone, replaced by a strange probing ache that radiated out from the center of his back.

"We have a strong connection!" Dell said.

A smattering of clapping and congratulations followed.

Billy pinched his eyes, quivering breaths sucked from the air. "My God," he gasped. "My God. Please don't do that again… please."

"It's going to be okay, Billy," Dell said. "That's it. You're in. Open your eyes."

Billy's eyes fluttered, blinking the tears away. He couldn't see a damn thing other than the damned pale yellow wash like the inside of a urine sample. Billy looked up and down.

"Am I in the toilet bowl?" he asked.

A few chuckles of laughter echoed inside his head.

"Still got your sense of humor, I see? That's a good sign," Dell said. "Otherwise, you're feeling okay? Maybe a little disoriented?"

"Yeah, and more than a little uncomfortable."

"It should pass," Dell said. "Tell me what you see."

"I'm suspended in a yellow... liquid."

"Good. That's the fluid containing you and your bots."

"I don't see them."

"Use your joystick to turn 180 degrees."

Billy pressed the analog stick. A blur of motion followed as the visual representation of his environment struggled to keep up. His whole body swung to the left, legs dangling in space. The headset screen shuddered, piecing together pixelated images. Motion sickness tightened his stomach. "Whoa."

"Your commander bot is highly responsive. So is the robotic arm holding you. Just ease on the sticks. The AI will auto stabilize to give you a sense of up and down, though that's not really a thing where you're going."

"Ease the stick. Got it," Billy said, giving the analog stick a slight nudge. A smooth spinning motion followed. He released the stick, astonished. There, floating suspended all around him, his medi-bot force—organic, capsule-shaped bots with wispy hair-like arms drifting in the solution.

"Holy hell," Billy said.

"Highly efficient biological machines, Billy," Dell said. "They're not engineered to look pretty."

"I can see that."

"Look to the lower right side of your screen. See the blue capsule shaped image with the number one hundred beside it?"

"Yes."

"There wasn't time to develop a complex heads-up display for you. We are working with the base prototype, which has no directional guidance and only shows the overall number of active bots. As bots are disabled or malfunction, that number will decrease until…"

"I'll be eating through a straw," Billy said dryly, tried to ignore his mounting anxiety.

Dell gave a little cough. "Um, yes. So, don't lose too many."

How many is too many? Billy thought, his chest cramping.

"Let's make sure the interface is working properly before we send you in to the host. Give them a command."

"Okay, uh… I just think it, correct," Billy said.

"That's right," Dell said.

Billy focused, imagining the bots forming into neat rows, repurposed attack bots in front, medi-bots in the rear. At a glance he could visually distinguish between the two through a variation in their color. The medi-bots seemed to have a rose gold-colored hue, while the attackers, when clumped together seemed to take on a color that was more akin to platinum. Billy wasn't sure if this variation was actual or part of the AI interface designed to assist him and it didn't matter as long as he was able to distinguish them. He marveled as the odd creatures pivoted and scrambled into position. In seconds, the force before him mirrored the same picture he'd formed in his mind.

"Amazing," Billy murmured.

"Isn't it?" Dell said, beaming like a proud parent.

"Ah, Professor Dell," Dr. Hakagi's voice filled Billy's ear. "We just registered a new signature on our scan of the host."

"What sort of signature?" Dell asked.

"I don't know, but we weren't detecting it before, and now we are," Hakagi said, breathless. "It's at the site of infection."

"Get me in there—that's him," Billy said, his heart rate quickening.

"Damn. I'd hoped we'd have more time to work out the

kinks," Dell said.

"We don't. Put me in." Billy flexed his fingers and regripped the joysticks.

"Okay, here we go," Dell said. "Doctor, you may proceed with the injection."

"Good luck, Vick," Reinhardt said. "We're rooting for you."

Billy didn't reply. The liquid around him shifted, his point of view rocked forward at a sharp angle.

Don't fuck this up, Billy.

"Injector is in position." The administering doctor's voice squeaked like chalk scratching on a blackboard. "We're clear in three, two, one."

Billy felt his body tilt, the arm cradle shifting to adjust to a change in angle. For a moment he hung there, waiting, that terrible pause at the top before the roller coaster drops over the edge. With a violent jerk, he and the rest of his medi-bots fired downward, accelerating at unbelievable speed. Billy knew his physical body was in a controlled environment, that this was all just a simulation. But he still couldn't suppress the whoop of excitement that emerged from his throat as his body pitched forward and he launched into the void. The image of the environment around him blurred, particulate streaking across the screen like a starship hitting warp speed.

In an instant it was over. Billy's body jerked upright, hovering. The screen before his eyes flickered. Fuzzy, digitized puzzle pieces knitted together. He squinted, trying to make out his surroundings.

"Billy?" Dell's voice rose in pitch. "The injection was successfully administered. How is your connection? Can you still hear me?"

Billy didn't answer, instead he gawped at the massive gray-pink spongey mass—Marie's brain—looming up before him and his considerable army.

"Bioluminescence appears to be working," Hakagi said. "He should have the same visual we see right now."

"Billy, this is not going to work if you don't tell us what you've got going on," Dell said, a touch of exasperation in her voice.

"I'm in. This is... incredible," Billy said at last.

"We don't have time to—" Dell's words cut short as a rake of static filled Billy's ears.

"Billy Vick?"

It took Billy a moment to process the voice, to realize it belonged to Evan Weyland.

"Why do you want to kill Marie?" Evan said, his tone cold.

Billy manipulated the controls, imagining where he wanted his bots to form up. He swiveled, slow, deliberate, until his goggles filled with the image of a hole opening up in a nearby artery.

A black horrible mouth pulled open in the vessel. Billy stared into the maw. Long gangly arms twirled, like some monstrous alien from a 1950s sci-fi movie. A long pellet-shaped cell popped through, then another, and another. They came slow at first, then burst through like a river breaking a dam. It was an army—Evan's army. And it was enormous. Billy's heart faltered as the bots seemed to double every second and fan out in front until the battlefield was set, and one last Endobot—larger than the rest—pushed through the gap, stretching it wide.

Evan's command bot.

"Billy Vick." Evan's voice wavered, raw emotion clinging to the words. "I heard your team. I heard they want to kill Marie."

"Evan, I need you to stop what you're doing and listen to me." Billy tried to keep his voice measured. "It's very important. I just

STU JONES & GARETH WORTHINGTON

need you to—"

"I know what you want. You're that soldier who tried to strong arm me, but you can't. Not here. Marie's life is at stake. I won't let you risk it."

Damn, Billy thought. *There goes diplomacy.*

Cellular particulate floated past, dust in the wind of the void-like space. Billy pivoted, aligning his command bot and taking in the scene. Ahead, Evan's forces mirrored Billy's formation—rank and file, multiple rows deep. Fear clutched deep into the warm spaces of his heart. He was outnumbered in a bad way, at least two to one. Maybe three to one.

He doesn't want to talk to me, Billy thought. *All he wants is to save his wife and he's ready to fight about it.*

"Evan." Billy swallowed. "I don't want to hurt you or Marie. But this has become bigger than us. I've seen this thing before. It's a bioweapon called Omega, and it's capable of mutating into something really nasty. Millions of lives could be at stake. Evan, you're right, there are people out here that would sooner just kill Marie and you, and end this all. But I don't want that. If you could just stop what you're doing, I'll help you and Marie any way I can—"

"I don't trust you," Evan said. "Leave now."

Billy watched as more of Evan's artillery bots disengaged from the bacteria to join the lines formed against him.

Professor Dell's voice scratched through the static. "Billy... important... copy?"

"No," Billy said. "We've got some sort of interference. I can't copy you."

"Billy, make sure you don't—" Static washed out the rest of Dell's transmission.

Don't what? Billy swore to himself.

He was on his own.

Billy studied the forces gathered against him. Evan wouldn't budge. There was only one way this would end. He'd have to destroy Evan's forces if he had any hope of stopping the man. *But how? If he's connected the way I am,* Billy thought, *can I do that without killing him?*

Nothing in his own experience on the battlefield had prepared him for this. As an infantryman and a Ranger, Billy had trained in small unit tactics and insurgent guerilla warfare. This was altogether different. Two massive armies facing off toe-to-toe on the field of battle like some antique theater of war.

That was it.

Billy wracked his brain trying to remember all the West Point classes on military history and classical battlefield strategy. Anything that might give him an edge against a superior force. If he could cripple the opposition, break the back of the enemy line, he might have a chance.

The answer hit him like a jolt of electricity, giving hope against insurmountable odds. *Defeat in detail,* Napoleon's wildly successful approach to dismantling larger forces. Napoleon utilized this strategy in his lightning campaign across Italy in 1796. As did Stonewall Jackson in 1862 in his Shenandoah Valley campaign, one of the most stunning upsets of the American Civil War and one of the greatest strategic defeats in recorded military history. Jackson defeated a superior Union force of fifty-thousand men with just seventeen thousand. In theory, the same principals could work here.

Billy closed his eyes, trying to remember the old battlefield diagrams of Napoleon's conquests, as well as the strategic attack and retreat and concentration of force employed by Jackson. In his mind's eye he constructed each position, spreading his entire company out and dividing them into four platoons of twenty-five bots each across the space. Each platoon contained a squad of twelve and thirteen, with the attack squad holding the larger number.

"What are you're doing?" Evan said. "Don't make me hurt you."

Billy opened his eyes and surveyed the field, his bot platoons spread out in just the way he'd imagined. With awkward movements, he swiveled the position of the command bot. Evan was right. Billy had no chance of physically out-maneuvering him. The guy had years of training and experience on him. Not to mention a gift for it. But what he didn't have was combat experience and a strong knowledge of tactical theory. Billy could out-*position* him. Numbers weren't everything.

Billy watched as Evan's forces divided, mirroring his own troops' positions, each section supported by infantry bots and defensive bots with artillery bots in the rear. At each position, Evan had superior numbers as well as the ability to engage Billy's forces from a distance.

Not good odds.

"You won't stop me," Evan said. "You shouldn't try. Go away. Last chance."

Billy didn't respond. His mind drifted, hazy, distant, his heart thundering in his ears. Somewhere in the dark corners of the battlefield he could hear Pete crying for help. A faint wafting of smoke and dust and blood filled his nostrils. Sweat prickled his brow. He was done talking. Possessing superior forces didn't hurt Evan, but it also didn't guarantee the victory for him.

Evan would have to learn this lesson the hard way.

238

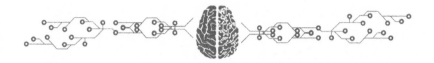

CHAPTER TWENTY-FOUR

CDC Quarantine

"What just happened?" Reinhardt stormed down off the command platform to the staging area. "Somebody tell me what the hell is going on? Why have we lost Billy?"

An electrical energy danced in her eyes, an intensity and singularity of focus no one would suspect as being a fear response. Except that's exactly what it was. Her heart fluttered, her knees weak. She gulped at the air, warm with electronics.

"We didn't lose him..." Dell began. "Hold on a second," she said, whispering something to Hakagi.

"I need some answers, people," Reinhardt said. "Nate?"

The chubby IT specialist bumbled from station to station, checking monitors and rechecking cables. "All I can tell you is it doesn't appear to be on my end." With a few clicks of a mouse he ran an internal diagnostic on their hastily assembled intranet construct. "All systems are operational. Everything's still connected."

"Then what the hell—" Reinhardt tried to hide the quiver in her voice.

"It's not us." Jeanine Dell turned from her frantic, whispered conversation with Hakagi. "At least, it doesn't appear to be."

Reinhardt's smart device vibrated in her pocket.

"Look," Dell continued, "it might be some sort of interference from Evan's unit. We never tested two of them in such close proximity. They aren't designed for this."

The phone in Reinhardt's pocket stopped buzzing. She cracked her neck and swiped a strand of hair from her face. She turned her attention to Billy, secure in the cradle of the arm, which swung to the right with a slow sweeping gesture. Inside the Plexiglas box, Billy continued to operate his bot army, lips pinched together in a determined grimace.

Reinhardt tapped her upper lip with her fingers. "Listen, I'm not telling any of you what you don't already know, but a man's life is on the line right now. We assured him we had his back when he took on this risk. It is not acceptable for us to leave him twisting in the wind. I need solutions." She turned, clearing off the end of a table with a swipe of her hand. A tablet and a stack of printouts hit the floor with a smack. "Dell, Hakagi, I need you both over here developing contingencies."

Amidst the hubbub of the busy makeshift command center, Reinhardt pulled over her laptop and opened it. In the top left, a pixelated video screen jumped and jittered, a pitiful representation of what Billy was actually experiencing. To the right a box measured and monitored Billy's vitals, his breathing and heart rate elevated. Below both, she looked at a close-up image of Marie's brain stem. Speckled groups of red indicated Evan's considerable force surrounding the stem at the center of the disease, while ringed around him and spread thin, Billy's much smaller force appeared in blue.

Reinhardt's eyes narrowed. She watched as the little blue blips jostled, reforming in a different pattern. Evan's red forces mirrored Billy's arrangement. There were so many of them. They'd grossly underestimated the force Evan and NeuroDelve together could marshal.

Dell, breathing deep, dropped her laptop down on the table with a *clunk*, grabbing for her tablet as it slipped from her arms. Hakagi followed, swiping through green streams of floating data hovering in the air, cast from a projection tablet.

"Okay." Hakagi pushed up the Plexiglas-thick lenses perched atop his nose. "We don't have communication with Billy. And it doesn't appear to be a problem on our end."

"NeuroDelve have a militia of sorts," Reinhardt said. "They could be using tech to hack our signal."

Dell bit her lip.

"Why can't we just open the door and talk to him?" Reinhardt asked.

"No." Dell's eyes grew wide. "Absolutely not. If he's alert to our presence, that would break the illusion for his brain. He'd be confused, distracted. A moment Evan could easily exploit. It could get him killed." She shook her head. "We can't open the door until he is clear of danger."

Reinhardt released a heavy sigh. "Any alternatives?"

Hakagi shook his head and pinched his lower lip.

"Maybe," Dell said, looking up.

"I'm all ears," Reinhardt said.

"Well, maybe we could type messages direct into his interface. We used to do this in our old beta test runs. It should show in the center of his screen, like a warning message." She shrugged. "He couldn't respond to us, but at least we could pass along vital information."

Reinhardt nodded and pulled on the back of her neck. She leaned forward on the cluttered tabletop. "It's worth a shot. How long to get it up and running?"

"I don't know. I'll have to get with Nate and rig something."

"Do it. We're out of time." Reinhardt glanced at Hakagi as Dell strode across the room to the IT specialist. "What are we missing, Dr. Hakagi? What does Billy need to know right now?"

"Well." Hakagi interlaced his fingers. Behind him, a hurried tech with an armful of cables bumped him as he squeezed passed. Hakagi adjusted his glasses. "If he didn't hear Professor Dell's last transmission, he needs to know not to engage the white blood cells attacking the disease."

"Okay. Why?" Reinhardt asked.

"Right now, due to the design of his bots, he's sort of cloaked," Hakagi said. "Her immune system doesn't recognize him as a foreign body. That could change very quick, and if it does, it'll be trouble he doesn't need."

"Good," Reinhardt said. "Work with Dell on getting that message to him."

"Got it," Hakagi said.

Reinhardt's phone buzzed in her pocket again. She retrieved her device and checked the screen. Her heart sank. The name the HSI Division Chief out of D.C., filled the display. She'd missed four calls from him already. She let this one go to voicemail. Again. The Chief calling was not a good sign. Sending him to voicemail for the fifth time wasn't going to help. She'd have to reach out, but she wanted to do it from a controlled environment. The operational command center was just too damn busy for her to focus. Needed her ducks in a row before she got on the phone with the boss.

242

"I've got to step out," she said to murmurs of acknowledgement and a wave from Dell. "Keep trouble shooting and do what you need to do to keep Agent Vick alive and operational."

She pushed through the door to the ops center, swinging it wide on her way out. Past the employee lounge and various offices and labs, Reinhardt marched toward the rear parking deck. Outside, at least, she'd be able to steal a minute of privacy.

"Everything okay?" Barrett said, a questioning look on his face as she blew past him down the hallway.

"No," she said, holding up her phone. "Division Chief keeps calling."

Barrett grimaced. "Rowley? Good luck."

"Yeah, right." Reinhardt pushed through the rear door and stepped past the two-man SRCAT detail at the exit. A chill November wind nipped at her exposed face and neck and she regretted having left her jacket back in Ops. She exhaled, then raised her phone. "Here we go." She tabbed the contact on the recently missed call list and placed the phone to her ear. It didn't even ring.

"Reinhardt, what the hell is going on?" The Division Chief's nasal whine buzzed from her phone speaker. Why did the man always sound like he had his nose pinched? "I've been trying to reach you for the last hour."

"Morning, Chief," Reinhardt said, her mouth dry.

"I need some answers, now. I've got the Pentagon breathing down my neck over here. The word on the street is you ambushed a military convoy and took one of their prisoners? Please God, tell me that's not true. I need to know what the hell is going on and I need to know right now."

Reinhardt winced, pulled the phone away to escape that horrific Jersey accent. *There's no way in hell he's going to understand,* she thought. "Chief, if you'll allow me, I'd like to try and explain myself."

"I'm all ears."

"Did you read the brief I sent over last night?"

"I scanned it. I assumed I was up to speed on everything until I woke up to this shit storm this morning."

"Sir, we had a development overnight that changed the scope of our operation. Army CID happened to be escorting a man, their agent Billy Vick, who is of vital importance to our investigation. We couldn't risk him going dark. We needed his cooperation and we didn't have time to go through the proper channels."

"What the Army does with the people under its command is their business, Reinhardt. Do you still have this man in your custody?"

"He's not in our custody. He's acting as a consultant in our investigation. I feel certain that I laid out in the brief how serious this situation is and how, if not resolved properly, we could be looking at some sort of global pandemic."

"I understand it's serious, but dammit, Reinhardt, there's just some things you can't do."

"Respectfully, Chief, I disagree. Millions, maybe even billions of lives might be at risk."

Silence enveloped the line.

"Listen to me," the Chief said, his voice taking on a soothing tone. "I'm not asking you to cooperate with the Army—I'm telling you, you must."

Reinhardt rolled her eyes, pulled the phone away from her ear then put it back. She glanced at Mike Barrett and the two SRCAT operators at the door, talking.

"You need to slow down and think how this affects you personally," the Chief said. "I've kept up with your career, Reinhardt. You are a shining example of what our people can be and you've overcome barrier after barrier when men tried to tell you what a woman could or couldn't achieve here. But now is not the time to prove your mettle. It's not the time to stand on principle."

"Chief listen—"

"No, I need to hear you say you understand," the Chief said, the nasal whine rising. "You are on the cusp of creating a major problem for the agency. A problem that could ruin you."

"I'm aware of that sir, and I stand by my decision," Reinhardt said, defiance bleeding into her tone.

Reinhardt could practically hear the Chief's blood pressure soaring. On the other end of the line he took a shaking breath, furious, but attempting to maintain some level of control.

"Let me make myself clear." The Chief's gentle tone was gone. "Your entire career, your future with this organization, rests on this single moment. I've already spoken with the Army's CID commander and he is willing to let this slide, if you release this Agent Vick back to his custody. His team is en route to your location at the CDC now. So help me, God, Reinhardt, if you don't release this man to them, I'll—"

Reinhardt terminated the call. The Chief still didn't understand what was at stake. She doubted he'd even read her brief, and she couldn't turn Billy over now even if she wanted to. That ship sailed long ago. Shivering from the cutting wind, Reinhardt entered back the way she'd come, passing Barrett and his guys.

"That bad, huh?" Barrett said with a smirk.

245

"Worse," Reinhardt said. "Look, this is going to get ugly. I asked you to come help. You did, as a favor to me. I'm releasing you from that obligation."

Barrett narrowed his gaze. "I don't like the sound of that."

"Mike, I'm going to get crucified for this," Reinhardt said. "I don't want you and your people to get drawn into that. You can head out now and say you agreed to help but when you saw what was going on you pulled your team out. My people can handle security."

Barrett gave her a scolding glance. "After all we've been through, you think I'm going to go for that? You know I'm not the type to ditch so easily." He motioned to one of his men, who handed him a tablet, digital files stacked atop one another. "Besides, check this out." He showed Reinhardt the screen and tapped open one of the files. "While we had some down time, I had my intel guys work up what they could on this Omega thing. Called in a few favors. It's not pretty."

"Not pretty, how?" Reinhardt said, glancing from the tablet to Barrett.

"Seems this thing was started by us. It went into development alongside the Russians with Russian funding and assistance coming in under the table. Uncle Sam got cold feet, thanks to Agent Vick back there, but the Russians didn't. They continued with the research. The dumb assholes put a shipment of it on a plane. But that's where it gets interesting." He double tapped on the tablet screen and handed it to Reinhardt. "The plane wasn't shot down by some terrorist faction."

"Who then?" Reinhardt asked. She looked down at what appeared to be a military flight log.

"The Russians wouldn't shoot down their own multi-billion

246

dollar bio-weapon." Barrett shrugged. "But we have fighter jets in the region all the time as a security presence. I think it was shot down by us."

Reinhardt blinked. "Us as in the United States? Why risk open war?"

"Seems our administration didn't want the heat associated with this thing," Barrett said. "Maybe they had regrets. They couldn't hit a Russian installation without it being an obvious act of war, but a cargo plane in transit? The motive and the means are there."

"The plane is shot down," Reinhardt said, "but the cargo is not destroyed, it's stolen. Our government can't have that either, so to avoid the fallout, they decided to burn the stolen cargo, and an entire village, to the ground. But no one counted on Marie Weyland."

"Right, and what no one's been thinking about is how much she's worth," Barrett said.

Reinhardt froze to the spot. "The Russians, or the terrorists, or even our people trying to cover it up, will come looking for their prize."

Barrett nodded, then flicked the page on the tablet. "Our analysts have been picking up a lot of unusual chatter on the dark web. Something is about to drop. If someone comes looking to take it back, you've got a bigger problem than a pissed off Division Chief. So, if it's all the same to you, me and my team are gonna hang around." Barrett crossed his arms.

Reinhardt offered a stoic nod. "Thank you, Mike. You might regret that decision before this is all over."

Barrett opened his hands. "And miss front row tickets to opening night at the shit-show?"

The two SRCAT guys laughed. Reinhardt could only manage

to shake her head and fake a smile, an icy dread swelling within her as she turned and headed back for operations.

CHAPTER TWENTY-FIVE

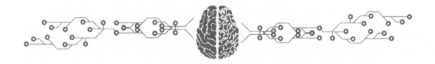

Marie Weyland's Cerebral Aqueduct

E van stared at the battlefield. Clinging to the meninges of Marie's medulla oblongata was a clump of bulbous bacteria that he surmised to be the infection killing her. Enormous white blood cells passed over the cluster and moved on, unaware of the threat. Whatever disguise this invading disease had, it worked well. Evan would have to attack the foreign bacteria, rip them apart.

To the left of center, Billy Vick and his army fanned out, ready to foil Evan's plans.

No time for this. Evan commanded a contingent of his infantry to head straight for the infection, while his remaining and sizeable army could fend off the unwelcome government agent.

Billy Vick, the man who had been chasing Evan for days now, had said something about Omega, some kind of infection. Governments wanting to kill Marie.

"What's Omega?" Evan said, his voice echoing inside the Sphere.

There was a long pause, but then Agent Vick's voice came, calm and collected, as if he were in Evan's head. "It's a bioweapon. Designed to hurt and kill specific people—people of Arabic descent—in order to beat the spreading terror attacks with no centralization. I don't know the specifics. You'd know how that would work better than me."

Evan's skin prickled. Marie did have Middle Eastern family, a few generations back. Was she sick because a certain percentage of DNA wasn't Caucasian? "How did she get sick?" Evan asked.

More silence, as if Vick weighed whether or not to answer.

"Screw it," Billy said. "The United States and Russia worked on it together. I shut it down last year. Or thought I did. But it seems someone, probably the Russians, carried on. A plane transporting a container of Omega went down over Syria. But the container survived. The U.S. government wanted the whole situation gone. So, they firebombed the village. Your wife discovered the planned bombing and went in to investigate. That's when she got exposed."

"You… tried to stop it getting out once before?"

"Yes," Vick said. "That's why I know how bad this thing is."

Was Agent Vick on Evan's side? How did he get bots? Did Dell give him access? If so, then he knew about Lai. Evan shifted his command Endobot to point the microscopic camera at his strike force making contact with the Omega bacteria.

"I didn't kill Lai on purpose," Evan said. "Lai fell."

"I know," Vick said. "You just wanted the nanobots to cure your wife."

A small weight lifted from Evan's chest, relief from a mental tick requiring forgiveness. As a kid he'd say sorry and keep repeating it until his father remembered to say, "don't worry." Evan couldn't be sure if the need was driven by real guilt or just an obsessive desire to complete an agreed transaction: say sorry, hear forgiveness.

"Evan, you have to call off your Endobots. Don't attack the

infection. Omega will defend itself and adapt."

"She's dying," Evan said, tears welling.

"I know, Evan," Billy said, his tone softer now. "And we'll save her, but not like this. Call off your bots, you're about to make things worse."

Evan thought for a second. Maybe ten. It could've been minutes or hours. There was no way to tell, given how Sharmila manipulated the perception of time in the Sphere. But his logic path was clear: if he didn't succeed, Marie would die. Right here and right now, he had a chance to destroy Omega.

A shockwave ripped through the cerebrospinal fluid, swirling the Endobots and nanobots into a maelstrom. The currents and eddies in the fluid dragged his command Endobot along, and smashed it against the wall of the cerebellum. Evan twisted over and over in the Sphere, catching his own reflection on the inner surface, tearing him from full immersion and hampering his ability to regain control.

"Evan, Marie's convulsing," Sharmila said. "You have to hurry."

"I'm sorry, Vick," Evan mumbled.

"Don't do this," Billy shouted.

For what seemed like time without end, neither force moved. Instead they floated in the cerebrospinal fluid, poised and ready to launch forward. Pawns in a microscopic game of chess. In the fading bioluminescence and murky detritus-filled liquid, Evan couldn't discern just how many nanobots Billy Vick commanded—but Evan knew *he* held the greater number.

Vick's army pivoted into action.

Evan's gut tightened. The simulated sound of sloshing, became loud and offensive. Locked inside his own head, and suddenly very aware he was man in giant Christmas bauble, Evan's commands to bloody well move went unheard by his Endobot army.

But, no strike came from Billy's force.

Instead, the enemy divided into four distinct groups and dispersed so wide that Evan's line of sight only contained one contingent, which seemed to be relatively small—maybe twenty-five bots. Behind them waited Vick's command nanobot.

Evan scrambled to follow suit, dividing his own army into four platoons that fanned out to meet their enemy head on.

The first clump of attackers straight ahead sank to the meninges lining the cerebellum, and hid among the folds. *Dammit*, he thought. *Need to be careful.* Damaging Marie's cerebellum would be disastrous. He would need pin-point accuracy to pierce each enemy nanobot. Evan commanded the majority of his first platoon to advance—keeping a few soldiers back as a defensive force. His Endobots descended upon Billy's squad, each individual cell lining up mano-e-mano for a strange, cell-to-cell combat. Nematocysts fired, extended like little swords as they clashed with the enemy. A storm of swirling cells sparred and twisted, each with their nematocysts stabbing and parrying. Cells burst open. The battle raged.

In a stunning show of force, Evan's bots were winning. The enemy legion hiding in the meninges suffered defeat after defeat, unable to keep up with the speed at which Evan commanded his units to maneuver, evade, and strike.

A sudden sharp pain dug into his brain like an icepick pushed through the eye-socket. Evan flinched and gasped.

"Evan? Evan, what the hell is going on? You're hemorrhaging numbers," Sharmila barked into his ear. "You're getting slaughtered in there!"

"What are you talking about? I'm winning."

"Check your readout, you're losing and your vitals show it."

Evan's heart raced in his chest. He glanced at his bot counter, down twenty-five percent. Another five percent slashed from the tally, followed by another three.

"What's going on?" Evan swiveled his command Endobot around, his own body pivoting in the Sphere, until his field of view filled with one of his platoons—now little more than a few individuals, executed one by one. Billy Vick syphoned some of his forces and banded together several of his original four legions into a single larger force capable of crushing each one of Evan's groups.

Evan stopped breathing, his vision dimming in the fading bioluminescence as the chemical energy in his bots dwindled. *No time, I have no time.* Few bots, no light, and an enemy that had somehow outwitted him. He needed the thirty-thousand foot view only Sharmila could provide.

"Sharmila, help, there's too many," Evan said, his voice breaking along with his resolve. "I can't beat him."

There was a long silence.

"Marie can," Sharmila said, her tone confident.

"Marie?" Evan replied, breathing labored.

Two more of Evan's Endobots exploded.

"Flood the whole space with your antigens," Sharmila pressed. "Call in her immune system. Make them work for you."

"But I can't guarantee they won't destroy my own bots."

"Just do it," Sharmila shouted. "The enemy of your enemy is your friend. It'll keep Vick busy and buy you the time you need. Take out the bacteria on her medulla and we'll pull you out as soon as you're finished."

Evan righted himself in the Sphere and connected with what

253

army he had left. With a single thought, the screen-wall of the Sphere filled with the image of a shower of antigen artillery fired in the direction of Vick's bots. The antigens attached to everything, cells, surfaces, and particulate, drifting in suspended animation like fired confetti at a parade.

It'll take a couple of minutes for the immune system to register that, Evan thought. *Got to make it to the medulla.*

Evan's command Endobot propelled forward, flagellum rotating as fast as possible, hurtling him toward the true enemy. *What had Vick called it? Omega?* He watched in horror as a group of his Endobots attacked and stabbed at the Omega infection with little effect. Evan's nematocysts glanced of the surface of the bacteria. He might as well try to pierce a knight's full plate armor with a sewing needle. He scanned closer to see if his antigens had adhered to the bacteria's surface, perhaps Marie could fight this. But their surfaces remained clear, as if designed to force antigens and other tagging molecules to slide from them. Impenetrable. Untaggable.

How was he supposed to beat this thing?

"No, no, no, this isn't possible," Evan said, rubbing his head inside the Sphere.

One of the bacteria seemed to grow tired of Evan's infantry Endobot scratching at it and with lightning speed it consumed the attacker—phagocytosis at a rate never before seen. The translucent Omega bacterium ingested his Endobot. As if to add insult to injury, the bacterium's own ribosomes set to work on the coiled up strand of DNA in Evan's Endobot and began unzipping it, pulling it apart. But instead of expelling the pieces, the bacterium's own DNA began to unfold. Tiny maneuvering molecules chivvied the two, foreign strands of nucleic acids together.

"The bacteria is incorporating the Endobots' DNA," Evan said aloud.

"Evan, stop!" came Vick's voice, sudden and close.

A jarring impact of Vick's command nanobot sent Evan's Endobot careening through the fluid and away from the infection. Evan clenched his jaw and righted himself inside the Sphere. As his bot spun, Evan's view panned over the arena now alive with conflict—Endobot versus nanobot versus Omega versus Marie's immune system. A free-for-all melee akin to a medieval battlefield.

Evan's cellular camera settled on the clump of bacteria along the medulla. Now, the disease fought back—phagocytosing Evan's soldiers—as if they had learned from each other that consuming the Endobots meant victory. One or two of the Omega bacteria had even constructed nematocysts inside their walls. The bacteria were adapting.

"I have to destroy them," Evan said.

"Evan, stop this," Vick yelled. "You don't understand what's at stake."

The agent's command Endobot maneuvered itself between Evan and the infection, while the battle raged around them.

"Get out of my way," Evan said, jaw set.

Another rumble coursed through Marie's body. Another convulsion.

"You know I can't do that," Vick replied.

Evan considered his options, but deep in his heart there was only one: he had to save Marie. That meant going through Billy Vick. Evan thrust his bot forward. The nematocyst shot out, hovering before him like a javelin, a jousting knight on horseback, charging the enemy.

"Evan, you reckless son of a bitch!" Billy shouted as his own rapier-like nematocyst swung forward to engage his foe. His vision blurred, the rapid twitch causing lag in the visual feed. He swiveled to the side just as Evan's command bot rocketed into the space where he'd just been, its nematocyte thrusting. Billy gasped, retreated as the thing jabbed at him like a massive hypodermic needle, once, twice. Pivoting to the left, his own nematocyst shot upward and connected with Evan's extended weapon.

High thrust, low thrust, straight down the center. Billy twisted away, retreated, and lunged forward again, his own blade counter thrusting and parrying his enemy's weapon. Like ancient honor-bound duelists with rapiers crossed, they clashed and evaded again and again.

"Evan, don't—"

Feigning right and spinning left, Evan caught Billy by surprise with a slashing strike. Unable to parry, Billy dodged, his visuals struggling to keep up. In a moment of blurred pixilated movement, he lost sight of Evan's bot.

The impact landed with the force of a car crash, a flaming brand of pain that slashed through Billy's left shoulder and into his chest. He screamed. The arm-like cradle that held him whipped savagely to the side, rocking almost upside down for a moment, before returning to the neutral position.

"Billy?" Dell shouted in his ears. "We've got you back, Billy. Are you okay?"

Billy gasped, the cradle rocking, his view of the dark, hostile territory reforming.

"Stop," Evan's voice crackled through the static.

Shuddered breath filled Billy's lungs. Limp and useless, his left arm dangled by his side. A searing wave of pain radiated outward from the wound, causing his whole left side to ache. He could smell the faintest tinge of smoke in the air, simulated cordite and dust sticking in his nostrils.

"Pete, I… I'm injured," he groaned, his mind pulled from the moment, lost in a nightmare of pain.

"Billy…?" Professor Dell said, her tone calm. "Billy, just keep breathing, you're okay."

With a groan, Billy tried to raise his left arm, his composure returning. "Why can't I move?"

"Evan landed a non-fatal cutting blow," Dell said. "Your bot is damaged and your brain is translating the injury to your physical body. You're fine, though—stay in the moment. The function in your arm will return."

"It's fucking not fine, Doc," Billy said through gnashed teeth.

"Stay in the fight, Billy," Reinhardt said.

With great effort, Billy moved the fingers of his left hand, still holding the controller. He couldn't fully raise his arm, but he didn't need to. All he needed was a thumb on the throttle. A wave of fresh pain rushed through him. But this pain was different, distant and obscure. The coppery taste of blood filled his mouth.

"What's happening?" he asked. "I feel like this rig is killing me!"

"You're losing bots, Billy," Dell said. "Your body is under extreme stress. You've got to issue new orders and change the momentum of the fight. But whatever you do, don't engage with Marie's immune response unless you have no other choice."

"New orders," Billy murmured. "Don't engage the white blood

cells. Okay."

Billy watched his biological war machines bump and jostle with Evan's forces. Nematocysts fired and Endobot sacs burst into a wash of hazy particulate. Billy turned his gaze to the bot counter in the corner of his HUD and watched as it ticked below sixty-five. A quick look back to the brain stem map and he noted that Evan's command Endobot locked in battle with the Omega infection. This was his chance to turn the tide.

Re-imagining the conflict, he issued fresh orders for the remaining medi-bots to engage with friendly forces, triage what units were salvageable, and provide aid. Then, along the left flank he marshaled up a large cobbled together platoon of his attack bots, which formed into a wedge and charged like mounted cavalry.

For an instant, elation filled his chest as his forces carved a swath through the center of Evan's lines. Endobots burst and came apart under the counter assault, their grainy insides dissipating into the fluid like sand in the wind.

Evan cried out in pain. "What are you doing?"

"Stopping you—" The words seemed to lodge in Billy's throat.

Marie's full immune response, a cavalry of white blood cells, stormed the battlefield. Side by side, the strange and translucent warriors collided with and swallowed Billy's medi-bots—even as his forces tried to revive injured and disabled units.

"No," Billy whispered. He shuddered with a fresh jolt of electrical pain and watched his nanobot counter drop below forty units.

"Billy, you're losing too many bots!" Dell shouted, her voice far away and dreamlike in his ears.

Billy opened his mouth to respond, but no sound came. The battlefield before his eyes morphed and bled like wet paint

running. The bacteria were now tanks, the membranes sandy
outcroppings and the fluid around him, a river of his brothers'
blood.

And then, Billy was no longer in the brain stem of Marie
Weyland, but once again crawling on his elbows, his legs dragging
in useless serpentine trails through the smoke and the fire, past the
screams of dying men.

He had to get to Pete. He had to know.

"Pete! Pete, where are you?"

"Billy."

*Time jittered and jumped, flashing forward at the speed of
thought. One moment Billy's limbs burned in the hot sand as he
crawled, the next he sat hunched, the broken skull of his friend held
together by blood soaked fingers.*

"Hang in there, brother. I've got you, just hang on." Tears
streamed down Billy's cheeks.

"They killed me, Billy."

"No. We're going to get you outta here, bro," Billy said.

Pete swallowed, blood and grime on his lips. "Promise me."

Billy waited, lips pinched.

*"Promise me you'll make it home. Don't die for nothin'... like
me."*

*Time jumped again as Pete took his last breath and an emptiness
filled Billy's chest. The void all consuming, wrapped its cold tendrils
around him, sucking all warmth and life and hope from his body.*

Billy shrieked into the air, long and loud.

"Billy!" Professor Dell's voice jolted him from his trance.
"They're going to kill you!"

The ticker plummeted below thirty bots.

Billy choked on a wet gasp for air, rivulets of blood streaming from his nose.

"Evan!" he screamed, as his command nanobot shot forward.

Evan's bot turned just in time to intercept him, nematocyst thrusting. Their sabers crossed again, flashing in the gloom. Teeth bared, Billy drove on, heedless of the danger.

"I have to save my wife," Evan shouted. His sword-like nematocyst plunged down.

Billy cried out as the blade pierced the surface of his bot. Fire flared in his chest. He pressed back, his own needle rising.

"Hit him. Do it now!" Billy screamed.

His bot fired its nematocyst. The blade launched out, deflected at the last moment by Evan's own biological blade.

Three of Billy's remaining bots slammed into Evan, clamoring and stabbing with their nematocysts. With deft, inhuman control, Evan parried and destroyed each in turn.

Billy's lungs heaved, a gurgled wheeze bubbling up from inside him.

Evan's wounded bot swiveled to face him once again.

"You can't beat me," Billy coughed.

"I don't have to," Evan said.

Was that pity in his voice? Billy thought.

Something slammed into Billy from behind.

The giant neutrophil exploded in a kamikaze attack, stringy web-like particles encasing the last of his bots. Billy screamed, unable to move. A second neutrophil exploded nearby, freezing him in a sticky net. Billy's heart stuttered as he watched the last lines of his bots immobilized by the discharging neutrophils, sacrificing themselves to contain the hostile invaders. Trapped in the sticky expanse, his forces twisted and flailed to no effect. And then Marie's immune cells descended upon them, swallowing them, tearing them apart.

"Billy, we're pulling you out!" Dell's voice was nigh incomprehensible.

A blast of agony crashed over Billy. His counter dropped below ten bots.

"No!" he shouted. "I. Can. Do it…"

Marie's immune cells, massive and terrifying, converged on him, consuming his command bot. His nematocyst stabbed with wild jerking thrusts, bursting one attacker, then another, but there were too many.

Billy convulsed and coughed, blood streaming from his nose and mouth as the creatures consumed his nanobot, pulling it—and his mind—apart from the inside out.

CHAPTER TWENTY-SIX

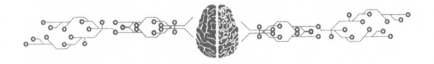

Marie Weyland's Cerebral Aqueduct

In the gloom, bioluminescent light now all but gone, Evan watched Agent Vick's command nanobot disintegrate, pulled apart by Marie's white blood cells. Attackers Evan himself had set upon the man. Evan's gut knotted. Lai had been an accident, but this act had been very deliberate. Was the agent's connection to his nanobots as deep as Evan's to Sharmila's Endobots?

Had he just murdered Billy Vick?

The last remnants of war petered out as Marie's immune system mopped up the smattering of nanobots—sucking them up, dissolving them and then spitting out the harmless biological scrap. Yet, in shadows, Omega clung to the membranes of Marie's brain. The bacteria pulsated, grew and then split into two new functional cells, doubling their numbers every few minutes. Omega had been docile, happy to merely kill Evan's wife. Now, having been attacked, they were pissed. Evan knew it to be unprofessional, anthropomorphizing single-celled life, but the way they moved and swayed—like a rabid dog trapped in an alley, waiting to strike— sent cold shivers down Evan's spine. Omega had mutated into something terrifying and it was all his fault.

One of the horrible invaders close to Evan's command bot

powered forward, now furnished with flagella, a tool adopted from consuming his own army. It rushed at him from the dark, a translucent demon.

Pain wracked Evan's body, his brain interpreting Omega's attack on his Endobot as an onslaught on his own limbs and organs.

"Sharmila," he wheezed.

Evan felt torn out of quicksand that fought to hold him in place, with no sound or light to help him distinguish up from down. His consciousness burst back to reality, floating in the Sphere, the curved walls no longer projecting the insides of his wife's skull, instead blasting out a singular harsh white light. The contents of Evan's stomach rushed up, through his esophagus, and forced its way through his nostrils and mouth. He heaved the fluid, and it spattered on the floor of the Sphere.

The electromagnets disengaged and Evan crumpled into a pair of arms that failed to support him. He and his would-be assistant crashed into the smooth floor and slid in his own vomit. The world spun, the open door to the Sphere whizzing past over and over.

"Evan? Evan, can you hear me?" Sharmila's voice, hot in his ear.

"Sharmila, you can't just yank him from the system," Sharmila's scientist said, hovering in the doorway. "It could cause serious brain damage."

"You want to talk about serious brain damage?" Sharmila barked. "Did you see what was about to happen to him?"

Sharmila's hands pawed at Evan's face and headgear until he was free of the device. The relief on his neck muscles was incredible, almost enough to outweigh the nausea still crawling up his throat.

"Evan, are you okay?" Sharmila asked. "What happened? Evan?"

"I... I destroyed... Vick's nanobot. His army."

"Evan, did you eradicate the infection?" Sharmila pressed.

Evan shook his head slow, his gaze falling on the woman's nose. "I think I made it worse."

"Worse?" Sharmila said, her bloodless face becoming even paler.

"It adapted to resist me. It fought back. Vick, he said the government engineered it to attack people of Arabic decent, but now it's changed into something else..."

"You can't be serious," Sharmila said. "Engineered? By whom?"

"I don't know," Evan replied, pushing himself from the floor to his knees. He wiped a dribble of blood from his nose.

"We got the data, Evan, maybe we can figure out a way to save her. Save anyone at risk."

He shook his head. "It's too late for Marie. I have to go to her, to be with her before..."

Sharmila recoiled and climbed to her feet. "Evan, it's a nightmare out there. Homeland agents are everywhere. Maybe others, too, dangerous entities you don't want to tangle with. I can't let you go."

"I'm not asking," Evan said, nausea pushed aside by a burning desire to be with his wife.-He stumbled out of the Sphere and into the trailer.

Sharmila's team stared at him, their gazes a mixture of concern and fear.

"Evan, you're too important," Sharmila said, following him out. "The data we have, it's like nothing I've ever seen. We need to continue the research. You'll lead it."

"No," Evan replied, his jaw set.

Sharmila grabbed Evan by the arm, poised to give another long speech, but was interrupted by a deafening whir that droned through the hull of the converted trailer, rhythmic and oppressive.

Evan covered his ears, as the sound drilled into his head.

An external camera flickered on revealing a Black Hawk helicopter landing on a dirt track nearby. On screen, Sharmila's security team exited the chopper and made a beeline for the rear of the trailer.

A squeal followed by a clunk and the door to the trailer opened. Cold air and the sound of rotor blades rushed into the room.

"We need to leave," Sharmila's merc shouted.

"I thought you'd left," Sharmila said.

"I had. We can talk money later," the merc replied, throwing a nervous glance over his shoulder. "Right now it's my job to get you out of here."

"What's the problem?" Sharmila grabbed a portable data storage device from one of the consoles.

"This whole area is burned," the merc said. "Military radio chatter is all over the place. Unknown operatives spotted on foot in the vicinity. Something's about to kick off. We've got to go, now, Sharmila. This is what you pay me for."

"Okay," she said, sweeping her index finger in an arc around the trailer. "Burn it to the ground. All of it."

"It's already rigged," the merc said. "We'll do it from the air."

"Already rigged?" Evan repeated, rubbing his head.

The merc ignored him and grabbed Sharmila by the elbow. "Look," he said, "we managed to get a tiny window of airspace from Dulles on a fake. We have no time to screw around."

A squad of the merc's men poured into the trailer, grabbed up the tech crew and Evan, and with weapons raised and eyes alert, ushered them out through the door. Evan squirmed and struggled as the soldiers pulled him along. He fell through the doorway and crashed into the dirt below. The helicopter engine shrieked, RPMs raising, and for a moment Evan thought the sound might cause his skull to implode.

Sharmila shuffled past, her head ducked and hair whipping about her face in the turbulence caused by the chopper blades. She met Evan's gaze as she passed. It was the first time that they'd ever met eyes, and in that moment, Evan realized why he hated it so much—it could reveal volumes about a person. Their innermost self, their true feelings, their panic. In Evan's case, in this moment, he knew she saw his plan to run.

"Don't do it!" Sharmila shouted, her voice drowned out by the helicopter. She twisted, reaching for Evan, but her merc's arm snaked around her waist and dragged her toward the waiting helicopter.

One of the merc's men pulled Evan up. Evan rose but then shoved the man and jerked in the opposite direction. His mind filled with the desire to see Marie one last time, Evan powered forward and ran as fast as his rubbery legs would allow. Past abandoned cement trucks and stacks of pallets. Past furrows in the ground made by huge tire tracks, and past disassembled crane pieces. All the while focused on the large structure encased surrounded by a ten-foot-high wall: the CDC quarantine building.

No one gave chase.

Instead, he heard the helicopter lift up and away. A series of pops made Evan glance over his shoulder. Coils of black smoke chugged from the open ports in the trailer now engulfed in dancing orange flames. The unmarked Black Hawk floated upward, turning away from him. Evan slowed to watch it disappear.

Something small, white, and cigar-shaped screamed up from the ground. It made a sound like tearing paper that scratched at Evan's inner ear. The helicopter banked hard to the left and the little white finger whipped after it, smashing into the tail section. A flash of fire followed a muffled *whump*, blasting a human figure from the hulk of the chopper, to fall pinwheeling. A second explosion lit up the sky, the resulting fireball descending in a meteoric streak back to Earth. The flaming mass smashed into the ground, the screech of warping metal and the crackle of burning bodies emanating from the wreckage.

Evan froze to the spot, wide eyed, half-nauseated, half-captivated by the dancing flames. Sharmila was dead. All her work. All that she tried to achieve. Gone in a single instant. And why? Because someone, somewhere wanted the bacteria inside his wife.

Marie.

Evan spasmed back to reality and tore off again with clumsy strides across uneven ground in the direction from which the missile launched. Back toward the CDC facility. The place now felt formidable and impenetrable—all high walls and concertina wire. It was foolish. Utter madness. They'd shoot him on sight. None of that mattered anymore. He had to see Marie.

Just one last time.

CHAPTER TWENTY-SEVEN

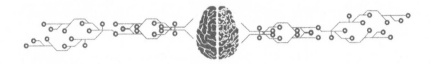

CDC Quarantine

Reinhardt flew from the platform, and took the stairs all at once—crashing into the wall at the bottom. She careened across the room to Dell and Hakagi who pulled at the Plexiglas chamber in which Billy Vick hung motionless, still in the grip of the giant claw.

Reinhardt gasped. "Is he breathing?"

"I can't tell," Hakagi groaned, as he and Dell leaned into the heavy case door.

"Billy?" Reinhardt shouted through the gap. "We'll get you out of there. Just hang on." She turned, eyes frantic. "I need the critical response medical team down here, now!" The door swung back and Reinhardt squeezed through the breach. She kicked over a box platform to stand on and reached up to feel his carotid. "Get in here! He's got no pulse."

A three-person medical Critical Response Team pushed into the space. Reinhardt stepped back against the Plexiglas wall and raised a trembling hand to her mouth.

"Unlock this thing," one of the medics shouted.

"I have it," Hakagi called back, and pulled the red emergency release lever.

With a clunk, the mouth of the claw disengaged. Billy's lifeless body lolled forward, blood dripping from his chin. The medics lowered and placed him on a stretcher then lifted him over the lip of the enclosure and out of the chamber.

Reinhardt's chest wouldn't inflate, her lungs and mind starved of oxygen. *What have I done?* She stepped with rubbery legs from the chamber and stood beside Professor Dell and Dr. Hakagi.

"Start chest compressions. I've got the auto-ventilator," the medical team leader called out.

The medics hovered, scanning the body of Billy Vick and checking his vitals.

"I believed he could do it," Reinhardt said, her voice frail. "I just knew he could."

A sad smile graced Dell's face as she touched the edge of Reinhardt's sleeve. "We all did."

"He's breathing," a medic called out.

"All right people, I've got a pulse," the medical team leader responded. "It's thready, but it's there. Let's get him out and stabilized."

Reinhardt surged forward.

"Let them work." Dell's touch was gentle, her voice understanding.

The medical team leader turned to Reinhardt. "We're going to move him to critical down the hall for further stabilization and assessment." The man didn't wait for her reply before he and his team wheeled Billy through the double doors at the far end of the room.

Reinhardt put her hands to her face, and exhaled a sigh between cupped palms. *Was this all for nothing?* she thought. *Is it over?*

269

"Did you see it?" Dell said.

"See what?" Reinhardt met the professor's gaze.

"The bacteria. Before we lost Billy's visuals, it had already started the mutation process."

"In response to Evan's tampering?"

Dell nodded.

"Exactly what Billy warned would happen." Reinhardt shook her head. "My God. What a mess we've made of things."

"Listen to me." Dell's eyes were glassy. "Whatever happens, we can't allow whatever it's become to leave this facility. We have no idea what it is now, or what it's capable of."

"Right." Reinhardt nodded. "Of course. I'll make sure the CDC knows what sort of situation they're dealing with."

"I've got to debrief with my team, troubleshoot our next steps." Dell nodded in the direction of the double doors through which Billy had been wheeled. "They'll take good care of him." She gave Reinhardt's shoulder a squeeze and turned to meet with Hakagi and the rest of her team.

Reinhardt's mind spun with thoughts of failure and the myriad consequences that would follow. Billy had almost been killed, his brain probably damaged.

Evan Weyland had forced an already dangerous bacteria to mutate into something worse.

"Ma'am."

Reinhardt turned to see one of her agents, a tired looking, out-of-breath woman with short strawberry-blond hair.

"What is it, Sarah?"

"The back gate, ma'am. There's a problem."

Reinhardt's attention snapped into focus. "What kind of problem?"

"A military unit forced its way in and is in a standoff with the team."

"*Forced* their way in?"

"Yes, ma'am," the young agent struggled to catch her breath. "Through the back gate. It's tense. No one could reach you on the radio, so I came."

Shit. Reinhardt grabbed a handheld radio on her way to the door. She twisted the knob and heard Barrett, the SRCAT team leader, barking at one of his men. "What's your count?"

"Twenty-two soldiers with rifles. Four armored Humvees with heavy weapon support," came the Homeland marksman observer's reply.

"Are they advancing?" Barrett asked.

"Negative," the marksman said. "Just a show of force right now. They want us to know it's not a problem for them to get in."

With a curse, Reinhardt marched down the sterile white hallway toward the rear lot. She clipped the radio to her pocket and grabbed a set of ceramic shell-plated body armor held out in readiness by her people. She shrugged into it, fastened the hook and loop straps secure about her midsection, and palmed the radio again.

"All units, do not engage," Barrett said. "I repeat, do not engage or we're going to have a blood bath on our hands."

"Copy," the marksman replied.

"Anyone been in contact with Reinhardt?" Barrett said.

"I copy you direct," Reinhardt replied, her heart picking up speed. "I'll be on you in sixty seconds."

She ran the rest of the long hall and pushed through into the rear entrance screening vestibule. Her mind whirled, all the looping, branching, intersecting possibilities only serving to create more problems than solutions. This was the doing of that Army Major, Billy's commanding officer. And he didn't plan on leaving without his man.

Reinhardt pushed through the rear doors and braced against the bite of the numbing mid-afternoon cold that seemed to be growing with the length of the day. She slowed her speed. Instead of a panicked run, she marched forward, shoulders back, chin up, the posture of someone in total command. Across the concrete parking pad with its rows upon rows of parked cars and trucks, Reinhardt stalked toward the rear gate. She passed the fanned out SRCAT team members in full tactical gear standing with their massive Bearcat armored vehicle, DHS SRCAT in big white letters down the side. She gave her former teammates a nod to hold steady.

With ten-foot-high concrete walls surrounding the back lot, the solid steel mechanical rollback rear gate framed the only way into the complex—and it hung open. In the gap sat two armored Humvees complete with manned M240 Lima machine guns in their turrets. Behind the first two Humvees were two more, surrounded by soldiers in full kit.

"How'd they breach the gate?" Reinhard said as she sidled up next to Barrett.

The SRCAT leader gave her a quick glance before returning his focus to the convoy. "I was checking in with our different positions when the detail at the gate called for support. Honestly, I think they were a little shocked at a confrontation with our own military."

"Understandable," Reinhardt said, rubbing at where her vest irritated her neck. She pulled the protective gear down and away from her throat with her free hand. "Any contact?"

"Nothing," Barrett said.

"Our people accounted for?"

"All but two of mine. They were manning the gate when this group showed up. Hesitated to fire on their own military personnel and got outnumbered, disarmed, and forced to open it. They're being held by whoever is in charge over there."

"I know who's in charge," Reinhardt said through pinched lips. "Get overwatch to cover me. Everyone else stays back."

"You sure?" Barrett asked.

Without replying, Reinhard walked out toward the Humvees and stone-faced Army soldiers at the steel rollback gate. Her hands raised, one still clasping her radio, she made great effort to walk at a relaxed pace and to keep her face free of any emotion—despite the maelstrom swirling inside.

"All units," she said, slow and clear into the radio. "We are federal agents lawfully occupying a federal facility involving legitimate federal business. We are in the right here and the Army is in the wrong. Do what you must to defend this facility and protect life." She paused. "Overwatch, do you have me?"

"Yes, ma'am," came the marksman's low reply.

"If they attack, take out their ranking officers first," Reinhardt said.

A pause. "Confirm?" the marksman asked.

"I know what I'm asking of you," she said. "That's only if they attack us."

"Yes, ma'am. Good copy."

With the confidence of knowing she was under the watchful eye of some of Homeland's best precision marksmen, she slowed, clipped her radio to her belt, and stopped before the gate. "Special Agent in Charge Reinhardt with Homeland Security. I'm in charge of the security for this facility and I'd like to know just what the hell this is about. Who's your commanding officer?"

The soldiers stood silent, their eyes fixed forward. A few shifted their position, anxious looks on their young faces. Reinhardt stepped in front of a thick concrete barrier blocking the exit lane. She was just feet away now. She eyed three men who stood out from the others, expressionless and dressed in black instead of the Army's urban camo. Something felt different, more lethal, about these men. Especially the one in front with eyes like fragments of cold diamond. No one said a word.

"Well, come on," she said, raising her voice.

The door to one of the Humvees popped open. Major Barclay stepped out. Though he presented himself, she couldn't help but notice the coward still stood well behind the ranks of his men. "You surely do have sound command of this installation, Ms. Reinhardt... well, except for the rear gate of course." He produced a malicious smile. "I'm sure everything else is secure."

Reinhardt felt herself flush, memories of being talked down to by men in positions of power, because she was a woman, flooded her brain. She pressed her teeth together and breathed through the building fury. "I'm quite sure it is, sir," she said, with an air of defiance.

"I'm here to collect Captain Billy Vick, the prisoner you unlawfully seized from us this morning."

For a moment Reinhardt's thoughts returned to Billy, a man who'd sacrificed himself for what might now be the most vital mission of their time. *Please be okay*, she thought. She gathered her thoughts and spoke with a measured tone. "His cooperation in our investigation is quite lawful, I assure you, and he is of vital importance to it. I cannot release him to you at this time."

The major shifted his weight from one leg to the other. "You don't seem to understand, *Ms.* Reinhardt. I've spoken with your division chief and he assured your cooperation. Billy Vick has committed crimes and must be held accountable to the military code of justice. We will collect him today with or without your help."

Reinhardt's skin prickled at the major's intentional misuse of her title. "*Mr.* Barclay," she fired back, "though current circumstances have enabled your unit to extend its powers into the civilian world, the United States military does not have absolute authority, and you are not a substitute for duly sworn federal agents upholding civilian law. If your claim to Captain Vick is legitimate, send your paperwork through headquarters and we will hold him for you once his involvement in our investigation is terminated."

"That's not how this works!" the major blurted out. "Release him to us, or my men will take him from you by whatever means necessary."

"Are you threatening me with violence, sir?"

The major looked to three black-clad, hard-figured men with no name tape or rank insignias. The one up front, wearing full black tactical battle kit, took a step forward. His eyes were glass blue, deep and cold as an arctic fjord. "Ma'am," he said, his voice low. "I admire your tenacity, but with all due respect, you're about to get all of your people killed. Is that what you want?"

"Excuse me?" Reinhardt didn't want to give the impression of retreat but couldn't resist the impulse to take a step back as the cold-eyed man inched forward. "And you are?"

"The consequence of your meddling," the man smiled—a terrifying and mirthless gesture.

A moment of silence passed, the chill wind electric with

275

expectation.

"I'm sure there's still room to discuss—" Reinhardt flinched, as the zipping whine past her ear caused an involuntary seizure of her shoulders.

The major coughed, a stream of blood sputtering from his mouth. He staggered and fell back. He was dead before his prostrate body hit the ground.

"We're taking fire!" one of the men in black, a big man with a big beard, screamed.

Shots rang out.

"No! Cease fire, damn you!" Reinhardt yelled, waving her arms overhead at her people, but the rippling staccato crack of gunfire drowned out her words. Two rounds struck deep into her rear armor plate, sending her sprawling forward and into the ground behind a concrete barricade.

Gasping, she shuffled to her knees and pressed the painful ache in her back against the barrier. "Spineless weasel," she said between breaths, her pistol in her hand. "Shot me in the back." She jerked upright, ripping off a blind string of fire over the top of the barricade.

The cold-eyed man, staggered by her attack, flung himself against the ground.

Did I get him? She fumbled with the flap on one of her pouches. *Can't say for sure.*

Rounds zipped and zinged, skipping off the concrete, blowing uneven chunks from it. Ducking low, Reinhardt pulled a yellow striped cannister from her vest, yanked the pin, and heaved the grenade over the barricade. It popped and gushed thick white smoke, which obscured the back lot of the CDC building. Reinhardt drew her knees beneath her, prepared to run for a better position, when a clattering sound scratched at the ground beside her. A fragmentation grenade. With a curse, Reinhardt grabbed the grenade and threw it back toward the soldiers. The thing detonated in the air.

Too damn close, she thought.

For a moment, the firing grew sporadic, mixing with the cries of the wounded.

Reinhardt rose and fired her pistol one-handed toward the Humvees as she ran back toward the building. Clearing the engine block of the SRCAT Bearcat, she half-fell, half-slid, striking her kneecap hard on the ground. Sharp pain stabbed into the joint. Crawling the rest of the way behind the bulk of the armored truck, Reinhardt leaned against the front passenger-side wheel. The sounds of war ringing in her ears, she gnashed her teeth together and pushed down her knee to quell the throbbing ache.

Behind the cover of full body shields, Barrett and another SRCAT member moved from their position toward her.

"Are you okay? Where are you injured?" Barrett asked as he reached her.

Reinhardt shook her head. "Just my knee. I landed on it."

"Can you move?" Barrett asked, glancing toward the back gate.

"Forget about it." She winced as several rounds pinged off the body of the Bearcat. "What the hell happened?"

"We're getting slaughtered," Barrett said.

"Who fired first? Overwatch?" Reinhardt said.

The SRCAT team leader shook his head. "I dunno. I can't reach overwatch. They've gone radio silent."

"Radio silent?" Reinhardt repeated. She strained her eyes to see through the smoke, searching the rooftop for where the Homeland snipers had been positioned. Movement. Reinhardt watched as

277

strange blurry silhouettes came into view. Figures that held the general shape of men but lacked the definition, as though seeing someone through a cloudy slice of handblown glass. One of the forms raised an object—a hazy shape resembling an RPG-7 rocket propelled grenade launcher.

"Give me your rifle," Reinhardt said.

"What?" Barrett balked.

"Your rifle!" Lurching forward, Reinhardt grabbed Barrett's rifle from him.

"Reinhardt, what the hell—"

"Get your people inside the building. Overwatch is dead. We're under attack." She loosed a volley of rifle fire on the rooftop, the hazy shapes ducking low. An RPG screeched across the back lot, slammed into a Humvee, and shredded its gunner in a blast of fire and smoke.

"Overwatch is down," Reinhardt called into her radio. "I've got threats on the roof to our six. They're using some sort of active camouflage. Fall back."

The droning, crackling hum of something electrical filled the air. A blue-white flash like lightning preceded the rolling crash of thunder. More screams as another Humvee, rocked by the blast, rolled on its side.

What the hell is happening? Reinhardt thought.

"All SRCAT units retreat to the facility," Barrett shouted into his radio. "I repeat, all units disengage and fall back. We're under attack by an unknown force."

Reinhardt tried to raise up to get a sense of things, but another spike of pain in her leg stopped her short. She swore, searching the smoke and fire. From the rooftop she heard the careening sound of jet engines as a large squad of the blurry humanoid-figures leaped from the edge of the roof. Dust and debris swirled beneath them as they floated in, spectral and terrifying. Touching down, they opened fire on both the remaining SRCAT members and the military convoy.

Reinhardt fired on the spectral figures and watched in horror as her rounds pinged in showers of sparks off the armor of the invisible warriors.

A multi-bang frag grenade exploded with a rolling five-concussion blast along the lines of the remaining army soldiers. The men screamed and fell, clutching at their wounds. Another Humvee exploded, fire gushing from its windows.

"Why can't I see them?" Barrett said, unclipping an MP-7 submachine gun from his gear.

"It's some sort of light-bending technology," Reinhardt said.

"Who are they?"

Reinhardt shook her head and fired off a few more rounds. "I don't know, but they got us to kill each other, and now they're mopping up."

Beside her, the shield man extended his ultra-compact sub gun in one hand. Brass cases launched in a stream into the air as he unloaded in the direction of the wraiths. A sizzling hum, like electricity snapping from a severed power line, ignited the air.

"Hey!" Reinhardt called. "Get down—"

The snap of something hot and close tore through the rear section of the armored Bearcat. Reinhardt screamed. She rolled to her side as the blinding blue-white flash struck the shield man, cutting through the level-four barrier like it was nothing. His terrible shriek cut short as skin, muscle, and bone came apart. Fragments of ashen bone, brittle and charred, scattered across her legs.

"What the fuck!" Barrett screamed, a snarl on his lips.

"Oh my God," Reinhardt said. "Mike, we can't stay here."

Barrett charged around the front of the vehicle, changing angles as he went. "Go! Get back to the facility!"

"Mike!"

Barrett threw a distraction device, the stunning detonation seemed to give him the window he needed. He changed directions again and unleashed a hail of bullets on the invading force. One of the ghostly figures staggered, active camouflage flickering as he clutched at his neck. The man fell.

The spectral figures fanned out, and approached the destroyed armored truck, communicating in clipped barks of a language she recognized all too well. *Spetznaz.* Reinhardt blinked. *The Russians have come for Omega.*

Another crackling zap and Barrett came apart with a twisted cry under the force of the terrible energy weapon.

And then Reinhardt was running.

Heedless of the pain in her knee, blind with the fog of war, she ran for the rear entrance of the facility, boots slipping on brass and pulverized asphalt. Smoke and terror clouded her senses, her ears ringing, her mouth bone dry. An explosion drove her from her feet, powdered concrete dragged away by the wind. She hit the ground, rolled and, with a groan, pushed to her feet once again.

Ahead at the door, a stiff-postured man with half-shaved, ash blonde hair pulled an ID card from the bloody chest of the lifeless curly-haired agent.

The odd man scanned the ID, popped the door, and disappeared inside.

That couldn't have been, Reinhardt thought, running for the door. *Evan? It's not possible.* She dropped Barrett's empty rifle, and produced her ID card. The door opened with the *thunk* of bolts disengaging. Bullets smacked against the heavy bulletproof glass. In two steps she was at the wall. Her palm slapped against the large red button marked *Containment Breach/Emergency Use Only.*

A piercing alarm shrieked through the building; a strobing red light flashed in her eyes. Massive steel shutters slowly released from the ceiling to seal off the rear entrance. Reinhardt kept moving.

CHAPTER TWENTY-EIGHT

CDC Facility, Dulles Airport

Evan ran, lungs laboring, to the edge of the rear lot behind the CDC facility, the outer concrete walls looming high. He'd planned to sneak in through the back entrance, figuring it might be less heavily guarded than the front—though frankly he had no real understanding of these things. He was wrong—both were aflame and clogged with soldiers. The whole complex was a war zone. He'd have to find a way to scale the wall to enter the compound.

Evan ducked into a dumpster alcove carved into the perimeter wall. The sour stench of unemptied refuse made his eyes water. Evan swallowed back the bile in his throat. He climbed onto the lid of a giant blue dumpster and balanced on the flimsy plastic flip-top lid that buckled beneath his feet. His ankles wobbled and he fought to maintain balance, until his perch became so precarious he had to jump to the lip of the wall and grab on with his fingers.

He pulled himself just high enough to peer between the razor wire down into the rear lot of the compound. The steel rollback gate lay open. Smoke and gunfire choked the air. On both sides of the conflict soldiers and armored vehicles exchanged sporadic gunfire. The sounds of grenades, screams, and warping metal filled his head, as if some higher power had designed this one final test of Evan's ability to manage his symptoms, overcome the sensory onslaught, and reach his wife. He squinted, attempting to focus on something, anything, to stem the flow of stimuli.

His gaze settled on flags. American flags. Stitched to the shoulders of every soldier.

Why would two American forces stand toe to toe, trying to destroy one another? Was this all because of Marie?

A lean woman in body armor crawled behind a concrete barrier near the gate. Mirroring her, on the ground in a pool of spreading blood, lie a tall man in an operational camouflage uniform. His soldiers moved to drag his lifeless corpse behind cover.

Evan shuffled for a better view. His fingers, clinging to the outer wall edge, ached. Was Billy Vick down there? Had he survived? *No, not likely.* The neural strain of defeat would have been too much. Evan's gut knotted again.

Something darted across the top of the wall toward the roof of the facility. An odd blur, almost human in shape, skittering in fits and starts. Others might think it a heat haze from the roof itself, or perhaps just the result of watery eyes in the blustery cold and smoke of the day. But not Evan. He cocked his head and squeezed one eye closed, tracking the apparition along the rooftop until it reached the edge, then disappeared from sight.

Gunfire echoed through the parking lot, each force scattering for cover. Volley after volley of bullets streaked across the parking lot and ripped through parked cars. A formidable and violent response rose from the defenders. Smoke chugged into the air and debris coughed from the walls as munitions pummeled the pockmarked concrete.

Now was his chance. In the disarray, he might be able to sneak in the gate.

If he didn't get shot along the way.

Evan's chest tightened again and the gunfire became somehow louder and more oppressive. Bullets ricocheted off concrete and the chassis of armored cars. Unable to cover his ears while hanging on the ledge, the high-pitched squeals and pings assaulted his eardrums and mind with their full force. Wild-eyed, he searched for something to boost his ascent over the wall and the jumble of twisting razor wire.

Nothing in sight.

He covered his ears with his palms, elbows stuck out, to muffle the cacophony of sound and the keen of dying men. On the other side of the wall, a screech followed by an explosion sent shockwaves through the air, and rattled Evan down to his bones.

On any other day, Evan would have been overwhelmed. Hell, a bar full with revelers had been known to send him into a spiral of panic. But here and now, Evan forced himself to remain calm. The single focus on finding his wife grounded him—allowed him to slice through the noise like a javelin in flight.

Find Marie, he told himself.

A scream from above. Evan's head jerked up.

A blurry figure, struck by gunfire, toppled from the roof and crashed headfirst into the concrete of the trash alcove. Evan's heart near jumped through his ribcage. With hands still covering his ears, he looked down to inspect the man-shaped ghost flickering in and out of the visual spectrum. The spectral shifting slowed to a stop and a soldier appeared, his entire body covered in a bizarre combination of protective armor Evan had never seen before. Even the helmet was full-faced, comprised of sharp angles and shielded slits where the soldier's eyes would be.

As Evan peered closer, the hair on his forearms stood up on end. A loud electrical hum was followed by a tremendous snap—as if the world's largest circuit breaker had shattered. The wall beside him disintegrated in a cloud of dust and tiny fragments of block. The force knocked Evan tumbling from the dumpster. He struck the ground flat on his back, driving the air from his lungs. He peered up. There was no large debris, no chunks of concrete. Only a hole, strange and symmetrical, in the outer wall.

His way in.

Evan scrambled to his feet and sprinted through the opening and into the fray.

Bullets snapped and whined off the concrete. Armored cars burned hot with licking orange flames. Men and women dragged their comrades to safety concealed by the whirling smog of dust and scattered debris dragged along by a cold wind.

Evan crouched low and scurried to the back entrance. Off to his right, the lean woman was hunkered down behind a large armored car alongside two other men—one of whom carried a human-sized square shield that read *Police* in stenciled white letters across the front. The other carried a huge rifle of some sort.

A bright blue arc of electricity ripped across the parking lot, jarring a row of parked cars in its wake. A terrible scream filled the air as the man with the shield and half the armored car evaporated in a flash. The rifle-toting man burst out from behind the burning remains of the half-evaporated armored truck, screaming and firing his weapon at everything and nothing.

But there *was* something. One of the man's bullets struck true and another ghost-like apparition slumped to the ground, his—or her—image fluttering in and out of existence.

A second arc of electrons ripped through the air and the rifle-toting man came apart in a charcoal mist of disassociated cells. Only charred black bones fell in a shower of tinkling ash across the empty parking lanes.

Evan, heart pounding and still covering his ears, made a rush for the door of the facility.

His fingers closed around the metal handle and he yanked down hard. It didn't budge. He needed an access card. Evan glanced over his shoulder at the advancing specters behind him.

Got to find a key!

Evan scanned the immediate area, ducking and flinching with every ping or zip of a passing bullet.

On the ground near the door lay a young agent, petite, with short curly hair, her eyes fixed wide. Blood pooled around her neck. A badge stuck up at an awkward angle from the flayed soft body armor beneath her rumpled suit. Evan grabbed it and ripped it from the woman's corpse with a single pull.

He scanned the card and with another quick glance back, darted inside. The door clunked shut behind, locking the raging war outside.

The clamor of battle was muted in here, only to be replaced by the sounds of screams and pained whimpers. Doctors—more accustomed to dealing with pathogens than triage—ran from one room to the next, tending to gaping wounds and missing limbs.

A woman crashed into Evan's shoulder, her stained lab coat smearing Evan with lumpy clotted blood. He recoiled, but the woman kept moving, calling out for an IV bag. No one cared he was here, too busy dealing with the horrific mess caused by the conflict raging in the rear lot.

Evan shuffled, his head on a swivel, peering through open doors to examination rooms and waiting rooms, searching for where they might hold his wife. Charred men and women, some missing limbs and screaming, others staring off into space in horrified acceptance of impending death, lay sprawled on gurneys or propped up against walls—all waiting their turn to be treated. One combatant, a young man no more than twenty-five-years old laid in a fold-up chair, caught Evan's searching gaze. He reached out a blackened hand, a silent plea for help.

Evan's gait slowed for a brief moment, but he shook off any notion of being a good Samaritan and quickened his pace—Marie was all that mattered. But, as he glanced through the gap in a set of double doors, he froze.

Inside, Captain Billy Vick lay on a gurney.

Evan wanted to push on, his heart pounding at the idea of not finding his wife before she died. His legs, however, didn't move. His body somehow willed him to check on the CID Captain. The moans and whimpers of dying men in the corridor melded into white noise as Evan pushed into the room.

The ECG peeped in a slow, sad rhythm—sounding out the failing heart of the agent who lay prostrate and limp, eyes closed. Evan scurried over, his gut pulling tight. He scrunched up his face and cocked his head, studying Billy. With eyes closed, and without his intrusive questioning, the agent looked like just another human, who lived his life and did his job like everyone else. Evan's gaze roved over Vick and the ECG until it came to rest on a digital intelli-wallet beside him.

Another scream echoed from somewhere down the corridor.

He should keep moving, but still he couldn't bring himself to leave. Not yet. He picked up the wallet and swiped it open. The background flitted to life. Evan stared at the image, studying the pretty woman and three young boys hugged up together with the smiling agent, their tagged names hovering above the image. Billy Vick and his family. He carried them with him, just as Evan carried Marie.

A hand closed down over Evan's wrist and he dropped the intelli-wallet onto the bedsheets.

"Ev... Evan?" Billy croaked, one side of his face moving very little.

Evan pried Billy's bloodless fingers away. The man's hand dropped to his side.

"Evan... how did..." Billy said.

Evan paused, examining the slack features of the agent. Vick had suffered some kind of stroke in the ordeal. There was no telling what other damage had been done. Evan's mind whirled. If Vick had a stroke, he'd be crippled for life. Because of Evan. Even if the agent survived, had therapy, he'd never be the same—not for his wife or his kids. *But he forced me,* Evan thought. *I just wanted to save Marie.* Still facts were facts. Evan had mutilated another person.

"You... gonna... kill me?" Vick managed.

Evan shook his head, tears welling hot in his eyes.

Vick released a long, withered sigh.

Evan screwed up his face, struggling to summon the words. "I'm sorry."

Billy's eyes fluttered closed and open again, his gaze weak and distant. "You... wanted... save your lady," he murmured, breathing labored. "I get... it."

"I love her," Evan said, tears now streaming down his cheeks.

Billy's fingers grazed the wallet laid on his gurney. "My Rosie..."

Evan swallowed the stone of guilt in his throat.

"Did you…" He swallowed. "Destroy it?" Billy grunted, life returning to the good side of his face.

Evan hung his head.

A rattled string of gunfire echoed through the building.

The sound seemed to waken Billy from his stupor, as if the sound of war somehow triggered a hidden reserve of adrenaline. The agent's eyes grew wide and he shifted on the cot, pulling the wires and tubes connected to him. His arms and legs jerked, perhaps the result of the stroke, but the look in his glazed eyes suggested something more—as if Billy Vick was no longer in the room, but somewhere far away. Somewhere that evoked pure panic.

Evan shuffled on the spot, a growing need to leave and find Marie pressing on his mind.

Another volley of gunfire.

"It's like a war outside," Evan said. "I don't know who. American soldiers, but others, too. They're all fighting each other."

Vick shuffled again, struggling to force himself onto his elbows and into a seated position. "Not safe. They're here for Marie… for the weapon."

"She's going to die," Evan said, almost unable to form the words.

Billy nodded. "But that's… not enough, Evan," he said, more words coming with his growing strength, even if they were slurred through his crooked mouth. "It must… be destroyed. No one… can have Omega. No… what it's become. "

"How?" Evan asked.

Billy studied Evan's eyes. "Burn her," he said, his tone firm but somehow empathetic.

"Burn her? How could I?" Evan said, backing away from Billy's

289

cot.

"You have to," Billy said. "The whole world... everyone could be at risk."

Evan opened his mouth to protest, then stopped. Vick was no longer focused on him, but behind him, his eyes full with recognition.

In the doorway stood a man in black minimalist tactical gear, his face obscured by a balaclava. A wound in his arm streamed blood. In his opposite hand he raised a pistol. Evan's heart stuttered.

A deafening bang. Brain matter scattered across the floor at Evan's feet.

The man in black slumped to the ground, a crimson fan spreading out and pooling against the baseboard.

In the attacker's place stood the disheveled, grim-faced athletic woman from outside, the muzzle of her weapon trained at Evan's chest.

"Reinhardt," Billy croaked from the table. "Damn... that was close."

"Hey, Vick," the woman said, still holding Evan in her sights. "You look like I feel. I thought you were dead for sure."

Evan's gaze darted between Vick and Reinhardt.

Billy coughed, and with a dry chuckle, sat forward, a pained look of determination on his face. "What's the play?"

CHAPTER TWENTY-NINE

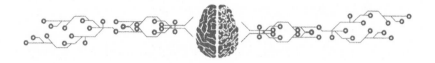

Spurts of red pumped between Ryder's blood-slick fingers. He fumbled one handed with the bulky pouch in the center of his plate carrier, stripped it free, and dumped the contents onto the ground. Rifling through the various sterile packets of rolled gauze and hemostatic wound dressings, the contents of the trauma kit mixed with pooled blood and a sea of still warm brass glinting in the cold gray light. Another string of rounds zipped past, tearing chunks from the poured concrete barrier, the only thing still shielding them from the hellish assault.

Ryder's phone buzzed in his pocket, but he ignored it to apply a tourniquet to Duke's thigh. Working fast, he cranked it down high and tight, years of muscle memory and training under stress doing the work for him. He pressed his knee hard into the femoral junction in Duke's pelvis. The big man let out a blood curdling scream and tried to push away.

"Stop fighting me," Ryder shouted. "A round clipped your femoral. I've got to stop the bleeding."

Duke's lips moved, words strained and lost beneath the blast and rattle of war.

Ryder leaned closer, his fingers slipping as he tore at the hemostatic dressing's outer package. "I got you man, just lie still."

291

"I'm dying, Ryder," Duke said, his face chalk white.

Another vibration in his pocket.

"Fuck off!" Ryder screamed at his phone.

Duke moaned, rolling on his side.

Ryder released the side buckle on Duke's carrier and exposed more wounds in the downed man's lower abdomen. A crimson wash bathed Ryder's hands. He swore, then pulled the hemostatic sponge from the packaging, and stuffed the dressing deep into the largest wound. He followed it with two full rolls of gauze.

Duke continued to scream, his voice trailing, weakening.

Pressing down with his full weight, Ryder watched the blood as it streamed from too many lesions. "You're not dying. Stay with me," Ryder shouted.

But Duke was already gone.

"Fuck!" Ryder slung a packet of gauze. Another bullet zinged off the barricade showering his hair with powdered concrete. He coughed, scrambling away in the filth for his rifle. *They'll all pay for this. All of them are as good as dead. Starting with that meddling bitch from Homeland. Her rounds were meant for me, not Duke.*

The critical stress and fog of war peeled away, revealing a clarity of purpose men only come to know when every good intention has failed. A darkness swelled inside Ryder. It was a feeling he knew all too well. The same pitch-blackness that was born in the heart of a young man so many years ago, fighting a war he didn't understand, for powers that sought to use and discard him. He wasn't sure why he liked it, but there, in those third world shitholes killing became as easy as breathing. Precious life, hand-in-hand with youthful innocence, lost its value in a sea of gray indifference. The decision to become a killer isn't always a conscious one. Sometimes it just happens.

Ryder's phone continued to buzz. He dug into his pocket. The device caught in the folds of the lining and flipped free. The screen cracked as it struck the ground. Ryder ducked with a curse as a shower of munitions speckled a nearby Humvee. His gaze fell on the cell phone laid face up. Squinting, he read the message glowing through the webbed slivers of fractured glass.

Changed my mind. I do want ice cream. Get home before it melts. Forget everything else, don't need them.

The message was clear: recover a sample, eliminate the loose ends. Why they wanted a sample of this thing now he didn't know. Maybe deep down he didn't want to know. In the end it didn't matter. This was personal. Duke was dead and Frank was nowhere to be found. Probably laying in a pool of his guts somewhere. The only thing left for Ryder was to settle the score with that bitch from Homeland. If Vick was still in there, he'd do him, too, then the Weylands. Then and only then, he'd try and retrieve a sample of Omega.

An explosion rocked the smoke-shrouded back lot drawing Ryder from his thoughts. Ryder searched for the way forward through the smoke, the dead, and the dying. Another soldier, a kid who hardly looked like he could grow stubble on his face, fell screaming. This elite Homeland unit wasn't a bunch of pencil pushers. They knew their job, how to execute the mission. Seasoned agents, every one of them, accustomed to hard work and the grit and grime of dealing with the underbelly of society. When the gunfire started, these experienced operators, not near as jumpy as the young army recruits working for Barclay, went to work. Tough, smart, adapting on the fly, they were just the sort of people Ryder would select if he were putting a team together. Which meant they'd be twice as hard to kill.

But there was something else, some other presence beyond Homeland he couldn't quite put his finger on. Ryder cinched the straps of his midnight black stealth pack down across his shoulders and shifted out to get a better view. He'd have to do this just right if he wanted in to that facility.

Surging from behind the barricade, rifle at the ready, Ryder got the jump on two SRCAT operators and dropped them fast with precision bursts from his colt M4. He scrambled to the next point of cover and laid down some suppressive fire. The rifle ran dry. Following a fast chamber check, he flicked his empty mag free and slapped in a fresh one. Then he was back out into the open, running for the next point of cover. He slowed, took aim, and fired twice, dropping a Homeland agent as the man ran for cover. Near the rear door, another agent in a suit wheeled on him, her gun up, eyes wide. She looked young, too young and terrified to be fighting.

His rounds found their mark and she toppled back in a haze of red, clutching at fatal wounds to her face and neck.

Four down, but not the ones he wanted. Dropping behind another barricade, Ryder scanned the battlefield, his body and mind mechanical, honed from years of operating in the most hostile warzones on Earth. Through the smoke, stretching in serpentine paths across the parking lot turned warzone, he saw the lead Homeland agent. At full tilt, Reinhardt slid like a baseball player behind an armored Bearcat. Two more tactical SRCAT operators joined her. Ryder chided himself to be patient. If he could see her, he could catch her.

Ryder bounded farther to the right, the zip-whine of gunfire in his ears. A screeching sound tore at the air. He hugged close to the rear quarter panel of a midsized sedan riddled with bullet holes as an RPG whistled overhead. It slammed in a concussive blast of fire into one of the Army Humvees obliterating the position he'd held with Duke just moments before.

An RPG? Ryder scrambled to the opposite front end of the shot-up car. *What the hell is Homeland doing with an RPG?*

In his guts he already knew the answer. *Foreign operatives on U.S. soil. But who, and where are they?* He stayed low, craning his neck for a better view. Scattered chunks of blasted concrete and rifle brass dug into his knee. He held still, constraining the desire to rush onward. Ahead, just a handful of the elite SRCAT operators remained, but that was it. What was he missing?

A shadow, like the shade of a passing cloud, crossed the open space ahead. Except it wasn't that. Ryder searched the area. There, again. A human-shaped apparition. *Active camouflage,* Ryder thought. Light-bending technology, experimental at best, was only used by the Russians.

The Russians. Spetznaz sent to reclaim their stolen bio weapon.

Ryder wasn't a man plagued by anxiety. He knew his measure. That didn't stop a cold sweat from prickling his forehead. He double checked his pouches. Still had a couple of loaded rifle mags, two frag grenades and one timed Semtex charge. Time to get to work.

A hissing crackle-pop, the sound of a power cable torn from a transformer coupling, caused Ryder's body hair to stand on end. A blue white electrical blast snapped across the parking lot and tore through the end of the Bearcat.

Ryder ducked. "Holy shit!"

No way in hell he was going toe to toe with these Ruskies and their crazy tech. He had to be smarter. Work faster. With SRCAT tied up with this invading force, Ryder identified two threats between himself and the back door of the facility. Both of them Spetznaz. Broken off from the group, they stalked toward his current position. He needed a diversion.

Ryder pulled the pins on a grenade, holding the spoon tight in one hand against his palm. With his free hand, he pulled the Semtex charge, shaped like the old potato masher grenades used by Germany in the second world war. Holding the handle, he pinched the paper wrapper encasing the end and pulled it free, exposing a rounded box shaped-end cap covered in adhesive gel. Ryder pivoted and from behind cover, threw the standard hand grenade as far behind his enemy as he could. The throw was left handed and weak, but it was enough. His bloodless white fingers, clenched down hard on the polycarbonate handle of the Semtex grenade. He primed the fifteen second charge, and waited.

A concussive *whump* sounded as the standard grenade exploded. The two men-shaped mirages swiveled hard to the rear, weapons scanning.

Ryder rose and sent the Semtex charge flipping end over end at the Russian soldiers. With a gooey smack, the charge stuck to the invisible rear armor plate of the closest soldier. Ryder ducked back behind cover and readied his rifle. The stuck man gave a shout, jabbering words Ryder couldn't understand.

The explosion, so close it rattled Ryder's teeth in his skull, launched the Spetznaz soldier twenty feet into the side of an SUV. Active camo defeated, the thrown man slumped to the ground. The other man struggled to his feet, his blurry cloak of invisibility fluttering in and out.

They're still alive? Not possible.

Stunned, but wild with the fury of battle, Ryder could see his enemy clear now for the first time. Heavy armor plate covered every surface. The soldier's face was concealed by a mask, alien in appearance, complete with sharp horn-like angles and slits for eyes. In his hands, a massive square muzzled weapon shone with an electric blue light. On his back, a power pack for the thing gushed cables and tubing that connected to everything.

No time to think. Ryder rose from behind cover and opened fire on the standing man. The rounds pinged and zipped off the heavy plate in showers of golden sparks. The man continued to climb to his feet. Ryder surged forward, flicked the selector switch on his Colt down to full auto. A raucous blaze erupted forth as he riddled the Spetznaz soldier with bullets.

No effect.

The end of the massive weapon glowed bright. A blistering crack followed. Ryder released his rifle and dove, rolling to the left. The trashed sedan he'd taken cover behind, tore in half and rolled on its side, scratching grooves deep in the asphalt.

With a scream, Ryder rose and slammed into the armored man, combat knife in hand. He delivered two quick stabs beneath the man's armpit before shifting to cut low and deep, slicing through the femoral artery at the hip joint in the armor. The man made a desperate sound, his body collapsing.

In Ryder's peripheral, twenty feet away, the other soldier blasted aside by the Semtex, stood, disoriented. Pivoting behind his wounded victim, Ryder delivered a brutal upward stab to the man's neck, just below the creases of his mask.

Desperate to kill Ryder, the thrown man opened fire on his comrade.

Taking cover behind the armor of his dead foe, Ryder struggled to raise the muzzle of the electrical weapon, still clenched in the dead man's hand. The barrel glowed a bright, stunning blue. The

STU JONES & GARETH WORTHINGTON

far soldier screamed, emptying his weapon as the electric flash tore him apart. The soldier's armor plate disintegrated beneath the force of the weapon. Flesh rent from bone. Severed at the thighs, pearly white femurs jutted upward from the exposed meat of two legs. The rest of the man was gone.

The smell of cordite and death carried on the cold wind. The pop and whiz of gunfire continued, echoing from the other side of the lot.

"My God," Ryder, covered in blood, gasped as he rolled out from beneath the stabbed man. The heavy weapon clunked against the asphalt. "I have to get one of those."

Across the parking lot, the battle raged as the last of the SRCAT operators clashed with the might of the remaining Spetznaz.

And then, there she was. His quarry, Reinhardt, ran through the chaos. Before Ryder could think, he ran after her, his muscles groaning as he pushed through the fatigue of combat. Rifle lost in the melee, he drew his Glock and pushed on.

Ahead of him, Reinhardt scanned her keycard, which popped the door to the building open.

Smoke stung Ryder's eyes, a round ricocheted off the ground somewhere close.

As Reinhardt darted inside, she slapped something on the wall. With a shriek of alarms and the flashing of white lights, the security blast doors began to shut.

Ryder dug in his cargo pocket and secured the fabricated key card with bloody fingers. He paused at the wall beside the door. He waited just a moment, watching the blast door come slowly down, waiting until Reinhardt had disappeared around a bend in the strobe-lit corridor. Then he swiped the key, jerked the door open, and rolled under the blast door with little room to spare.

298

Ryder's chest heaved with exertion and droning alarms stabbed at his inner ear. He sucked in a deep breath, checked his Glock, then stood.

Only one task remained.

CHAPTER THIRTY

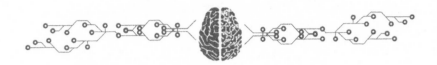

CDC Facility, Dulles Airport

Billy watched as several lab techs ran past the opening to his room, speaking in breathless, panicked whispers. In the ceiling, an amber light strobed in cadence with the lockdown alarm, and far beyond he could hear the pop-rattle of exchanged gunfire. He understood bad things were happening, and yet, felt himself struggling to keep up with the gravity of the situation. His head ached but felt detached, empty. He tried to shake it away without success. A dream-like fog covered everything. He swallowed and blinked hard a few times, then dragged his arm across his face and smeared crusted blood beneath his nose and across his lips.

With her pistol still leveled on Evan, Reinhardt reached down and snatched the torn balaclava from the dead man's head. Released from the cloth, the bloody mohawked skull *thunked* back against the floor.

Evan, still frozen, mouth moving with silent words, was white as the sheet beneath Billy's legs.

"Damn," Billy murmured.

"You know this guy?" Reinhardt looked from the dead man back to Billy.

"It's one of three guys I tied up with in Evan's townhouse." Billy blinked again, hard, sorting his thoughts. "Spec ops or a contractor... I don't know. They're dangerous, though. They're here to bury this whole thing... us. All of it."

"Well, this one won't be a problem anymore," Reinhardt said, tossing the mask onto the splayed body. "Another one of these bastards shot me in the back out there. Now this one just tried to execute a man in a hospital bed. Cowards." She turned her eyes to Billy and Evan.

"Assassins," Billy said.

"It's bad outside, Billy." Reinhardt wiped a strand of dark hair from her face. We're under attack by more than just these guys." She kicked at the downed man. "We don't have much time."

"Then we have to get moving if we want to see this through." Billy struggled to focus. He raised a hand and motioned for Reinhardt to lower her weapon. "This is Evan Weyland, by the way. He's not our enemy... anymore."

Reinhardt looked from Billy to Evan, and lowered her weapon. "Just like that?"

Billy nodded.

Evan rubbed his hands over one another and glanced in Reinhardt's direction. "I just need to see my wife before she, um... she..."

Billy groaned as he pulled at the last of the various cables and cords designed to monitor his condition. The heartrate monitor flatlined with a sustained beep as he yanked it free. "Evan's going to find Marie and say goodbye." Billy worked his tongue, dry like jerky, around in his mouth, trying to summon the moisture to swallow. "After she's... gone, he's going to roll her body into the incinerator. You and I are going to cover him."

301

Evan clutched his hands together.

"Isn't that right?" Billy said, looking to the bewildered researcher. "You can do it... you have to."

Evan managed a slight nod, his body rail straight.

"It's the right thing," Billy continued in a soothing tone, though his words were slurred. "Omega must be destroyed. No matter the cost."

"Whatever the hell we're going to do, we'd better do it now," Reinhardt said, moving to Billy's side and helping him from the stretcher.

Evan took a step toward the door. "I have to see Marie."

"Okay, let's go, Captain," Reinhardt said.

Reinhardt reached for Billy. He shrugged her off.

"I can do this." Billy tried to swing his legs over the edge of the cot, his left side failing to cooperate. Caught in the strap of the gurney, his left foot refused to move. He tried to reach across his body with his right hand. A gasp of pain and frustration escaped his lips and the hot prickle of embarrassment tickled across his scalp.

Reinhardt laid a hand on his shoulder, her voice gentle as she spoke. "Billy, I think you've suffered a stroke. Let me help you. We don't have much time."

A stroke. The idea loomed over him like a shadow, smothering his hopes for a future. For the first time since waking, the weight of it all descended upon him, squeezing like a vice. *What's left for me now? What's left for my family? My country?*

A moment passed, his jaw ached from clenching. He nodded.

Reinhardt unhooked the caught toe of his left boot, helping his legs over the side. She looped his useless left arm over her shoulder. Helping him stand with a groan. He took a step, his knees buckling. Beneath his arm Reinhardt, her arm around his waist struggled to help him regain his footing.

"Come on," she said. "I've got you."

Evan shuffled on the spot. "Please hurry."

Billy swore. "This is useless. Why are you helping me? Where are we going to go anyway?"

Reinhardt shifted to look him in the face. "Evan and I need your help. We've got all sorts of threats trying to get in here to either silence people or steal a doomsday bioweapon, or both. One of these groups might be a team of Russian spec ops. They destroyed us out there, Billy, and they've got some crazy tech that frankly scares the shit out of me. I need you switched on."

They took a few more stumbled steps.

Billy shook his head in disgust. "Look at me. What good am I to you?"

"Stop it," Reinhardt grunted from beneath his arm. "This was your plan. See it through. You're an Army Ranger. Surrender isn't a Ranger word, remember? Now give me everything you've got. We have to buy Evan as much time as we can." She pushed a pistol into his good hand.

Billy huffed out a pained laugh. Morbid thoughts swarmed his brain. "Yes, ma'am."

The going was slow. She stopped at the door to the hallway, did a quick peek for threats, then ushered Billy down the hall toward Marie's containment. Evan shuffled close behind, his hands still clutched tight.

"Come on," Reinhardt muttered. "We'll cut through operations to containment. It's not far."

They paused at the T intersection in the hallway. To the right, in the direction of the rear parking lot, an electrical buzz-snap was followed by a flash and the groaning of warped steel.

Billy flinched. "What was that?"

"You don't want to know," Reinhardt said, breathless. "Hold tight. Can you stand?"

Billy managed a pained nod. He leaned against the wall and watched, helpless, as Reinhardt peeked the corner.

"Son of a bitch," she said. "They're coming through. The Russians. Zapping the steel shutter with that crazy electric weapon."

"What the hell are you talking about?" Billy said.

"We have to hurry." Evan shivered like the last leaf on a long dead tree.

Reinhardt ignored them both, the strobe and flash of emergency lights, illuminating the indecision on her face.

Another crackling blast-flash rent the air.

She peeked again and shook her head. "It's melting through, but the weapon isn't as powerful as it was. Maybe it's running out of juice, I don't know ..."

"We gotta keep moving," Billy groaned.

"No, we've got to slow them down. Give Evan more time." She jerked her thumb in the direction of the Russians. "There are two more shutters. If we drop at least one of them and that lightning weapon is underpowered, it could buy Evan the time he needs."

"We stick together," Billy said.

"Billy we're out of time." Reinhardt's face was stern. "If Evan is going to finish this, he's gotta go it alone. We can give him the time he needs."

Billy held her stare. Acute nausea swarmed over him, his body failing, dying. He swallowed it back. "Okay."

"Here," Reinhardt said, handing a keycard to Evan. "Take this.

I've got another. It'll get you in to her. Go left here, then right into operations. It's the double doors. On the far side of that room, scan this card and you're in to the hallway that leads to containment. Got it?"

Evan nodded and took the card with trembling fingers.

"Good luck, Evan," Billy said, reaching into his pocket. He extended his intelli-wallet to Evan. "If you make it out, find my wife, Rosie. I've had something set up in case things went south. Get my family out. You, too. You hear me? Don't wait to see what happens here. Get out."

Evan touched the wallet, cupping it with his palm as though it were fragile. He looked at the digital image of a happy family, met Billy's eyes for just an instant and nodded. "I will."

"Go now," Reinhardt said. "Destroy this thing. We'll buy you as much time as we can," She squeezed Evan's arm. "Everyone on the planet is counting on you."

Evan pulled away and pressed his lips together and, without another word, slipped into the hallway.

Another blast hit the door, flashing the hallway with brilliant white light.

"Come on!" Reinhardt shouted, grabbing Billy around the waist.

They pushed around the corner. Billy's shuffling gait stuttered, his left leg refusing to raise and step. A sense of terrible wonder struck him. The steel roll down door melted and buckled. White hot, liquid metal sagged and dripped from the metal shutter as another weaker blast of electrical energy struck it. As soon as it opened, he and Reinhardt would be exposed.

"It's right here," Reinhardt said, pulling Billy with her to a panel set into the wall. "Cover me."

With his good hand, Billy trained his pistol on the glowing hot shutter.

Fifteen feet away a small rift opened in the center of the melting door, but the metal cooled fast. Beyond, Billy saw the shifting of armored men in high-tech battle suits. Heard the clipped bark of Russian shouts.

"Whatever you need to do, do it quick," Billy groaned, his hand shaking with the outstretched pistol.

Reinhardt pried the panel open with her fingertips.

An armored hand shot through the gash in the cooling door, grabbing the flimsy edge and peeling it back.

Billy fired, rounds pinging off the shutter. "Now, Reinhardt!"

"I got it!" She slapped the release. The shutter responded clanking down slow. Too slow. On the other side, light poured into the hallway through the ever enlarging port. The sounds of shouted Russian, louder.

Bullets struck the lowering shutter causing Billy and Reinhard to flinch back.

"It won't hold them forever." Reinhardt said, pulling Billy away from the clanking steel shutter. "Come on, we can still help Evan."

"Yeah," Billy said, mind warped by pain. "If he's still alive."

Rounding a bend in the hall, muffled pleas for mercy proceeded more gunshots. Billy and Reinhardt shrank back against the wall, eyes scanning the flickering amber corridor.

At the entrance to the makeshift operations center, the double doors lay cracked open. Just beyond, sprawled out on the floor Billy could just make out someone's legs.

"Oh no," Reinhardt murmured.

Billy held on to the door as Reinhardt stooped to examine the lifeless body of the young agent, Sarah, twisted in a heap, her face disfigured by a single gunshot through the eye, blood spatter reaching up into the strawberry-blond bangs. Reinhardt hung her head. She reached over and pulled the short-barreled AR-15 rifle from Sarah's frozen grip. Tabbing the release, Reinhardt checked the magazine and shook her head. "Only three rounds." She re-inserted the magazine into the long gun and stuffed the pistol in her waistband. After tucking the rifle beneath her arm, she grabbed Billy.

"Take it slow," Billy murmured. "Whoever did this is still here."

"Yeah," Reinhard said, her face grim.

They pressed into the operations center, the muzzles of their weapons sweeping back and forth. Inside, the bodies of doctors, technicians and Homeland agents lay strewn about in a whirlwind of violence. The space, just minutes ago a hub of bustling activity, was now a mass grave, silent and foreboding. Papers and equipment scattered the white-tiled floor, and bullet holes riddled the walls and punctured flickering computers.

In a pile, strewn atop one another, were the bodies of Hakagi and Dell, their blank stares locked open. In their final moments they'd tried to shield one another.

A sick feeling of *déjà vu* covered Billy. The burning of the sand on his forearms. The stench of death. An acidic sting of rising bile tickled the back of this throat. So many bodies.

"Who the hell did this?" Billy said.

"He did," Reinhardt said, motioning with her rifle.

At the far end of the room a cold-eyed man in full black tactical kit, stood before the containment lock. A gas mask jangled at his waist. In his hand a stack of pinched ID cards, some of them speckled or smeared with blood. He swiped one card, then the next, the movement becoming more furious as the red light on the panel flashed with each pass. Scanning the last one, he swore and flung the remaining cards to the ground. He stood facing the heavy containment lock portal, his head lowered, shoulders rising and falling.

"Ryder," Billy said.

"You know this asshole?" Reinhardt asked.

"We've met," Billy replied.

"Was wondering how long it would take for you two to show up," Ryder said, shrugging free of a slim tactical backpack and dropping it to the floor. "For what it's worth, Agent Reinhardt, your people put up a good fight."

"You shot me in the back," Reinhardt said, leaving Billy leaning on a bench table and separating to get a better angle. "Like a dickhead coward."

"I did." Ryder chuckled. "I needed the distraction."

"Why the hell would you kill all these scientists?" Billy asked. "They weren't a threat to you."

"Captain Vick, you look terrible, brother. I must admit, even back at Weyland's place, I never wanted this fight with you."

"I'm not your brother," Billy said, his voice low. "And you and your people picked this fight by acting like criminals."

"It wasn't always like this, you know. There used to be rules. There used to be good guys and bad guys. We used to all be Americans." Ryder shook his head. "We should all be on the same team. We still can be, Billy."

Billy felt the man's cold gaze cutting through him.

"Help me destroy it," Ryder said.

"You don't want to destroy it," Billy said. "Not all of it. You're here to do the same thing those Russians are—steal it back."

"Can't begin to admit to yourself how much alike we are, can you?" Ryder said. "We're both good soldiers. We both love our country. We're willing to do anything to protect her."

"I don't kill civilians," Billy said.

Ryder inclined his head. "Mission first, my friend. We've all got orders. You know that."

"A lot of bad shit has happened throughout history in the name of *just following orders*," Billy said.

"Be that as it may." Ryder shrugged, drawing his pistol from his rig. "I'm going to complete my mission. I really wish you hadn't tried to stop me."

A deafening explosion rocked the facility. The ceiling tiles shook and fell, the lights flickering.

Ryder's face hardened. "In about two minutes those fucking Russians are going to come in here and take this thing if I don't get in there first. Is that what you want?"

Reinhardt and Billy said nothing, their weapons trained on the black ops leader.

"Fools. Just as well, I guess." Ryder brass-checked his weapon and looked at Reinhardt. "None of these dead people have clearance for containment, but I'm betting you do, Special Agent in Charge. So, what's it gonna be?"

A terrible stillness filled the air. Billy's heart pounded in his temples, the smell of old smoke and dust in his nose. The pistol in his hand shook with violent tremors.

In a display of stunning speed and grace the black ops leader fired first and lunged to the left, two rounds landing true in the center of Reinhardt's armor plate. She screamed and fell back, her rifle firing into the ceiling.

With a shout, Billy opened fire, the pistol bucking and jerking in his good hand as he tracked the black ops leader across the room. The man ran perpendicular to Billy, scrambling and ducking as rounds punched into the walls and tore through the table tops, scattering documents and destroying equipment.

The slide of Billy's weapon locked to the rear. He thumbed the magazine release, and flicked the empty mag from the weapon. He threw himself on the ground, as the man in black opened fire. Crawling, one arm and one leg pushing, he inched toward the nearby body of a downed agent. Bullets ripped through the lab, gouging holes in an overturned tabletop, Billy's only concealment.

He reached the downed agent, the dead man's head lolling as Billy probed his carrier. Only a flashlight and a pair of handcuffs. No extra magazines.

"Come on!" Billy shouted.

Bullets zipped lower through the table, punching holes in the wood and stone with the efficiency of a laser.

He rolled the agent toward him and pulled the man's body, the all too familiar smell of death, swarming his senses. Suddenly, it was hot, fucking desert hot, the Syrian sun baking him in a shallow grave filled with hundreds of bodies. He had to get out.

The dead agent rocked as bullets riddled his body armor and flesh. Billy clamored, returning to the moment, his left hand and leg crippled and useless.

In an instant the shooting stopped, and in that same moment, Billy saw the heel of the dead agent's Glock wedged beneath the man's hip. With a grunt he pulled it free, wracked the slide on his belt to clear the malfunction, and pushed himself up and onto his one good leg.

Behind a heavy conference table, the black ops leader searched for a fresh magazine.

Hobbling forward, Billy opened fire. Each flash of the pistol illuminated the wild look of fury on his bloodstained face. Eating away the man's cover with each blast, Billy closed in for the kill shot.

With a *shink*, the slide of the Glock locked back, empty.

Ryder surged from behind the table and collided with Billy, spear tackling him to the ground. Rolling, he centered himself over Billy and drew his hands to his chest, jerking a combat knife from his rig. Raising high, he stabbed down.

Billy's good hand flinched, grabbing the honed steel of the blade as it pressed in on him. He screamed as the knife sliced through the meat of his palm.

"Is that all you got, Ranger?" Ryder spat through gnashed teeth.

Blood dripped from Billy's hand across his face as the tip of the blade closed in on his eye.

Then he saw Pete standing there in nothing but his shorts, kit, and helmet, having hastily thrown it on one morning when their FOB got shelled with mortars. He had that stupid goofy smile on his face, one hand clenching his rifle, the other throwing up a hang ten.

I hope I did good, brother. I hope I earned it.

The attacker's knife flipped into the air, clattering across the floor. Ryder's head jerked up and he made a strangled sound as Reinhardt peeled him backward in a rear naked choke. Locking it in, she grabbed her bicep and clamped down with her free hand behind his head. The man in black gasped, flailing.

Stiffening, Ryder toppled, his full weight slamming Reinhardt's back against the floor. The special agent grunted with the impact. A pistol clattered from her waistband. Her teeth bared, she sank her heels into the pelvis of the black ops leader. Arching her back, she stretched him out. Spittle frothed on Ryder's lips.

Billy forced himself from the floor, wiping the blood from his eyes. His vision cleared, clarifying the life and death struggle just feet away. It was then he saw the smaller double-edged boot knife clenched in Ryder's hand.

"Reinhardt!" Billy croaked.

Reinhardt screamed as the knife entered her side. Once, twice, thrusting and twisting. She gasped, her grip loosening.

Billy clamored across the floor, desperate to help, his body ineffectual. He squirmed, his one good leg pushing.

Another stab-twist and Reinhardt released her hold with an agonized gasp. Ryder pulled himself free, his face purple. He hacked and sucked at the air, then spun, pushing the knife to her throat.

"Bitch… almost… killed—"

The gunshot, hot and close, rocked Ryder's head to the side, flinging blood and brain in an arc across the space. He flopped backward and thrashed for a moment, a crimson stream pumping across the waxed white tile.

Reinhardt's gun clattered from Billy's wounded hand to the floor. He pulled himself alongside the Special Agent in Charge.

"How bad is it?" he asked.

Reinhardt squirmed. "It's not good." She pressed down hard on the wound in her side pooling with blood.

"Let me help you." Billy sat forward and unclipped Reinhardt's armor, pockmarked with bullet strikes. "Come on."

"I thought I was helping you." Reinhardt raised her arms with a groan. The armor carrier clacked to the ground behind her.

"You did," Billy said, squeezing her arm. "Now let's get a dressing on that thing. Can't pack your abdominal cavity. It's going to have to be a chest seal for now."

Billy grabbed Reinhardt's armor and zipped open the pouch labeled IFAK. He extracted a package of sterilized gauze, tore it open with his teeth, and made quick work of wrapping his palm. Pulling the rest of the contents of the trauma kit onto the floor, he located the chest seal and peeled the backing off.

Reinhardt gasped again, raising her shirt to expose the nasty wound in her lower ribcage.

Billy wiped off as much blood as he could and slapped the seal over the wound. "That knife could have clipped something," he said. "You'll need critical care."

Reinhardt winced. "I don't think that's happening—"

Electrical static snapped at the air. Shouts burst forth on the far side of the room; the rippling crack of a half powered blast of lightning and a wave of gunfire followed.

Reinhardt grabbed Billy by his shirt and jerked him to the floor, a blinding blue-white flash, a twisting bolt struck the table behind them, rending it apart. The computer equipment shredded, chewed to pieces by light machine gun fire.

"Go!" Reinhardt shouted.

Crawling on their bellies, Billy and Reinhard made for the containment lock.

Behind them, rifles opened up from the opposite side of the room in a concussive wave of gunfire that seemed to shred everything. Heavily armed and armored, the Russians spec ops soldiers stalked forward terrifying in their alien aspect.

Scrambling side by side to the containment lock, Reinhardt flicked her badge against the scanner. It blipped and turned green, the heavy door sliding back.

"Come on!" she shouted.

Billy grabbed the black ops leader's backpack and dragged it with him toward the hatch.

Crouching, Reinhardt seized Billy beneath the arms and dragged him groaning the rest of the way through the threshold. Bullets zinged off the doorframe and zipped down the short hallway. A blast of electrical energy snapped across the space, but seemed to dissipate before reaching them. They fell to the floor and with a *thunk*, the heavy door sealed shut.

For a moment, they just sat there clutched together, labored breaths heaving in rhythm. The hollow thud of bullets striking the outer surface of the door was replaced by the clipped murmurings of the frustrated assault team.

"They'll get in… eventually," Reinhardt said between breaths. "And when they do, they're going to mow through us on their way to collect Marie."

Billy sat up and unzipped the satchel, spreading the mouth of the bag wide. Inside, were stacked bricks of cream-colored plastic explosive coupled with a remote detonator.

"So we set up a nice little surprise for them." Billy smirked, the left side of his face failing to move.

With what energy they had left, Billy and Reinhardt set to work, stacking bricks of C4 along the entranceway and covering the choke point with whatever junk they could find. The effort was excruciating, flooding Billy's senses—every nerve ending set aflame with a white-hot burning that never seemed to abate. He looked at his bandaged palm, the gauze already soaked red. Vision blurred, he stumbled to the corridor wall and slid to the floor. Across the space, Reinhardt moved slowly, fingers pinched over the sealed wound in her side.

On the other side of the door, the voices murmured, growing louder, then drifting away as the Russian soldiers worked to defeat the three-inch-thick steel door. Marie's secure containment room was hardened. Going through him and Reinhardt at this point of entry was the Russians' only way in. He pulled his knife from the damaged keycard scan panel sparking from the wall.

"Is that door into containment sufficiently disabled?"

"Yep." Reinhardt grunted with pain and placed a brick of C4. "They'll have to blast or cut it, same as this first one if they want to get in there." She motioned to the door they'd come through, jumbled with carts and tables and other piled debris. Reinhardt stretched with a grimace and placed the last brick of C4 along the baseboard. "That good?"

"It'll do," Billy said, wishing he could see that digital photo of his wife and three boys one last time.

"That's the last one." Reinhardt eased down onto the floor beside him.

Billy noted Reinhardt's pale, sweaty brow and pained features. A look of misery crossed her sweat damp features as she cupped the sealed wound in her side. She saw him looking and forced a smile.

"It's fine," she said.

Internal bleeding. How much time does she have? Billy pushed away the thought. *Not that it matters now anyway.*

A methodical series of clunks knocked against the door. A strange humming followed.

Reinhardt pulled her phone from her pocket. The cracked screen winked to life bearing the image of Reinhardt and a young woman laughing.

Billy glanced at the picture. "Your little sister, Elena?"

Reinhardt nodded.

"You should call her," Billy said.

Reinhardt shook her head. "She's out of the country. I already sent her a message." She pushed the unlocked phone into Billy's hands. "Call your wife."

"No… Shouldn't you use it?"

"Billy," Reinhardt said, meeting his gaze. "Let her hear from you."

Billy swallowed and took the phone.

The whining outside the door intensified, a dripping blue metallic glow beginning at the lower right seam.

Billy punched in the number and held the phone to his ear. It rang twice.

"Hello?"

"Rosie."

"Billy? My God, Billy where have you been? What's wrong with your voice?"

"Hey, honey."

"After they took you this morning, I couldn't get anyone to tell me where you were. I've been sick over it. Where are you?"

"I know, baby, things have been a little crazy." Billy watched the glowing blue seam stretch and rise. Liquid metal dripped from the smooth cut in the door, and formed a lumpy pile on the floor.

"When are you coming home?" Rosie asked. Something in her tone told Billy she already knew.

"Soon. I have a few things to wrap up here first," Billy said, his

316

stomach sour with the lie. "I need you to listen to me. Don't ask any questions. Just listen. Can you do that for me, Rosie?"

"Yes." Rosie's voice was small, childlike on the other end.

"I'm afraid something bad is about to happen stateside." Billy tried to swallow the lump. "Look in the safe for the red folder. It's a packet of information I put together a while back to get you and the boys out of the country in the event of an emergency."

"Billy Vick, I don't like this. You're scaring me," Rosie said.

"Remember a name for me: Evan Weyland. He's a friend. He might reach out to you if I get busy. Just a precaution, okay? I'll handle what I need to handle and I'll be right behind you."

The line was quiet.

The door popped, groaning, as the seam traced around the top and began its descent. In seconds the Russians would be through.

"Rosie?" Billy said.

"I love you, Billy," she whispered.

"I love you too, baby. So very much. Give the boys my love and tell them I'll see them soon." Billy didn't wait for her to reply. He ended the call and wiped at his eyes with the back of his hand, still clutching the phone.

Reinhardt placed her hand on his leg. "To give them some comfort. It's worth the lie."

"I guess," Billy said. He took a shaky breath. "Well, Reinhardt, this is it."

The glowing cut streaming with little tendrils of smoke closed in on the bottom of the door.

"Laura."

"What?" Billy asked, meeting the gaze of his friend.

"My name, it's Laura," she said.

Billy held up the detonator. "It's been an honor, Laura."

"Pete would be proud of you," she said, her eyes welling with tears.

Billy clenched his jaw and managed a sad smile.

"Together?"

She nodded, her hands encasing his around the detonator. "Together."

CHAPTER THIRTY-ONE

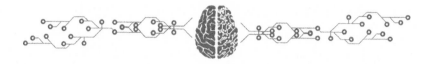

Marie's Isolation Unit, CDC Facility, Dulles Airport

Evan stood at Marie's bedside, staring through the plastic shielding surrounding her. Tubes of medical ivy wound around her limbs and face. She hung by a thread—only machines keeping her body from collapsing. A ventilator, an IV pushing a cocktail of drugs to elevate her heart rate, a dialysis machine. Though she might only look like a shade of the vibrant woman he loved, this was still Marie. His everything. How could Vick suggest *burning her* like biological waste?

The rhythmic sound of the ventilator's turbine pushing air through the flow valve, punctuated by the out of sync peeping of the ECG monitoring her heart, grew louder and louder in Evan's head. He pressed his palms to his ears to muffle the oppressive sounds, but to no avail.

It was selfish, but still he wanted Marie to be awake to comfort him, help him hold it together.

Another seizure took hold of Marie, her body stiffening and shaking.

Evan jerked to action, pushed through the opening in the plastic, and held his wife down until the convulsion passed. Then he lay his head on her warm chest and wept.

He'd tried so hard, and still he'd failed. He couldn't save her. The one thing he was good at, controlling the damn nanobots, wasn't enough. *He* wasn't enough.

And now, at the end, he didn't even get to tell her he loved her. He needed to say it. She needed to hear it from him.

The muffled pop of gunfire resonated through the walls. A firefight. How long would it be until those terrifying soldiers found his Marie? Would Billy Vick and that Agent Reinhardt really help him after everything he'd done?

You're on your own, Evan. Get up.

Evan pushed himself up from the bed, wiped his face, and stormed about the room. He rifled through cupboards and drawers, flinging their contents to the floor until he found what he was looking for: adrenaline and a syringe. Evan drew up a large dose, squirted some out to remove air bubbles, then half-stumbled to Marie's IV bag. He found the Luer lock and three-way stopcock, then attached the syringe. A last glance at Marie's gaunt face, then he turned the tap and pressed down on the plunger, forcing the adrenaline into the line.

A moment passed with nothing.

Then Marie's eyes burst open and she spasmed, choking on the tube filling her airway. The ECG screamed with rapid beeps. Evan pulled free the tape holding the ventilator tube to her face, then, trying to hold her down with one hand, slid the tube from her throat. Marie hacked and gasped as her lungs struggled to work on their own for the first time in days. She clawed at the bedsheets, her gaze darting about the inside of her plastic prison.

"Marie," Evan said, holding her down with just enough force to prevent her falling from the gurney. "Marie, it's me."

His wife's struggling slowed and her head lolled in his

direction, her stare not quite fixing on his face.

"E-van," she said, brow creasing.

Evan gave a thin smile.

"Ev... wh..."

"In the hospital," Evan said. "In the U.S. You're very sick."

"Sy ... ria?" she asked.

He bobbed his head again. A tear ran from the corner of his red-rimmed eyes.

Marie shook her head as if to ask: *with what?*

"A weapon," Evan said, clasping her hand as tight as possible without squashing the IV needle. "It doesn't matter now. I'm sorry." Evan's smile slipped from his now quivering lips.

"For..." Marie's voice seemed to gurgle, her lungs already filling with fluid.

"I couldn't save you," he said. "I tried so hard."

"Ba... by," Marie said, her voice just a whispered rattle.

Evan burst into a sob, spittle hanging from his chin.

"I lo—"

"No," Evan interrupted. "No, I need to say it first."

Marie frowned.

"I love *you*," he said. Of all the words Evan had to use, had struggled with for so long just to get along in the world, those three little words were the easiest that had ever come from his mouth.

Marie squeezed his hand, tears running down her cheeks.

A concussive boom sounded close, somewhere near the secure access entrance corridor. They both looked up as the shockwave ripped through the concrete and rattled the lights and ventilator machine. The shrill sounds of screaming followed, words shouted in a hard stabbing dialect that could only be some form of Russian.

"They're coming," Evan said.

Marie's brow creased, her gaze wandering off, but Evan understood the question.

"I don't know. Some military men. They want the bio-weapon inside you."

The voices grew louder. A *clunk* at the door to the room. Then, a bright blue seam appeared along the lower frame. It rose fast, tracing its way across the top in a widening arc.

"They're cutting their way in," Evan murmured.

Marie didn't respond, already slipping away as the adrenaline wore off.

Vick's words rolled around in Evan's head, over and over until it was all he could hear.

You have to burn the body. Evan shook his head, fresh tears rolling down his cheeks. "I can't."

"Ba... by?" Marie wheezed. "Some... thing's... wron—"

Marie's eyes rolled back into her head until Evan could only see white. His wife convulsed, back arched, foam spewing from between gnashed teeth.

"Marie! Marie!" Evan screamed.

The sound of metal slamming against metal echoed in his ears. The drifting smell of acrid smoke filled his nose. But he didn't care. He clutched at his wife, tears running in rivulets down his anguished face.

Behind Evan, a deep voice barked something in Russian. He stood and turned, still clinging to Marie's hand.

Before him stood two soldiers wearing strange heavy armor, alien in appearance. One of the men flickered in and out of the visual spectrum, the same spectral camouflage he'd seen earlier. Their equipment looked damaged, pockmarked with bullet strikes and deep gouges. Neither wore a helmet. One brandished a stubby machine gun and wore a messenger bag. The other held a large strange, square-shaped weapon emitting a glowing blue light that sputtered in and out arrhythmically at the nozzle. He shook the weapon with a curse. Unsuccessful in powering it back on, he dropped the heavy thing to the ground and shrugged off the giant backpack connected to it. He drew a sawed-off shotgun from a holster strapped to his thigh.

Vick and Reinhardt are dead, Evan thought. It was the only way these two made it in.

"Your comrades back there kill my whole squad," the man with the machine gun said. "I am not in mood for games. Step aside from specimen." He moved one hand to his messenger bag, fumbling around inside.

Evan lifted his chin. "She's not a specimen."

The soldier with the shotgun stepped forward and shoved Evan away from the bed. "Get back from specimen—"

Marie's hand shot out, her fingers grazing the man's weapon.

The soldier jerked and gave a startled shout. The stubby shotgun barked and Marie's face came apart in a mist of flesh that spattered against the lead soldier's face. The man gave a shout and wiped at it, spitting.

Evan bawled, his body shaking with wild tremors as he stared at the mutilated face of his beloved. All colors and shapes in the room melded into a single amorphous sludge, tinnitus screamed in his ears, the air suddenly too thick to breathe. Evan palmed his ears and blubbered huge tears. Inside him, his heart stuttered to a standstill.

The assailants paid him no heed, their voices rising in clipped chatter as they argued with each other. A shove. A finger jabbed at the bloody faced soldier. The soldier with the shotgun turned it on

323

the squad leader and keyed up his radio. The head man, a snarl on his blood-covered face, rattled off three rounds into his subordinate's skull.

An electrical energy filled Evan's chest, the sensation as wild and furious as a trapped bull released from its pen. A wounded howl erupted from somewhere deep inside him, a madness that silenced the storm of sensations attacking his mind. Evan locked his furious, tear-filled stare on the remaining soldier and charged.

With the full weight of his body Evan rammed into the soldier, swinging his arms in wild furious arcs. The barrel of the submachine gun clacked against the soldier's face, splitting his forehead open.

The powerful man seized Evan and slung him to the floor, but Evan clung to the soldier with all his strength. They fell to the ground together, then rolled over the body of the squad leader's blood-soaked comrade. A cannister dropped from the messenger bag and rolled across the floor.

The soldier grabbed Evan by the throat and squeezed. Evan gasped, flailing, the corners of his vision turning dark. He bucked and fought, his arms whipping about in an undisciplined melee. Evan's hand scratched against the sidewall of the soldier's sub-machinegun, and his finger hooked through the trigger guard.

A rippling crack tore the air between the two men.

The soldier shrieked. He released Evan and fell back, clutching at his upper thigh. Evan's hands slid free from the soldier's weapon. The man clawed at the terrible wounds squirting blood onto the floor.

Evan stood on shaking legs, watching as the terrified squad leader yanked a tourniquet from his kit, then tied it around his thigh, desperate to staunch the flow of blood. Evan knew an arterial bleed when he saw it. This man could hold a gun on him or he could choose to save his own life, not both.

The soldier's radio squawked with digital static, shaking Evan from his stupor. The soldier initiated his mic and spoke a few breathless words into the radio, then fired a panicked glance in Evan's direction. His team were coming for him, and Evan couldn't be there when they arrived.

Evan turned to face his wife one last time, but collapsed against the wall. The flayed face and chest of his dear wife gaped open. He shielded his eyes with an arm, bile rising into his mouth.

"Marie," he whimpered.

Evan's far away gaze roamed from his wife, to the Russian soldier and finally the cannister that laid on the floor. He cocked his head and stared at it, concentrating on the metallic cylinder despite another trill of gunfire echoing somewhere in the building.

They want to take it, he thought.

Evan swallowed away the acidic taste in his mouth and fought against the knot in his gut. He stumbled to the counter and, with trembling hands, grabbed a bottle of ethanol. Then, he rifled through the cupboards until he found a box of matches. Without looking at the Russian still crumpled on the floor, he shuffled back to Marie's corpse.

Eyes pinched shut, Evan squeezed the plastic bottle, spraying his wife and the cot with ethanol. Then, careful not to let his gaze fall on Marie's corpse, Evan struck the match. The smell of sulfur filled his nostrils and he stood there swaying on the spot. The flame touched his fingertips and Evan dropped the match.

Marie and the bedclothes caught in a *whoosh* of flame.

"I'm sorry," he whispered.

Evan turned and ran toward the still smoking hole cut in the door. He ducked through the hatch, choking on the airborne debris. The interior hallway, distorted by the detonation of some sort of explosive device, was filled with yet more black smog. He blinked away the sting in his eyes and picked his way through the rubble. Using his sleeve as a filter for his nose and mouth, Evan navigated the bodies of several dismembered Russian soldiers littering the space and around an overturned gurney against the far wall.

The sound of men shouting in Russian somewhere ahead grew louder.

Evan dashed to the back corner of the hall and hid behind a series of jumbled crates and charred bodies. A new team of Russians—three men all equipped in the same strange gear—pushed through the destroyed door at the far end of the hall. Evan sat still, limbs numb. They were headed to Marie's room and their fallen comrades. The image of Marie's burning body filled Evan's mind. He clamped his eyes shut and put his hands over his ears to block it all out.

What do I do? What would Marie want me to do?

Evan looked down at one of the burnt corpses, blackened and rolled on its side away from him. He stared at it long and hard. Though distorted and gnarled now, Evan realized the charred remains belonged to Billy Vick.

Evan froze. He'd never intended any of this. So much death and destruction, and for what? It was all his fault. Evan pulled Billy's intelli-wallet from his own pocket, opened it, and fixed his stare on the image of Rosie and the children. He disappeared into a place he hadn't been since he was a child, his safe place where outside things couldn't hurt him—not the smell of fire and burning flesh, or even the howl of the alarms. And in that place

Marie's voice called out: *You're a good man, Evan.*

"A good man," Evan whispered. That's what she believed he was. That's what he should strive to be.

The squeal of warping metal and the shouting of men brought Evan out of his trance. He glanced down the corridor one last time to ensure the Russian soldiers weren't coming out, then stuffed the intelli-wallet back into his pocket and disappeared into the wailing, strobing shadows of the CDC facility.

EPILOGUE

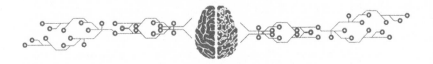

Somewhere on the Yenisei River, Russia

"The mystery surrounding a downed Russian military plane in France continues today as hospital workers who attempted, and failed, to revive the crew are now dying themselves from an unknown disease. Both the hospital and the crash site have been quarantined. The French Prime Minister has assured NATO and the UN that the situation is under control. Meanwhile, the Kremlin has said an investigation is underway regarding the plane's presence in French airspace. Amidst the escalation of terror attacks in the last three weeks, speculation continues to grow that this may be yet another planned attack by one of the many terrorist splinter cells—"

Evan pulled out his headphones and switched off the news app. It had started. The spread. He'd doomed humanity by forcing the infection to protect itself, to mutate into something horrible and unstoppable. Now he could only run, to a remote, frozen corner of the world, in hopes Omega couldn't take hold there.

Evan wrapped his fingers around the railing of the dilapidated old boat on which he stood. Bundled in layers of wool and a down-filled coat, he shivered until he thought his bones might break. He stuffed the cheap pay-as-you-go phone into the outer pocket of his jacket, then pulled up the thick wool scarf around his face. The itchy sheep fleece rubbed against his fortnight-old beard, and was almost as maddening as the cold. Evan peered over the edge into black water. The reflection of the bleak snow-covered landscape distorted as it slipped under the rusty bow of the vessel. A dizzying sensation rose from the pit of his stomach like a quiet voice encouraging him to jump.

Just do it and it'll all be over. The cold will kill you.

And he wanted to die. To be with Marie again, assuming an afterlife even existed.

Not now, Evan, he told himself. *You can grieve later.*

Evan sniffed back hot tears and swallowed the stone in his throat. Even though his heart felt heavy and lifeless in his chest, there was no point crying here—the tears would just freeze on his cheeks and draw unwanted attention. No, he'd come this far and had to carry on. Had to do this one thing, because he couldn't let his last act in this world be failing to save his wife and releasing a horror like Omega upon the world. There had to be one thing of which he—Marie—could be proud.

"How much longer, do you think?" came a woman's soft voice from behind.

"A few days, at most," Evan said, though he couldn't bring himself to turn to face his traveling companions. "We'll moor-up soon and meet our contact. We'll drive the rest of the way"

"That's good, right?" the woman asked.

"Mmm," Evan replied.

"Is something wrong?"

Evan rubbed at the back of his head and turned around.

Rosie Vick pulled her three young boys against her. They nuzzled close, looking up to their mother for strength—and she looked to Evan for the same.

Evan's stomach clenched.

For the first time in his life, Evan had lied. Not a little white lie, like the ones Marie had explained were told to spare someone's feelings—*You don't look fat* or *Your spaghetti was great*. No, this was a massive lie, a fabricated story to ensure Rosie would follow him to deepest Russia.

He'd told her he was Billy's friend and he'd been sent to get her and the children out.

Rosie was of course no fool. Evan had scripted out what he'd say. The intelli-wallet had been the first piece of evidence to confirm his story. The second had been a forged digital image of Billy and Evan together. The retelling of Billy's heroic sacrifice together with Evan's knowledge of the Omega bacteria and the need to flee as far north as possible had added enough truth to be convincing. Evan didn't know if Rosie believed his story. Maybe Billy had said something to her. Maybe it was his gentle nature that had swayed her, just as it had once convinced Marie. Whatever the truth, Rosie had gotten on a plane with him—boys in tow—headed for a small town in Siberia.

Norilsk, their destination, was an ex-gulag turned mining colony. Not the kind of place he'd imagined living out the rest of his life, or where he'd take a woman and her three children to live. But it made sense on multiple levels. The escalating war with terror cells was unlikely to bleed into what was called *the most miserable place on Earth*. More importantly, the combination of few people traveling there, together with the blistering cold slowing bacterial growth, led Evan to believe Norilsk to be a haven from Omega. At least, he hoped so.

"Evan, is something wrong?" Rosie repeated.

"Just want to get there," Evan said. "Do you have your new passport ready?"

"Well, kind of an old one really," Rosie said. "Haven't gone by my maiden name in a long time. And only my mother ever called me Ruža."

Evan stared blankly.

"Slavic version of Rosie," she said with a smile.

"Oh," Evan said. "It's nice."

The boat jerked to a stop, the bow scraping along the riverbank. Rosie clamped onto her children and Evan near fell into the railing. Their captain gave a nod of apology, then shut off the engine and scurried away to tie off the vessel.

Evan rubbed at his ears. With the thrumming of the outboard now gone he realized he'd managed to suppress the annoying sound for the whole journey.

A new person, wrapped in a thick coat with a fur hood, scarf and goggles stepped to the end of the jetty. The scarf was yanked down revealing cold, blue, shapely female lips.

"Ruža? Ruža Solokoff?" the woman asked.

Rosie glanced at Evan, then her boys, and back to the woman. "Yes, yes, that's me."

"Good, okay, I am Olga. We have place for you." The woman gestured to a truck some twenty feet away, already fading into the white wall of snow falling from the gray sky. "Please, come. Careful of ice on wood. Very slippery."

Rosie helped each of her boys from the boat and into the arms of Olga who escorted them through the deepening snow to a clapped-out vehicle. Then Rosie turned to Evan. "You coming?"

"Sure," Evan said.

Rosie hopped onto the jetty, then trudged off to the truck.

STU JONES & GARETH WORTHINGTON

Olga returned and held out a hand, gave it an expectant shake. Evan took it and heaved himself over the lip of the deck onto the little wooden pier.

"You are the scientist, correct?" Olga asked.

"Yes," Evan said.

"Good, we could use more scientists. Come, Doctor Weyland."

Evan stared at the snow-covered truck, Rosie and the kids now tucked inside. He'd gotten them here. He'd done good. Tried to make right his failures. Marie would be proud. Now the future laid before them. Cold and desolate as it was, they were in the safest place they could be in a world that was poised to tear itself apart.

With hot breath misting around his face, Evan braced himself against the biting wind and started up the hill, boots crunching in the snow. *Maybe, in time*, he thought, *we'll all find a way to start again.*

About the Authors

A veteran law enforcement officer, **Stu Jones** has worked as a beat cop, an investigator, an instructor of firearms and police defensive tactics and as a member and team leader of a multi-jurisdictional SWAT team. He is trained and qualified as a law enforcement SWAT sniper, as well as in hostage rescue, close quarter combat and high-risk entry tactics. Recently, Stu served for three years with a U.S. Marshal's Regional Fugitive Task Force - hunting the worst of the worst.

Known for his character-driven stories and blistering action sequences, Stu strives to create thought-provoking reading experiences that challenge the status quo. When he's not chasing bad guys or writing epic stories, he can be found planning his next adventure to some remote or exotic place.

Stu lives in Alabama with his wife, two children, and a golden-doodle who thinks he's human.

www.StuJonesFiction.com

Gareth Worthington holds a degree in marine biology, a PhD in endocrinology, and currently educates the World's doctors on new cancer therapies. Gareth has hand tagged sharks in California; won in the Science Fiction Category at the 2017 London Book Festival and won honorable mention at the New York Book Festival  2012 and 2013 for his writing; and trained in various martial arts, including Jeet Kune Do, Muay Thai, and MMA at the EVOLVE MMA gym in Singapore and Phoenix KampfSport Switzerland.

Born in Plymouth UK, Worthington currently resides outside of Zurich, Switzerland.

www.GarethWorthington.com